THE BROKEN

IRINA SHAPIRO

Storm
PUBLISHING

This is a work of fiction. Names, characters, businesses, places, events and incidents are either the products of the author's imagination or used in a fictitious manner. Any resemblance to actual persons, living or dead, or actual events is purely coincidental.

Copyright © Irina Shapiro, 2019, 2025

The moral right of the author has been asserted.

Previously published in 2019.

All rights reserved. No part of this book may be reproduced or used in any manner without the prior written permission of the copyright owner. This prohibition includes, but is not limited to, any reproduction or use for the purpose of training artificial intelligence technologies or systems.

To request permissions, contact the publisher at rights@stormpublishing.co

Ebook ISBN: 978-1-83700-244-3
Paperback ISBN: 978-1-83700-245-0

Cover design: Debbie Clement
Cover images: Shutterstock

Published by Storm Publishing.
For further information, visit:
www.stormpublishing.co

ALSO BY IRINA SHAPIRO

Echoes from the Past

The Lovers

The Forgotten

The Unforgiven

The Forsaken

The Unseen

The Condemned

The Betrayed

The Lost

The Invite

A Tate and Bell Mystery

The Highgate Cemetery Murder

Murder at Traitors' Gate

Murder at the Foundling Hospital

Murder at the Orpheus Theatre

Murder on Platform Four

Murder on the Prince Regent

The Carnival Murders

Murder on Devil's Ridge

Wonderland Series

The Passage

Wonderland

Sins of Omission

PROLOGUE

She never saw it coming. The blow was so forceful, it lifted her up, and for a few terrifying moments, she was airborne, hurtling through the dark night on wings of excruciating pain. And then she landed on the ground with a sickening thud, her limbs splaying at odd angles, as if she were a broken doll. Her head rolled to the side, and a trickle of blood ran down her chin and onto her shoulder. The pain was so visceral, she thought her heart would stop from sheer shock, but then all sensation began to recede, replaced with a creeping chill that spread from the tips of her fingers and toes inward, toward her major organs.

She began to tremble as tears of white-hot terror slid down her cheeks. This time, there'd be no dramatic rescue, no second chance. This was it. Her life was at an end, and what a legacy she was leaving behind. A trail of tears. She'd cut a swath through life with her angry sword, had taken what she wanted, leaving nothing but carnage in her wake. Well, now she was the carrion, left mangled and defenseless to be picked over by the crows that wore the disguise of family. Perhaps she deserved it, she thought with uncompromising clarity, for what she'd done couldn't be forgiven, or forgotten by those she'd hurt. She'd tried to destroy something precious and sacred, and this was her punishment, her just reward for her vanity.

"Why did you do it?" she whispered hoarsely, staring blindly at the star-strewn sky. For she knew the face of her executioner, had seen it for just a second before the devastating impact.

As death cradled her head in its gentle hands, she stepped into its comforting embrace, leaving behind a woman who'd been irreparably broken long before this night.

ONE
JUNE 2015

London, England

A miserable drizzle fell from a leaden sky as Quinn left the house, making her hair damp and coating her face with a sheen of moisture. It was nearly the middle of June, but it was cold enough to wear a thick cardigan. She unfurled her umbrella and hurried toward the tube station. She'd have loved to take a taxi, but traffic always slowed to a crawl when it rained, and it would take longer to travel cross-town by car than by tube. Rhys was meeting her at an address in Spitalfields, not an area she was overly familiar with.

Quinn descended into the station and consulted the map. Nearly half an hour later, she emerged on Shoreditch Road and walked to the address Rhys had texted her. The building was modern, but not very attractive, and had a discreet sign that proclaimed it to be the City Mortuary. Quinn looked around, wondering what on earth Rhys wanted to show her here. He said they had a new case, but nothing that resembled an archeological find could possibly be located here.

Fishing her mobile out of her bag, Quinn checked her messages. She'd left Alex with a childminder, a twenty-year-old college student who preferred to take evening classes and work during the day. Nicola had stayed with Alex three times to date and seemed to be taking good care of him. Still, Quinn worried and checked her phone multiple times to make sure there were no frantic calls or texts from Nicola. She didn't want to annoy Nicola, so she rang Gabe instead, but the call went directly to voicemail. Quinn returned her mobile to her bag and looked up and down the street, hoping Rhys would get there soon.

A few moments later, Rhys emerged from a taxi and greeted Quinn with, "Filthy weather. I prefer a good downpour to this pissing rain any day."

"Good morning to you too," Quinn replied. She'd been sheltering in the doorway but would be glad to get inside and out of the rain, which was beginning to come down in earnest. "Rhys, what exactly are we doing here?"

"You'll see. I didn't want to spoil the surprise."

"Nothing you do surprises me anymore, so no danger of that."

"All the same," Rhys replied as he held the door open for her.

The interior of the building wasn't any more pleasant than the exterior, and the familiar smell of carbolic and death accosted Quinn's senses as soon as they advanced down the narrow corridor. A fluorescent light flickered overhead, threatening to go. It was like something out of a bad horror film.

"Nice place," Quinn commented. Her sarcasm wasn't lost on Rhys.

"Not all mortuaries are as upscale as Colin Scott's. This one's used primarily by the local Criminal Investigations Department, and from what I understand, there's no shortage of bodies."

"Lovely," Quinn replied, wishing desperately to be out in the fresh air, even if the rain was coming down. This place gave her the creeps. A short, portly man came out to greet them. Quinn placed him somewhere in his sixties, but the bald pate and the sizeable paunch probably added years to his appearance. His thick horn-rimmed spectacles made him look like a wise old owl.

"Mr. Morgan, a pleasure to meet you," the man said, extending his hand.

"Dr. Clegg, this is Dr. Allenby," Rhys said.

"Dr. Allenby, an honor. I'm a great admirer of your program. I'm fascinated with anything that has to do with human remains. Occupational hazard, I'm afraid," he said, chuckling. "You have a real talent for bringing history to life. It's almost as if you'd known those people and had spent time with them. They seem so heartbreakingly alive when you speak of them."

"Thank you, Dr. Clegg. I'm so glad you're enjoying the program," Quinn said, still unsure of why Rhys had brought her to this seedy mortuary.

"Dr. Clegg, if you would be so kind as to fill Dr. Allenby in on the details before showing her the remains."

"Of course. Let's talk in my office, shall we? Can I offer you both a cup of coffee?"

"Yes, thank you," Rhys replied. Quinn nodded. She hadn't had any breakfast, per Rhys's suggestion, but thought a coffee would be safe enough. Dr. Clegg guided them to his office and left them to chat while he went to get the coffee.

"Were you alerted to this case by someone who rang the *Echoes from the Past* hotline?" Quinn asked. Rhys's assistant had been fielding a surprising number of calls since Rhys set up the hotline a few months ago.

"No. As a matter of fact, I received a call from your pal, Drew Camden, a few days ago. He thought I'd find this one interesting. He'd heard about it from a mate of his on the Met."

"Drew called you about a case?" Quinn asked with some surprise.

As far as she knew, Rhys and Drew Camden had never met, but they were very much aware of one another, given Quinn's search for her twin and their respective roles in locating Jo Turing. Quinn sighed. She hadn't heard from Jo since she had so suddenly departed a fortnight ago, after their trip to Leicester in search of Jo's daughter, whom she'd given up at birth. Whatever Jo had learned from the letter her father had left for her seemed to have sent her running, but Jo had never so much as said goodbye or provided even the most basic of explanations. Quinn had tried calling her several times since that day, but her mobile was off, and her agent, Charles Sutcliffe, remained mum, although he had assured Quinn that Jo was fine and off on a new assignment somewhere in the Middle East.

"Drew is a fan of the program," Rhys replied. "He thought we'd be all over this one."

"And will we?"

"Oh, I think so. Not a pleasant sight though, from what I understand."

"It rarely is."

Rhys turned to look at Quinn. "It's a baby."

"We've come across babies before," Quinn replied, puzzled by Rhys's sudden need to coddle her.

"Not like this one."

Any further questions were forestalled by Dr. Clegg, who returned with three mugs of coffee. The coffee was surprisingly good, and Quinn drank it quickly, grateful for its warmth.

"Right," Dr. Clegg said as he reached for a file and opened it in front of him. "The remains were discovered just over a fortnight ago at a property owned by Mr. and Mrs. Brock. The Brocks had lived at that address for nearly fifty years, but it seems they weren't keen gardeners and never bothered much with their back garden. Having recently retired, Mrs. Brock decided it was high time she planted some flowers in her garden and put her elderly husband to work, digging. The Brocks had successfully planted two rose bushes before coming across something wrapped in oilskin. Upon unwrapping the find, which they hoped would be buried treasure, they came across the remains of a child, wrapped in what remained of a woolen shawl. Naturally, they called the police."

Dr. Clegg took a noisy sip of coffee and adjusted his spectacles, which were sliding down his nose. "I was called in to examine the remains."

"And what have you discovered?" Rhys asked. He seemed eager to get to the more pertinent details.

"Given that the body had been wrapped in oilcloth, it was insulated from the moisture in the ground, and therefore better preserved than a body that had been buried without would have been. The assumption was that this might have been a recent burial, but upon closer examination, I determined that this child died over fifty years ago, so no official investigation has been opened."

"What makes these remains so remarkable?" Quinn asked. She could see that both Rhys and Dr. Clegg were bursting with something akin to excitement, their coffee forgotten.

"Allow me to show you."

Dr. Clegg led them to the lab, where several bodies were laid out, awaiting postmortems. Quinn averted her gaze. As an archeologist, she dealt with death on a daily basis, but not recent death. Coming face-to-face with the recently deceased still shocked her, and she didn't relish the reminder that no matter how well a life had been lived, it still ended up in pretty much the same way: cold, ugly, leaking bodily fluids and bloated with gasses. She recalled one particularly gruesome detail she'd read about Victorian mortuaries. The morticians often made holes in the bellies of the deceased and inserted tubes to allow the gasses to escape. If the corpses weren't claimed for burial quickly, they held a match to the tubes, making them glow like candles, the flame fed by the noxious gasses that had built up in the body.

"This way, please," Dr. Clegg said, directing them to the furthest slab. The remains were covered with a sheet, but Quinn's heart nearly burst with sadness at the tiny shape beneath the cover. The child had to be a newborn.

Dr. Clegg ceremoniously drew back the sheet and Quinn stared at the skull and torso of a baby. "Where is the rest of it?" she asked, turning to look at the doctor, who was now practically bursting with glee.

"This is it."

"Had the surrounding area been excavated?"

"Yes, the entire garden had been dug up, newly planted rose bushes and all. This is all there was."

Quinn stared at the slab, speechless with horror. She knew what she was looking at but couldn't fathom how the child would have come to be in such condition. "You said on the telephone there were no signs of violence?"

"This child appears to have died a natural death."

"What became of its limbs?" Quinn asked, her gaze glued to what was left of the baby.

"They must have been removed postmortem, and whoever did it had extensive medical knowledge."

"But why would someone dismember a child before burying it?"

"That is for you to find out, Dr. Allenby. It's what you do, isn't it?" Dr. Clegg replied, smiling at her. "It's a historical mystery," he added for good measure.

"Yes, I suppose it is," Quinn muttered. She'd never been overly squeamish or easily affected by cases, but since having Alex all of that had changed. Mothers and babies held a special place in her heart, and the sight of this poor, mutilated child made her want to weep. What had happened to it? How did it die, and why would anyone remove its limbs before burying it in the garden, like a dead dog? These are questions she would have to answer if Rhys decided to make this find the subject of the next episode.

"I'll just wait outside. I need some air," Quinn said and fled the laboratory.

"Be right there," Rhys called after her.

He came out several minutes later, a cardboard box beneath his arm. "I assume you'll want Dr. Scott to examine the remains," he said as he handed Quinn the box. "No doubt he'll run more tests and be able to give us greater insight into when this child actually lived and what killed it. And then you can work your magic," he added with a grin.

"How can I? I have nothing to go on," Quinn replied, accepting the box despite her better judgment.

"Oh, but you do." Rhys pulled a plastic bag out of his pocket. "The baby was buried with this. It had been used to secure the shawl."

Quinn reached out and took the bag from Rhys, holding it up to see the brooch more clearly. It was small and plain, the type of piece that would be owned by a working woman who couldn't afford to spend much on jewelry. Perhaps it had belonged to the child's mother, or grandmother. Quinn would soon find out, but she didn't want to. She did not want to see what happened to this poor baby. She knew it would break her heart.

"Buck up, Allenby," Rhys said with a smile. "You've seen worse. Surely, this is not as gruesome as a man who's been crucified."

"I don't know about that. Anytime I hear of something happening to a child, I think of Alex and Emma, and I feel like my heart will burst. As a mother, I can't imagine anything more devastating than losing a child."

Rhys nodded in understanding. "There are far fewer children dying now than at any time throughout history. Think of that. You've nothing to fear."

"Every parent has something to fear, Rhys."

Rhys's face transformed, his smile fading. Quinn hadn't meant to point out that he had no children of his own, but having recently lost a child he'd been anxiously awaiting when his former girlfriend suffered a miscarriage, Rhys was acutely aware of how fickle life could be, and how easily a child could be taken, even in today's day and age.

"I'm sorry, I didn't mean..." Quinn said, but Rhys waved the apology away.

"You've nothing to be sorry for. Life goes on, and this case will capture the hearts of our viewers. No one can resist a baby, so get on it."

"All right. I'll deliver the remains to Colin and see what he can discover. It doesn't seem like Dr. Clegg ran any tests beyond those needed to establish if this was a recent death."

"Keep me posted," Rhys said. "I can't wait to hear what that little brooch has to tell us."

Quinn stowed the brooch in her bag. Sometimes she hated her ability to see into the past when holding an object that had belonged to the deceased. She saw the joy, the love, and the hope, but she also experienced the suffering, the loss, and the heartbreak that inevitably stalked every life, and every death.

"The person this belonged to might not be dead," Quinn said as she followed Rhys toward the junction. "If this child died fifty years ago, then it's very possible that its mother is still alive."

"Well, we won't know until you try, will we? I have every hope that she's pushing up daisies somewhere."

"Rhys!" Quinn exclaimed.

"Don't take it so personally. It's just business, Quinn," Rhys replied as he leaned in and kissed her on the cheek before hailing a cab. "Can I give you a lift somewhere?"

Quinn was going to take the tube, but it would be a bit awkward with a box of bones beneath her arm. "Can you drop me at Colin's mortuary?"

"Of course. In you get," Rhys said as he held the door of the taxi open for her, then settled next to her and immediately took out his mobile. "Excuse me, but I have some work emails I need to respond to."

"Don't worry about me," Quinn said. She was in no mood to carry on a conversation, so she turned to look out the widow, the rain-drenched streets slipping by unnoticed as she tried to force the image of the baby from her mind.

TWO

"Delivery," Quinn announced as she walked into Colin Scott's office less than an hour later. He was behind his desk, entering data into the system. Colin looked up and smiled, but the smile did little to hide the sadness in his eyes or the unusual pallor of his skin. He had dark shadows beneath his eyes and his normally smooth cheeks were covered with dark blond stubble.

"Colin, are you all right?" Quinn asked.

"I'm fine. Thank you for asking. Hadn't slept well, that's all, and I had an early-morning postmortem, so had no time to shave," he explained as he accepted the box from Quinn. "That's very light," he commented as he lifted the lid. "Where's the rest?"

"That's all there is. According to Dr. Clegg of City Mortuary, this baby died of natural causes. The limbs must have been removed after death."

"I see. Well, leave it with me. I'll see what I can find out. It'll have to wait though. I'm a bit short-handed just now."

"Has Dr. Dhawan not returned from India?" Quinn asked. Sarita Dhawan, Colin's trusted assistant, had gone to her brother's wedding in Mumbai, but that had been several weeks ago.

"Unfortunately, Sarita's grandmother took ill the day after the wedding. She's not expected to make a recovery. Sarita wanted to remain with her family for a little while longer. I have a temporary replacement, but he's nowhere as competent as Dr. Dhawan."

"Handsome though," Quinn replied as she spotted a dark-haired young man with a designer beard walk out of the lab. He was tall and lean with startling blue eyes beneath sinfully long lashes.

"That he is, and charming. Just ask your brother."

"What does that mean?" Quinn asked carefully.

"Nothing. Forget I said anything. I'm just tired. I'll ring you as soon as I have anything to report."

"Colin, do you ever wish you'd chosen a different aspect of medicine?" Quinn asked, her gaze still glued to the tiny skull in the box.

"No, why do you ask?"

"I don't think I could ever do what you do. How can you focus on life when you're always in the midst of death?"

"It's all in how you look at it," Colin replied with a shrug.

"How do *you* look at it?" Quinn asked.

"Working with living patients reminds you of how fragile and irrational human beings can be. Many people could avoid serious illnesses altogether, or hold them at bay for years, if they'd only live sensibly. You know—eat well, not smoke or drink in excess, go for a walk once in a while, do something to lower their stress level. Instead, people pretend they'll live forever until their body reminds them, they won't, and then they go to pieces and expect miracles from their health professionals, who're supposed to reverse the effects of decades of boozing, overeating, and sitting on the sofa watching reality TV while puffing on a fag."

Quinn smiled. Colin, who was trim and fit, wouldn't be caught dead sitting on the sofa with a fag hanging out of his mouth. He watched what he ate, ran three times a week, sometimes with Logan, and did yoga to destress. Quinn had heard him berate Logan once for eating a bag of crisps, to which Logan had responded with a rude gesture accompanied with a sweet smile.

Colin shook his head and continued, "The dead, on the other

hand, are very amiable. They lie quietly while you do your work and then get wheeled off without uttering a word of complaint. They also remind you that every day is precious and you should live your life to the fullest before it's your turn on the slab."

"I see you're feeling very cheerful this morning," Quinn replied, a tad sarcastically.

"Like I said, I'm not good company," Colin replied, smiling apologetically. "Logan and I had a bit of a tiff last night. I'm still smarting."

"I hope everything is all right between you two."

"It will be. We just need some time to cool off."

Quinn didn't ask any more intrusive questions. She had no wish to pry. Her brother's love life was his own business. If he wanted to talk to her, she was always there, but Logan wasn't one to come running when he was in a foul mood. That simply wasn't his style. The only time he really needed to talk was when things got rough with Jude, but since Jude was still cooling his heels at a very posh rehabilitation facility, Logan wasn't over worried. The facility had top-of-the-line security and vetted every person who came to visit the patients, checking their bags and pockets for contraband. As long as Jude was inside, he had no chance of getting his hands on any heroin, or even a leather belt, which he might use for erotic asphyxiation if he was in the mood for a wank. He wasn't allowed so much as shoelaces, much less anything that could be wrapped around his neck, like the wire from his earbuds. All patients were issued with wireless headphones.

Quinn made a mental note to ring Logan, said goodbye to Colin, and headed for the door. She was due to meet Jill at a bridal boutique in an hour and needed to grab something to eat before trying on her dress. Despite the melancholy that had dogged her since seeing the tiny remains for the first time, she was starving and had to eat before her blood sugar dropped and she became dizzy. Quinn found a Costa and ordered a large coffee and a breakfast sandwich. That would tide her over until after the fitting, and then maybe she could have lunch with Jill, if Nicola was all right with staying with Alex for an extra hour.

Jill was already at the shop by the time Quinn arrived, standing like a statue while a seamstress with her mouth full of pins worked on the hem of her frock. The empire waist cleverly concealed Jill's growing baby bump, and she looked truly radiant, except for the scowl on her face.

"What's wrong?" Quinn asked as she took a seat across from Jill.

"Brian and I went at it hammer and tongs last night. This is supposed to be a happy time in my life, but it seems that everyone is on a mission to ruin my wedding."

"Who's everyone?"

"Oh, let's see," Jill said, holding up her hand and folding down the fingers one by one as she recited the list of offenders. "Well, there's Brian's mother, for starters. She's not happy with the caterer and our choice of band. Brian's dad has suggested shooting something for the main course."

Quinn let out a guffaw of laughter. "I never realized Brian's dad was so fond of hunting."

"Neither did I, but there it is. Brian's sister, whom I've met literally twice before we got engaged, wants to bring some bloke she met on Tinder last week, and my brother is not sure he's in the mood to wear a morning suit."

"And your mum?" Quinn asked. It wasn't possible that the mother of the bride had nothing to say.

"Mum's been an angel, believe it or not, and she's forbidden my dad to utter a word. They just want me to be happy. Oh, I do wish your parents were coming for the wedding."

"They'd love to be here for your big day, Jilly, but funds are tight, from what I understand. Retirement is a careful balancing act of one's savings and living in Marbella is not cheap."

"No, I don't imagine it is. Neither is having a wedding. I cannot believe the prices people charge for playing a few songs or putting together a dozen flower arrangements. Brian thinks we should ditch the band and have his cousin DJ our wedding." Jill looked like she was about to cry. "And he doesn't think there's any need for exotic flowers. 'They'll just die,' he said. I've always fancied having orchids and lilies as my centerpieces. Brian thinks we should cut corners and put the money we save toward buying a flat."

"Jill, every bride goes through this. It's a rite of passage, of sorts. It'll all work out in the end."

"Not every bride is five months pregnant. I'm weepy, hormonal, and bloated, and Brian's mind-blowing male obtuseness is about to set me off like a bloody hand grenade."

"It's Brian's wedding too, and his finances. Surely, he has some say in how the money is spent. Perhaps you can compromise."

"On what?" Jill demanded.

"On the less important things. I wouldn't be overjoyed if Gabe's dad had offered to shoot the entrée, but maybe spending less on flowers is not a bad idea. Brian is right; they die, and orchids are quite expensive. Maybe you can have orchids in your bouquet and choose something less pricy for the tables. And having a DJ instead of a live band is not the end of the world. What would be the difference in price?"

"About two thousand quid," Jill admitted.

"Brian is thinking about your future. You have a baby on the way. You'll need a bigger place, and if you plan to continue to work, you'll eventually need to consider the question of childcare. At least you'll now have paid maternity leave," Quinn pointed out. Having closed her clothing shop several months ago, Jill was back in the corporate world, where she'd get up to a year paid leave.

"A silver lining if there ever was one," Jill agreed, no longer scowling. "I'm beginning to understand why you decided to get married on a hilltop in a roofless tower. Brian and I should have just gone to the registry office and had a supper for our nearest and dearest afterward. But no, I wanted a church wedding with a reception to follow."

"Jill, hopefully, this will be your first and last wedding, and if it's a church wedding you want, then a church wedding you should have. And the reception will be great fun as long as you allow yourself to relax and enjoy it. It will all come together; you'll see."

"Thanks, Quinn. I know you're right. I'm just a bit overemotional right now."

"Been there, done that, as Seth likes to say."

"Okay, we're done here," the seamstress said as she stuck in the last pin and got to her feet. "Are you ready for your fitting, Mrs. Russell?"

"Yes." Quinn sprang to her feet. She was eager to get the fitting over with. "Lunch after?" she asked Jill.

"Sure, but it'll have to be a quick one. I have a doctor's appointment at two. I hope she'll do a scan. I want to see this little one," she said, patting her belly.

"Do you know what it is yet?" Quinn asked.

Jill grinned happily. "It's a girl."

"Congratulations. I can't wait to meet her."

"Now we just have to agree on a name," Jill said with a comical expression. "I've suggested several beautiful names, but Brian has his own ideas."

"Such as?"

"Don't even get me started," Jill replied and marched off to get changed.

THREE

By the time Quinn got home, Gabe was back from work. He was in the kitchen, with Alex on his hip, crooning to Ed Sheeran's "The Shape of You," which was playing on speaker on his mobile, as he did a little dance. Alex was giggling like mad and swaying in time to the music. Quinn kissed her boys and set her bag on the worktop.

"Was Alex all right when you got home?" Quinn asked.

"Fine. Nicola was on the floor with him, building a tower. She's a nice kid."

"And speaking of kids, where's Emma?"

"In her room. She said she was tired and needed a lie-down."

"Emma? A lie-down? Is she sickening for something, do you think?" Quinn asked.

"No, she seemed fine. She wasn't running a temperature. I think she was just upset."

"About what?"

"She had a row with Maya. Is it wrong of me to say that I don't care for that girl?" Gabe asked, making a face.

"I'm not a big fan either. Maya is years ahead of Emma in her thinking. It's like she's six going on sixteen."

"She has an older brother and parents who are on the verge of divorce, from what Emma says. Her home life is very different from Emma's," Gabe replied. "I almost miss Aidan."

"So do I. Aidan had a smart mouth, but at least he didn't make Emma feel bad. I think Maya is a bit of bully."

"I'm going to have a chat with Emma's teacher when I bring her to school tomorrow," Gabe said. "Ask her to keep an eye out for any signs of bullying."

"Yes, I think that's a good idea. An impartial judge."

"If there's reason for concern, we'll talk to the head."

"I'll try to talk to her after dinner. Maybe she'll tell me more than she's told you," Quinn offered.

"Yes. Emma likes girl talk. By the way, I hope you stopped by the shops. We have nothing to make for dinner," Gabe said as he settled Alex in his high chair with a teething biscuit.

"I'll make some pasta," Quinn replied airily.

"Sounds good," Gabe replied. "Cup of tea?"

"Yes, please." Quinn sat down at the table next to Alex and made a silly face at him.

"How was your day? What's this new case Rhys has you working on?" Gabe asked as he filled the electric kettle with water and set it to boil.

"It's a baby," Quinn replied, desolation sweeping over her as she recalled the little skeleton.

"And?"

"An elderly couple found the remains in their garden. It looked like a recent crime, so the police pathologist was called in. He determined the remains are older than fifty years and that the child died a natural death."

"So, what's Rhys's interest in this?" Gabe asked. He took out Quinn's favorite mug, a sweet gesture not lost on Quinn, and reached for the tea bags.

Quinn sighed. "There's definitely a story there. I just don't know if I care to find out what it is. The child was buried with some care, which shows that it had been loved. It had been wrapped in a shawl, which was fastened with a brooch, and then covered with an oilcloth to protect the remains from the moisture in the ground. What makes it odd is that the child's limbs are missing. There's just the skull and the torso."

Gabe set the steaming mug in front of Quinn. "So, you think this child was dismembered?"

"It would appear so. The police dug up the entire garden but found no trace of the other bones. They might have been buried separately, for whatever reason, or a dog might have dug them up, for all we know."

"Why would someone bury the remains of a child with such care, but not bury all of it in the same grave?"

"That is the question, and Rhys thinks there's a juicy story there."

"There probably is, if not a very pleasant one. Where are the remains now?"

"I left them with Colin. He'll run the usual tests and see what he can find out. He was in a mood today."

"Oh?"

"He had an argument with Logan last night," Quinn replied. "And Jill had a massive row with Brian. Planning a wedding can turn the most easy-going individuals into raving lunatics."

"Is there a full moon or something?" Gabe asked with a smile. "For the rest of the night I'm going to be saying, 'Yes, ma'am,'" he joked. "I don't want to argue with you."

"I'm too tired to argue," Quinn replied.

"Why don't you go have a lie-down as well. Alex and I will take care of dinner."

"You are going to make us pasta?" Quinn asked, her eyebrows rising in surprise.

"It's time I expanded my culinary skills. Just forward me an easy recipe."

"All right. I'll send you the one for pasta primavera, but don't cock it up."

"Thank you for your vote of confidence. Or, should I say, 'Yes, ma'am'?"

Quinn laughed. "Sorry, I'm just feeling a bit off. I'm sure it will be delicious. I'm going to take a bath and then take a closer look at the brooch that was pinned to the shawl. I'm curious about it."

"All right," Gabe replied and lifted Alex's hand to wave Quinn off. "Say bye to Mummy."

Alex grinned. "Bye," he said very clearly.

"Wow. He said it."

"We've been practicing. Alex say 'Mummy'," Gabe told him.

"Ma," Alex exclaimed gleefully.

"You are brilliant," Quinn said and kissed the baby's sweet-smelling head.

"I was the one who taught him," Gabe said sulkily.

"You're brilliant too."

"Yes, ma'am," he said with enthusiasm.

FOUR

JUNE 2015

London, England

Having finished her bath, Quinn toweled herself dry and walked into the bedroom, where she got dressed and brushed out her hair. She had a few minutes until she had to return downstairs, so she pulled on a pair of latex gloves and took the brooch out of the bag. It wasn't crusted with dirt, as the artifacts Quinn normally found were, but it was tarnished.

Quinn ran a finger over the surface. She'd held the pin in her bare hands for only a moment when she'd first brought it home, long enough to ascertain that the owner was deceased. If she were still living, Quinn would have seen nothing, but an image of a young woman had immediately floated before her eyes, and Quinn had dropped the pin, unprepared for the secrets it had to tell.

Helen, as the woman was called, had been what people used to refer to as "plain." She had a trim figure and fine dark eyes, but she wasn't beautiful, or even particularly pretty. She had a nice smile and a pleasant manner, but she was self-effacing, the type of person who melted into the background and was quickly forgotten by those who'd come across her. There had been an air of disappointment about her, but then, ten years after the end of the Second

World War, there were still many women whose hopes had been dashed, and whose hearts had been torn to shreds by the losses they'd suffered.

Quinn held the brooch up to the light. There was a design of some sort etched into it. She dabbed some facial cleanser onto a cotton disc and carefully wiped the surface. It took a few tries, but eventually the pattern became discernable. The letter *H* was carved into the brooch, executed in beautiful, old-fashioned calligraphy, so it looked flowy and whimsical.

H for Helen, Quinn thought as she returned the brooch to the bag. "Was it your baby, Helen?" she asked the phantom of the woman who'd fastened the shawl with her pin. "What happened to it? To you?" Quinn whispered into the silent bedroom.

"Discover anything?" Gabe asked when Quinn walked into the kitchen a few minutes later.

She nodded. "The brooch is inscribed with the letter *H*. It must have belonged to Helen, the woman I saw when I first held the brooch in my hands."

"Why do you look so forlorn?" Gabe asked as he came up behind her and wrapped his arms around her waist, his lips brushing against her neck. Quinn relaxed into Gabe as shivers of pleasure ran down her spine. She didn't want to talk about Helen yet, but she needed to explain.

"All the other people I've seen came long before. They've been gone for centuries. Helen might have died as recently as a few months ago, for all I know. It feels odd knowing that our lifetimes might have crossed."

"Yes, I can understand that. It feels more personal somehow."

"Exactly. I feel like I'm intruding on something private, like a peeping Tom. The child's father or siblings might still be alive, and they might not wish to have its story told."

"I think whoever buried that unfortunate baby at the bottom of the garden gave up their right to privacy when they denied the child a proper burial, which they would probably not have done had its death not been the result of a crime. Whether they're alive or dead, you will give this baby some measure of justice."

"Much good it will do it," Quinn replied. Every time she thought of the tiny skeleton that fit into a container the size of a shoebox, she felt tears welling up in her eyes. "It's long gone, its remains buried like those of a pet dog. There was no marker to even commemorate its existence."

"If the child's parents were going to put up a marker, they'd probably have buried it in the cemetery, not in the garden."

Quinn shook her head. "It doesn't make sense. It was buried with care, with love. What in the world happened to it, and where are its missing limbs?"

"I think we'd best shelve those questions for the time being. Dinner is almost ready."

"It smells good," Quinn said with a smile. "You seem to have used every vegetable in the refrigerator."

"And cheese," Gabe added. "To hide the vegetables from Emma."

"She'll find them. She has a nose like a bloodhound."

FIVE
MAY 1955

London, England

"Nurse Brent, I need your assistance," Dr. Waterson called out as he walked by. Helen set aside the chart she'd just finished updating and followed the doctor at a brisk pace. He walked into one of the examining rooms, where a man was waiting patiently, his face greenish in the mercilessly bright light streaming through the window. His forearm was wrapped in what looked like a tea towel, which was soaked with blood. He wore the clothes of a laborer and his heavy leather boots were covered with mud.

"Let's take this off and have a look, shall we?" Dr. Waterson said as he reached for the bloody towel. The man winced, and Dr. Waterson immediately drew his hand away. "Nurse, let's moisten this towel. It's stuck fast to the wound."

"Yes, Doctor," Helen said and filled a small basin with warm water.

She gaped at the nasty gash on the man's arm once the towel had been carefully removed. Dr. Waterson examined the wound and gave the young man an encouraging smile. "You were very lucky, Mr. Edevane. It's not very deep. We're going to clean it, disinfect it, and apply a few stitches, and you'll be as good as new."

"Thank you, Doctor," Mr. Edevane replied. His color had improved somewhat during the examination, but he paled again at the mention of the stiches.

"It's not as bad as it sounds," Dr. Waterson said, clapping the patient on the shoulder. "Just a pinch, really. Nurse Brent, clean the area thoroughly," Dr. Waterson instructed and walked to the other side of the room to collect the supplies he needed to stitch up the arm.

Mr. Edevane sucked in his breath when Helen touched his injured arm.

"This won't hurt," she assured him as she began to carefully clean the area with warm water. She'd have to swab it with alcohol once she finished, but she decided to keep that information to herself for the time being.

"Thank you, Nurse," Mr. Edevane said. "You have a gentle touch. If you weren't covered in my blood, this would almost be pleasurable."

Helen smiled and got on with her work. Flirting with patients was strictly forbidden by the ward matron, and she had no wish to get into trouble. She finished cleaning the wound, then moistened a ball of cotton with alcohol and quickly disinfected the area. Mr. Edevane's sharp intake of breath didn't surprise her, nor did the swear word that slipped between his clenched lips.

"I beg your pardon," he said. "That took me somewhat by surprise."

"Mind your language, young man," Dr. Waterson said as he filled the syringe with the anesthetic. "This is nothing compared to the injuries our boys sustained during the war." He gave Mr. Edevane a questioning look. He would have been old enough to enlist at the onset of World War II. "You did fight for your country, did you not, son?" he asked when Mr. Edevane didn't immediately reply.

"Yes, sir. I was lucky enough never to be wounded."

"Had a good war, did you?"

"I suppose you could say that. I was in the Royal Navy, sir. The HMS *Nelson*."

"A fine ship. Saw her in the harbor once," Dr. Waterson said wistfully. He had been too old to join up, but he'd fought his war on the home front, tending the wounded nearly round the clock without uttering a word of complaint.

"Buck up, then, sailor. This is naught but a scratch," Dr. Waterson said with a smile.

Mr. Edevane remained stoically silent for the rest of the procedure, grinding his teeth as Dr. Waterson administered the stitches. Helen watched the muscles in his jaw clench and felt sympathy for the man. Pain was pain, and everyone experienced it differently.

"I will give you a note for your employer," Dr. Waterson said once he'd finished. "You are not to return to work for at least a week. If the area should become swollen and hot, come back immediately. If not, I'd like to see you in a week's time. Nurse Brent will provide you with clean bandages and some disinfecting ointment to take home. You are to change the dressing tomorrow, then again in two to three days, as needed. Your wife can do it for you."

"I'm not married, sir."

Dr. Waterson made a dismissive gesture. "Your mother, your landlady, your mate. Makes little difference as long as they clean their hands before touching the area and do a competent job. If you need assistance, just stop by the hospital. Any nurse will be happy to help you."

"Thank you, Doctor."

"Off with you, then."

Mr. Edevane jumped off the examining table and walked toward the door. "Thank you, Nurse," he said softly before letting himself out.

Helen disposed of the bloody water and washed out the basin, then deposited the soiled linens in the hamper and tidied the room before returning to her duties. The ward was nearly full, and she had a busy day ahead of her. After work, she'd have to stop by the shops and get something for supper. She'd be happy with a fried egg and toast, but her mother liked a proper meal. Helen hoped the butcher would have some chops left, but they tended to sell out by midafternoon.

Maybe some sausages, then, Helen thought. It was nearly noon, and she was hungry, having had only tea and toast for breakfast nearly six hours ago. She'd brought a cheese and pickle sandwich for lunch, but as her stomach growled in displeasure, she wished she could splurge on some fish and chips. *Maybe when I get my pay packet,* she thought and turned her mind to the task at hand.

SIX

"There's a patient asking for you by name, Helen," Sarah said as Helen walked out of the linen cupboard with a stack of fresh sheets. "Here, let me have those." Sarah reached for the linens in order to free Helen's hands. Sarah wasn't on her ward, but the two wards shared the linen cupboard and women's lav, where Sarah occasionally snuck a cigarette. The men's lavatory was located some way down the corridor, closer to the doctors' lounge. The doctors, who were all male, enjoyed comfortable leather armchairs, little tables with ashtrays, should they wish to smoke, and fresh tea, which they never had to make themselves.

Helen made her way to the admissions desk. Mr. Edevane was standing by the window, gazing up the stairs expectantly. He smiled when he saw her. Having presumably come from home, he wasn't wearing the clothes he'd worn to work. He was dressed in a dark-gray suit with a white shirt and a tie in shades of navy and aqua. His hair was neatly brushed, and he held a brown fedora in his hands.

"Mr. Edevane," Helen said. "Are you quite all right?"

"Yes, thank you, Nurse Brent. It's just that I couldn't get anyone to help me with the bandage, and I was wondering if you might..." He allowed the sentence to trail off and smiled guiltily.

"Yes, of course. This way, please."

Helen led Mr. Edevane into an empty examining room and took out some cotton, alcohol, and a clean bandage. She carefully unwound the soiled linen and examined the arm. "It's healing well. No infection."

"That's a relief. I need to get back to work. The floor supervisor is not happy with me taking time off, even if the injury was through no fault of my own. Someone had left an exposed metal spike sticking out of the wall."

Helen finished securing the bandage and smiled at Mr. Edevane. "All done. I'm sure Dr. Waterson will give you the all clear when you come back next week."

"Nurse Brent, I hope I'm not being too forward," he said as a telltale blush bloomed on his lean cheeks. "But I was hoping you might join me for a cup of tea. There's a tearoom not far from here."

"Mr. Edevane," Helen began but stopped. She had been about to decline the invitation but suddenly realized she had no good reason to turn down the offer.

At twenty-six, she had not only been left on the shelf, as her mother liked to point out repeatedly, but she was covered with an inch of dust. Invitations from eligible men didn't come often, and these days, her prospects were practically nonexistent. She met plenty of men in her line of work, but it was unprofessional to carry on with a doctor and an infraction punishable by dismissal if she flirted with any of the patients. The porters and the ambulance drivers never paid her any mind, always zeroing in on girls who were younger and had fewer inhibitions.

Helen wasn't the type of woman who let down her guard easily, and she didn't go in for men who became overly familiar or tried anything the first time they took her out. She dreamed of a man who'd respect her and treat her with kindness and consideration, not someone who'd expect her to go to bed with him at the earliest opportunity and then only call on her whenever he felt the urge. She didn't want an affair, she wanted love—tender, loyal love, the kind that lasted a lifetime, not a fortnight.

Helen sighed. Mr. Edevane was a nice-looking man in his mid-thirties, a widower or a bachelor, since he'd admitted to Dr. Waterson to having no wife. He'd been nervous to ask her; she'd noticed the anxiety in his gaze and the stiffening of his shoulders, as if he'd expected to be rejected. Why not have a cup of tea with him and see where it went?

"My shift finishes at four," she finally replied, an answering heat blooming in her cheeks.

"I will meet you by the main entrance," Mr. Edevane replied. "And it's David," he said shyly. "My name is David."

"Helen."

"That's a lovely name. Well, I won't keep you from your duties. Till four, then."

"Till four."

Helen looked at the watch pinned to her shirtfront. She had four hours to question the wisdom of agreeing to tea with David Edevane but decided to put him from her mind and concentrate on her work. There was no sense in second-guessing herself. It was just tea, after all. They might spend a pleasant half hour together or discover early on that they had little in common and make their excuses. Either way, it didn't obligate her to anything. And she was lonely. She'd enjoyed several close friendships since enrolling in the nursing course and applying for the job at the hospital, but most of her friends had eventually married and left. Few women continued to work after getting married, and even fewer kept in touch with their unmarried work friends.

Sarah was the only friend she had who still liked to go to the cinema or get a cup of tea on their days off. But their carefree outings would come to an end soon. Sarah had met her current beau, Albert, several months ago, when he came to read the gas meter in place of the man who usually covered Sarah's street. The relationship had progressed swiftly, and Sarah was expecting a proposal any day now. If it came, she'd leave her position at the hospital, and Helen would be left all alone, a prospect she didn't relish.

"Nurse Brent, stop mooning about and return to your duties," Dr. Waterson said, not unkindly, when he saw Helen gazing out the window.

"Yes, sir. Sorry, sir," Helen mumbled and scurried down the corridor toward her ward.

SEVEN

JUNE 2015

London, England

Quinn had just finished setting the table for dinner when the doorbell rang. Rufus, who'd been lying quietly beneath the kitchen table, jumped up and raced to the door, eager to sniff the visitor. He stood with his paws on the door, his tail wagging like a windscreen wiper. Even Alex turned his head toward the front door, displaying an awareness that made Quinn realize just how much he'd changed in the past few weeks.

"Expecting someone?" Gabe asked as he handed Alex a sippy cup full of juice.

"Not that I know of," Quinn replied as she went to answer the door. She was surprised to find Logan on the doorstep, a knapsack slung over his shoulder. His normally spiky hair looked even more disheveled than usual, and he looked tired and upset. He patted Rufus absentmindedly and gave Quinn a perfunctory peck on the cheek.

"I hope I'm not disturbing you," he said as he stepped into the foyer. "I need a place to crash."

"Eh, yes, of course. We have a spare bedroom. Is everything all right?" Quinn wondered why Logan had chosen to come to her house rather than going to his mother's, where he still had his own bedroom. Sylvia would be glad of the company, even if it was temporary.

"I don't want to have to explain things to Mum," Logan said in response to Quinn's unspoken question. "Colin threw me out."

"Colin threw you out?" Quinn gaped at Logan. Colin had said they'd had a tiff, but this appeared to be a lot more than that. "Want to talk about it?"

"Can we talk later?" Logan asked quietly as Emma came down the stairs.

"Uncle Logan," she exclaimed. "Have you come for dinner? Daddy made pasta. He put all sorts of vegetables into it," Emma added with distaste. "I don't much like vegetables, but if they're covered in melted cheese, I'll give it a go."

Logan stole a peek at Quinn rather than answering.

"Yes, Logan's come for dinner, and he's going to spend the night," Quinn replied cheerfully, as if she'd known Logan was coming all along.

"Why? What's wrong with your house?" Emma asked with her usual directness.

"Nothing. Colin is away, and I felt like a bit of company," Logan lied smoothly.

"Can we play a game after dinner?"

"Sure. What kind of game?" Logan asked eagerly.

"We can play beauty salon. You'll be the customer and I will be the beautician," Emma replied with a sly grin.

"Oh, I see where this is going. Are you going to give me a makeover?"

"You could use one, to be honest," Emma said.

"Emma," Quinn said in a warning tone.

"No, it's quite all right. You are absolutely right. I'm ripe for a new look. Tell you what—we can play beauty salon after I have a chat with your mum."

"All right. But don't forget. You promised."

"I will not forget. On my honor," Logan added and carried his knapsack into the guest bedroom.

Gabe graciously pretended Logan had been invited to dinner all along and served his creation with panache. He'd even made a salad.

"Gabe, this is really good," Logan said as he tried a forkful of pasta. "You've come a long way from making toast."

"I'm a man of many talents," Gabe replied. "Not too bad, if I do say so myself."

"I can still taste the vegetables," Emma complained.

"Eat up. They are good for you," Gabe replied.

Emma made a face but continued to eat. Alex leaned forward in his high chair, staring at the pasta on Quinn's plate.

"I think Alex wants some vegetables," Emma said. "He can have mine."

"Don't worry, there's plenty for everyone." Gabe filled a small bowl with pasta and set it in front of Alex, handing him a plastic baby spoon.

Alex was just learning to eat by himself, and the spoon would probably go unused as he scooped up the pasta with his hands, but it was worth a try. Alex instantly threw the spoon on the floor and grabbed a fistful of pasta, shoving it into his mouth. He chewed on a bit of broccoli, then fished for another piece, holding it up to his face for a closer inspection before putting it in his mouth.

"I can't believe he likes it," Emma said under her breath, spearing a piece of broccoli and studying it as if seeing it for the first time. "Oh well," she said and followed Alex's example.

Logan and Gabe kept up a lively conversation all through dinner, with Quinn chiming in occasionally so as not to be rude, but her mind wasn't really on football or the film Logan was telling Gabe about. She wasn't into science fiction, and Logan's false cheeriness worried her. Quinn felt a wave of relief when the meal was finally over and Gabe took the children into the other room to give Quinn and Logan a chance to talk.

Quinn began to stack the dirty plates in the dishwasher while

Logan collected the cutlery and brought it over to the sink. Having finished, he leaned against the worktop and looked at Quinn like a dejected puppy.

"Colin's angry with me," Logan finally said.

"Yes, I gathered that. I saw him this morning."

"Oh?"

"Yes, new case."

Logan nodded. "He thinks I'm cheating on him."

"Are you?"

Quinn expected Logan to deny the charge immediately, but instead he looked away, his gaze fixed on a colorful biscuit jar.

"It didn't mean anything. It was a one-off," he finally said, turning to look at Quinn. She saw a flare of defiance in his eyes and was surprised by how much his admission upset her. A one-night stand was still cheating. She didn't subscribe to this idea that something didn't mean anything. Everything meant something, and if someone was up for a casual shag, they were obviously sending a message to their partner.

"Are you sorry?" Quinn asked at last. Logan didn't look all that remorseful.

"I'm sorry I hurt Colin," he replied.

"But not that you have cheated on him?"

"I never set out to do it. I went out with a couple of mates from work after my shift. We went to a pub, had a few drinks, other people joined us. There was this bloke..."

Quinn remained silent. She loved Logan, but her heart ached for Colin. He was so good, so decent. She hated to see him hurt, and now she understood why he'd suddenly felt threatened by an attractive young man. She wasn't sure if his new assistant was gay, but she supposed it didn't really matter. He was young, good-looking, and a potential temptation for Logan.

"I love Colin. I really do," Logan said, his expression pained. "But our life has become so—" He stopped talking, his gaze thoughtful as if he were searching for just the right word. "Quiet," he said at last.

"How do you mean?"

"We're like an old married couple that has an established routine. We hardly go out anymore. We rarely try new things. And the sex—"

Quinn shut the dishwasher and fixed her gaze on Logan. She wasn't sure she was comfortable with this much honesty, not when she had to interact with Colin professionally, but she could hardly tell Logan not to share his troubles with her. He was her brother, and this was what she'd dreamed of all her life—a close relationship with a sibling.

"The sex has become stale, you know? Predictable. Routine."

"That's what often happens in long-term relationships," Quinn replied.

"I know, but I'm not sure I'm ready for that. I'm only twenty-seven, and I haven't been with anyone new in years, well, except for that bloke last Friday. Lord, I don't even know his name. He was hot though. Really hot."

"Logan—"

"Are you ready yet, Uncle Logan?" Emma asked as she walked into the kitchen.

"Go on," Quinn said to Logan. There wasn't much more she could say. Logan had to decide for himself whether he wanted to work things out with Colin or break things off. It sounded to Quinn as if Logan had already moved on, both mentally and physically. She followed Logan and Emma into the lounge, where Emma had already spread out her makeup palette and brushes. She stood back, studying Logan's face, her head tilted to the side as if she were appraising a work of art.

"I think you need a bold new look," she said to Logan.

Quinn thought Logan's look was pretty bold already, what with the spiky hair, sleeve tattoos, and several piercings, but she was sure Emma had something very different in mind, and pink was going to feature prominently.

"Make me beautiful," Logan said. He closed his eyes and turned up his face, giving Emma free rein.

"This is going to be fun," she said.

"Better you than me," Gabe said to Logan as he lifted Alex off the floor and carried him upstairs for his bath. Quinn trailed behind him.

"What's going on with Logan?" Gabe asked quietly.

"Colin threw him out."

"Why?"

"Logan had a one-off."

"I see," Gabe said. "Think they'll get past it?"

"I don't know. To be honest, I feel for them both. Colin is so lovely, but he's older than Logan and ready to settle down. Logan's a bit wild, which is probably what attracted Colin to him in the first place, but it seems like Logan's beginning to chafe at the restrictions of a committed relationship. Why must everything always be so complicated?" Quinn complained.

"Because human nature is complicated. A happy ending is never guaranteed."

"No, I don't suppose it is. We'll have a happy ending though, won't we, Gabe?" Quinn asked. She recoiled at the desperation in her voice, but she needed reassurance. Everyone around her seemed to be having an existential crisis. What if Gabe grew tired of her? He was surrounded by beautiful, young female students who made no secret that they found him attractive. She trusted Gabe, always had, but trust was such a fragile thing that could be so easily broken. She should know; she'd trusted Luke, and he'd been playing away behind her back for longer than she cared to imagine.

Gabe turned to face her, Alex still on his hip. "Quinn, every relationship is unique, so you can't compare anyone else's experience to your own, but what every relationship has in common is that it needs work to thrive and endure. I'm prepared to put in the work, and I know you are too. That gives us the best possible chance of a happy ending," he said, smiling into her eyes.

Quinn rested her head on Gabe's shoulder. It would have been a tender moment had Alex not grabbed a fistful of her hair and yanked as hard as he could.

"Ma-ma," he said. "Ma-ma."

Quinn's heart swelled with joy. "That is the first time he's called me Mama," she gushed. "Darling, say it again."

"Bah!"

"Take what you can get," Gabe said, laughing. "I've yet to have the pleasure."

"Da-da," Alex promptly said.

"Where is Dada?" Gabe asked, testing him.

Alex pointed a chubby finger at Gabe. "Dada."

Quinn grinned from ear to ear. "He's actually starting to talk."

"According to the childrearing manuals, ten months is about the time babies start saying words consciously," Gabe said. He sounded like an academic, but the smile on his face was anything but scholarly. "I love being a dad," he said and gave Quinn a meaningful look.

"I'll see you later," she replied and left the bathroom. She had told Gabe she was on the pill, and he'd accepted her decision, but there were times when she felt as if she were betraying him by preventing another pregnancy. She wanted another baby as well, but she simply wasn't ready. Alex wasn't even a year old yet. What was the bleeding rush? She needed time, and she wished Gabe would simply give it to her without making her feel guilty.

Quinn went down the corridor to prepare the spare bedroom. She moved Logan's knapsack off the bed and put on fresh linens. He came in just as she was fluffing the pillows.

"Wow, thank you. I'm sorry to put you out."

"You're not putting me out, but I hope you'll wash your face before you go to bed." Logan was wearing electric blue eyeshadow, and his lips were a sparkling pink. Bronzer shimmered on his cheeks, and there were tiny purple bows in his hair. "You're a sight."

"I think Emma was determined to use every single color in her palette. Will this goo even come off?" Logan asked as he touched his lips. "It feels disgusting."

"Yes, it's made specially for children, so there's nothing harmful in there."

"Right." Logan sat on the bed. Despite his colorful appearance, he looked awfully sad. "I miss Colin."

"So, call him."

"And say what?"

"Tell him you're sorry," Quinn suggested.

"I'm not though, am I?" Logan argued. "I need to figure out what I want before I mess him about any more than I already have. I love him too much to toy with him."

Quinn nodded. There was a certain logic in Logan's reasoning. "Logan, have you heard from Jo?"

"No, and I'm not expecting to," he replied as he kicked off his boots. "To be honest, I hadn't even thought about her until you just asked me."

"Don't you care?"

Logan shrugged. "I have enough to deal with. Jude's rehabilitation is costing more than I expected."

"Let me contribute."

"No! Jude is not your responsibility. You have a family to look after."

"Then let me give you a loan. You can pay me back whenever you're ready. With interest, if it makes you feel better."

Logan shook his head. "Look, Jude's been in the rehab center for several months now. I can't afford to keep him in there forever. He has to want to get clean. If he doesn't, no amount of time at a posh facility will cure him of the desire to get high. I think I'm going to have him discharged."

"Are you sure he's ready to come home?"

"He'll have to be," Logan replied. "Mum agrees with me."

"Does she ever ask about Jo?" Quinn asked, wondering if Jo and Sylvia had got past their mutual wariness.

"Not anymore. She knows better. Let her go, Quinn."

"How do you mean?"

"I mean that Jo knows we are here. If she wants a relationship with us, all she has to do is pick up the phone. She's been MIA for weeks. Maybe she'll ring us when she gets back, and maybe she won't. Either way, the ball's in her court. Stop blaming yourself for whatever happened."

"I'm not blaming myself."

"Aren't you? You think Jo took off because of something you said or did. She would have left anyway. That's her nature."

"And what's my nature?" Quinn asked, wondering how Logan perceived her.

"Your nature is to wish for more. You crave emotional intimacy more than most people, not that there's anything wrong with that, but that leaves you vulnerable to being hurt."

Logan stood and wrapped Quinn in a warm embrace. "I love you, Quinn, and I'm so glad to know you. No matter what happens, you'll always be my sister, the one sibling who hasn't let me down."

Quinn held Logan close. "It'll be all right, Logan. You'll see. No matter what you decide to do, it will be for the best. Things usually are."

Logan nodded against her cheek. "I know. It just takes time to come out on the other side and see the situation with more clarity." He pulled away and laughed bitterly. "I'd better wash up. Half your face looks like a fairy threw up on it."

"That could be said for your whole face," Quinn replied. "Let me get you a towel."

She returned with the towel, then went downstairs to speak to Emma. It was time for her to go to bed. Emma was on the sofa, organizing her makeup box. She looked up and grimaced.

"I know, I know, it's time for bed. I'm coming," she drawled. She'd picked that up from Seth.

"Em, is everything all right between you and Maya?"

"Yeah, everything is grand. I don't want to talk about it. I'll get ready for bed myself," she said and walked toward the stairs, dismissing Quinn as if she were already a teenager.

"Are you sure?"

"I'm not a baby. I'm almost six."

"All right. Call me if you want me to read you a story."

Emma didn't reply, but the tension in her little shoulders suggested that she wasn't as indifferent to whatever had happened with Maya as she liked to pretend.

Well, this has been a weird day, Quinn thought as she trudged up the stairs. If it wasn't for Alex's sweet surprise, she'd say it had been a bloody awful day.

Thankfully, the night that followed was uneventful, and Quinn got up bright and early, ready to make breakfast for the troops. She reached for the cafetière and poured Gabe a cup of coffee when he walked into the kitchen.

"Alex is still asleep," Gabe said, his surprise evident. Alex was usually up by six, ready to have his breakfast and watch his favorite children's program while Gabe and Emma got ready for school and work. "Have you checked on him?"

"Sleeping peacefully," Quinn replied. "Maybe his routine is changing. Wouldn't that be something?"

Gabe nodded. "Not being woken till seven is quickly becoming a cherished dream of mine."

"Mine too. Remember when we slept in on the weekends?" Quinn asked wistfully.

"And then stayed in bed for another hour or two," Gabe replied with a seductive smile. "And then Emma came, and just like that —" He never got a chance to finish the sentence.

"Came where?" Emma asked as she sauntered into the kitchen, disheveled from sleep. She wore a pink terrycloth dressing gown Phoebe had bought for her, and pajamas with unicorns on them. "I'm hungry," she said. "Can I have a fried egg for breakfast?"

"No soldiers?" Gabe asked, amazed. Emma's favorite breakfast was a boiled egg with strips of toast to dip into the yolk.

"Soldiers are for babies," Emma replied. "I want sausages too."

"All right," Quinn replied. "Why don't you go ask Uncle Logan if he'd like some breakfast."

"He's gone," Emma said as she settled herself at the kitchen table.

"I didn't hear him leave," Quinn said, turning to look at Gabe.

"Me neither," Gabe said.

Quinn reached for her mobile, which was charging on the worktop, but pulled her hand away without picking it up. Logan had been right in what he'd said to her last night. She got too involved. He'd probably left early because he needed space, and she'd be respectful enough to give it to him. If he wanted to talk to her, he'd ring.

EIGHT

MAY 1955

London, England

Helen studied David over the rim of her cup. She hadn't paid him much attention while Dr. Waterson had been dressing his wound or when she'd changed his bandage, but now that she had nothing else to distract her, she could observe him at her leisure. His hair, which at first, she had taken to be brown, had coppery highlights that shimmered in the afternoon sun that shone through the window behind him, and his eyes, which she had thought were brown as well, were hazel with flecks of gold. His nose was a bit too long, and his face too thin. He was a man that needed feeding up, as her mother would say—looking after. There was an aura of neglect about him. His cuffs were slightly frayed, his trousers a little wrinkled. But, on the whole, he was attractive and pleasant to be with. He was quick to smile and easy to talk to.

"How long have you worked at the London?" he asked as he reached for a fish-paste sandwich.

"Since 1945. I lied about my age to get the job," she admitted. "I think they knew I was only sixteen, but they were desperate for help since many volunteers had left after the war, and no one who was willing to work was turned away. I started out rolling bandages

43

and taking out the bedpans," she reminisced. "I didn't mind. It made me feel useful and needed."

"What about your family?"

"I'm an only child. My father died in forty-nine. Lung cancer. Both my parents had siblings, but they died young. My mother's brother, also named David, died at the Somme, and my father's sister, Ellen, died of influenza the year I was born. I'm named after her. So, it's just my mother and me these days."

"Are you and your mother close?"

Helen thought about that for a moment. She really wanted to say that they were, but the truth was they'd never really seen eye to eye. They loved each other and had clung to each other during the terror-filled days of the war, but they'd never really understood each other, and probably never would.

"We get on," Helen said. "What about you? What of your family?"

"I have none," David replied. "I grew up in an orphanage. My mother left me there when I was an infant. She did provide the orphanage with my name but didn't leave her own. I suppose it was a way for her to find me, if she wanted to, but also a way to prevent me from looking for her. Can't say I ever wanted to. Life at the orphanage wasn't too bad," he said with a wistful smile. "I didn't have a family, but I had dozens of friends. We still see each other, those of us who survived the war," he added.

"And you work on a construction site?" Helen asked.

"I'm a foreman at a shipbuilding plant. I've only recently been promoted to the position. I worked there before I joined up in 1940, but times were hard after the war ended—too many returning men, not enough jobs. I had to take any job I could find. I worked as a day laborer for several years, then there was finally an opening at the plant, and the floor supervisor contacted me, since he knew I wanted to return. It's a good job," he added, his eyes becoming anxious. "It's not like being a doctor or a solicitor, but it pays the bills."

Helen wanted to reassure him that she hadn't meant to sound

disdainful. There was no shame in working at a plant, especially if David held a managerial position. Work was work. She'd never felt ashamed of washing bedpans or changing soiled linens. It was better than sitting idly at home, reading countless books about other people's lives and listening to her mother reminisce about happier days.

"It sounds like a very good job, indeed," she said. "We both work with our hands. To be honest, I much prefer what I do to sitting behind a desk, typing someone's correspondence eight hours a day. I can't think of anything more boring," Helen added with a chuckle. "I'd actually considered doing a secretarial course before settling on nursing. My mother thought it was more genteel, better suited to a well-bred young lady."

"That type of thinking sounds positively Edwardian," David joked.

"My mother was born at the onset of the century, so her formative years took place during the Edwardian era. I'm afraid she still holds on to the beliefs of that time. I, on the other hand, want to embrace everything modern."

"Me too," David agreed. "Do you like jazz?"

Helen nodded. "My mother won't allow me to listen to it in her presence. She thinks that kind of music is degenerate. She prefers classical music, but I do love jazz. I have several records, but I don't get much of an opportunity to listen to them."

"Who's your favorite?"

"I love Duke Ellington, and Sydney Bechet, and anything American, really. Their music is so—oh, I don't know—fun, I suppose. It just makes you want to dance."

"Or brood," David replied. "Some songs by Billie Holiday and Nina Simone, they just rip your heart out, don't they? They're so full of longing and pain."

"Yes," Helen agreed. "They're bursting with raw human emotion. I enjoy classical music, but I think it's had its day. The world has changed, and music has changed with it."

"When's your day off?" David asked as he reached for another sandwich. The poor man looked half-starved.

"Sunday," Helen replied. All her Sundays were the same. She attended church with her mother, then came home, cooked lunch, and spent the rest of the day catching up on her washing and ironing. On fine days, she did a bit of gardening, or went for a walk with Lynn, who lived two doors down. They'd been friends since childhood, but Lynn was married now and had a baby. She couldn't get away too often, so their walks usually took place when Lynn took little Charlie out for a bit of air and ended when it was time for his tea.

"Would you like to go to the cinema this Sunday?" David asked shyly. "*In a Lonely Place* is playing at the Odeon."

"I would love to." She'd been wanting to see that film but had been reluctant to go on her own, since Sarah spent her Sundays with Bertie, and Lynn couldn't bring a toddler to the cinema. She'd asked her husband to mind Charlie for an hour or two, but he'd said that raising children was women's work, and she had no business gallivanting all around town with her girlfriends when she had a family to look after. Lynn had never brought up the subject again.

David's smile lit his gaunt face. "Splendid. Shall I come to collect you, or would you prefer to meet by the cinema?"

"Let's meet by the cinema," Helen replied. It was nice of David to offer, but she had no desire to introduce him to her mother. She wanted to keep this new friendship to herself for now. "I really must get home. My mother will be worried."

"May I walk you?" David asked after he signaled for the bill.

Once again, Helen found herself about to decline when good sense kicked in. She was enjoying David's company and there was no reason to cut their date short. It was a pleasant day, and the walk home would take at least a half hour. Why not?

"Yes, I'd like that," she replied as they rose to leave.

NINE

"Is that you, Helen?" Edith Brent called out.

"Yes, Mum."

"I was beginning to worry," Edith said when Helen came into the parlor. Her mother was sitting in her favorite spot, by the window, close to the wireless. Since taking a spill down the stairs three years ago and breaking her hip, she rarely went out, claiming that the injury hadn't healed properly, and she was in constant pain. Edith spent her days watching the street and listening to whatever was being broadcast on the wireless, her only relief from utter boredom the visits from her friends, Agnes and Joyce, who'd known her since Edith and Harry had moved into the house the year Helen was born. They came by on Saturday afternoons to play a hand of bridge and fill Edith in on all the neighborhood happenings. Edith loved the gossip and passed judgement quickly and harshly, her moral code too lofty to allow any sympathy for mere mortals. By the time they finished drinking their tea, with whatever treat Agnes had baked for them, they'd put the world to rights, and Edith was ready for another week of near solitude.

"I went for tea with Sarah."

"You could have told me you'd be home late," Edith admonished her.

"We'd only just decided this afternoon. And we're going to the cinema on Sunday."

Edith didn't reply. She hated it when Helen left her alone on Sunday afternoons but could hardly begrudge her a few hours to herself.

"I'm really tired, Mum. I'm going to have a bath and turn in." It was too early to go to bed, but she simply wanted to be on her own for a bit, to reflect on her date with David, and maybe read for a little while before going to sleep.

"Good night, then," Edith replied, her attention already on the radio program that was just beginning.

Helen trudged up the stairs to the bathroom and turned on the taps, then went to her room, undressed, slipped on her dressing gown and slippers, took a pair of clean knickers and a towel from the cupboard, and returned to the bathroom. The tub was half full, but she decided not to wait. She lowered herself into the water and rested her head against the back of the tub, closing her eyes. Her back and bum were nice and warm, but her breasts and belly were chilled, and she felt ridiculously exposed, even if she was alone. Helen tried to rearrange her body so that the water covered more of her and stared at the sprig of fake flowers sitting on a shelf in a tiny vase. They were violets, made of stiffened purple silk and wire stems wrapped in green felt. Edith had made them herself years ago, when decorating the house had still been a pleasure for her.

The water finally got deep enough to cover Helen completely and she sighed with pleasure as it warmed her through. She felt guilty about lying to her mother, but had she told her the truth, the revelation that she had gone for tea with a man she'd met at the hospital would have been followed by a stream of questions. Who was he? Who were his people? What did he do for a living? Why wasn't he married, and was she *sure* he wasn't married? Why hadn't he walked her to the door, as a gentleman should? Would they see each other again? Was she meeting him on Sunday?

Edith sounded like any well-meaning mother who was preoccupied with her daughter's unmarried state, but beneath her overwhelming concern lay blatant self-interest. Edith was terrified that Helen would find someone who intended to stick around. The few men who'd been interested in Helen in the past had been torn to shreds, made to sound like depraved bounders who were only after Helen for sex or money, or both. Given that she had nothing to her name beyond about forty pounds in the bank, she was hardly the plum target her mother made her out to be, but she had been right once, and that knowledge had done much to sour their already difficult relationship.

Edith never missed an opportunity to remind Helen how she'd been taken in, and Helen felt just as heartbroken and humiliated as she had when she'd found out that the charming captain she'd been seeing for six months, who'd spoken to her of marriage and family, turned out to be a married father of two. Captain Hastings had been conducting an extramarital affair not only with her, but with two other women, while his wife and children were biding in the country, safely away from war-ravaged London and rationing that had still been as stringent in 1948 as it had been just after the war. Neil had used his deceased parents' London flat to entertain his lady friends, having removed any traces of his family.

Not only had he lied to Helen about being married, but he had often been short of funds, and Helen, being a naïve girl of nine-teen, had used her wages to keep him in cigars and whisky, and her rations to pay for the food she bought to cook him dinners. They had rarely gone out, something that should have alerted her to the fact that Neil didn't want to be seen with her in public, but he had kissed her tenderly and told her how much he wanted to spend the evening alone with her, away from the hustle and bustle of the city after spending all day surrounded by the buffoons that inhabited Whitehall, where he worked.

Helen no longer thought of Neil as often as she had after she first discovered his perfidy, but when his name did crop up, she had to fight down a wave of shame that threatened to drown her. She'd been so foolish, so naïve. She'd loved Neil and trusted him, had believe him when he'd promised to marry her and told her that sleeping with him was no sin since they were practically man and wife already. He'd been very careful not to get her pregnant, citing his concern for her health and reputation, while all along the only reputation he'd been worried about was his own. He'd walked away from her without a backward glance when a casual acquaintance of his mistook Helen for his wife, Nancy, and a confrontation ensued.

It was that same evening that Helen had discovered she wasn't the only woman he was stringing along. They'd rowed, and the truth had come out, a truth that she'd stupidly shared with her mother when she came home, shattered and crying her heart out. Edith had been quick to point out how ignorant Helen was of the ways of men and how easily she'd fallen for the oldest trick in the book. She'd been kind enough not to tell Helen's ailing father what their daughter had been up to but had used her inside knowledge to manipulate Helen into doing a hundred little things for her, knowing that Helen could hardly refuse. The subject came up again and again when they were alone together, and Edith went over the same ground, skillfully squashing what remained of Helen's dignity like a bug beneath her shoe.

"And why would he marry you even if he were free?" Edith had asked, pinning Helen with her self-righteous gaze. "He's taken what he wanted off you. Had you behaved like a decent woman, you'd still have your good name, but now, you've been cast aside like the tart that you are, and he's no worse off, your precious captain. He's still got his family, and you are alone, used up, and no good to anyone."

Helen had been shattered by her mother's cruel words, but in retrospect, she'd realized that Edith had her own reasons for wanting to crush her spirit. Her father having mere months left to live, Edith had been terrified of being left on her own after Harry died. Edith didn't really need the space, but she'd never want Helen and her family to move in. The house was hers, and she would live there, on her own if it came to that, until she died. Helen was told time and again that should she marry, her husband had better be able to provide for her, or she'd end up homeless and penniless, and full in the belly, most like.

Edith wouldn't be pleased to know someone had taken an interest in her daughter, so it was best to keep mum. She would tell her mother about David if there was still anything to tell in a few weeks, or a few months, come to that. David might turn out to be a delightful surprise, or just another spark of potential that quickly burned out. It was too soon to tell. She was looking forward to Sunday though. It'd been a while since she'd been to the pictures and having someone to go with and then discuss the film with afterwards was a rare treat.

She always envied the couples who looked comfortable with each other and talked nineteen to the dozen as they left the cinema, eager to share their opinion and hear their partner's thoughts on the film. She wanted someone to talk to, someone other than Sarah, who was always rushing off after the film to give her mother her tea. Helen wanted to walk arm in arm, maybe go out for a meal, and be escorted home rather than take the bus on her own and hurry home in the dark.

Helen sighed with contentment as the hot water finally reached the tips of her breasts. It was pure bliss and she intended to stay in the bath until she resembled a prune. It was the only physical pleasure she indulged in these days. Helen soaped herself leisurely, running her hands over her breasts and legs. She hadn't been with a man since Neil—seven long years. Perhaps she'd been punishing herself for her bad judgement, or perhaps she'd been afraid to trust anyone that way again, but suddenly, she longed to be touched, to feel loved and cared for, if only for one night. Who was she saving herself for, and what was the point? What if she never married or had children? Would she wind up just like her mother, old and bitter, and jealous of anyone who still had love in their life? Had Edith ever had love in her life? Edith and Harry had got on—or "got on with it" would be the more accurate description of their marriage—but she'd never felt genuine affection between them.

Edith hadn't been particularly affectionate as a mother either. It was Harry who'd doted on Helen and made her feel special. He'd often said that she reminded him of his younger sister, that she had the same spirit and the same kindness Ellen had possessed before she died at the age of twenty. Helen had never felt truly loved by her mother, not even as a child. Edith had smothered her, but not with affection. She was a brittle woman who always needed to be in control. Everything had to be just so, even the fake violets in the bathroom whose green felt leaves cleverly picked up the green of the vines on the wallpaper. Helen had always been beautifully turned out, her hair neatly plaited, and her shoes polished to a shine, and Edith had been equally well groomed.

She'd been beautiful once, before two wars had robbed her of her health and vitality. Edith still took pride in her appearance. She had the hairdresser come in once a fortnight, a pricy indulgence Helen paid for out of her wages since the woman charged extra for the house call, and a seamstress from whom Edith ordered several new dresses every year. Edith liked real silk stockings, which she guarded jealously and wouldn't allow Helen to borrow, and wore bright red lipstick, a shade that would be more appropriate on a woman of twenty-five. She believed she looked good for her age, but at fifty-five, Edith hovered on the brink of old age. Her hair was streaked with gray, her face pinched and crisscrossed with tiny lines, and her lips, when not slathered with her favorite lipstick, were pale and thin. She'd put on weight too, despite watching her diet. After Harry's death, she hadn't been as strict about avoiding Agnes's treats and often allowed herself a second helping, a well-deserved treat in her opinion.

Edith had gone downhill since Harry died. There was no man to compliment her on her looks or escort her to church. There was no husband to impress with freshly baked scones or nearly meatless shepherd's pie made with vegetables from her victory garden. There was no one to keep her warm at night. Edith was a woman who needed a man at her side, and if she couldn't have a husband, she'd cast her daughter in the role of companion and try to keep her tied to the house for as long as she could, using any means necessary to assure her compliance.

The water had grown cold, so Helen got out of the bath. She pulled on clean knickers, followed by her virginal nightgown, and donned her dressing gown and slippers. Suddenly, she felt very old, as old as her mother. If she didn't find a way out soon, she'd quietly fade away as her mother had done, her life ending before it had ever truly begun.

TEN

JUNE 2015

London, England

Rhys poured a cup of coffee, added sugar and a splash of cream, and handed it to Katya, who'd just come out of the shower. Her hair was damp, and she had no makeup on, but to him she looked just as beautiful as when she was fully made-up. They'd been seeing each other for only a couple of weeks, but he felt more comfortable and settled than he ever had with any woman in the past. Katya was that heady mixture that made her the ideal modern woman: independent, forward-thinking, and undemanding, yet warm, affectionate, giving, and unbelievably sexy. Sometimes, when he saw her walking toward him or when he woke to find her sleeping next to him, his heart melted like butter on a hot skillet.

He was smitten. He'd lost his heart but found unexpected joy. He wished he'd met Katya earlier in his life, but maybe they wouldn't have clicked then; maybe they would have had other priorities, or not been as attracted to each other as they were now, having had multiple partners who'd disappointed them in the past. At times, they seemed to be on exactly the same page, or singing from the same hymnbook, as his mother liked to say. He liked that analogy. There was beauty in singing, and harmony, and that was what he felt with Katya—harmony. The feeling was new to him, since he'd never felt truly in sync with any of his previous partners, but he recognized it for what it was—beautiful and rare.

Katya accepted the coffee and smiled. She wasn't a morning person and didn't engage in any serious conversations until after the first cup of coffee and something to eat. She always had breakfast, and he loved making it for her. She'd taught him to make Russian cheese pancakes with cottage cheese, raisins, sugar, egg, and flour. She always ate them with a dollop of sour cream topping each pancake. Rhys put three pancakes on each plate and set a plate in front of Katya before sitting down across from her with his own breakfast. He watched as she added the sour cream then gave him a questioning look.

"Why not?" he said and moved his plate toward her. She added the sour cream to his pancakes as well and took a long sip of coffee before refilling her cup.

"Mm. Delicious," she said as she took the first bite. "No Russian man would serve me this kind of breakfast."

"Russian men don't cook?" Rhys asked.

"They do, professionally, but they prefer to be served at home. It makes them feel loved."

"Do you feel loved when I cook for you?" Rhys asked.

"I feel loved even when you don't cook for me," she replied, smiling into his eyes. "Do you have plans for the weekend?" she asked as she continued to eat her breakfast.

"Actually, I was thinking of going to visit my mum. I haven't seen her in nearly three months, and her birthday is next week."

"I always judge a man by the way he treats his mother," Katya said with mock seriousness. "Go see Mama."

"Come with me," Rhys said. He'd never brought any woman to meet his mum. Not even Haley. He'd instinctively known his mother wouldn't approve of the too-young, too-thin, too-preoccupied-with-her-career woman he'd planned to marry, and she would have been well within her rights. Had it not been for the baby, Rhys would never have considered his relationship with Haley anything more than a fling, always knowing it had a sell-by date.

"I think you should go on your own," Katya replied, "but I do appreciate the offer."

"Why don't you want to come?"

"Because it's your mother's birthday, and she'll feel like she must cater to me and make me feel comfortable instead of enjoying her son's long-overdue visit. Give her your full attention, make her feel special. Is it a significant number?"

"Seventy-five. My brother has planned a little party."

"All the more reason. Everyone will be too curious about your new girlfriend to pay attention to the birthday girl."

"Next time?" Rhys asked, disappointed. It had been a spur-of-the-moment decision to invite Katya, but he'd become attached to the idea.

"Absolutely. Have you got your mum a gift?"

Rhys smiled, pleased with himself. "I had Owain send me all the home movies he could find. There weren't many, but enough to work with. There are several of my parents when they were newly married, and then there was one of me and Owain as toddlers, and then as little boys. They were shot on an old video recorder, the type that's been discontinued for decades. He also sent me some more recent videos, ones he'd made over the years. I asked one of the techs at work to clean up the old films, add color and music, and put them on a disc, followed by the newer footage. Mum will love it. She'll be able to watch the film anytime she likes."

"That's a bittersweet gift," Katya said.

"Yes," Rhys agreed.

Katya pushed away her empty plate but made no move to get up. She reached out and slipped her hand into his. "What do you have on at work?"

"A new case for *Echoes*. A dismembered baby."

Katya's face fell. "That's awful. How do you deal with such sadness?"

"It is awful, but it makes for good television. I actually want to talk to Mum about it."

"Why?"

"I remember her mentioning a case when I was about ten. She said there was some deranged woman in London who stole babies from their prams and pretended they were her own. Once she grew tired of looking after them, she smothered them and buried them in her back garden."

"Did she dismember them?"

"She dismembered a few of them, I think, presumably to make them fit inside the box she was using to bury them in."

"That's a horrible story, Rhys. Why would you want to remind people of something so tragic?"

"I don't. I only want to make sure the baby we found isn't one of her victims."

"How many babies did she take?"

"I can't recall."

"There's no worse crime than taking the life of a child. My grandmother never got over having to kill babies."

"What?" Rhys exclaimed. "Your grandmother murdered babies?"

Katya looked away for a moment, her gaze fixed on the London skyline, her eyes shimmering with unshed tears. "My grandmother was a gynecologist, back in Kiev. This was during the Stalin era, when everyone lived in fear of being denounced and taken away in the middle of the night, never to be seen again. Like everyone else, she had to toe the party line. She said the edict came down in 1949. It had never been made public, and she'd get arrested if she ever told anyone outside of the hospital she worked at."

"What did this edict say?" Rhys asked, surprised to discover that he had been holding his breath.

"It said that if a child was born severely physically or mentally deficient, it was to be dealt with at birth. The Soviet Union needed strong, healthy citizens, not people who'd undermine morale and require lifelong care. My grandmother said that she was required to keep a bucket of water beneath the birthing cot. If such a child was born, she had to plunge it into the water and drown it before it had a chance to cry. The mother was told that the child was born dead and immediately wheeled back to the ward. The corpse was cremated before anyone could make any inquiries, not that they would. People accepted what they were told. To make waves was to put yourself and your family in danger."

"Did she have many such cases?" Rhys asked.

"She said that, thankfully, she had only two. One child was born with mongolism, which was unacceptable in communist Russia, where every face had to be perfect, and the other was born with its heart on the outside. It would never have survived, given the primitive level of Russian medicine. My grandmother never got over it though. She thought of those children every day of her life, and begged God's forgiveness for her sins on her deathbed. Now, religion was still outlawed when she died, but neither the doctor nor the nurses made any mention of her deathbed prayer. They'd known her for years, and everyone loved and respected her. They kept her secret."

"I hope she found peace," Rhys said, his brow furrowed. This conversation had grown awfully macabre, and he wanted to talk of something light.

"Meet me after you finish for the day," he said as he began to clear the plates. "Let's go see a film—something uplifting and funny. There's some American comedy playing. Rhiannan said she laughed so hard she nearly wet herself."

"Well, if that's not a ringing endorsement, I don't know what is. I'll call you," Katya said with a grin. "Since we'll be seeing something base and unsophisticated, can we continue the theme by going to a pub for dinner?"

Rhys clapped his hand over his heart as if he were having chest pains. "Fish and chips? Chicken pot pie? Kill me now."

"Aw, come on, you pretentious snob. Surely you can handle uncouth plebeian cuisine for one evening. Pretty please. I want something salty and greasy, washed down with a pint of bitter."

"All right. Whatever you like. I will take one for the team."

"You're an angel," Katya purred.

"Hardly," Rhys muttered as he collected the dirty dishes and stacked them in the dishwasher. He couldn't leave a kitchen untidy, even if it wasn't his kitchen.

ELEVEN

Gabe opened a new document and faced the blank screen. Blank screens could be terrifying, but they could also be exciting and full of promise. Now that the spring term was finished, it was time he got to work. In the past, he'd spent his summers at digs or teaching a course at the institute, but this summer, he planned to do something different. The discovery of Kate de Rosel's remains beneath the tiled floor of his parents' kitchen had reignited his interest in the Wars of the Roses and he'd decided it was high time he did what an academic was supposed to do—write a book. There had been countless books written on the subject, but Gabe's contribution would be different.

Thanks to Quinn, he had the kind of insight no scholar could hope to possess, and he meant to use the information to set his book apart. Now, all he had to do was find an angle that hadn't already been analyzed ad nauseum. Quinn thought he should focus on the women of noble houses and how the ongoing conflict had affected them, especially when their men suddenly switched sides and married them off into the houses of people they'd only recently considered their enemies. And then, when their fathers and brothers changed allegiances once again, the women were torn between loyalty to their families and duty to their husbands and children. It was an interesting idea, and the more Gabe considered it, the more he warmed to it.

With Alex napping and Quinn and Emma out with Jill, this was the perfect time to begin. Gabe took his notes out of the desk drawer, reviewed the points he intended to address in the introduction, and began to type. He had just finished the first draft of the introduction when the doorbell rang, making him lose his train of thought. Gabe reluctantly left the study and went to see who was at the door. He wasn't expecting anyone and hoped it wasn't some overzealous local business owner, offering a discount for a service Gabe had no use for. Rufus barked happily and preceded Gabe to the door, eager to see who'd come to visit them.

Jo Turing stood on the doorstep, her face deeply tanned, and her dark hair pulled into a ponytail.

"You're back," Gabe stated unnecessarily.

"Your powers of observation are extraordinary," Jo replied. The comment would have sounded like an insult had she not been smiling coyly at him, her eyes dancing with mirth. "May I come in?"

"Eh, yes, of course." Gabe stepped aside to let Jo into the foyer.

She leaned down to pet Rufus, then looked around. "Where is everyone?" She took a step forward, gazing up at Gabe with an expression he didn't care to name.

He took an instinctive step back. "Alex is asleep, and Quinn and Emma had a dress fitting."

"Dress fitting?"

"For Jill and Brian's wedding. It's in less than a fortnight," Gabe explained. "Emma's to be a flower girl, and Quinn is the maid of honor, of course."

"Ah, yes. I forgot all about that. I do hope I'm not invited," she drawled as she followed Gabe into the lounge. "I can't imagine anything more boring."

"Where have you been?" Gabe asked, ignoring her rude observation. He lowered himself into an armchair, and Jo sat on the sofa across from him.

"Syria. God, what a bloody mess. Of course, it's the civilian population that always suffers. I got some excellent shots though. Charles has been able to sell a couple to major American publications. *Time* magazine paid top dollar. What a coup," she said, smiling.

Clearly, the suffering of the civilian population was of high value, especially if the photos were of terrified children, their faces covered with blood and dust from the explosions. "Congratulations," Gabe said. "How nice for you."

"It is, rather," Jo agreed. "Someone's got to tell their story."

"Lucky for them, they have you to champion their cause." Gabe hadn't meant to sound sarcastic, but he couldn't help himself. She was so cocky, a lot more so than she'd been a few months ago when she'd first returned from Germany, having undergone neurosurgery after her near-death experience in Kabul. "I hope you weren't hurt this time."

"Not a scratch," Jo replied with a bright smile. "And how have you been? You look well," she added, her gaze turning predatory.

"I'm well, thank you. Quinn and the children are well too," he added. He was annoyed and wished Jo would leave. "Quinn won't be back for several hours."

"I don't have anywhere to be," Jo replied as she settled more comfortably on the sofa.

"Jo, I'm sorry, but I can't devote time to you at the present. I was working when you arrived," Gabe said, his tone implying that she should have rung instead of just coming round as if it were the most natural thing in the world for her to drop by.

"Sorry. You're right, of course. I'll leave you to it," Jo said, clearly irritated by his rebuke. "Please tell Quinn I stopped by."

"I most certainly will." Gabe stood, ready to walk her out.

Jo waited until he'd reached the sofa and stood suddenly. Her face was inches from his, and she pressed a hand against his chest, as if to steady herself.

"Sorry," she purred.

Gabe didn't respond. He simply stood aside and let her go first, following her to the door. Rufus trailed behind him, his soft brown eyes on Jo's backside.

"It was good to see you," Jo said and leaned in to kiss his cheek. "My sister is a lucky girl."

Gabe closed the door behind her and swore under his breath. *What in the bloody hell was that?* He returned to the study, the introduction to his book forgotten. Jo had made no secret of her attraction to him before she left, but this had been yet another guerilla attack. What had she hoped to accomplish? Did she really think he'd respond to her advances, or was she just having a bit of fun at his expense? Gabe sighed and ran a hand through his hair. Not for the first time, he realized that being an only child wasn't as unfortunate as he'd once thought.

Having given up on writing for the moment, Gabe reached for his mobile and rang Quinn. "Hi. How's the fitting going?" he asked, starting from afar.

"Great. Emma looks like a princess," Quinn gushed. "She's going to steal the spotlight."

"She must be pleased."

"Oh, yes. She doesn't want to take the dress off. Jill looks beautiful as well. She'll be a lovely bride."

"You'll be the prettiest one there, as far as I'm concerned," Gabe said, smiling. "What color is your frock?"

"You'll see it soon enough," Quinn replied. He could hear her smiling too. "Jill's invited us to lunch. Are you and Alex okay on your own for another few hours?"

"Sure. Have a good time. Alex and I have our own plans."

"All right. See you later," Quinn said.

"Eh, Quinn, Jo stopped by."

"What? She's back? Where had she been?"

"Syria."

"Did she offer any explanation for her abrupt departure?" Quinn asked, her voice strained.

"No, and I didn't ask. To be honest, she was being a bit abrasive," he said and instantly regretted the comment.

"Really? In what way?"

"Never mind. I shouldn't have said anything," Gabe said.

"All right. Kiss Alex for me."

"Will do," Gabe replied and ended the call. He hoped having Jo back wouldn't rattle Quinn. Jo seemed to have that effect on his wife, and as much as he hated to admit it, she had that same effect on him.

TWELVE

MAY 1955

London, England

David was waiting by the cinema when Helen arrived. She was secretly glad he'd got there first and she wouldn't have to stand by herself, waiting and worrying that he might have changed his mind and wouldn't show. Helen felt a bit awkward, unsure how to greet him, but David leaned in and gave her a light peck on the cheek. The kiss wasn't intimate or romantic, but it made her feel as if she and David were a couple, a unit, and not just two people going to see a film together.

It felt nice to have someone waiting for her, someone who was clearly glad to see her. She was getting ahead of herself, she knew that, and her neediness surprised her. She was used to being on her own—independent, capable Helen, "a brick," as some of her fellow nurses described her, who could be relied on in a crisis and who was always available, since she didn't have a family of her own to see to. She couldn't help wondering how David saw her, and what he hoped to gain from their association.

"Shall we get the tickets?" Helen asked, in an effort to mask her sudden insecurity.

"Got them," David said, holding up two tickets. "Ready to go inside?"

"Yes."

Helen allowed herself a small smile of satisfaction when David held the door for her, then escorted her to their seats. He waited until she was seated, then took his place next to her. The one time Neil had taken her to the cinema, he'd walked ahead of her, plopped himself into a seat, and planted his arm on the armrest, his elbow pressing into her side for the duration of the film. David clearly had better manners, despite having been raised in an orphanage. Helen experienced a brief moment of annoyance at herself. Why was she thinking about Neil today of all days?

"What did you do this morning?" David asked while they waited for the film to begin.

"I went to church with my mother, then we had Sunday lunch. You?"

"Just some housekeeping."

"Do you have anyone to do the washing for you, or cook your meals?" Helen asked, wondering what type of an arrangement David had with his landlady.

"I'm used to looking after myself. Been doing it for years," David replied cheerfully. "I like to cook, although sometimes it's too much of a bother to cook for just myself."

"So, what do you eat?"

"There's a small café just around the corner from where I live. The food is good, and the prices are reasonable. I eat there when I want a hot meal. Other times, I just make a sandwich and a cup of tea. It's easier that way."

"I'd probably do the same if I was on my own. My mother likes a proper tea."

"It's nice to have someone to eat with," David said. "That's one thing I miss about being in the Navy, the camaraderie."

Helen was about to reply when the lights went down, and the heavy velvet curtains parted to reveal the screen. She settled more comfortably, looking forward to the film. She thoroughly enjoyed it, all the more so because about halfway through, David covered her hand with his own and left it there, his fingers intertwining with hers in a way that made her feel warm and tingly all over. It was the perfect thing to do, in her opinion—not overly forward, but intimate enough to reaffirm that he liked her and was glad to be there with her.

"Did you like it?" David asked once the film finished and they stepped outside.

"Oh, yes," Helen exclaimed. "It was wonderful."

"You know what else would be wonderful?" David asked, smiling down at her. "Something to eat. I'm famished. Shall we get some supper?"

Helen hesitated. She wanted to have supper with David, but she didn't feel comfortable with him spending all this money on her. It made her feel beholden. Besides, she didn't think he could afford it. His suit looked freshly pressed and the collar of his shirt had been starched, but it was the same suit he'd worn when he came to the hospital, and the same tie. He was clearly on a budget, and she didn't want to put him out.

"Will you allow me to treat you?" she asked shyly.

David's face clouded over, and his gaze turned hard. "I asked you out. That means I pay."

"I'm sorry. I didn't want to presume," Helen stammered.

"You think I can't afford to take a girl out to a film and some supper?" he asked, clearly insulted by the insinuation.

"No, really, I don't," Helen replied. Hot tears stung her eyes, but she blinked them away before David could notice her discomfort. She hadn't meant to offend him, but given his reaction, she could see she'd made a terrible mistake. Now he'd walk away, and she'd never see him again. She tended to cock things up, but this was a record even for her. Maybe that was why she was still unmarried. She never took the fragile male ego into account and blundered in without thinking, eager to show the man how independent and forward-thinking she was.

David smiled and reached for her hands. "You are a lovely girl,

Helen, and so thoughtful. I appreciate your generous offer, but I really would like to take you to supper. Will you let me?" he asked gently.

Helen nodded miserably. "I didn't mean to offend you."

"You haven't. I mistook your generosity for a rebuke of my circumstances. I'm sorry." He smiled contritely and Helen smiled back. He wasn't angry, and she felt tremendous relief. She'd have to be more careful how she phrased things if they were to continue seeing each other.

"What would you like to eat?"

Helen shrugged. She didn't care if they went to a chippy, but saying that would imply that he couldn't afford anything better, so she kept quiet.

"Would a pub be all right? A friend of mine tends bar at the King's Arms. It's only a few streets over."

"Yes, that sounds lovely," Helen replied.

"Grand. Let's go, then."

They walked to the pub, chatting about their favorite films and books, the earlier tension forgotten. And David once again held the door for her and put his hand on the small of her back as she entered the pub. It was a bit run-down, but the patrons didn't appear to mind. The pub was busy this evening, and there weren't many empty tables. David found one toward the back and went up to the bar to place their order. Helen saw him talking to the barman, who peered toward their table and gave her a friendly wave.

"He'll come by and say hello later," David said once he returned with their drinks. "He's a bit busy at the moment."

"How do you two know each other?" Helen asked as she took a sip of her cider.

"We go way back. Olly and I know each other from the orphanage. Then we enlisted together in 1940."

"How old were you then?" Helen asked carefully, wanting to know his current age.

"I was twenty-two. I'm thirty-seven now," he said, smiling at her. "How old are you, if you don't mind me asking?"

"Twenty-six," Helen replied.

"The perfect age," David said, taking a sip of his bitter.

"For what?"

"For everything. You're old enough to know your own mind, but not too old to follow your dreams."

"I never had any dreams," Helen said. "I always assumed I'd get married and have a family. Then the war came, and the world changed overnight. Suddenly, women were working in factories and offices and were even joining the army. I was too young, of course, but I was inspired by women who wanted to do their bit, and didn't just cower in the country, growing turnips and knitting socks."

"The war's been over for some time now," David pointed out.

"Yes, it has, but the world will always need nurses. Besides, there's nothing for me to do at home."

David nodded, probably too polite to ask why she'd never married. She'd been too young to lose a sweetheart in the war, but by the time she'd come of age, men were thin on the ground, and the country was rebuilding, the returning soldiers bitter and angry at having no good jobs to come back to. Things had changed in their absence, and women who'd been holding their own during the war years resented being told to go back to their domestic responsibilities. Some had wanted to hold on to their jobs and put up a fight when they were unceremoniously dismissed to make room for the men. The status quo had shifted. Girls were no longer marrying as soon as they were out of the schoolroom. There were many young women in London who shared flats and held full-time jobs. Most of them still wanted to marry at some point, but they realized they didn't have to settle down imme-diately. There was fun to be had, and there were wild oats to be sown.

Helen wanted to ask David about his own situation but didn't know how to phrase the question in a way that wasn't prying. He was thirty-seven, an age when most men were married and had children. The war had been over for ten years, and there were plenty of single women to choose from. Why had he remained single? Or was he? Helen sat up straighter, squaring her shoulders. She couldn't fall into that trap again. Just because David said he wasn't married didn't mean he wasn't.

David seemed to notice her change of mood. "Is there something you'd like to ask me?"

Helen braced herself for his displeasure, but she had to know. She had a right to ask. "Why are you not married? Or are you?"

David smiled at her. He didn't seem offended by her insinuation that he might be lying to her. "I'm not married, Helen. Never have been. I had a sweetheart when I joined up, but she was married to someone else by the time I was finally discharged from the Navy. To be honest, I wasn't exactly heartbroken. Not seeing someone for years can either reaffirm how much you love them or make you realize that you'd never loved them enough. Mine was the latter."

"I see," Helen said. "And you haven't had anyone since?"

David blushed. "There was someone, but things didn't progress as I might have hoped. There's been no one since."

"I had someone as well," Helen confessed, "but things didn't progress as I might have hoped," she said, repeating his words back to him. That made him smile, and he reached for her hand.

"I believe things happen as they should, and people meet each other when the time is right. Just because something didn't work out doesn't mean it wasn't worth experiencing. It's made you and me the people we are today."

"You mean older and wiser?" Helen joked.

"Yes, but also more cognizant of what we need to be happy with someone long-term. I, for one, need to be with a woman who's honest with me. You see, my lady friend turned out to be married, a fact she withheld from me for nearly a year. She no longer lived with her husband, but they were both Catholic, so divorce was not an option. She was more than happy to cohabitate with me, but I wanted to get married and have a family, so I ended it."

So, we've both been burned, Helen thought, her heart going out to David. There was nothing worse than being lied to.

"Are you still angry with her?" Helen asked.

"No. We were happy for a time, but life goes on. I don't believe in looking backward."

"Neither do I," Helen said, glad he wasn't pining for his lost love.

"Ah, here's our food," David said, beaming at the server. "I'm hungry."

They were done with their meals by the time David's friend came over to the table. "May I?" he asked as he pulled a chair over.

"Helen, this is Oliver Greene, or just Olly. He's my oldest and dearest friend."

"Pleased to make your acquaintance," Helen said, discreetly studying Oliver from beneath her lashes. Oliver Greene was short, stocky, and balding, but he had a warm smile and eyes that shone with good humor.

"No, it is I who am pleased. David never introduces me to anyone. You must be very special."

Helen's cheeks grew hot. "We've only just met," she replied.

"I'm sorry, I didn't mean to embarrass you. I'm just so glad to see David happy. It's been a while."

Helen noticed the glint of a wedding ring on Olly's finger. Perhaps David didn't have too many friends with whom he could spend time.

"David was my champion at the orphanage," Olly said. "It's hard to believe now, but I was very small and thin. A strong wind could blow me over. I always got picked on. David looked after me, and I looked up to him. I thought he was so lucky."

"Why is that?" Helen asked.

"David was one of the few children at the orphanage who had his own name," Olly explained. "Most of us had been named by the people who worked there. They'd just take one look at an incoming child and name them based on what they thought the poor kid looked like. I suppose I reminded them of Oliver Twist," he joked.

"What about the girls?" Helen asked, intrigued by this naming system.

"Same went for girls. The prettier girls always got beautiful names, like Amelia, Violet, or Elizabeth, while the plainer girls were saddled with names like Dorcas or Ethel. The girls resented it more than the boys, who didn't even notice until some of the girls pointed it out," Olly said, grinning. Helen thought he might be having her on but didn't question his story.

"Would it have mattered if you'd known your name?" Helen asked. Greene was a good name, in her opinion. No worse than any name he might have been born with.

"It wasn't so much the name itself, but the knowledge that it was a dead end," Olly explained. "David could have searched for his birth parents if he chose to."

"And why would I do that?" David asked, annoyance flickering in his eyes. This probably wasn't the first time Olly had brought up the subject. "I wasn't wanted. End of story."

"I still can't believe you're not even curious," Olly said. "Edevane is a Welsh name. I looked it up. Not very common either."

"Leave it, Olly," David said, his tone laced with warning.

"Sure. Sorry," Olly said. "Well, I'd best get back to work. It was good to meet you, Helen. I hope to see you again soon. Perhaps we can all go out one night," he suggested.

"Olly's wife, Alice, was one of the pretty girls at the orphanage," David said, grinning at Olly. "I looked after Olly when he was young, but Alice took over as soon as he started showing signs of promise. She snatched him up before any other girl even had a chance."

"She knew what she was about, my Alice," Olly said jovially before he departed.

"He seems nice," Helen said.

"I'd trust him with my life," David replied. "I *have* trusted him with my life," he added quietly. "He'll have my loyalty and gratitude for the rest of my days, even if he is an annoying little twerp."

THIRTEEN

"So, what's he like, this David?" Sarah asked as she unwrapped her sandwich. They'd decided to take their dinner break outside, since the day was too lovely to miss out on. It had rained in the morning, but by noon, the clouds had parted, and the sun had come out, quickly drying off the bench Helen and Sarah favored.

Helen poured a cup of tea from her thermos and took a sip. They only had a half hour for their dinner break, but it was a half hour she looked forward to all morning, since Sarah took her break at the same time. Sarah was on the maternity ward, but Helen had been moved to post-op about a year ago. She was told she radiated calm and reassurance and soothed the patients who were in pain after their operations and needed patience and understanding.

"He's nice," Helen replied carefully.

"Is that the best you can say for him?" Sarah asked her, arching a dark brow.

"There's something about him..." Helen replied, allowing the sentence to trail off. She wasn't sure how to put it into words and had no desire to sound foolish.

"Such as?" Sarah prompted.

"Something solid, I suppose."

"Hm?"

"Trustworthy," Helen elaborated. "He seems like a man who doesn't like to play games."

"They all like to play games," Sarah replied. She bit into her sandwich and chewed thoughtfully. "Take my Bertie, for instance. Sure, he says he loves me and wants us to get married, but if I were willing to forgo the legalities, he'd have no incentive whatsoever to rush to the altar."

"You reckon?" Helen asked, surprised by Sarah's confession.

"He's a man, Helen. That's what they all want—pleasure without responsibility. Unmarried women take care not to get into trouble, but as soon as they marry, all precautions go out the window. Before you know it, there's a baby or two, and the woman who devoted herself to the pleasure and comfort of her man is now a younger version of his own mother. She's no longer a lover, she's a wife—the ball and chain, the noose around his neck, the woman who keeps his bollocks in her pocket," Sarah finished dramatically.

"And they said romance is dead," Helen joked. "Come, surely marriage can't be that bad."

"It's not, but it's not the bed of roses we're led to believe it will be, your every need fulfilled by this one man who can barely pick his socks up off the floor or remember your birthday. Marriage is hard work, for both parties, but it's the best alternative. Living your life alone is a fate worse than death, according to my mother, and I tend to agree with her. I like my job, and I like earning a wage, but I will gladly give it up for a home and a family of my own. I want children, Helen."

"So do I." Helen sighed.

"Not every man is like Neil bloody Hastings. There are some good ones out there, honest blokes who want more than a quick roll between the sheets."

"Yes, I'm sure there are," Helen agreed.

"So, tell me more about him," Sarah invited. She'd finished her sandwich and looked wistfully at the empty wrapper. Despite her petite frame, she was always hungry.

"He has this way of looking at me," Helen began.

"What way is that?"

"Like I'm the only person he can see. The few times I was out with Neil, his eyes rarely stayed on me for long. He was always scanning the room. I stupidly thought it was part of his military training, to be aware and alert, you know, but he was probably just checking out the other women or trying to avoid being caught."

"But it happened anyway," Sarah said with some satisfaction.

"Yes, when he least expected it. David looks directly at me and pays attention when I talk. He tilts his head to the side and has this thoughtful expression on his face, like he's really listening, and I know he is because he asks questions and then goes back to something I said hours later, as if he'd only just thought of something relevant to add. He seems like the kind of man who means what he says."

"You be careful, Helen. Don't trust too soon. A man in his thirties is bound to have his secrets."

"We all have our secrets. I'm not about to enlighten him about what happened with Neil. I only hope my dear mother doesn't blurt something out. You know how she relishes telling the truth, but only when it's about someone else's failings." Helen hadn't meant to sound bitter, but she couldn't help herself. Her mother's lack of sympathy still stung, and she was wary of sharing anything with her, even the most mundane of details.

"Your mother is scared of being alone," Sarah said wisely. "Same as mine. She keeps saying she'll move into the smallest bedroom and keep house for us as long as Bertie and I don't leave when we get married. I feel sorry for her. Bertie won't be happy to have her living with us, but she's my mother, and I'm the only one she's got left. She's lost her husband and two sons; it'd be cruel to leave her on her own."

Helen nodded. "I won't leave my mother on her own either, but I wish I felt more than a sense of duty toward her."

"We'd best be getting back," Sarah said as she stood. "There were three women in labor when I took my break. I wonder if they've delivered by now. I do envy them sometimes," she said as they walked toward the main entrance. "I wish it were my turn. I long to hold a baby in my arms, one that's mine."

"Yes, I know just how you feel. That's the one thing I'll really feel badly about if I never marry. I've always wanted to have children."

Sarah stopped and squeezed Helen's hand. "You will, Helen. You will."

Helen nodded, hoping Sarah was right. She wasn't getting any younger, and her window of opportunity was closing fast. Another few years and it'd be too late to think of having children.

FOURTEEN
JUNE 2015

London, England

Jo poured herself a glass of wine, took it into the lounge, and propped her feet up on the coffee table. She always felt a sense of displacement when she first returned from an assignment. There were no bombs whistling overhead, no explosions, no danger, no frightened, miserable people who reminded her how lucky she was to have a safe, comfortable home to come back to, and no desperate need for sex. People tended to give in to their urges when faced with danger, and she'd found companionship nearly every night in the arms of foreign correspondents who'd been flocking to Syria since the start of the civil war.

The sex had satisfied a physical need, but this time, Jo craved something more. Every night as she fell asleep, whether she was alone or with someone else, her thoughts turned to Gabe and she yearned for just a glimpse of him. For the first time in a long while, she wanted the man and not only what he could give her. She was like a schoolgirl who had found photos of her crush online and poured over them endlessly. She had no access to Gabe's Facebook page, but she was friends with Quinn, and she scrolled through her photos, grinning like an idiot when a particularly sexy photo of

Gabe caught her eye. If she didn't focus on Quinn's face, she could pretend it was her in the picture, holding a baby in her arms as she leaned against her amazing husband, whose arm was draped protectively over her shoulders.

Jo fell asleep with Gabe's face swimming before her eyes and woke with his name on her lips. She was sick with longing for him. Jo laughed out loud when the name for her illness became apparent to her. She was in love—truly, madly, deeply, and wrongly. She'd gladly give up her career, stay at home and have babies, and stab her own sister in the heart if she could only have him all to herself.

How pathetic can you be? Jo had asked herself with disgust as she packed her case in Damascus, ready to return home. To lust after your sister's husband was bad enough, but to dream of playing happy families with him was even more laughable. Gabe was in love with Quinn, in love with his children, and in love with his life. It was obvious. He wasn't on the make, and judging by his response to her, he wasn't interested in a one-off either. He had too much to lose, and too little to gain.

She had succeeded in catching Gabe on his own when she'd dropped by the house, but she'd behaved like a fool, and Gabe's lack of response made her seethe with frustration. He'd been cool and polite, and made it clear in every possible nonverbal way that he wasn't interested. Why would he be? He had his perfect Quinny. What did Jo have to offer him that Quinn hadn't already given him? He wanted more children; Quinn had mentioned that. God, Jo would gladly give him half a dozen babies if he'd have her. She never wanted to be pregnant again, not after that first time, but she'd gladly accept all the pain of childbirth if the child was Gabe's and he wanted it. The thought of him looking at her with tenderness, worrying about her well-being, and supporting her unconditionally was enough to make her weep with longing. For the first time in her life, she truly understood why women wanted to get married. It was all about possession, and she wanted to possess Gabe. She wanted to proclaim to the world that this gorgeous man was hers and hers alone, and she'd eviscerate any woman who so much as looked at him the wrong way.

Jo sighed with frustration. Gabe wasn't hers, but there was someone who belonged to her, in an abstract sort of way. She leaned forward and flipped open the laptop that had been lying dormant on the coffee table. She'd been stalking Daisy on Facebook for weeks, drinking in her daughter's every post and photo. She'd sent her a friend request, and Daisy had accepted, assuming the request had come from her elusive aunt and not her birth mother. Jo briefly wondered if Michael knew of the tenuous new connection. He could hardly come out and tell Daisy the truth, so he'd just have to sit on his hands and wait to see what Jo had in store for him. The thought made her grin like the Cheshire Cat. She had no plans to tell Daisy anything, but knowing that she could torment Michael from afar held a certain appeal.

You had no desire to be a part of her life, the more honest part of her brain argued. *You never even thought about her until a few months ago. Michael has been a true parent to her, despite his many failings.*

Still, Jo replied to herself, *I should have been told. I had a right to know.*

Jo logged in to Facebook. There, on her screen, was a picture of Daisy, wearing a wreath of flowers and a flowing lemon-yellow dress. She looked like a 1960s flower child—so beautiful. It had been someone's wedding, her stepmother's niece, by the looks of it. Daisy and her stepsister, Michael's wife's daughter from a previous relationship, had been in the bridal party. Jo stared at the picture. If she could produce such a lovely girl, she could have more children, but only with the right man.

"Gabriel," she whispered. "Gabe." A bolt of desire shot from her belly downward and she felt the familiar heat between her legs. She'd take him on any terms. Even if he promised her nothing but an occasional shag, she'd take it and call herself blessed. She'd take any part of him, even if that meant eating the scraps from Quinn's table. She was that starved.

The buzzing of a text message startled her. She reached for her mobile and checked the screen. The message was from Quinn:

> Welcome back. Sorry I missed you. Would love to see you and catch up. Ring me.

Jo tossed the phone aside. She'd call Quinn, but not today. Today she needed something a bit more satisfying. She picked up the phone again and scrolled through her contacts. Callum McBride had said he'd be in London for a week. Jo grinned slyly at the memory of the big, brawny Scot. He'd been the best shag in Syria by far. Yes, he'd do—do her, again and again until he pounded Gabe out of her mind, at least temporarily.

FIFTEEN

JULY 1955

London, England

"Off again, are you?" Edith asked as she came into the kitchen to find Helen making sandwiches.

Helen wrapped the sandwiches in brown paper, laid them carefully in a small basket, then added two apples.

"We're going to Hyde Park for a picnic," Helen explained. She'd been seeing David for over a month, but still hadn't told her mother. She'd meant to, but every time she made the decision to come clean, some deep-rooted sense of self-preservation stopped her and told her to keep mum about the new relationship. Helen felt heat rising in her cheeks. She hated lying, wasn't good at it, but the past few weeks had filled her with hope and an excitement for the future she hadn't experienced in years, and she couldn't bear to have those budding feelings tarnished by Edith's skepticism and well-meaning advice.

"You've grown awfully close with Sarah this past month. I thought she had a young man," Edith said, watching Helen closely.

"She does, but Bertie is travelling a lot for work and Sarah is at a loose end on her days off."

"Hmm, in my day no one was at a loose end, as you put in,"

Edith said, her reedy voice sharp with disapproval. "Young women married and had a family to look after. Nowadays, no one seems in a rush to do the right thing."

"Things have changed since the war, Mum. People want to have a bit of fun before they settle down."

"You can have fun with your husband," she replied, pronouncing *fun* as if it were a dirty word that she had to force past her lips.

"I know things were different when you were my age, but you can't begrudge me a bit of time on my own."

"Time on your own?" Edith asked, her brows knitting in displeasure. "I'm on my own all day long. Thank God for Agnes and Joyce, or I'd probably die of loneliness. I know you must work, having no husband to support you, but I would think you'd spend a bit of time with me on your days off."

"Mum, I spend every evening with you. I will be back later, and we can have supper together and listen to the wireless, just as we always do on Sunday evenings. But if I don't spend time with people my age every now and then, I'll go mad."

"I never knew spending time with me was such a hardship," Edith snapped. "I always considered myself blessed, having a daughter instead of a son. Boys go off to war, and if they're lucky enough to return, they marry and forget that their mother was the first woman to have loved them. Girls look after their mothers; they do their duty."

"I've been doing my duty by you my whole life," Helen retorted. "What more do you want? I'm twenty-six years old. I'm entitled to a life of my own."

"You're a spinster, Helen. You've missed your chance for a life of your own. This is your life now. Sarah's young man will return, and she'll forget all about you as soon as she's got better things to do, like plan a wedding. You wait and see. And then you'll come running back to me with your tail between your legs. Well, don't imagine I'll quickly forget how you've treated me."

Helen glanced at the clock. She had to go, and this conversation was not one that needed finishing. Her mother had carried on like this any time Helen had gone out with a group of nurses after work or went on the odd date. Her mother was a selfish woman who thought everyone owed her something, even her friends. She always expected them to call on her, as if she were the queen, and bring by a treat when they came. She carried on like an invalid, when in fact, there was nothing stopping her from going for a walk, or to the shops.

Getting out of the house would do her good. The only time Edith left home was to go to church, and even then, she made a show of suffering, leaning heavily on her cane and stopping every two minutes as if she were in unbearable pain. Helen might have felt more compassion for her mother had she not been a nurse. She'd spoken to Dr. Ross several times after he'd called in on her mother, and the man had assured her that Edith's injury had healed years ago. Her real ailment was that she lacked the attention she needed to feel important, and her symptoms had worsened considerably since her husband had died.

"I'll see you this evening, Mum," Helen said as she slung the basket over her arm and headed for the door.

Edith didn't reply but leaned on her cane hard enough for the wood to creak in protest and retreated to the parlor, where she turned up the wireless, as if to drown out the sounds of Helen's departure.

Helen hurried to catch the bus and took a seat on the top deck. Despite the confrontation with her mother, she was in good spirits. It was a lovely morning. Gentle sunshine glowed in a cloudless blue sky and the birds chirped joyfully, their song echoing in Helen's heart as she anticipated her meeting with David. She enjoyed spending time with him, and she liked having something to look forward to at the end of the week. Despite Dr. Waterson's orders, David had returned to work weeks ago, so getting together in the evenings became tricky since his shift ended several hours after hers, but they had their Sundays, and she wouldn't allow her mother's sour mood to ruin the best part of her week.

Helen removed her hat and turned her face up to the sun, enjoying its warm caress. It was as if the sun were shining just for her, and that was how David made her feel, as if he had eyes only for her. She'd never been the kind of girl to inspire mute admiration in men. She was average at best, but David looked at her as if she were the most beautiful woman in the world, and the warm glow that he'd lit in her heart continued to grow, more so because David didn't seem like the kind of man to take an interest in many women. He was serious and solemn, someone who gave honesty and expected nothing less in return. And it was his unflinching ability to see things for what they were that had inspired Helen to take a good look at her own choices.

She'd spent her life trying to please others—her parents, her teachers, her employers, and even Neil. She was always afraid to disappoint, to be made to feel like her best wasn't good enough. She'd allowed Neil to take her to bed because that was what he'd wanted, and their relationship had been all about her trying to satisfy him. He'd never taken the time to ask her what made her happy, or what she might have wanted. David wasn't like that. He never put his needs first. In fact, it brought him pleasure to make her happy, and she wanted to please him in return. She wanted to see his face break into that slow smile that always reached his eyes. She wanted to feel his hand covering hers, making her feel safe, and she wanted to feel his lips on hers.

She'd been nervous the first time David had kissed her, frightened that she'd feel disappointed, but the kiss they'd shared had been everything a kiss should be—shy and gentle at first, hot and demanding as it deepened. She'd leaned against David as his arms slid around her, pulling her closer, molding her to his body. It was the kiss of a man, not the fumbling of an inexperienced boy or the next step in a practiced seduction. When Neil had kissed her, it had been a means to an end, an attack meant to breach her maidenly defenses. David didn't need to breach her fort. She'd laid down her weapons and opened the gate, inviting him in and making him feel welcome. She was no longer a naïve girl of nineteen; she was a woman of twenty-six who'd been used and discarded, who'd been supporting herself without the help of a man for the past eight years, and who was ready for more.

She was past worrying about her mother's disapproval or her reputation. What good was a pristine reputation if she wasn't happy, if her life was as sterile as the bandages she rolled in her spare time? It was time to start living her life on her own terms. She had yet to figure out exactly what those terms might be, but deep down, she knew she was on her way. It was now or never. Helen smiled to herself as an idea sprang to mind. It was so shocking and forward that she couldn't believe she was thinking along those lines, but today she felt reckless. As the bus approached her stop, she jammed her hat on her head and grabbed her basket, eager for her real life to begin.

David was standing at the curb, his eyes anxious as he scanned the faces of the disembarking passengers. Helen was nearly half an hour late, and he'd become accustomed to her punctuality. She came down the steps to the lower level and got off the bus. David's face lit up at the sight of her and he leaned forward to kiss her cheek as he relieved her of her burden. The basket wasn't heavy, but she appreciated the gentlemanly gesture.

"I was afraid you wouldn't come," he said as they turned toward the park.

"I'm sorry. I got held up and then had to wait for the next bus."

"Is everything all right?"

"My mother was a bit put out. She thought we'd spend the day together," Helen explained.

"I would have understood," David replied, but his eyes told her he'd have been crushed if she failed to show up.

"I know, but I wanted to come. I've been looking forward to this all week. And it's not raining," she added, grinning like a loon. It had rained nearly every day that week and she'd thought they'd have to forgo the picnic and do something indoors.

"It's a glorious day," David agreed. "What do you say we rent a boat after lunch?"

"I'd love that. I've never been on a boat."

"What? Never?"

"I've never even been by the seaside," Helen said, watching David for a reaction.

"Oh, that's a shame. I love the sea. The orphanage used to take us to the seaside for one weekend every summer. It was the highlight of the whole year, even better than Christmas."

"What was Christmas like at the orphanage?" Helen asked. She liked it when he told her stories about his life. It made her feel closer to him, and she was glad to see that despite being abandoned, he felt no resentment.

"Christmas was nice. We decorated the dining hall with pine boughs and tinsel, and on Christmas Day, there was a special dinner after church, followed by gift-giving."

"You got gifts?"

"Everyone got the same thing. It was either a pair of socks, a new pen, or something equally innocuous, but it was the gift-giving between the children that was fun. We all had our friends, and we gave gifts to each other that we'd obtained through black market trade," David explained, grinning. "Oh, yes, there was a thriving black market at the orphanage. Some children were very enterprising and managed to get hold of cigarettes, magazines, even gin."

"So, what did you get for Christmas?" she asked.

"Olly always got me books. I liked to read. Still do. And I got him magazines and cigarettes, which he shared with me. His last Christmas at the orphanage, he managed to procure a small bottle of scent for Alice. She was over the moon."

"What did you do for Christmas after leaving the orphanage?" Helen asked, curious how a single man spent his holiday.

"There were several Christmases spent in the company of other sailors," David replied, "and once the war ended, I always went to Olly and Alice's flat for Christmas. They looked after me, made sure I wasn't on my own," he added with a rueful smile. "What about you?"

"I used to love Christmas when I was a child, but after my

father died, it became just another day to get through. Since everyone was with their families, it was just my mother and me, putting on the pretense of being happy. It became exhausting after a while, since neither of us felt anything that could be mistaken for joy."

"Yes, I can understand that. Joy is not an emotion that can be forced."

I feel joy now, Helen thought as David spread the blanket he'd brought beneath a leafy tree and set down the basket. It felt deliciously cool in the shade. David stretched out on the blanket and folded his arms behind his head. He looked like a man who didn't have a care in the world. *Maybe he doesn't*, Helen thought as she folded her legs beneath her and set her hat atop the basket. She turned away from him as she tried to work up the courage to broach the idea she'd thought of on the bus. Once she uttered the words, there'd be no going back. It was probably a mistake, but a small voice inside her head told her she mustn't give in to her fear.

"Hungry?" she asked instead.

"Hmm," David replied lazily.

I'll mention it later, Helen thought as she reached for the basket. *Much later. Or not at all.*

SIXTEEN

AUGUST 1955

Bournemouth, Dorset

A lovely breeze blew through the open window, filling the net curtains and making them billow like sails in the wind. The air smelled of sand and sea, the glorious aroma of summer at the seaside. Helen pressed her body closer to David's, enjoying the solid warmth of him. She had a lover, and it was delicious. Despite her ill-fated association with Neil, Helen had never known physical pleasure. The lovemaking had been for Neil and was a predictable affair—a little groping followed by a few minutes of missionary intercourse. Neil had never asked her if she'd enjoyed it or if there was anything he could do to make it more pleasurable for her. Making love to David had been a sensual feast where she got to try different kinds of delicacies before even getting to the main course, followed by a pudding so delectable, she thought she'd never experience its like again.

Lying next to him afterward, their limbs tangled and their hearts beating in unison, she felt so sated, she didn't think she'd ever be hungry again, but the memory of what they'd done not only suffused her cheeks with heat but shot bolts of desire to the very core of her, making her yearn for him again. He seemed to sense her need and met it with his own, this time taking her swiftly and urgently, and bringing her to a shattering climax that left her quivering like a bowl of jelly.

"I hope you're not sorry you invited me," David said, a lazy smile stretching across his sweat-dampened face as he moved his hand down her side and rested it on her hip, as if it were the most natural place for it. Helen smiled in response and buried her face in his shoulder, suddenly embarrassed.

David had been taken aback when Helen suggested they spend a few days by the sea. It had been a bold thing to do, and risky, but she had taken a calculated risk. Helen didn't think David was the kind of person who'd think less of her for acting on her feelings. He was a simple, down-to-earth man who didn't aspire to any lofty ideals or unrealistic spiritual or moral standards. He took every day as it came, living it as if it might be his last. He said he'd learned to do that during the war, when there was the danger of his ship being torpedoed at any moment. He'd lost friends, who'd met their end when they had least expected it, and had come home to find no one waiting for him.

Helen understood how he felt only too well. She'd been only nine when the war had broken out, but London had been a war zone as much as any battlefield. She'd survived the Blitz that had nearly pulverized the city, cowering in air raid shelters with Edith as explosion after explosion shook the walls of the overcrowded cellar, the vibrations dislodging pebbles and thick dust that coated their hair and faces. Every time they'd gone down to the shelter, they'd had no way of knowing if they'd be coming back up, or if their house would still be there when they returned. Miraculously, it had been, but once the explosions came too close to the shelter and a loose beam had knocked Edith on the head. Helen had held her mother's hand until the all clear, and then several men helped her get Edith to the surface and hailed a passing ambulance.

Waiting in the foyer of the hospital, Helen had seen the steady stream of ambulances pulling up in front of the hospital, one after the other, disgorging their bloody contents, the victims either half-dead and unconscious or wide awake and in agonizing pain, trying to put on a brave face for the nurses, who were so tired they could barely stand. It was then that Helen had decided to become a nurse. She wanted to do something that mattered, something that might make a difference to someone's life. Some of the people she'd seen arrive had left the hospital in bags, but their final moments had been made less harrowing by the stoic compassion of the nurses.

She'd taken to the streets with the others when the news finally came down that the war was over, waving a Union Jack and singing loudly along with the crowd. There'd been such exaltation, such hope for the future, but very little had changed in the coming months, or even years. She'd returned to the hospital, as a volunteer this time. The wounded had stopped coming, the adrenaline-filled hours of chaotic urgency replaced by orderly shifts on the ward, but life did not return to normal. London was gray and forlorn, the people who'd been dancing in the streets only a few months ago downtrodden and tired of never-ending hardship.

Rationing continued, as if the war hadn't ended at all, and returning soldiers trickled into the city, expecting to resume their interrupted lives and reclaim their livelihoods. A new threat loomed in the East, Stalinist Russia whispering words of terror into the ears of post-war Whitehall, warning that the threat wasn't only without, but within. Rumors circulated that individuals close to the seat of power were spying for the Soviet Union and planning to betray their country. A known enemy, who'd worn a recognizable uniform and the insignia of the Third Reich, morphed into shadowy back-alley spies, people one might work with or sit next to on the bus. The world had changed, and nothing would ever be the same.

People often reminisced about the war, recalling close calls, brief but passionate affairs spurred by fear of dying, and a sense of purpose they now seemed to lack. They grumbled as they stood in bread lines and walked with their shoulders stooped once they received their allotment of butter or flour. It was as if those first few years had been stolen from them, lost in rebuilding and regaining their equilibrium. For Helen, they had been years of hard work, domestic economy, and bitter romantic disappointment. But as she lay next to David, the world seemed full of promise. The golden sunshine that streamed through the window warmed her, the sea beyond sparkled in gorgeous shades of blue and green, and the gentle breeze caressed her skin like the hands of her lover, who smiled and pulled her closer, brushing his lips against her flushed skin. His stubbled jaw felt rough against her cheek and his stomach was rock-hard against her pink softness, but lying next to him felt so right, so natural.

Helen wondered if David felt it too, as she closed her eyes and gave in to the drowsiness that seemed to weigh down her limbs and cradle her in its embrace. Once they returned to London, their idyll would be over. David's landlady didn't allow lady friends in the gentlemen's rooms, and Helen could hardly invite David to spend a night at her house. They would have to come up with some sort of arrangement, but she would leave that up to him. He'd made no mention of the future, and she hadn't asked, preferring to enjoy the lazy days of their getaway.

She'd lied to her mother, telling her she was going on a training course offered by the hospital, but she was sure Edith suspected that wasn't exactly the truth. It didn't matter; she'd carved out three days for herself and she would enjoy them. She felt truly alive for the first time in years, and the feeling was heady. They had only been in Bournemouth for two days, but already her face looked less pinched in the mirror, and her shoulders weren't hunched with tension. She felt carefree, wanton, and sophisticated.

"Helen," David whispered as he tenderly pushed a stray lock of hair out of Helen's face. "My beautiful Helen."

Helen had never thought of herself as beautiful, and the compliment sent shivers of pleasure down her spine. She was plain, ordinary, and easily overlooked, the type of woman blessed with good sense and a strong constitution. But when David looked at her, she felt pretty, and sensual, and interesting. He gave her his full attention when she spoke, and even when she was quiet, his gaze caressed her as if the mere sight of her gave him untold pleasure.

For so long, she'd dreamed of belonging to someone, and now that she was with David, it felt even more wonderful than she'd ever imagined. She lifted a hand to his face, cupping his cheek with all the tenderness of her love-starved soul. She was still floating on a bubble of contentment when David abruptly brought her back to Earth.

"I think it's time I met your mother," he said, watching her from beneath hooded lids.

"Why?" Helen asked. She supposed she should be glad he wanted to meet her mother. That meant she wasn't just his tart, but his sweetheart; but for some reason, she wanted to keep him a secret just a little bit longer.

"Because I love you, and I see no reason for us to hide our relationship, unless you have reservations about me," he added, studying her face.

Helen shook her head. She couldn't seem to find her voice. David had said he loved her. No one had ever said that to her, not even her parents, who'd been reserved at the best of times. She wanted to tell him how much she loved him, how much his words meant to her and how she wanted nothing more than to bask in the glow of his affection, but instead, all she managed was, "All right. I'll arrange something."

David reached over to the nightstand and took a little brown packet out of the drawer. He handed it to Helen. "I saw it in a shop window yesterday when I went out to buy a newspaper and thought of you. I hope you like it," he said shyly.

Helen opened the package with shaking hands. It was a pewter brooch. A whimsical letter H was carved into the round surface, the curlicues entwined with flowers and vines. It was beautiful. "Thank you, David." She beamed at him. "It's lovely. I'll treasure it always."

"You deserve to be happy, Helen."

"I am."

He nodded. His eyes were shining with love and warmth, and he bent his head to kiss her.

Dear God, so this is what happiness feels like, Helen thought as she wrapped her arms around his neck.

SEVENTEEN

JUNE 2015

London, England

Quinn set aside the brooch and let out the breath she'd been holding. She'd almost expected David to spring some awful truth on Helen, but his feelings for her seemed genuine. Unlike the other tortured romances she'd witnessed over the past two years, this one seemed pretty straightforward. Helen and David looked right together and enjoyed the kind of effortless connection that defined most successful couples of Quinn's acquaintance. They should have had every chance of a happily-ever-after. What had gone wrong for them and the child, whose remains now lay tiny and incomplete in Colin Scott's mortuary?

Since Quinn was able to see Helen's memories, she had to be deceased, but what about David Edevane? He'd be close to a hundred now, if he still lived. Quinn was tempted to go online and do a cursory search but decided to wait. She needed to learn more before scouring the internet for any trace of David.

Quinn returned the brooch to the drawer of her bedside table and reached for her mobile. She'd sent Jo a text but hadn't heard back. She longed to talk to her sister, but instinct told her not to push Jo too hard. She clearly wasn't ready to speak to Quinn, so it was best to give her some space. It seemed that everyone was in need of space these days. She'd texted Logan as well but received a terse reply several hours later, assuring her he was fine and would ring her when he had time.

Quinn selected the one number where someone was always happy to hear from her. Susan Allenby answered the phone, her voice breathless. "Quinn, I'm so glad you rang," she exclaimed. "Your father is running me ragged on the tennis court and I need to take a break without having to admit that I'm winded."

"Glad to help," Quinn replied, smiling to herself. She was glad her parents had become so active since moving to Marbella a few years ago for her father's health. They'd traded in the cloudy skies of England for the blue vistas of Spain, and the change seemed to suit them both. They'd made friends with other English expats and had a busy social life, enjoying wine and tapas and day trips along the coast.

"How are my grandchildren?" Susan demanded. "I long to see them, Quinny. You said you'd come see us this summer."

"Mum, we've been a little snowed under, what with the program and the new house. I think we might be able to come at the end of July, if that's all right."

"We'll be happy to see you anytime you can make it. Oh, I long to hold Alex in my arms. He's growing so fast. And Emma... I do wish we lived closer to one another. I'd love to spend more time with her. I keep remembering all the fun things you and I did when you were a little girl. You were so sweet," Susan crooned. "How quickly childhood goes by."

"I'm still sweet," Quinn assured her with a joyful chuckle. She missed her mum and dad dreadfully, and even though she was happy they were well, she wished they lived closer too.

"Have you spoken to that woman?" Susan asked. Sooner or later she always returned to the topic of Sylvia. For some reason, she didn't feel nearly as threatened by Seth. Maybe it was because he was in New Orleans, or because she trusted him not to hurt

Quinn. Sylvia, on the other hand, was not to be underestimated, in Susan's opinion.

"Yes, I've spoken to her, but I haven't seen her in a while. I've been very busy with the program. Cases are coming fast and thick."

"Your Mr. Morgan is a genius," Susan gushed. "Imagine, creating a hotline for people to call in their discoveries. Given England's long history, I bet there are a lot more unexcavated burial sites than we care to imagine."

"There are plenty, but many of the calls are cranks," Quinn replied. "People long to be on television, so they call in all kinds of rubbish in the hope that it will turn out to be something of interest. Every rusted piece of metal is Excalibur, and every bone might have been a fallen knight or a Celtic warrior princess. Rhys keeps a full-time archeologist on staff just to check out all these claims. I tell you, Mum, he's not a happy camper."

"'Happy camper'? Is that another silly expression you picked up from your, eh...Seth?"

Quinn giggled. "Seth is full of them. Some of them are quite clever. On the money, as he likes to say."

"It's all about the money with the Americans, isn't it?" Susan grumbled. "Vulgar, is what it is."

"Mum, come off it. Seth is great. You'd like him if you ever spent any time with him. He's not like Sylvia. Or Jo," Quinn said, instantly regretting bringing her into the conversation.

"Have you heard from that sister of yours?" Susan asked, her tone implying that she'd be much happier if Quinn hadn't.

"She's back. Seems she'd gone off to Syria. She stopped by two days ago, but I wasn't at home. I texted her, but she hasn't responded yet."

"Not in much of a hurry to see you, then?" Susan asked. "Can't say I'm surprised."

"Mum, Alex is awake. I've got to go."

"I'll ring you next week, darling. Do book your tickets soon. Tourist season is in full swing here in July and August. All the flights will be booked."

"Don't worry. I'm on it."

Quinn said goodbye and hung up. Alex was still asleep, but she didn't have the patience to continue the conversation once it turned to Quinn's birth family. She could understand her mother's feelings. Susan couldn't help feeling displaced after years of being Quinn's closest relation, but no matter how many times Quinn assured her that no one would ever take her or her father's place, she still tried her best to remind Quinn that these people weren't her real family, despite their blood ties.

"Ma! Ma!" a cry came over the baby monitor.

Quinn's face split into a happy grin. Hearing Alex say "Mama" made her heart soar. She went to his room and lifted him out of his cot. He was warm and sleepy. She inhaled his wonderful scent and held him close. "Would you like to go to the park after lunch?" she asked him. "We can go on the swing and the slide. Would you like that?"

Alex's eyes opened wider, and she was sure he'd understood the question.

"Can you say 'park'?" she asked as she settled him in his high chair.

"Pa," Alex said.

Rufus came trotting into the kitchen, wagging his tail when he saw Alex, or maybe because he'd heard mention of the park.

Alex leaned over the side of the chair and pointed a chubby finger at the puppy. "Dog," he said, clear as a bell. "Fus."

"Rufus," Quinn automatically said, correcting him.

"Fus," Alex repeated.

Rufus gave a contented woof and settled beneath Alex's chair. Quinn smiled affectionately at the two of them as she prepared Alex's lunch, grateful that her life wasn't as tragic as those of the people she saw in her visions.

EIGHTEEN

Getting to know Sylvia had never been the plan, but Jo found herself outside Sylvia's neat little house, a box of chocolates in her hand as a peace offering. She'd called to ask if she could come round, and Sylvia had cautiously agreed. Jo wasn't sure what she hoped to accomplish by seeing Sylvia again, but their story felt unfinished. There had to be a third act to this drama, a final scene in which they either forged a tentative relationship or cut all ties. She'd been in favor of cutting ties from the moment they'd met but had found herself frequently thinking about Sylvia during her time in Syria. She had been shocked to discover that the arctic layer of ice around her heart had begun to thaw. Her worldview had shifted, thanks to Daisy, and she had come to realize—not without some bitterness—that she shared a strange kinship with her birth mother.

After all, how was Jo any different? She'd always assumed her daughter's adoption would go through the proper channels and her child would have a good home, but she'd never bothered to find out what had become of her. For nearly fifteen years, she'd been at peace with herself, not giving her daughter a second thought. Daisy was a part of the past, not a bridge to the future. Now that she knew the truth, she couldn't believe she'd never considered the possibility that her adoptive brother, Michael, who was Daisy's biological father, might have taken it upon himself to raise their daughter.

Michael had proved to be a better person than her, a better parent. Jo had seen numerous photos of Daisy on Facebook and Instagram. She was a happy girl, surrounded by a loving family and countless friends. She looked like her, Jo had thought as she'd studied Daisy's face for the first time. She had her eyes, and the shape of her mouth was just like Jo's, and there was the way she stared pointedly into the camera, the way Jo always did when photographed by someone else.

There were lots of selfies too. Daisy wasn't shy. Jo wished she could speak to her and ask her all the questions that had been multiplying in her mind since she'd seen her face for the first time, but it was too late. If she were to give Daisy one gift of maternal love, it would be to not disrupt her well-ordered life. She had no right to march in there and turn Daisy's world upside down.

Jo frequently wondered what Daisy had been told about her birth mother. What would she think of the woman who had never even asked what became of her baby? Against all hope, Jo prayed that Michael hadn't been too truthful. Perhaps he'd spun some yarn about a girl who wasn't ready to be a mum, or even killed her off in Daisy's imagination. If Daisy believed her mother to be dead, she wouldn't look for her, would never spend hours lying in bed at night, wondering why her mother didn't want her and had never even asked for visitation rights or inquired how her little girl had been. Jo's resentment of Sylvia had colored her entire existence, but while cowering in a shelter during a bombing raid in Syria, she'd suddenly realized that she was exactly like her—cold, calculating, and selfish.

Daisy was better off without a mother like her. Michael was probably a great dad. He loved children. He was a giver by nature, a nurturer. He'd tried to nurture Jo when she'd been an awkward, sullen preteen and then a resentful, selfish teenager, and she'd taken advantage of his love and had nearly destroyed his medical career. She'd wanted to punish him, to hurt him for disappointing her. She'd wanted so much more than a drunken tumble in her bedroom. Michael had been in his thirties, a grown man who'd had his share of sexual experiences. He'd been married. She'd thought he'd know how to love her, would be so much better than some sloppy teenage boy who had no experience of the female body. But Michael had been drunk that night, thanks to her, and he'd been aroused. She'd teased him for hours, had straddled him and wrapped her arms around his neck, sliding her tongue into his mouth and kissing him with all the intent of a grown woman. Michael had kissed her back, but then he'd lifted her off him and set her down on the sofa.

"Enough," he'd said. "This has gone too far. Go to bed."

But Jo had been nowhere near finished with him. She'd given him a slanted look before sliding down to her knees, her fingers deftly unzipping his jeans. Michael had been shocked, but not as shocked as when she'd wrapped her pretty pink lips around his swollen cock and begun to suck slowly, deliberately, taking him as deep as she could, while undoing her shirt to give him an eyeful of her bare breasts. She wasn't going to be rejected, told to go to bed like a little girl. She'd meant to lose her virginity that night, and she'd lose it to Michael, whom she'd wanted since she was old enough to understand that what she felt for him was more than sisterly love. Had Michael given her what she needed that night, had he enjoyed the sex, she'd have done everything in her power to continue the relationship, but Michael, who'd come to his senses a few minutes too late, had been horrified and remorseful. He'd thrown a duvet over her blood-stained thighs, his beautiful eyes filling with tears of shame.

"Oh, God, I'm sorry," he'd cried. "I'm so sorry. I never meant for this to happen. Please, forgive me. I'll do anything to make this right."

"You've done enough," Jo had said, angry and disappointed. She'd wanted earth-shattering sex, and all she got was a few minutes of uninspired intercourse followed by Michael's tearful apologies. "Get out, Michael."

She should have kept their tryst a secret, should have taken her share of the responsibility for what happened, but she'd thrown Michael to the wolves. She'd accused him of rape and demanded that her parents press charges. She'd wanted to see him brought down, humiliated, and destroyed. When she'd discovered she was pregnant, she had been almost glad, eager to punish Michael and their parents, since they'd refused to betray their son, and to remind them every day that they'd let her down. Instead, she'd destroyed herself. The girl she'd been before that night no longer existed. She'd been replaced by a younger version of Sylvia, but even Sylvia had managed to find redemption. She'd married, had a family, and enjoyed more than twenty years of peace before her past came calling.

Some days, it felt like Jo's past had never gone. She'd left home, had changed her name, had even fled the country, but she carried the damage with her, the insecurity, the self-loathing, the inability to form healthy, lasting relationships. All these issues had brought her to Sylvia's door because some childish part of her still longed for closure, still wanted to be loved by the woman who'd thrown her away. Perhaps it was pathetic, or perhaps it was the first step to finding a way forward. If she could find a way to forgive Sylvia, then maybe, one day, Daisy would find it in her heart to forgive Jo. Maybe, someday, it'd be Daisy standing in front of her house with a stupid box of chocolates, worrying about making peace with the mother who'd betrayed her.

Jo could almost hear her adoptive dad's bitter laugh as she stepped onto the path that led to Sylvia's door. She'd repaid his kindness with hatred, had made her cancer-stricken mother's last months on Earth a living hell. She'd destroyed everything that was good in her life, and there was no forgiveness, not even in death.

Yes, I know, Dad, I was a bitter disappointment to you, Jo thought, recalling her father's final letter to her. She'd burned the offending missive, but the words were imprinted on her heart, the ink seeping into her blood like deadly poison. She hadn't realized until the night she'd read the letter that she still longed for her father's approval, or in this instance, his forgiveness. That was why she was here, and that was why she wouldn't cause Daisy any unnecessary pain.

Unfortunately, her newly discovered goodwill didn't apply to Quinn. Unlike Sylvia, who was tragically flawed, Quinn was like Mary Poppins—practically perfect in every way. Jo knew her jealousy of Quinn was petty and unfounded, since Quinn had done nothing but try to forge a relationship with her and help her find her daughter, but for some reason, Quinn's innate kindness irritated Jo to no end, especially since it seemed to have won her Gabe's love. Perhaps if Quinn had been married to some terminally dull, balding doughball, she'd love Quinn with all her heart, but Jo's desire for Gabe skewed her feelings and played up her competitive streak.

Jo chuckled when she recalled the wicked little fantasy she'd indulged in on the flight back to London. What if Quinn became trapped in one of her visions? What would happen? Jo had never allowed herself to get caught up in anyone's life, past of present—it hurt too much— but Quinn mentally time-travelled routinely, using her psychic ability to dupe unsuspecting viewers, who watched her program and lapped up her assumptions without ever questioning how someone could deduce so much about a victim's personal life from a dusty pile of bones. Quinn could have stuck to scientific facts and painted a more abstract picture of her subjects' lives, but she used her gift and put herself through an emotional wringer because, at the end of the day, she was desperate to be liked and admired. Perhaps Gabe was like that as well; maybe that was why they got on so well. Did he think himself superior to others because he was an academic rather than a bus driver or a civil servant? Well, Jo would be happy to stroke his ego, and anything else that needed stroking, as long as she got what she wanted.

As Jo finally walked up to the door of Sylvia's house, she briefly wondered how Sylvia felt about Quinn. Was she the president of the Quinn Allenby-Russell fan club, or did she secretly want to slap that self-confident smile off her face? She was probably proud as hell, given the mediocrity of her other children. Logan was nice enough, but at twenty-seven, he'd most likely reached the pinnacle of his potential, and Jude would be lucky to see his next birthday, at the rate he was going. Perhaps it was Seth's DNA that had imbued both Jo and Quinn with intellect and ambition. How she wished she'd met Brett. She bet they'd have lots to talk about, given their mutual resentment toward Quinn. She'd gladly take a trip out to New Orleans just for a chat with the evil little fucker. It'd be fun to get into his head.

Jo raised her hand and rang the bell. For a moment, she hoped Sylvia wouldn't be home and she could tell herself that she'd tried and failed, but then she heard the click of the lock and braced herself for the awkward meeting.

NINETEEN

Sylvia was cautiously friendly when she opened the door. Jo registered the glimmer of satisfaction in her hazel eyes, and thought she noticed a hint of smugness in Sylvia's less-than-welcoming smile. Sylvia had known Jo would come back. The daughters she'd abandoned were drawn to her like moths to a flame, desperate to understand the woman who'd given them life and blithely walked away from them as soon as she was able.

Jo handed Sylvia the box of chocolates and followed her into the kitchen, where Sylvia put the kettle on and went through the ritual of preparing tea. She had no clue whether Sylvia liked chocolate, but it seemed rude to come empty-handed and she couldn't be bothered to ask Quinn what might make an appropriate peace offering.

Jo was surprised when Jude walked in. She hadn't expected him to be back at home. Jude's hair was tousled, and his jeans were sliding down his hips in a way that showed off his chiseled abs and sharp hipbones. Despite his unkempt appearance, he was a good-looking bloke, and surprisingly fit after weeks of stewing in rehab. He looked healthier and stronger than when they'd first met, and his gaze, which had been clouded and unfocused, was sharp as a razor when he gave her a casual once-over.

"Hey, Jude." She couldn't help humming a couple of bars of the Beatles song in her head, before forcing her brain to focus. "Been working out?" Jo asked. It was a stupid question, but she had no idea what to say to him. She supposed it was better than, *Been shooting up since you got out?*

"Yeah, there was a gym at the rehab facility. Thought I might as well take advantage," Jude drawled lazily.

"So, what are you doing home?"

"Haven't you heard? I've been sprung. Too expensive to keep me on ice for this long. It's time I faced my demons and took control of my life," Jude said, clearly mimicking something he'd been told in one of his therapy sessions.

"Oh yes? So, how's that going?" Jo asked. She'd meant to convey interest but instead came off sounding sarcastic.

"As well as can be expected," Jude replied and accepted a mug of tea from his mother. "Clean as a whistle, me; and will stay that way even if it kills me." He grinned, grabbed a piece of chocolate from the box on the table, and left the kitchen without bothering to ask Jo anything about herself.

She wasn't surprised. Jude had still been recovering from his overdose when they'd met and couldn't give a toss about a sister who'd appeared out of the blue. Jo did get the feeling that Jude was close to Quinn. He'd mentioned her several times during that first conversation, and there was a softening in his gaze when he mentioned something Emma had said. Emma was a hoot; Jo would give her that. She was the kind of child Jo wouldn't mind having—smart, sassy, and observant, and the fact that she wasn't Quinn's biological child made her even more appealing. In Jo's eyes, Emma was entirely Gabe's, her dead mother a nonentity as far as Jo was concerned.

"I was glad you called," Sylvia said as she placed a mug of tea before Jo. "I wasn't sure we'd speak again after the last time."

"I've had a lot of time to think," Jo replied.

"Oh?" Sylvia asked noncommittally as she sat across from her and reached for a chocolate.

"I have a daughter, Sylvia. I gave her up nearly fifteen years ago and never bothered to ask what had become of her. I guess you and I are not so different after all."

Sylvia didn't say anything, which irritated Jo. She wanted Sylvia to tell her that she understood and sympathized, and that there had to be a good reason for what she'd done. She wanted Sylvia to give her permission to forgive herself, but Sylvia continued to drink her tea, as if Jo hadn't just informed her that she had another granddaughter.

"I found her," Jo continued. "She lives with her father. She's happy."

"And does that make you feel better?" Sylvia asked, her head tilted to the side and her gaze narrowed in speculation, as if she were taking Jo's measure.

"Yes, I suppose it does, although it makes me angry too."

"Why?"

"I don't know," Jo lied.

"Don't you?" Sylvia asked. "You don't strike me as the type of person who doesn't know what she's angry about."

Jo exhaled loudly. She resented Sylvia's tone and the implication that she was holding back, but she needed to talk to someone about this, and it wasn't until she'd seen Sylvia a few minutes ago that she'd realized how much she missed her adoptive mother. She hadn't given her much thought over the years; it had always been her father who'd done the haunting, but there was something comforting about sharing your troubles with another woman, one who hopefully wouldn't judge you too harshly since she'd been through a similar experience.

"All right, I do know," Jo admitted. "I never wanted the baby, not for a moment, but finding out that her father has been there for her all this time, has raised her and been loved by her, makes me feel irrationally jealous, and cheated. You must think me a terrible hypocrite," Jo said, raising her eyes to meet Sylvia's thoughtful gaze.

"I don't think anything of the sort," Sylvia replied. "You did what you thought was best at the time. In retrospect, it might have been the biggest mistake of your life, but you wouldn't know that when you were sixteen. Life has a way of changing one's perspective, and one's priorities. When I was seventeen, all I wanted was to feel unencumbered again. At forty-eight, all I want is to keep my children around me, since I know my time with them is not guaranteed. Quinn doesn't need me; she has a mother who's loved her all her life and thinks I'm a dirty little slapper who doesn't deserve a second chance. Logan has a life of his own, and whether his future is with Colin or not, he'll still go his own way regardless, as he should; he's a grown man. And Jude won't stick around here for long. He's an adrenaline junkie who needs to walk the knife edge of danger to feel alive. I pray that whatever he does next won't be the end of him. I wish I'd appreciated my children more when they still needed me, instead of wishing I had more time to myself, but it's too late now. Now, all I can do is wait until they ring me and make myself available to them for the brief period of time I'm useful to them."

"You're very forthcoming," Jo said, taken aback by Sylvia's candor.

"Isn't that why you came here, to hear some home truths?"

"I suppose. I'm not sure what to do, Sylvia."

"About what?"

"About any of it. I'm nearly thirty-two. I have a daughter I'll never have a relationship with, a sister who annoys me because, if I'm honest, I'm desperately jealous of her, brothers who'd be just as happy without me in their lives, and I'm in love with a man I can never have."

"Oh dear," Sylvia replied with a knowing smile. "Well, let's break this down into bite-sized morsels, shall we? Makes it easier to digest. Whether you have a relationship with your daughter is up to you. I'm not suggesting that you barge into her life and ambush her with your needs, but perhaps, in time, you can begin to lay the groundwork for a reunion. She might not want to have anything to do with you at first, but time is on your side, and nothing is impossible when it comes to human relationships. Just look at us."

Jo smiled in acknowledgement. She had never imagined being able to have such a frank discussion with Sylvia, and she was pleasantly surprised to discover that Sylvia was not only showing something of her own vulnerability but was eager to help Jo with her problems rather than just dismissing her as a heartless bitch. "And Quinn?" Jo prompted.

Sylvia smiled, her gaze soft with understanding. "It's only natural that you should be jealous of Quinn. Sibling rivalry is par for the course, even more so with twins, and Quinn is a tough act to follow. She drives me mad at times, but I am proud of her. Quinn is the type of person who will always win at the game of life because she's smart and kind, which is not to say that you don't have your own strengths. You are intelligent, ambitious, and fearless, a quality few people possess. Most people settle for the known, the comfortable. You just returned from Syria. What you do takes a lot of courage and self-sacrifice. Don't sell yourself short, Jo. You're just as successful as Quinn, and the personal side of things will come, in time."

Sylvia took a sip of tea and popped another piece of chocolate into her mouth. Seemed like that was another thing they shared—a love of sweets. "Your brothers don't dislike you; they don't know you. There's still time to build a relationship with them, even with your brother in the States. You can write to him, if you wish. And this man you're in love with, what's the story there?"

"He's married, and he loves his wife," Jo replied gravely.

"I see. What is it about this man that makes you love him? Could it be his unavailability?" Sylvia asked.

Once again, Jo was taken aback by Sylvia's astuteness. Would she still want Gabe so badly if he were available, or would she dismiss him as another dull academic who was soft as white bread beneath his starched shirts and tragically repressed where it mattered most? Jo smiled to herself, shaking her head. No, she'd want him just as much because he wasn't dull or soft or asexual. He was a rare man, the kind that came along once in a lifetime.

"He's everything I think a man should be: intelligent, kind, ambitious, and unbelievably hot. I've never met anyone like him, and I don't think I ever will."

"Does he know how you feel?"

"I think he's beginning to suspect. What should I do? What would you have done in my place?"

"I would have pursued him," Sylvia confessed. "I'm not proud to admit that, but I wasn't one to walk away from something I wanted. My husband was married when we first met, and he fancied himself in love with his wife. I helped him see that maybe he didn't love her as much as he thought he did."

"Did he love you?" Jo asked.

"He did. We had our ups and downs, but he loved me. You see, I never gave him all of me, and that kept him intrigued for over twenty years. I never meant to keep myself from him, but there were too many things I simply couldn't tell him, and he instinctively felt that there were walls left to breach. Men like a challenge. Nothing bores a man quicker than a needy, naggy woman."

"Did he have children with his first wife?"

"No, he didn't."

"Would you still have gone after him if he had?" Jo asked.

"At that time in my life, probably. I was too selfish to think of anyone else. Does this man have a family?"

"Yes, he has small children, but I would never try to prevent him from being their father."

"Jo, it's not for me to tell you what to do. You'll do what you think is right anyway, but you can't break up his family, only he can do that, and if he's willing to walk away from his wife and children, that's his decision, not yours. It takes two people to start a relationship. I'd tell you to walk away from this, but somehow, I don't think you will, so instead, I'll tell you to beware. If you pursue this, you're risking a lot more than he is."

"I can't walk away as long as I think there might be a chance for us," Jo replied. She briefly wondered what Sylvia's advice would be if she knew Jo was referring to Gabe but decided to withhold that particular bit of information. If, in time, Quinn discovered that Jo had been acting on Sylvia's advice, she'd have kittens. The thought nearly made her smile.

"And is there a chance for you? You just said he loves his wife."

"He does, but that can change. People fall out of love all the time."

"Then perhaps you should go all in. Confront him, tell him how you feel, and see if there's any chance of a future. If not, then walk away and don't waste any more time on something that can never be."

"Yes, I just might do that. Thank you for listening to me."

"I'm glad you felt you could confide in me. I never dreamed we'd meet, much less be able to talk like this. You've made me very happy."

Jo felt a momentary urge to hug Sylvia but fought it down. She'd become dangerously emotional since discovering this new family, and she didn't like it, not one bit.

TWENTY

SEPTEMBER 1955

London, England

Helen felt a flutter of nervousness in the pit of her stomach as she prepared Sunday lunch. She'd splurged on mutton chops and was going to serve them with mashed potatoes and peas and carrots. She'd even made a plum duff for pudding. Several bottles of beer were cooling in the ice box, and there was cider for Edith.

Helen untied her apron and went into the parlor to check on her mother. She'd caught a summer chill while Helen was in Bournemouth and had taken to her bed. It had taken her nearly a fortnight to recover. Had it not been for Agnes's kindness, Helen might have had to take a sabbatical from work to care for her. Agnes stopped in every day at noon to heat up the lunch Helen had prepared in advance, help Edith to the bathroom, and update her on the latest news. After work, Helen cooked supper and took it up to her mother, who pushed the food around on her plate and complained that it was either too cold, too hot, too bland, or too peppery. Most of her dinner wound up being next day's lunch. Helen then helped Edith bathe, and back into bed. The two of them listened to the wireless, which Helen had brought up from the parlor, until Edith began to nod off sometime around nine.

Edith still complained of achiness and fatigue and spent most of her days sitting by the window, but she felt sufficiently recovered to finally meet David.

"All right, Mum?" Helen asked as she poked her head into the parlor. "Do you need anything? I'll just go meet David from the bus."

Edith shrugged, her expression disdainful. Helen could easily guess what she was thinking. Why did a grown man need to be met off the bus like a child? He didn't, but Helen hadn't seen him for more than an hour or two since they'd returned from Bournemouth and wanted to spend a few minutes alone with him, not something she'd be able to do with Edith in the house. She missed him and wished they could find a way to be together for even a few hours, but neither of them earned enough money to start spending their wages on hotel rooms. Now that Edith was on the road to recovery, they'd find a way to pick up where they'd left off.

Helen's heart skipped a beat when David alighted from the bus. He smiled broadly when he saw her and reached for her hand, since to kiss or embrace her in public wouldn't be proper, more so because the stop was so near her house and someone who knew her might see. Helen was pleased to notice that David had taken extra care. He was wearing a new shirt, and a tie she hadn't seen before, and his suit looked freshly pressed. His hat had been brushed, and he was cleanly shaven and smelled of cologne.

"I'm so happy to see you," he said. "I was beginning to despair." They hadn't seen each other since Tuesday, when David had taken two busses just to spend her dinner break with her and get back to his own post before his allotted time had elapsed.

"I'm sorry. I couldn't get away," Helen explained once again. Thankfully, David's landlady, Mrs. Bush, had a telephone, so Helen was able to ring from a call box by the hospital and leave a message for him, or sneak out in the evening and ring just to hear his voice. The landlady stood next to David the whole time he was engaged in conversation, partly out of curiosity, and partly because she didn't want him tying up the line in case Prince Phillip, of whom she was inordinately fond, according to David, came to his senses and called to tell her that he was leaving Her Majesty the Queen for one Gladys Bush of Clerkenwell. She also charged David for the use of the phone, even when Helen rang just to leave a message.

"Have you told her yet?" David asked, his gaze anxious.

Helen shook her head. "I couldn't bring myself to spring it on her when she was so ill. I thought we'd tell her together."

David let out the breath he'd been holding. "I was beginning to think you'd changed your mind."

"As if I would," Helen exclaimed, arching her eyebrow. "I could barely keep the news to myself."

David had asked her to marry him on their last morning in Bournemouth. They'd been walking on the beach, their feet chilled by the rolling surf. The beach had still been empty at that time of the morning, the seagulls the only witnesses to what had been the happiest moment of Helen's life. She'd sensed a change in David that morning, a reticence that she'd attributed to a change of heart. When he'd suggested they take a walk on the beach before breakfast, she'd braced herself for the worst, steeling herself to the disappointment that seemed to stalk her every relationship. David had been silent and pensive, but his hand was warm on hers and he walked as close to her as decency would allow. Helen had been quiet as well, affected by his solemn mood.

When he stopped walking, the sun was behind him, adorning his head with a halo and making his expression difficult to read, but she instinctively knew that whatever he was about to say would change everything. "Helen, I know it's awfully fast, and I have no right to ask anything of you, since I don't have much to offer in the way of worldly goods, but I must tell you how I feel, and I place myself at your mercy in the hope that you might welcome what I have to say."

Helen arranged her face into a mask of calm and lifted her gaze to meet his. She had yet to comprehend the full import of the moment, or grasp the roundabout meaning of David's words, but her heart beat wildly against her ribs, and her breath came in shallow gasps as David took his time getting to the point.

"I don't think I'm being presumptuous in saying that there was a connection between us from the moment we met. It's as if we've known each other for years, not mere months. I want to be with you always. I want to wake up next to you for the rest of my life. What do you say?" he said, smiling into her eyes. He looked at her expectantly, his smile wavering when she didn't immediately reply.

"David, you haven't actually asked me," Helen reminded him gently.

David smiled sheepishly and sank down on one knee, wetting the leg of his linen trousers. "Helen Brent, will you do me the honor of becoming my wife?" he asked breathlessly, his gaze fixed on her face. "I love you," he added.

"Yes," Helen whispered. "Oh yes."

David stood, grabbed her around the waist, and swung her around, to the amazement of the seagulls, who scattered with squawks of displeasure. "I am so happy," he said simply, echoing her own thoughts. "I'd forgotten what it's like to feel this happy."

They'd spent the remainder of the day walking on air, their eyes finding each other as their fingers intertwined, words inadequate in the face of their newfound joy. It was too soon to make any plans or share their news; Helen had yet to tell her mother and that was a hurdle she wasn't looking forward to, but once they secured Edith's blessing, they'd set a date and go about figuring out the myriad details that their newly married status would entail. But that day, they allowed themselves just to be, and not think of anything that might put a damper on their soaring spirits.

Helen released David's hand as they approached the house. It was still fully light outside, but the glaring sun of the afternoon had given way to a soft glow that made the street and the modest little house seem almost magical. Edith was watching for them, her nose almost touching the windowpane, and Helen gave her a happy wave before unlocking the door. She led David, who was holding his hat in both hands like an errant pupil, into the parlor.

"Mum, I'd like you to meet David Edevane," she announced.

Edith stared at David, her eyes and partially open mouth nothing more than three black holes in a face shadowed by the dimly lit parlor. The window was behind her, the afternoon sunlight illuminating David's tense face. He gripped his hat harder, his fingers whitening at the knuckles.

"Pleased to make your acquaintance, ma'am," David said, bowing his head respectfully.

"Yes," Edith replied. Helen wasn't sure what she was saying yes to, but it didn't seem as if she were about to elaborate.

"I was glad to hear you're feeling better," David tried again.

"I suppose I'd better, since Helen obviously has more pressing things to do than look after me," Edith replied rudely.

"Mum, why don't you come to the table? Dinner is almost ready," Helen suggested, desperate to fill the awkward silence that had fallen in the wake of Edith barb.

"Something smells wonderful," David said. "Is there anything I can do to help?"

"Perhaps you can escort my mother into the dining room."

David offered Edith his arm. She took it, but Helen saw the fleeting look of panic on her haggard face. Her reluctance wasn't lost on David, who looked to Helen for help. Helen gave him a watery smile. She hadn't expected Edith to love David on sight, but she hadn't expected such obvious hostility either. Edith was a woman who enjoyed being liked, and was usually gracious and charming, at least until their guests left. It was only later, once she'd had time to consider her opinion, that she let Helen know exactly what she thought of whoever she'd invited.

Helen brought out the platter of chops and mash and the dish of vegetables, then returned to the kitchen for bread and butter, and a sharp knife. They'd need it to cut the tension, she thought hysterically. David offered to pour Edith a glass of cider and she accepted by inclining her head as if she were the queen. She took a small sip, then set her glass down and fixed her eyes on her still-empty plate. David tried his best to engage Edith in conversation, but she replied in monosyllables, asked him nothing about himself, then excused herself as soon as pudding was finished.

"I'm tired," Edith said. "Helen, help me upstairs?"

Helen rose to her feet. She tried not to allow her emotions to get the better of her, but she was angry and confused. "Mum, before you go up, there's something David and I would like to tell you. We are to be married. Soon," Helen added.

Edith's expression was stony. "Congratulations," she snapped. If Helen hadn't heard the actual word, she might have thought her mother said, "Damn you." She seemed so angry that she didn't even bother to glance at Helen's waist to see if she might be up the duff or make a caustic remark about the reason David was willing to marry her, and so soon.

"Thank you," David said, rising to his feet. "It was lovely to meet you."

Edith nodded in his direction and turned to leave the room. Helen helped her up the stairs but didn't utter a word of reproach. The conversation she'd meant to have with her mother would come later, after David left.

"I'm sorry," David said once Helen came back down the stairs and into the lounge, where he was standing by the window. "I seem to have done something to offend your mother."

"You haven't done anything, and it is I who am sorry. My mother's behavior was unforgivable, and I intend to ask her why she thought it acceptable to treat you as if you were beneath contempt."

"Helen, don't. I don't want to come between you and the only family you have left. Give it time. I'll try harder; I'll win her over."

"And if you don't?" Helen asked, fearful that Edith's derision might cast a cloud over her happiness.

"And if I don't, then at least we'll both know that I tried. If your mother continues to dislike me, we'll deal with it then."

Helen walked into David's arms and he held her tight, his lips brushing lightly against her temple. It felt so good to have someone to hold, someone who was willing to put aside his own feelings for the sake of hers. David didn't need to tell her he loved her. She felt it in his every gaze, his every smile, and his every gesture toward her.

"I wish you could stay," Helen whispered.

"I do too, but I think we both know this is not the time or the place."

Helen nodded into his shoulder. Edith wouldn't come out of her room, even if she heard something untoward, but to make love with her in the house would be disrespectful and embarrassing. Instead, David and Helen sat on the sofa, Helen's head on David's shoulder, his temple resting against her hair. He had his arm around her, and she felt more at peace than she had since returning from Bournemouth and finding her mother ill. Soon, they'd spend all their evenings together, and then go up to bed without feeling furtive or ashamed.

"I'd like to set the date," Helen said defiantly.

"Why don't we give your mother a few weeks to come round to the idea?" David suggested. "In the meantime, we can begin to plan."

"All right," Helen agreed. "No one says I can't go shopping for a frock or draw up a menu for our wedding breakfast. Whom would we even invite?" she asked, realizing that between her and David they'd only have a handful of guests.

"We don't have to invite anyone, if you've no wish to. It can be just you and me, a hotel room, and a bottle of fizz. What do you say?"

"I say I'll think about it," Helen replied. She'd always dreamed of having a church wedding with white flowers and a lace dress, but in her fantasy the pews were always filled with friends and family, the guests happy and smiling, and wishing the newlyweds a long and happy life. Given her mother's reception of David, she didn't think she'd be smiling or wishing them well. The only other guests would be Sarah and Bertie, and Olly and Alice. Perhaps they could all go out for a drink after the ceremony before David and Helen went off on their own. It would certainly cost less, Helen mused as she snuggled into David's side. "It'll be beautiful, no matter what we do," she said softly.

David kissed the top of her head. "That it will be."

After David left, Helen finished tidying up the kitchen and made her way upstairs. A part of her wanted to confront Edith there and then, but she resisted the urge and went to her own room. She was tired and angry. She'd had such hopes for this evening. She'd actually imagined that her mother might be happy for her and offer to help plan the wedding. What a fool she'd been. Of course, Edith wouldn't be happy, since Helen's needs conflicted with her own. Helen lay awake for a long time, but eventually, fatigue overtook her and she fell into a fitful sleep.

TWENTY-ONE

Helen woke to driving rain. It hammered against the windowpanes with surprising force and leached all the light out of the room. More than anything, Helen wished she could stay in bed. She was tired, not having been able to fall asleep immediately last night, and a barely perceptible hint of David's cologne on her skin reminded her just how much she wished he was lying next to her on this miserable day. Helen peered at the clock. Seven. Time to get ready for work. She swung her legs out of bed, shoved her feet into slippers, and headed to the bathroom. Having seen to personal business, she brushed her teeth and washed her face with cold water. It was a shock to the system, but it helped her to fully wake up.

Helen left the bathroom and was about to go get dressed when something made her pause just outside her mother's room. Edith was usually awake by the time Helen got up for work, and when Edith was awake, she made noise. Now that Helen thought about it, she'd been unusually quiet last night as well. Helen heard the groaning of the mattress springs when Edith shifted her weight, the padding of Edith's slippers, and the flushing of the commode when she got up to go to the toilet during the night. She also liked to have a cup of tea first thing in the morning. No sounds came from the kitchen, and Helen experienced a frisson of alarm. She stood in the corridor, unsure what to do. She really had no desire to see her mother this morning and would have gladly left for work without coming face to face with her, but her instinct warned her that something wasn't quite right. She rapped lightly on the door but received no reply.

"Mum?" she called softly, in case Edith was still asleep. No answer.

"Mum, are you all right?" she tried again. When she heard nothing, she turned the knob and opened the door a crack.

Edith lay on her back, her eyes wide open, her hand over her heart. Her face was frozen in a grimace of pain and her mouth was open, as if in a silent scream.

"Oh my God," Helen exclaimed as she hurried toward the bed. She reached out to check for a pulse, but her fingers met with cold, lifeless skin. Edith had been dead for some time. A sob tore from Helen's chest as her hand flew to her mouth in shock. She'd been angry with her mother last night, had resented her cool indifference most of her life, but at this moment, she wished only that her mother would wake up. Edith had been difficult and selfish, but she was the only family Helen had left after her father died, and she suddenly felt orphaned, as if she were a small child left to fend for herself. She wished David were there. It wasn't that she didn't know what to do. She saw death in all its forms nearly every day, but this was different. This was personal and frightening, and unexpected.

Helen allowed herself a few moments of grief, then left Edith's room and returned to her own. Normally, she dealt with problems by focusing on the small tasks that made up everyday life; they soothed her and gave her a sense of purpose at a time when everything seemed uncertain. This was no different. Although a tragedy, death had its own protocol and came with a list of things to be attended to. Helen dressed in a somber gray dress and pulled a navy-blue cardigan around her shoulders, grabbed her purse, and stepped out into the street. The rain had stopped, but the sky was dark and broody, and the gutters ran with dirty rainwater. Making sure not to step into any puddles, Helen hurried toward the phone box and made several calls. The first one was to the hospital to tell the matron she wouldn't be coming in to work. The second was to Dr. Ross. Mrs. Ross informed her that her husband had been out on a call all night, but she expected him back shortly and would give him the message as soon as he arrived.

"I'm very sorry, Helen. Your mother and I were friends once."

"Thank you, Mrs. Ross," Helen replied woodenly. Now wasn't the time to wonder why so many of her mother's friendships had fallen by the wayside. Now was the time to accept condolences and keep her heart from succumbing to grief. She'd deal with her feelings later, when she was ready.

Helen's third call was to David's lodging house. Mrs. Bush informed her that David had left for work a few minutes ago. "I'll be sure to give him the message when he returns, Miss Brent," she promised. "I'm sorry for your loss," she added.

"Thank you," Helen replied and ended the call. She returned to the house and went into the kitchen, where she made herself tea and toast. She wasn't sure what to do next, so she sat at the kitchen table and nursed her cooling tea until Dr. Ross came by.

He looked tired and a little disheveled, but his warm brown eyes were filled with sympathy and understanding. "I'm sorry I couldn't come sooner, Helen. I was called out to a difficult birth last night." He sighed heavily and looked away.

"One or both?" Helen asked.

"Just the baby. The cord was wrapped around its neck, but the head was already in the birth canal. I couldn't do anything to loosen it without cutting the mother open then and there. I would have too, except that by the time she'd consented, the child was already gone. The parents are devastated. It was to be their first."

"I'm sorry," Helen said automatically, although, at the moment, she didn't feel much of anything.

"Tell me what happened," Dr. Ross invited. "I could do with a cup of tea," he added, seeing Helen's empty cup on the table.

"Yes, of course. You must be exhausted."

"I am, rather. And hungry," he confessed. "Didn't have any dinner or breakfast this morning."

Helen made fresh tea and offered Dr. Ross the remains of the plum duff, which he gratefully accepted. After all, there was no rush. There was nothing Dr. Ross could do for Edith, but having a companionable cup of tea with him brought Helen comfort.

"Excellent," Dr. Ross said as he finished the duff and took a last gulp of tea. He gave Helen an expectant look.

"Last night a friend of mine came to dinner. Mum was snippy and abrupt with him," Helen confessed. For some reason, she found it difficult to tell Dr. Ross that David was, in fact, her fiancé. Now wasn't the time to share her happy news. "Then she went to bed. When I didn't hear her moving about this morning, I went into her room. She was already gone. I think she might have passed early last night."

"What makes you say that?"

"I didn't hear any sounds from her room after I'd gone to bed, and I was awake for some time. All was silent." Edith must have passed while she was in the parlor with David, enjoying a few minutes of quiet intimacy.

"I see." Dr. Ross pushed away his plate and stood, ready to examine the deceased. Helen opted to wait downstairs.

He returned a few minutes later and washed his hands at the sink before speaking. "Myocardial infarction," he announced. "But I think you already knew that. I'd say she died at least ten hours ago, based on the level of rigor. It would have been quick, Helen."

"How can you tell?" Helen asked, although she thought she already knew.

"She had no time to call for help, and you would have heard her distress, being next door. It probably took her no more than a few minutes to die, the first few of which she was most likely still asleep. By the time she woke and realized something was wrong, it was too late. If you stop by the surgery later today, I'll have the death certificate for you."

"Thank you, Doctor. I suppose I'd better start arranging the funeral."

"Gibson and Sons is reasonably priced and very efficient."

"Yes, they buried my father. I'll go over there after I speak to the vicar."

Dr. Ross shook his head. "I think you'd best head over to Gibson's first if you want them to collect the body today. I believe they have two funerals scheduled for this afternoon, both my patients, unfortunately. I don't expect you'd like to spend the night with your mother's corpse still in the house."

"No, I wouldn't," Helen agreed.

"Go on, then," Dr. Ross said as he walked to the door. "If there's anything you need, Sandra and I are happy to help. I've been treating your family since your parents first moved here after the Great War. Your father was a good friend, and your mother... Well, I'm sorry she's gone."

Helen grabbed her coat and handbag and followed the doctor out the door. The funeral parlor was several streets away and in the opposite direction from the church. It was bound to be open for business, since it was past nine. Helen was greeted by the elder Mr. Gibson, who expressed his condolences, showed her around the showroom, and filled out the details of her order. Helen settled on a modest burial package, which Edith would have hated. She'd been forced to exist on a tight budget her entire life and had been resentful of not being able to splurge on tea at Claridge's or a new hat every Easter. On her final journey, she would have loved to ride in a glass hearse overflowing with white flowers, pulled by a pair of black-plumed horses, and driven by a solemn-looking coachman decked out in a frock coat and top hat. Alas, her funeral would be as modest as her life had been, and Helen didn't expect there'd be too many mourners.

"We will collect the body around four," Mr. Gibson said. "We have two funerals today, so we're rather busy."

"Of course. I understand."

"Please prepare the clothes you wish Mrs. Brent to be buried in. Don't forget undergarments, stockings, and shoes."

"I won't. Thank you, Mr. Gibson."

"It's my pleasure," he replied, looking as if it really was.

Helen then made her way to the church, where she scheduled a burial service with the vicar for Wednesday morning, after which she paid a visit to Agnes to inform her of Edith's passing. Agnes insisted Helen stay for lunch and fed her a hearty slice of pork pie, followed by fruit compote and tea.

"Would you like me to come back to the house with you?" Agnes asked. "I can prepare your mother's things, if you'd rather not."

"Thank you, but I'll be all right," Helen replied. She appreciated the offer but felt the need to see to Edith herself. "I'll see you at the funeral."

"Of course, dear. If there's anything you need..."

Helen thanked Agnes and returned home, where she selected Edith's favorite dress, a pair of silk stockings, undergarments, and Edith's best shoes. She also added her mother's pot of rouge and lipstick to the bag. She wouldn't want to be buried with an unmade face. Helen considered the question of jewelry. Would Edith want to be buried in her pearls? She didn't think so. She'd see burying her valuables with her as wasteful. Helen removed her mother's watch but left her wedding ring. She'd want to be buried with it.

A strange hush fell over the house after the undertakers had gone, taking Edith with them. The house felt empty and dark, and watchful somehow. Helen considered going for a walk but felt unexpectedly tired. She heated some leftovers and sat down in the kitchen without bothering to turn on the light. Yesterday, at this time, David had been there, and her mother had still been alive. How quickly one's life could change, Helen reflected as she cut into her mutton chop. How quickly joy could turn to sorrow.

A knock at the door distracted Helen from her thoughts. She was relieved to see David standing on the threshold.

"I came as soon as I heard," he said, putting down his satchel and taking Helen into his arms. "Is there anything I can do?"

"You can keep me company for a bit. It's been such an awful day."

"What was it that—?" David left the question unfinished.

"Heart attack. Dr. Ross said it would have been quick."

"Well, that's a blessing at least."

"I suppose so." Helen's glance fell on David's satchel.

"I mean to stay the night," he said softly. "You shouldn't be alone."

"What will the neighbors say?" Helen said, but she knew she'd let him. Her need for him was far greater than the desire to observe propriety.

"Helen, we are to be married. What difference does it make what the neighbors say? I'm here to support you in your time of need."

"I think you should move in," Helen blurted out. "It makes no sense to maintain two residences."

"I agree. We can be married as soon as the mourning period is over."

"I want to be married now," Helen replied.

"Before the funeral?"

"No, after. We can go to the registry office on Thursday and be done with it."

"Don't you want a wedding?" David asked.

Helen shook her head. "My mother was my only family, and you haven't got any relations. We can invite Sarah and Bertie and Olly and Alice. Sarah and Olly can be our witnesses. What do you say?"

"I say it's a fine idea, if you're sure and it's not just the grief talking."

"I'm sure. Tomorrow I will prepare for the funeral. On Wednesday, we'll bury my mother and have some people over to the house afterward. On Thursday, we'll start a new life, you and I."

"I like the way you think," David said. He leaned forward and kissed her tenderly, bringing tears to her eyes. "I love you, Helen," he said.

"I love you too," Helen whispered into his shoulder. Knowing that he was there made her loss seem less devastating. Out of death came life.

TWENTY-TWO

JUNE 2015

London, England

Gabe stepped out into the garden, carrying a bottle of wine and two glasses. He wordlessly poured, then handed Quinn a glass, which she accepted gratefully. She stared up into the star-strewn sky, marveling that she could see the heavens so clearly despite the bright lights of the sprawling city. The evening was balmy, with the scent of flowers and freshly cut grass carried on the gentle breeze. The children were already in bed, and Alex's even breathing came over the baby monitor, which stood on the wrought iron table.

"Tell me about the case," Gabe invited as he settled in and took a sip of wine. She was glad he hadn't asked about Jo or Logan, neither of whom she'd heard from.

Quinn shrugged. "There's not much to tell. Helen and David seem like a nice, ordinary couple. There's genuine devotion between them."

"No one is displaying homicidal tendencies?" Gabe asked with a smile.

"No. They're almost boring compared to my usual subjects. There's no loveless marriage, no unrequited passion, no immediate threat to their safety. Helen's mother's sudden death, sad though it might be, paved the way forward for them. Once married, they would have the house and whatever assets Edith Brent left to her only daughter. Their life should have been ordered and comfortable."

"And yet, there was a dismembered child buried in their back garden. It is the same house, isn't it?" Gabe asked.

"It appears to be. I don't understand it, Gabe. That baby was buried with love. What on earth happened to it? And what became of Helen and David? The couple who found the remains have been living at the house for more than fifty years, which means that Helen and David sold the house not long after they married, if they married."

"Have you looked up David?" Gabe asked.

"No, not yet."

"Quinn, are you all right?" Gabe asked, his eyes searching her face anxiously. He always knew when something was on her mind and drew it out of her, and although Quinn had tried valiantly to keep it from him, he could sense her unease. "Is it Jo again?"

"No, not this time."

"So, what's troubling you?"

"I had a call from Seth while you were putting Alex to bed." Quinn reached for the glass of wine and drained it. She almost laughed out loud at Gabe's astounded expression. Normally, she drank her wine one sip at a time, savoring the pleasure. "The appeal hearing took place this morning. Brett's conviction has been overturned."

Gabe swore eloquently. "I was afraid this would happen since Seth beat a confession out of Brett. Had Brett's court-appointed lawyer been more competent, he might have argued that it was inadmissible in court."

"Well, he had a more competent lawyer this time, the best Seth's money could buy. Brett is free."

"I'm sorry. I can't imagine how you must feel," Gabe said softly.

"I'm happy for Kathy and Seth; I really am. They have their

son back, but I find it maddening that a person can get off on a technicality after trying to kill his own sister. Everyone knows he did it. The only difference this time was the legal mumbo jumbo that was pulled out of a hat, like a rabbit in a magic trick. It's not about justice, but about the skill of the legal team. Nothing new there, I suppose. Many a murderer has gone free, and many an innocent man has been convicted due to lack of competent counsel."

"I'm sorry," Gabe said again.

"You know, it's funny, but *Echoes* has completely changed my life."

"How so?"

"Had I not taken Elise and James's belongings home after their remains were found in that chest, there'd have been no break-in. Sylvia would not have seen my name on the news and attempted to make contact. I'd never have known about my possible fathers or gone looking for them. I'd never have met Seth, or Brett, for that matter, and I'd have never known I was a twin. I'd have blithely gone through my life, believing I was an only child. On the whole, finding my birth family has brought me a lot more grief than joy."

"Quinn, at the risk of sounding like a complete ass, I have to argue that life is all about managing expectations. Your expectations were never realistic. There is no such thing as a perfect family. People are people, in any part of the world, and in any century. They are flawed, and they lash out when they feel threatened. You backed Brett into a corner and threatened to expose something he needed to keep secret. You blundered along without ever asking yourself what impact your televised revelations might have on other members of the family. Now, I'm not saying that I sympathize with him or feel he was justified in what he tried to do, but people have killed for less. You of all people know that."

"Are you saying it was my fault?" Quinn asked, incredulous that Gabe would even suggest such a thing after what she'd been through.

"No, of course not. I'm only saying that you never know what will tip someone over the edge, and you have to tread carefully when it comes to someone's secrets."

Quinn sighed. "You are right. I should have told him what I'd discovered, and asked Brett and Seth's permission to make our personal history the subject of an episode instead of assuming they'd be okay with it," Quinn admitted. "I was so excited to finally learn the truth of my family that I never imagined Brett would feel so rattled."

"What you discovered changed not only the way the world saw him but the way he saw himself. He couldn't handle it."

"Gabe, what are you getting at?" Quinn asked, suddenly realizing that there was a point to this conversation.

"I'm saying that you should find David Edevane or his descendants and ask for their consent before you commit to telling this story. This is not something that happened four hundred years ago; this happened only a generation ago and shining a spotlight on this family might have repercussions."

"But I don't even know what happened yet," Quinn argued.

"No, but you know something did."

Quinn inclined her head in agreement. "I give you my word that I will put this to the Edevane descendants before any decisions are made. Rhys has already consulted legal anyway. Any living descendants will have to sign a release, allowing us to tell their family's story." She held out her glass for a refill and fixed Gabe with a gimlet stare.

"And what about Jo? Are my expectations off the mark with her as well?" she demanded. "You might as well tell me, since you seem bent on brutal honesty." She took the sting out of her words with a smile. She wasn't upset with Gabe. She valued his opinion and appreciated his candor. Few people would have the courage to tell her the truth, and sometimes, she needed to hear it.

"All right, but you're not going to like it," Gabe replied, smiling back. "Jo has issues that have nothing whatsoever to do with you. I think a part of her genuinely wants to like you, but a part of her needs to reject you to feel whole. You bring out her insecurities."

"Is that why she left without saying goodbye, do you think?"

"Possibly. Or maybe she left because she discovered something she wasn't quite ready to deal with."

"Like what happened to her child?" Quinn mused. "Then it must have been something tragic for her reaction to be so volatile."

"I won't try to guess, but I don't think you should ask her for an explanation. She'll tell you herself if she wants to."

"She won't."

"Then there's your answer."

"Logan's not returning my calls either," Quinn complained.

"He will. Once he's ready to talk."

"You know, you're only this rational because you don't have siblings," Quinn said, annoyed despite having asked for the truth.

"You're probably right. But my mum has several, and I've had a front-row seat to that particular drama all my life. I know the reality of having a large family."

"And yet you still want one," Quinn remarked.

"I do. My mum and her siblings go at it hammer and tongs, or used to when they were younger, but they love each other to bits, and there's no one in the world who can come between them, especially in a crisis."

"Thank you," Quinn said, smiling tenderly at Gabe.

"For what?"

"For being honest. For putting life in perspective. For reminding me to keep my feet firmly planted on the ground. You're a very useful person to have around."

Gabe gave her a seductive smile. "Allow me to remind you just how useful I can be. Come to bed."

"I don't need reminding," Quinn said as she stood and walked into his arms. "And I don't need a bed."

She pulled him toward a cushioned chaise and lay down, pulling up the skirt of her summer dress inch by inch.

"I think you forgot to put on knickers," Gabe said as he took in his wife.

"I never forget anything."

TWENTY-THREE

JANUARY 1956

London, England

Helen stood in front of Edith's door, her hand hovering just above the brass doorknob. She was determined to go in this time instead of making up an excuse and walking away as she had done several times over the past few months. It'd been four months since her mother's death, but Helen had done nothing more than strip the bed and air out the room after the undertakers had taken Edith's body away. David had made no mention of Edith's room until that morning, and now there was no avoiding the unsavory task.

"Darling, do you think it might be time to clear out your mother's room?" he'd asked over breakfast.

"I'll get round to it eventually."

"Don't you want to prepare the nursery?" he'd asked, his gaze sliding to her rounded belly. "I can't paint it until you clear out your mum's belongings."

It wasn't as if she didn't have the time. She'd had to resign from her job at the hospital once she learned she was pregnant, and spent her days cleaning, cooking, and visiting with her friend Lynn, who was glad of the company. Sometimes, when Helen got bored, she even went to see Agnes. She wasn't accustomed to spending so much time on her own and needed projects to fill her time. She'd reorganized every cupboard, thrown away some of her mother's dusty silk flowers, and purchased new curtains for the parlor. She'd asked David to move the furniture and hung a new picture in their bedroom. It was a nautical scene that reminded her of the beach in Bournemouth where David had proposed to her. There was nothing left for her to do except turn her attention to the nursery.

"All right, I'll do it today."

"Don't overtire yourself. A little at a time. Would you like me to get a couple of boxes on the way home?"

"Yes, please. I'm going to donate most of Mum's things to the charity shop."

"That sounds like a good idea. I'll take everything down whenever you're ready."

David had finished his tea, given her a sweet kiss, and headed for the door. "Have a good day," he'd called out before closing the door behind him.

Helen had put away the butter and milk, stowed the remaining bread in the bread box, and washed the breakfast dishes. She'd swept the floor, dusted the furniture, and walked to the butcher's and greengrocer's to pick up something for their supper. Having returned, she'd made herself a cup of tea and stared morosely out the window. There was nothing left to do, and no excuses left to make. Having several hours before she needed to start on dinner, she'd finished her tea, rinsed out her cup, and headed for the stairs, feeling as if she were ascending a scaffold.

As she stood outside the room, poised to enter, Helen reflected that she didn't miss her mother, exactly, but Edith was frequently in her thoughts, especially when she was doing housework. Her mother had been very particular, and Helen often felt as if Edith were standing next to her, grading her performance. Thankfully, she didn't conjure up Edith when she was in bed with David. Edith never intruded on that side of her marriage, but Helen had never heard anything in all her years of sharing a wall with her

parents that would lead her to believe that they had ever been intimate. Her mother would have been surprised to learn that Helen
quite enjoyed that side of things. Pregnancy seemed to have awak-
ened an insatiable hunger, which David was only too happy to
satisfy. Once they had grown more comfortable with each other,
David had become eager to try new things and pleased her in ways
she'd never imagined, and she was happy to return the favor,
secretly enjoying her ability to bring him so much pleasure.

Helen dragged her mind out of the bedroom and pushed open
the door, finally ready to tackle the task at hand. The room looked
exactly as it had when Edith was alive. Helen had even made up
the bed, although no one was likely to sleep in it. Edith's reading
glasses were still on the nightstand, atop the book she'd been reading. Helen sighed. Disposing of a person's effects was never a
pleasant task, especially when one had no desire to hold on to
anything. Helen would keep Edith's jewelry, but she'd never wear
any of her things; she was sure of that.

Starting with the wardrobe, Helen pulled out Edith's dresses,
coats, and hats. A few items were too threadbare to donate, but
most things went into a pile on the bed. The charity shop would be
only too happy to accept such a bounty. Most of Edith's things still
had years of wear left in them.

Helen had nearly finished with the wardrobe when she spotted
an old biscuit tin at the back of the shelf where Edith kept the hat
boxes. She couldn't reach it, so she fetched a broom and used it to
move the box forward until she could retrieve it more easily.

The box was full of papers. There was a neatly tied packet of
letters, sent by Harry Brent to his wife from France during the
Great War. There were also several sepia photographs that Helen
had never seen before. One was a picture of her mother, aged about
twenty. She looked young and pretty, her expression coy. A small
smile tugged at her lips, as if she had been trying to keep a straight
face for the photograph but failed. Helen had never seen her
mother look like that. Playfulness was not a trait she'd ever associ-
ated with Edith.

The second photograph was of a man dressed in a tweed suit and cap. He looked directly into the camera and smiled, his eyes crinkling at the corners. Helen's breath caught in her throat. Had the picture been recent, he could have passed for David's younger brother. Helen turned the photograph over. There, in faded ink, was an inscription: *Edward Edevane, October 1916*. With trembling hands, she set it aside and continued rifling through the contents. She found her parents' marriage certificate and her father's death certificate, but not her birth certificate, which Edith must have kept in a different place.

All the way at the bottom of the box was a blank envelope. She pulled it out and looked inside, extracting a single sheet of paper. It was still crisp to the touch. Helen unfolded the paper and stared at the neat writing. It was a certificate of birth. The mother was listed as Edith Brent, but the father's name was left blank. The child had been born in London on March 21, 1917—David's birthday—and his name was David Edward Edevane.

Helen's hand flew to cover her mouth as a gasp of shock tore from her chest. The typed letters danced before her eyes. How was this possible? How could Edith be David's birth mother? She'd been married at the time of his birth, and Harry had been far away, in Verdun. He hadn't returned home until the following year. Helen had been born years later. Her mother had confessed once that she hadn't been able to conceive for a long time and had never become pregnant again after giving birth to Helen. Helen had been Edith and Harry's miracle baby—a wonderful gift, her father had called her.

Harry Brent clearly hadn't been David's father, or Edith would have kept the baby. Helen picked up the photograph of the young man in the tweed suit. Now she understood the resemblance to David. The man was his father, but who was he, and what had become of him? Did he know he had a son?

Helen began to tremble as the magnitude of her discovery finally sank in. David was her brother. No wonder they'd experienced such an immediate connection. They got on incredibly well, even now that they were living together as man and wife. In all their time together, they'd never once had a serious argument. They were so in tune, it amazed her sometimes that they'd been lucky enough to find each other. But their compatibility wasn't random; it was written in their blood. They were committing incest, and their baby would be a child conceived in sin.

Helen bolted from the room and got to the bathroom just in time. She sank to her knees and was violently ill, heaving until there was nothing left in her stomach. "No," she moaned. "No."

She remained on the floor, pressing her forehead to the cool porcelain of the toilet, too weak to get up. There had to be a logical explanation. It was all a terrible mistake. Edith had been the most proper, unyielding woman Helen had ever known. She couldn't reconcile the mother she'd known to a married woman who'd indulged in an affair while her husband was fighting for his country, then dumped her child in an orphanage as if he were unwanted baggage. It simply didn't add up. David had said that he was one of the few children at the orphanage to know his birth name. Perhaps Edith had meant to come back for him.

A strangled moan escaped Helen's lips as the pieces of the puzzle fell into place. Yes, Edith would have come back for him if her husband never returned, but Harry had survived. Harry had come back to his wife, unlike so many others whose remains still rested in French soil, so Edith had had no choice but to forget about her child and play the loving wife. How could she tell her husband that she'd been unfaithful to him and given birth to her lover's child? Harry would have never forgiven her, nor would he have let her go. He'd loved her, more than she'd ever loved him, if Helen was any judge of human behavior. He would have fought to save his marriage, and Edith might have stayed because she had been too frightened of the consequences to ask for a divorce.

Divorce was scandalous, especially at that time. Edith's name would have been dragged through the courts, possibly even published in the papers. It would make for a sensational story, especially if her lover had been married as well. Edith would have sooner died than suffer such humiliation, so she'd sacrificed her love child for her own security and reputation. She'd never visited David, as far as Helen knew. She'd simply forgotten all about him. Or maybe not. She'd kept his birth certificate and the photograph of his father. Perhaps Edith had suffered the pangs of a guilty conscience, or perhaps she'd really loved David's father and had spent the rest of her life mourning a love that could never be, and a child who was forever lost to her.

What had it been like for Edith to see David walk through the door that fatal Sunday? No wonder her heart had given out. To be faced with the son she'd abandoned was shocking enough, but to discover that he was engaged to her daughter was probably more than she could take. To tell Helen the truth would have taken great courage, but to withhold it would be paramount to sanctioning her children's incestuous marriage. How could Edith have stood by and allowed her daughter to marry her own brother and have children by him?

"Dear God," Helen moaned miserably. "What am I to do?" Her hand instinctively went to her belly, where her unsuspecting child was kicking viciously, not best pleased by Helen's hunched position. She finally stood and forced herself to wash her hands and face. She went downstairs and sat down at the kitchen table, her mind enveloped in a fog of misery and disbelief. She had to tell David. She had to show him the indisputable proof of their relationship. Besides, he had a right to know who his parents were. Maybe his father was still alive, and it wasn't too late for them to get to know each other.

Whatever for? a small voice asked inside her head. *What will you accomplish by telling him the truth? You're already married. You have a child on the way. The truth will destroy all three of you. Your baby will be branded a child of incest, and your divorce proceedings will make the papers. Everyone will know your name and your story. Everyone will learn of your shame.*

Helen slowly got to her feet. Her limbs felt unbearably heavy, and her head was pounding. She needed someone to talk to, but she could hardly confide in the vicar, or Dr. Ross. They might demand that she dissolve the marriage immediately, or they would report her to the authorities. Could she confide in Sarah? She was newly married herself and expecting her first child. She would understand. She would advise Helen what to do.

Helen went out into the corridor, put on her coat and shoes, took her umbrella and handbag, and let herself out. She'd be back before David returned from work, and by the time she saw him this evening, her mind would be made up, one way or the other.

TWENTY-FOUR

Helen divested herself of her coat and shoes, dropped her umbrella in the stand, and walked into the parlor, where she poured herself a small sherry from a decanter on the sideboard. No one had touched the sherry since Edith had died. It had been her drink of choice, and she'd allowed herself a small glass once a week as a treat, usually on Saturday night. Helen sipped the sherry, enjoying its cloying sweetness as it slid down her throat. She hadn't eaten anything since breakfast, and the sherry went straight to her head, making her feel a bit woozy. She sat down on the sofa and stared at the ticking clock. She had three hours until David returned home from work. She'd have to get started on dinner soon, but she had a few minutes.

She'd never made it to Sarah's house. In fact, she hadn't even walked as far as the bus stop. Having taken a dozen steps, Helen had realized that if she told Sarah what she'd learned, she'd never be able to take it back. Sarah would surely tell Bertie, and maybe even her mother. Bertie might tell a mate over a pint, and Sarah's mother would share the story with her friends over her weekly game of bridge. Sarah herself might tell one of her neighbors, or even someone they'd worked with at the hospital. Before the week was out, at least a half dozen people would know, for who could keep such a juicy tale to themselves?

Helen couldn't bear for anyone to know the truth, to talk about it, dissect it, shake their heads in astonishment, and pronounce their judgment. No, the secret would die with her. Not even David would learn the truth. She loved him too much to burden him with the knowledge that could destroy their marriage and taint his love for their baby before it was even born.

Helen set down her empty glass on the sideboard and trudged up the stairs. Retrieving the tin from the top shelf of the wardrobe, where she'd left it only a quarter of an hour before, she brought it down to the kitchen and took out David's birth certificate and the photograph of his father. She left the rest of the papers in the tin. They held no interest for her.

Striking a match, Helen set the certificate alight, and watched it burn until the flame nearly touched her fingers. She dropped it in the sink, then did the same with the photo. It broke her heart to watch David's beloved features turn to ash, but she had no choice. She could never show him the likeness of his father or explain how she'd come by it.

The ashes littered the bottom of the sink, and Helen turned on the faucet and washed them away, watching in mesmerized silence as the evidence that could destroy her life slid down the drain. She opened the kitchen window to let out the smoke and turned her mind to more important things. By the time David came home, dinner was ready, Edith's room had been cleared out, and Helen smiled serenely at her husband, glad to have him home.

"Well, I see you've been busy. Are you not keeping anything?" he asked as he took in the pile of dresses and coats on the bed. "Not even any of her jewelry?" he asked when he noticed a small jewelry box next to the clothing. "Surely you'd want to hold on to something."

Helen shook her head. "Maybe you can sell it. I don't want any of it."

Edith's jewelry felt tainted to her now, especially the pearls, which she'd worn in the photograph that now rested at the bottom of the tin. Her lover might have touched those pearls, and David's tiny fingers might have reached for the pearls when she held him in her arms before giving him away. No, Helen could never bring herself to even take them out of the jewelry box, much less put them on.

"You might regret it later. Maybe you should hold on to it for a while?"

"No."

"All right. I'll see what I can get for the lot. Should be enough to buy a grand new pram, and then some."

"Yes," Helen agreed. "Those pearls are worth quite a lot. Maybe we can buy ourselves new bedroom furniture. We can use a bigger bed now that there are two of us," Helen said. She and David slept in her childhood bed, which was way too narrow for a couple to share.

David grinned. "I think that's a smashing idea. Who needs pearls when you can have a roomy new bed? I'll go tomorrow before work. Is that soon enough for you, Mrs. Edevane?" he asked, pulling her into an embrace and kissing the tip of her nose.

"Yes, that will suit," Helen replied with mock seriousness. "And make sure to haggle. Don't accept the first offer."

"I wouldn't dare. I will get a good price. I promise. Enough for us to get new furniture, a pram, and a cot and bureau for the nursery."

"Good man," Helen replied. "Wash your hands. Dinner's ready." Helen watched as David walked away, loosening his tie as he went, then she returned to the kitchen.

Later, she drew a bath and soaked for a long while, staring at the empty space where the silk violets had been. No amount of bathing would ever wash her conscience clean. Their lives were forever tainted, and those of the children to come. How little she'd understood of her parents' marriage and how ignorant she had been of her mother's true nature. And now, through no fault of her own, she'd been forced to become just as duplicitous. She would have to hide her secret for the rest of her life, and make sure David never discovered the truth of what she'd done. He was a man who valued honesty, who'd rather know the very worst rather than be kept in the dark. He'd never forgive her if he found out. He'd no longer love her.

That night, when David reached for her, Helen told him she was too tired after clearing out the room, so he simply held her and went to sleep. It felt odd to be held so closely by a man who was really her brother.

I mustn't let this change me, change us. I must put this poisonous knowledge out of my mind, Helen thought as she lay sleepless in David's arms. But the idea of making love to him made her feel dirty and sinful. Her love, which until that morning had been pure and true, was now something to be ashamed of. Her desire for him made her cringe with embarrassment.

Over the next several months, Helen worked hard to retain a sense of normalcy. She didn't refuse David, but their lovemaking no longer brought her joy. David assumed she was tired and irritable due to advanced pregnancy, but Helen couldn't put the secret of his birth from her mind. The knowledge festered, and she wished she could share her burden with someone, but there was no one she could confide in. She hadn't seen much of Sarah, who was busy with her own life and hardly noticed Helen's lack of communication.

The one person Helen felt comfortable with was Agnes. She was a kind soul who never judged anyone rashly and always spoke of Edith with great affection. When in Agnes's company, Helen could almost forgive Edith her sins. She'd been a young woman who got caught unawares. She wouldn't be the first woman to have a baby outside of her marriage, and she'd done the only thing she could think of at the time. How was she to know that nearly four decades later, her sin would come back to haunt her? The shock had been enough to kill her. Not even Edith, who'd been something of a cynic, could have predicted such a cruel twist of fate.

Was it a strange coincidence that Helen had met her brother, or had it been part of some divine plan, love disguised as retribution? Helen tried to convince herself that a kind, loving God wouldn't take his wrath out on their baby, but as her due date approached, she grew more and more fretful. She became convinced that there was something wrong with the baby, and that she or the child, or both, would die during childbirth. By the time Helen's pains came, she was almost relieved. She couldn't take the strain any longer. If God was to take her, so be it. She was ready to bow to his will.

TWENTY-FIVE
JUNE 2015

London, England

"Brother and sister?" Gabe asked, his brow furrowing in disbelief. "My God, that's one I hadn't expected. If it wasn't so tragic, I'd say that was the ultimate cosmic joke. Imagine, meeting and falling in love with the one person in the whole world you shouldn't be with. What are the odds?"

"Not very high, I'd imagine," Quinn said. She pinched the bridge of her nose, but the vicious headache that seemed to reside just behind her eyes wouldn't let up. Quinn reached for the bottle of paracetamol in the kitchen cupboard and shook out two tablets. Gabe handed her a glass of water. "Thank you," Quinn mumbled as she swallowed the medicine.

"So, you think the child buried in the garden is the baby Helen was carrying?" Gabe asked.

"It must be. Perhaps she experienced some form of sixth sense. She believed something was wrong with the baby, and maybe there was."

"Or maybe nothing was wrong, and she whipped herself up into such a state that she killed it."

"Oh God, I hadn't thought of that," Quinn replied. "She just didn't seem like someone who'd be capable of such a thing. Helen was so sensible, so practical."

"Some things can drive even the most practical people over the edge."

"What would you do if you found out I was your sister?" Quinn asked, a small smile tugging at her lips.

Gabe shook his head in bafflement. "I don't know. Throughout history, cousins were permitted to marry, even encouraged to marry to retain the purity of the bloodline. Helen and David were half-siblings, so almost like cousins. Had they lived in a different time and place, no one would have batted an eyelash."

"No, I suppose not, but they lived in 1950s Britain. Eyelashes would bat and stones would be cast if anyone discovered the truth of their situation. They might even have faced a prison sentence."

"Poor Helen," Gabe said, shaking his head. "What a burden to carry. I wonder if she ever told David."

"She wanted to spare him. She loved him too much to burden him with the knowledge." Quinn sighed. She'd dropped the brooch as soon as Helen had gone into labor. She couldn't bear to see what happened next, but she'd have to. Rhys was demanding an update. He needed to decide whether Helen's story was dramatic enough to engage viewers, and now Quinn finally had something to tell him. He'd be thrilled.

"Rhys thinks the child was dismembered by someone other than the parents," Quinn said. "His mother recalled a news story from years ago, about a woman who murdered babies and dismembered them. I was able to find the case she was referring to."

"Really? Tell me."

"A woman by the name of Cynthia Reed lost her three children in a bombing raid. The remains of the children were recovered several days later. Their limbs had been torn off by the blast. The children had been aged four months, two, and four years old. Over the next five years, several corpses of small children without limbs were discovered, all within three miles of where Cynthia Reed lived. They'd all been buried with some care. Ms. Reed's doctor swore under oath that Cynthia Reed had lost her wits after the death of her children and wasn't competent enough to stand trial. She was shut away in an institution instead. Till her dying day, she swore she was innocent of the crimes and would never have hurt anyone's children."

"Do you think the baby could be one of the victims?" Gabe asked, his head tilted to the side as he considered this new theory.

"No, I don't," Quinn replied. She began ticking off reasons by folding a finger for each. "One, Helen's brooch was pinned to the shawl. Two, Helen's house was way outside the range of the other burials. Three, Cynthia Reed had already been committed by the time Helen's baby must have died. I have no doubt that the baby we found was Helen's, but what I don't know is how it died, what happened to its limbs, and why it wasn't properly interred."

"I have a feeling you're about to find out."

"I don't want to, Gabe," Quinn whispered, her eyes welling. "I can't bear to see children suffer. It's bad enough when the victim is an adult, but when it's a helpless, vulnerable baby, I just feel like my heart will break."

"Maybe you can ask Rhys—" Gabe began, but stopped speaking when Emma walked into the room, Rufus at her heels.

"Can we go to the park?" she asked. "Rufus needs a walk."

"I thought Maya was coming over for a playdate later," Quinn said. She'd spoken to Mrs. Cooper, who'd promised to bring Maya round at two o'clock.

"Not anymore," Emma replied.

"Have you two had a row?" Gabe asked.

"No," Emma replied defiantly. She folded her arms across her chest and her lower lip trembled, as if she were about to cry.

"Emma, what happened?" Quinn asked gently.

"Maya said she's going to Jessica's instead."

"Why? She had plans with you," Gabe said.

"She said Jessica is more fun. She's more mature," Emma muttered.

"Is she now?" Gabe growled. Quinn threw him a warning look.

She didn't much care for Maya and wasn't terribly upset that she wouldn't be coming over, but she felt awful for Emma, who was experiencing her first real rejection.

"And she called Rufus 'Doofus.' On purpose," Emma added, bursting with indignation.

"Em, what Maya did isn't very nice, and it's not your fault this happened," Quinn said, opening her arms to Emma, who immediately walked into them, desperate for comfort.

"Maya says I'm too babyish. I don't understand things."

"You understand exactly the right amount of things for someone your age," Gabe said. Quinn could see the anger bubbling beneath his calm façade. At five, Emma had suffered more than most children. She'd lost her mother and grandmother, had to come and live with a father she'd never known existed, and had to adjust to life in London after spending the first four years of her life in Edinburgh.

"I think Maya is angry," Emma said as she rested her cheek against Quinn's shoulder.

"With you?" Quinn asked.

"No, with everyone. Her parents are getting a divorce. They're going to sell the house, so she'll have to go to a new school."

"That must be very difficult for her, but people move all the time. We moved, and you like your school."

"I miss Aidan," Emma said. "Aidan was a real friend."

"Em, I know you like Maya, but there are lots of children at your school. You'll make other friends. And if you like, I can ring Aidan's mother and see if you two can get together. Would you like that?"

"I suppose," Emma said half-heartedly, still smarting from Maya's abrupt change of heart. "I just want to go to the park and play with Rufus."

"All right," Gabe agreed. "Let's go for a walk. Shall we bring Alex?"

"No."

"You go on," Quinn said. "Have a nice time. Alex and I have errands to run."

"How's your head?" Gabe inquired when Emma went to put on her shoes and fetch Rufus's lead.

"Much better. I can use some fresh air though. I'll pop over to the shops, and I need to stop at Boots. I'll go once Alex wakes up."

Gabe leaned down and kissed Quinn. "I'll see you later. Try not to take this case so personally."

"Easy for you to say," Quinn mumbled once Gabe left the room.

TWENTY-SIX

After Gabe and Emma had gone, Quinn went upstairs to check on Alex. He was sleeping peacefully, his lips stretched into a tiny smile. Her heart melted at the sight of him. He was so sweet, so perfect. How could anyone murder a child, especially a child conceived in love? She'd do anything to protect her baby, would suffer any hardship without a word of complaint if it meant keeping Alex and Emma safe. She could easily understand how someone could go mad after losing their kids. She hoped she'd never lose Gabe, but if their marriage came to an end, she would recover in time. But she would never recover from losing the children, Alex especially. He was a part of her, her heart, her soul, her reason for being. Now that she had a baby of her own, she could understand the lengths people went to in order to protect their children, even when their children were truly evil.

She could understand Seth and Kathy's relief at finally having Brett back with them, and although, somewhere deep inside, she felt as if Seth had chosen Brett over her, she knew without a shadow of a doubt that Seth would move mountains to help her if she were ever in need. Being a parent was the most rewarding and the most heartbreaking thing in the world. It made you strong, but it also made you more vulnerable than you'd ever been and could destroy you if tragedy ever struck.

Quinn looked down at her sleeping baby. "Dear God, please keep him safe," she prayed silently. "Please, don't ever let anything happen to him." She tiptoed out of the room and returned downstairs.

Unsettled by the direction her thoughts had taken, she decided she could use a distraction, so she rang Logan. She'd kept her promise to herself to give him space, but she was getting worried, especially since Jude was no longer at the rehab facility. When she'd called, she'd been informed that Jude had been checked out.

Logan answered on the second ring. "I'm sorry, Quinn," was the first thing out of his mouth. "I've been an absolute tosser."

"I just wanted to make sure you're all right."

"Are you busy right now?"

"I was going to run a few errands, but they can wait."

"Want to meet for a cuppa? I'll come to you. Costa on Brompton Road in about an hour?" Logan suggested.

Quinn was about to tell him that it'd have to be later when she heard Alex's babbling over the child monitor. "Sure. See you there."

Quinn fed and changed Alex and set off. The day was lovely, and she enjoyed the walk. Alex was enjoying it as well, his mouth open in wonder as he spotted each new thing. He nearly shot out of his buggy with excitement when a police car with its siren on went by.

Costa wasn't too crowded, and Quinn found a seat by the window after getting her tea. She settled Alex in a high chair and gave him a toy to play with to keep him from getting fussy. Logan arrived a few minutes later. He looked well, if a bit tired. He planted a kiss on her cheek and waved to Alex, who waved back.

"I've taken on a few extra shifts at the hospital," he explained as he set his coffee on the table. "Can't stand being at home."

"Are you back at Sylvia's?" Quinn asked, stunned by this turn of events.

"For the foreseeable. I need to keep an eye on Jude, and things with Colin are... well, you know."

"Have you spoken to him?" Quinn asked, against her better judgement.

"Yes. No."

"What does that mean?"

"I tried to explain how I feel, but it came out all wrong, and if he was hurt before, now he's gutted. I really cocked it up, Quinn. I'm not sure where to go from here."

"Where do you want to go? Do you want to get back with Colin or would you prefer to remain single for a while?"

"The truth is, I don't know. I miss Colin. A lot. I think about him a hundred times a day. Every time something funny happens, or I get upset, or just want to sit on the sofa in companionable silence watching telly, I miss him. But I also miss not knowing exactly what the day will bring. I miss meeting new people and having new experiences. Colin is set in his ways. He's domesticated."

"I thought you were too."

"So did I, but I'm not ready—" Logan looked away, an odd expression on his face.

"Logan, what is it?"

"It's nothing. Forget it. I'm happy to see you, and this little guy." He made a silly face at Alex, and Alex laughed with delight. "I need some advice, actually. Jude's back home."

"I know. I called for him and they told me he'd gone. Does he have a plan?"

"No, that's the problem. Jude has no idea what to do with himself. He's moping around the house, sleeping half the day away, and watching endless hours of TV. If he continues like this, he'll relapse out of sheer boredom."

Quinn shook her head. "I'm afraid I can't suggest anything. He needs a purpose, something to fill his days."

"I suggested going to school, but he refused, and he has no interest in the types of jobs open to him. I don't know what else to offer. And, of course, Mum is coddling him as if he were an invalid. She's dancing attendance on him because it gives her something to do."

"I'm sure she's worried sick after what happened last time."

"She is, but babying him won't help. He needs to figure out what he wants to do with the rest of his life and take the first step toward that."

"Easier said than done."

"Yes," Logan agreed. "I'm hardly a shining example of self-awareness."

"Few people are."

"You and Gabe seem to have it together. I envy you guys. By the way, Jo's been by."

"Really?" Quinn asked. Jo still hadn't called her back, and she was shocked to find out that she'd gone to see Sylvia, or her half-brothers. She hadn't shown much interest in them, and anytime Sylvia was mentioned, she grimaced, as if even hearing her name was painful.

"She wanted to talk to Mum. Apparently, they had a nice visit."

"I'm glad they're getting to know each other," Quinn said, turning to take a sippy cup out of Alex's diaper bag to hide her surprise.

"Yeah, I guess." Logan consulted his watch. "Gotta run. I have a shift."

"All right. It was good to see you."

"You too, sis. Thanks for listening."

"Ring me anytime." Quinn stood and gave Logan a hug, then watched as he left the café and dashed across the street. Alex waved to him, but Logan didn't see.

TWENTY-SEVEN

Quinn was surprised to find Jo waiting for her when she returned home. Jo was sitting on the top step, phone in hand. She was casually dressed in a pair of torn jeans, a moss-green T-shirt, and a pair of trainers. Her hair was pulled into a ponytail, which swung when she turned her head, and a pair of designer shades hid her eyes from view. Quinn was glad to see her, but this habit of turning up unannounced didn't sit well with her, especially after weeks of complete radio silence. She was beginning to realize that erratic behavior might be the norm for her sister.

"Hey," Jo called out, as if they'd just seen each other yesterday. "I was beginning to think I'd have to wait for hours."

"You could have rung," Quinn replied. She didn't mean to sound sulky, but she didn't like to be ambushed. "Come in."

Jo followed Quinn into the kitchen and tossed her handbag on the worktop. "Any chance of a cup of tea?" she asked. Not waiting for a reply, she went to fill the kettle and turned it on.

Quinn settled Alex in his high chair and turned to Jo. Gabe had advised her not to interrogate Jo about her motives for leaving, but Quinn was too annoyed to heed anyone's advice. Jo's behavior was unpredictable and at times infuriating. She did what she wanted, when she wanted, without taking anyone else's feelings into account. Quinn plucked an apple from the fruit bowl and began to peel it, needing something to occupy her hands. She'd been about to cross her arms in front of her chest, just as Emma had done earlier. She supposed that to some extent, Jo had the same effect on her as Maya had on Emma. She made her feel destabilized. Quinn cored the apple and cut it into thin slices before placing it in front of Alex, who instantly picked up a slice and began to chew on it.

"What happened, Jo? Why did you leave so abruptly?"

"Nothing happened. I just decided it was time to move on," Jo replied tersely. She leaned against the worktop, crossing her ankles and sliding her hands into the pockets of her jeans. On anyone else, the posture would look casual and relaxed, but Jo seemed more tense than she was letting on.

"Was there nothing in your father's letter?" Quinn asked gently. She thought the letter was the key to Jo's sudden change of heart about finding her daughter, but Jo stubbornly shook her head.

"No. Let it go, okay?"

Normally, Quinn would let the matter drop, but in this instance, annoyance won out. She turned to Jo, pinning her with a steely gaze. "You were the one who asked for my help. Then you disappeared without a word of explanation."

"There was nothing to explain. I'd left it too long, Quinn. I should have asked my father while he was still alive, but I didn't. The trail went cold."

Every instinct told Quinn to accept Jo's explanation and move on to a safer topic, but for some inexplicable reason, she plowed on. "There's still someone left who might know what became of your daughter."

"No," Jo cried. "I don't want to speak to Michael, and I don't want anyone approaching him on my behalf. Don't you get it? I don't want to pursue this. It's too late for me to be a part of Daisy's life. The water's boiled," Jo said.

Quinn turned to take two mugs out of the cupboard, glad to have an excuse to avert her face. Jo had called the child Daisy.

Before, she'd said she didn't know her daughter's name. So, either she'd known all along, or she'd found something out and decided she didn't want to share it with Quinn and Drew.

Quinn plopped the teabags into the mugs, poured the boiling water, and handed a mug to Jo. Their eyes met and Quinn registered the uncertainty in Jo's gaze. She'd realized she'd slipped up and was wondering if Quinn had noticed. Quinn tossed her teabag in the rubbish bin, then went to sit at the kitchen table. She wasn't going to ask Jo about Daisy, not now, not ever. Jo clearly didn't want to tell her what she'd learned, and Quinn was done trying to be helpful.

Jo sat down next to Quinn. "He's grown," Jo said, referring to Alex.

"Yes."

"Is he walking yet?"

"No, it's too early, but he's pulling himself up in his cot. He's started saying some words."

Jo nodded. She didn't ask anything else, and Quinn didn't volunteer any information, sipping her tea in silence. There was a sort of manic energy coming off Jo that made Quinn feel uneasy. Suddenly, she wished Jo would leave. She'd wanted so badly to talk to her, but now that she was here, there didn't seem to be much to say.

"Jo, I—" she began, when the key turned in the lock and Rufus came trotting into the kitchen, his little pink tongue hanging out. He gave Jo a perfunctory sniff, then continued on to his water bowl.

"Hi, Aunt Jo," Emma exclaimed. "Where've you been?"

"I went away for work, but I'm back now. How are things with you?"

Emma shrugged. "All right, I suppose."

Jo's face broke into a winsome smile when Gabe walked into the kitchen.

"Oh, hello, Jo," he said. "Have we interrupted something?"

"Not at all," Jo replied. "I just stopped by to talk to Quinn."

"We'll leave you to it, then." Gabe put a hand on Emma's shoulder to steer her out of the kitchen, but Jo preempted him.

"Stay, please. I wanted to see you too," Jo said sweetly.

Her abrupt change of mood took Quinn by surprise, but not as much as Gabe's reaction to her. He removed his hand from Emma's shoulder and smiled as if he wanted nothing more than to spend a few minutes chatting with Jo, but Quinn had seen the spark of irritation in his eyes, and his desire to leave the kitchen hadn't been lost on her. She scrambled for something to say, wondering what reason he could have to be annoyed with Jo. When Quinn had returned home, she had planned to start on dinner, but if she began to cook now, she'd have to invite Jo to join them. She wasn't in the habit of being mean-spirited, but she didn't want Jo to stay any longer than necessary.

"Have you a new assignment lined up?" Gabe asked. He leaned against the doorjamb instead of coming back into the kitchen.

"Not yet. I'm going to be in London for a few weeks at least. What about you? What are your plans for the summer?"

"We're going to see Grandma and Grandpa Allenby," Emma announced. "I can't wait. I'm going to go swimming every day."

"Sounds lovely," Jo replied, but her gaze wasn't on Emma. She was still looking at Gabe, her gaze direct and hungry.

Gabe left his spot by the door and lifted Alex out of his chair. "Alex and I have a block tower to build," he said, settling Alex on his hip. "If you'll excuse us."

"Gabe's an amazing father," Jo said as soon as Gabe was out of earshot. "Most blokes I know would rather go to the pub for a pint than play with their children."

"Gabe loves being a dad," Quinn replied. "So, I hear you've been to see Sylvia," she said, eager to change the subject. She had no desire to discuss Gabe with Jo. It made her feel as if she were betraying him somehow.

"Yes. We had a nice chat."

"How's Jude? I haven't seen him in a few weeks."

Jo shrugged. "All right, I guess. We didn't exactly bond over tea and scones."

"He's a good sort," Quinn said. "You just have to find a chink in his armor."

"You seem to find a chink in everyone's armor." She smiled, but Quinn sensed the cattiness in the remark.

"I try to. Jude's my brother. I'd like to have a relationship with him."

Jo didn't reply. She gazed out the window, her expression unreadable. "I'd best be going," she said and stood, scraping the chair against the floor tiles. "I have things to do."

"All right," Quinn replied, getting to her feet. She tried not to show it, but Jo seemed to sense her relief.

"I'm sure you'd rather spend time with your family. Your husband looks like he could use some attention."

Quinn walked Jo to the door and watched her walk down the path toward the street, where she hailed a passing taxi. An unpleasant heaviness settled in her chest. For the first time since meeting Jo, she realized that a loving relationship between them might not be in the cards.

TWENTY-EIGHT

JUNE 1956

London, England

Shy rays of the morning sun crept into the room, the pink glow of the sunrise painting the scene in rose-colored hues. Helen lay back on the pillows, her eyes hooded with fatigue. She was still bleeding, and in some pain, but she hardly noticed the discomfort. A perfect baby boy lay nestled in her arms, his eyes closed against the quickly brightening light of the new day, his little hands balled into fists. He yawned, and Helen's heart nearly burst with love. He was the most beautiful baby she'd ever seen, and he was all hers.

"May I come in now?" David asked as he opened the door a crack.

"Come on in, Mr. Edevane," the midwife replied, smiling at David's uncertainty. "Your son is here."

David approached the bed and sat down carefully. Helen had expected him to focus on the baby, but he was looking at her, his gaze searching her face. "Are you all right, love?"

Helen nodded. She really was. She'd been so frightened, but the birth had been fairly easy, and the child in her arms was glowing with good health. "Would you like to hold him?"

David nodded, and Helen carefully placed the baby in his

arms. "Oh, he's perfect," David whispered, as though fearful of disturbing the baby.

"He is, isn't he?" Helen agreed.

"What did I do to deserve such happiness?" David asked as he studied his sleeping son. "I never imagined..."

Helen blinked away tears. If he only knew the price at which his happiness had been bought.

"You should get some rest," David said. "I'll look after the baby."

Helen sank deeper into the pillows. Her limbs had grown heavy, and it was becoming more difficult to keep her eyes open. "What shall we call him?" she murmured drowsily.

"Would you like to name him after your father?" David asked.

"Yes, but as a second name. How about David Henry?"

David beamed with pride. "When we have a daughter, we'll name her after you."

"You're already planning a second one?" Helen asked with a smile.

"And a third." David grinned. "Helen, we are a family," he said, his voice filled with wonder. "A real family, the kind I never had."

"Yes, we are, and nothing will come between us," Helen said fiercely.

She felt a little more confident after her ordeal. She'd survived the birth, and so had the baby. Perhaps God didn't hold her accountable. After all, it had been an honest mistake, a situation thrust upon them without their knowledge. To share their secret with the world would ruin all their lives and posthumously tarnish her parents' reputation.

I've done the right thing, Helen thought as she began to drift. *We'll be all right now. Everything will be all right.*

TWENTY-NINE
DECEMBER 1960

London, England

Despite her belief that everything was going to be fine, Helen remained nervous for the first few months of Davy's life, but as time went on, she finally came to accept that no bolt of lightning was going to strike her or her boy. Davy was thriving and making his parents very happy. Against stern advice to the contrary, Helen and David often took the baby into bed with them and spent many happy hours together, cuddling and playing. Every Saturday, David took his son out for a long walk, giving Helen time to catch up on housework and get some much-needed rest. Helen appreciated the time to herself but missed the baby and waited anxiously for her boys to return.

Time flew by, and before long, Davy was walking and talking, babbling to himself as if he were having an animated conversation. He was a sturdy little lad who exhibited signs of independence from an early age. He hated to be coddled and followed his father around like a devoted puppy. Helen was secretly a little jealous but couldn't begrudge David the adoration of his son. The two were inseparable, and as Davy grew from babyhood into boyhood, they spent time on more manly pursuits. David was good with his hands and had made toys for Davy when he was a baby, but now that Davy was four, they made things together.

"Well, aren't you clever," Helen exclaimed when Davy presented her with two Christmas tree ornaments. They were intricately painted, the horse and sleigh looking very realistic. "They're beautiful, Davy."

Davy beamed with pleasure. "Can I put them on the tree?" he asked.

"Of course, you can."

Helen watched Davy, smiling to herself. She had a present for them as well, but she wouldn't tell them till Christmas Day. She'd been keeping it to herself for a few weeks now, waiting for just the right occasion, and what better time than Christmas morning to spring her surprise? By the week of Christmas, she was on pins and needles, barely able to keep from blurting out her news, but she wanted to make her announcement special, and so bit her tongue and waited patiently.

At last, it was Christmas, and the family gathered around their little tree in the parlor. Davy was on the floor, still in his pajamas, ripping into the brown-paper wrapped gift Helen and David had left for him. It was a toy truck, the cab painted a shiny blue and the tires made of real rubber. Davy was in raptures. There was also a new jumper, but he wasn't as excited about that. Helen had also knitted a new jumper for David and had bought him a new tie.

David reached down and picked up the last gift. He handed it to Helen, smiling shyly. "I hope you like it. I saw you admiring it in a window a few months back."

Helen tore off the paper and gasped. It was the handbag she'd been craving for months, made of supple brown leather and adorned with a clever clasp. Helen opened it and examined the inside before setting it aside to be examined in greater detail later.

"I have a present for you two as well," she said, instantly getting the attention of her men.

"But there are no more presents beneath the tree," Davy pointed out. "Where is it?"

"It's here, in this room," Helen said, smiling at him.

Davy looked around, craning his neck to see all the corners of the parlor. "I don't see anything."

"We are going to have a baby," Helen announced.

"A baby?" Davy asked, peering at her in disbelief. He set his truck on the floor and climbed into Helen's lap, as if he were already marking his territory. "Well, where is it, Mum?"

"It will be here by June."

"That's too long to wait. I want it now," Davy protested.

"June will be here before you know it, sport," David said, lifting Davy off Helen. "We have to take extra special care of Mummy now. No more climbing into her lap."

"But I like Mummy's lap. She reads me stories," Davy protested.

"She'll still read to you, only you have to sit next to her, like a big boy."

"All right," Davy agreed. "I'll look after Mummy."

David wrapped his arm around Helen and kissed her temple. "I'm so pleased," he whispered into her ear. She could feel the joy coming off him in waves and leaned against him, enjoying the moment. She was glad she'd decided to wait. Her news made their Christmas even more special, especially since she suspected that David had begun to despair of ever having another baby. They'd tried and tried, but Helen had been unable to get pregnant until now. Her earlier reservations about being intimate with David had slowly evaporated after the baby's birth, and she had begun to enjoy their lovemaking again, confident that God had forgotten all about them. They were a family like any other. She'd even reconnected with Sarah, who had two little girls, aged one and three and a half. Helen and Sarah met for tea from time to time, grateful to their husbands for allowing them the infrequent luxury.

"I'm so happy for you, Helen," Sarah said when Helen shared the news with her in January. "Maybe you'll have a girl this time. Girls are such a pleasure. Stella is not yet four, but already she wants to imitate everything I do. She begs to help me in the kitchen. She loves to bake. And Deborah only wants to be close to her sister. They're so sweet when they are together. No rivalry at all."

"And how's Bertie?" Helen asked. Sarah rarely spoke of him.

"Bertie is Bertie. He likes to come home, light his pipe, and read the paper. He says girls are a mother's responsibility. Perhaps if we had a boy, he'd be more involved."

"Would you like to have another child?" Helen asked. Sarah made parenting look easy, but Helen knew what it took to look after a family and fully expected the new baby to add another layer of responsibility to her already full days.

Sarah shrugged. "Yes and no. I'd like to have a boy, for Bertie's sake, but I'm happy with my girls. They're enough for me. Some women enjoy pregnancy, but I'm not one of them. I was sick around the clock the first few months. I don't relish going through that again."

"I felt well with Davy, but this baby is different. I feel sick nearly every morning, and sometimes for the rest of the day. I'd hoped the nausea would abate by now. And I'm so tired," Helen complained. "I go to bed thinking I'll sleep like the dead, and then I end up tossing and turning all night long. I wake up more tired than when I went to bed."

"You need your rest, Helen. You should mention this at your next checkup. Are you still registered with Dr. Ross?"

"I go to him when I'm ill, but I've been seen by a midwife, the same one who delivered Davy," Helen replied.

"Midwives can't prescribe," Sarah said wisely. "If Bertie and I decide to have another baby, I'm going straight to my GP. No more suffering for me, not if he can offer me a safe sleeping aid, or maybe something for the nausea."

"It's not that bad, really. The sickness will pass."

"Well, if it doesn't, go see Dr. Ross. I'm sure he would be happy to furnish you with a prescription."

"I will," Helen replied and reached for the teapot. At least she could still enjoy her tea. While pregnant with Davy, one cup of tea had resulted in at least three trips to the lav, so she'd had to start rationing her liquids as early as four o'clock during the final months.

Helen inhaled the wonderful fragrance of Earl Grey and reached for a cucumber sandwich. She was pleased to note that she wasn't feeling nauseated just then and had to savor the moment. As Sarah continued to talk, she allowed herself a brief fantasy in which the child she carried turned out to be a girl. She cared only about delivering a healthy baby, but in her heart, she longed for a daughter. *Annie*, she thought dreamily. *Little Annie.*

THIRTY

JUNE 2015

London, England

"So, the baby wasn't Davy?" Gabe asked as he joined Quinn in bed. The children were already asleep, and Quinn had spent an hour in Helen's company while Gabe worked on his book in the study.

"No, but Helen became pregnant again in 1960," Quinn replied. "She seemed to have made peace with the situation. In fact, she'd almost forgotten about it. She was happy," Quinn added wistfully.

"Have you heard back from Colin?"

Quinn shook her head. "I texted him yesterday, but he replied that with Sarita still away, he's a bit behind and will get to the remains as soon as he's able. I don't think he trusts his new assistant to work independently."

"It takes time to get comfortable with a new person."

"Yes, I suppose it does, but Colin hasn't been himself these past few weeks. I can't say I blame him," Quinn said.

"Is it truly over between him and Logan, then?" Gabe asked as he returned the brooch to the bedside table.

Quinn shrugged. "It seems to be. Logan's back at Sylvia's, and he's picking up extra shifts at the hospital. I think he might have moved out his stuff from Colin's flat."

"It's a shame, that," Gabe said. "I thought they were good together."

"So did I. Maybe they'll still make a go of it, but somehow, I doubt it," Quinn replied sadly. "Funny how you can never predict the outcome of a relationship. I would have put my money on Colin and Logan, were I a betting woman."

"And speaking of volatile relationships, things seemed pretty tense between you and Jo earlier," Gabe said.

Quinn sighed dramatically. A part of her wanted to talk to Gabe about Jo, but another part wanted to think things over privately until she could figure out exactly what was happening between them. The Jo she'd met in Germany a few months ago was nothing like the woman she was dealing with now. Fear and uncertainty had been replaced with irritability and, at times, aggression. It was as if Jo was blaming her for something, but for the life of her, Quinn couldn't figure out what she'd done to offend her. Could Jo still be upset that Quinn had told Gabe about her child? But she'd apologized for that, and Jo seemed to have moved past it. Quinn thought Jo's sudden abrasiveness had something to do with her father's letter, but that theory was based on nothing more than speculation, since she had no idea what the letter had said. It might have had nothing whatsoever to do with Jo's sudden animosity.

"I just don't understand her, Gabe," Quinn replied at last. "She asked me to help her find her daughter, then she left London without a word of explanation, and now she's acting as if I overstepped some unseen boundary. If she's changed her mind about looking for her child, that's her affair, but why is she angry with me?"

"Because now you know."

"Know what, exactly?"

"Now you know that she abandoned her child, much as Sylvia had abandoned you two. Perhaps she doesn't like the parallels and thinks you're judging her, as she herself judged Sylvia."

"But I'm not. Many women give up their children for adoption. They have their reasons, and it's not for me to judge them."

"No, but Jo's story bears striking similarities to Sylvia's, and given how both you and Jo felt about Sylvia all your lives, she probably assumes that you feel much the same about her."

"Yes, you're probably right, and there's very little I can do to change her mind," Quinn conceded. "Gabe, I think Jo knows where her daughter is."

"Why would you think that?"

"Because earlier today, she called her Daisy. I think it was a slip of the tongue. That letter from her father revealed more than she's letting on," Quinn explained.

"Maybe so, but she clearly has no wish to tell you what it said. Quinn, I know you're bitterly disappointed, but you can't force Jo to be who you want her to be."

"She seemed so different when I met her in Germany."

"She was hurt and alone, and probably more than curious about you, as well. She's not nearly as vulnerable as she was then."

"You mean, she doesn't need me."

"Probably not as much as you need her, love," Gabe said gently. "I'm sorry. I know how much this hurts you."

Quinn laid her head on Gabe's shoulder. "It does hurt, but just as with Sylvia, I have to adjust my expectations." Lifting her face to Gabe's, Quinn gave a bitter chuckle. "Judging by the expression on your face, I think I should probably give up any expectations I have altogether. Of everyone."

"You said it, not me," Gabe replied. The fact that he hadn't contradicted her told Quinn everything she needed to know. "Have you spoken to Seth?"

"Not since he told me about Brett's release." As much as Quinn could understand Seth's feelings, she felt as if her soul had been laid bare in the past twenty-four hours, the shadowy corner where she kept her fears locked up blown open, and a searchlight directed into its murky depths.

"Quinn, you have nothing to fear," Gabe said, gently stroking her back as if she were a colicky baby.

"I know, but knowing that he's out there, free to do as he wishes, makes me feel surprisingly vulnerable."

"New Orleans is a long way from London. Brett will never trouble you again, not if he knows what's good for him."

Quinn lifted her face to meet Gabe's gaze. "Gabe, if Brett had known what was good for him, he'd simply have told me how he felt instead of trying to erase me from his life, like a persistent stain. No matter how threatened they feel, few people will cross the line between wishing someone dead and taking steps to kill them. I know I have nothing to fear from him, but there's a part of me that will never feel completely safe again. He's taken that from me. He's stolen the sense of security I took for granted for more than thirty years. And I don't think I'll ever get it back, especially now that he's free."

She expected Gabe to talk her out of her fears, but Gabe simply pulled her closer and brushed his lips against her temple. "I know," he said softly. "I know."

THIRTY-ONE

The following morning, with rays of June sunlight pouring through the wide windows of the study and shining a light on the gloomy thoughts of last night, Quinn decided that she was ready to do some online research into the Edevane family. She'd intended to wait for Colin's report, but that didn't seem to be forthcoming, and she needed to verify if there were any living descendants Rhys needed to consult. Gabe and the children had just left for the park, and she had at least an hour to herself. No sooner did she power up her laptop than a text from Jude popped up on her mobile.

Can I come round?

When?

Now.

Sure.

It made no sense to get started if she was to get interrupted in a few minutes, so Quinn went down to the kitchen to make some coffee. Not five minutes later, Jude was at the door. He'd got a haircut, and his dark blond locks, which usually framed his face in artful disarray, were now shorn close to the scalp, making him look more mature. He'd also given up his uniform of jeans and a T-shirt for a pair of smart trousers and a cambric shirt. Had he been wearing a tie, Quinn would have been seriously suspicious.

"You're out early," she said as she invited him into the kitchen. "Want some coffee?"

"Yeah, thanks."

"I'll bring it out into the garden. It's too nice a day to remain indoors."

Jude stepped outside, and Quinn followed with two steaming mugs a minute later. She set them on the wrought iron table and took a seat across from Jude. He looked different somehow, and it wasn't just his unusual attire and short hair. Quinn studied him from beneath her lashes as she took a sip of coffee, and then it came to her. Jude usually looked dejected, but today there was determination in his face and a defiant set to his shoulders. He also had a faraway look in his eyes, as if he were seeing something in his mind that both frightened and excited him.

"Are you all right?" Quinn asked. It was a banal question, but she wasn't sure how to broach the subject of his recovery.

"I've come to say goodbye, Quinn."

"Where are you going?"

"Away." Jude set down his mug and rested his elbows on his legs, his hands dangling between his knees. He stared straight ahead, as if he were working himself up to some big declaration. "I've joined the army."

"You did what?" Quinn cried. Had Jude announced that he'd joined the circus, she'd have been less shocked.

"You heard me. I signed my life away an hour ago."

"I don't understand. Why would you join the army? You're a musician, for God's sake."

Jude looked at Quinn and grinned, his light eyes sparkling with amusement. "Quinn, Logan burned through his life savings to help me. He can't even afford a place of his own, thanks to me. I owe it to him not to cock this up, and if I remain here, at home with Mum, I'll relapse for sure. The army will keep me on the straight and narrow. I'll have no access to my old friends or dealers. I'll have no choice but to remain clean. And I will acquire marketable skills that I can rely on once I've been discharged from the army. I'll always love music, but I can't make a career of it, not if I hope to stay off drugs for any length of time. I'd like to become a medic," Jude said shyly.

"Really?"

"Yeah. I want to help people, as people have helped me. I want my life to mean something, Quinn. I don't want to be a cautionary tale."

"Do Sylvia and Logan know what you've done?" Quinn asked carefully.

"Logan does. I told him this morning, but I haven't told Mum yet. She won't be best pleased and will probably make this all about her and how she feels, but my mind is made up."

"Jude, for what it's worth, I'm really proud of you. The army is not what I would have imagined for you, but you're right, maybe it's exactly what you need."

"I have to get going. I have a few more stops to make. I'm going to see Bridget."

Quinn nodded. She could understand Jude's need to say goodbye to the girl who'd been his kryptonite for the past few years. She only hoped that Bridget wouldn't sweet-talk him into one last hit, or one last shag.

"She blames herself for what happened," Jude explained. "I have to tell her it wasn't her fault. I'm the one to blame. For everything."

Quinn's gaze strayed to Jude's neck. The scars left by the belt were no longer visible, but the emotional scars would take longer to heal. "Be safe, Jude, and come back to us soon."

They both stood. Jude smiled awkwardly before reaching out to embrace her. The hug was warm and heartfelt, something Quinn had never expected from Jude.

"I was annoyed when Mum first told us about you, but I'm glad she found you, Quinn," Jude said as he released her. "I like having a sister."

"Sisters," Quinn corrected him.

"No, sister," Jude replied, erasing Jo from the equation with a single word. "Kiss the children for me and tell Gabe I'm sorry for everything. I never meant to hurt anyone."

"I know."

Quinn walked Jude to the door and watched him walk down the path. He hadn't started training yet, but he was already walking like a soldier—head held high, shoulders back, spine ramrod straight. Quinn sighed and shut the door, wondering what other surprises her siblings had in store for her. She would have never imagined Jude in the army, but now that the idea was beginning to settle, she saw its merit and appreciated Jude's newfound maturity. At long last, he was fighting for his life. She only hoped he wouldn't lose it fighting for his country.

She'd just put the mugs in the sink when the doorbell chimed again. Quinn wiped her hands on a tea towel and hurried to get the door. "Did you forget something?" she asked as soon as she opened the door, assuming Jude had come back. Her heart nearly stopped when she saw the person standing on her doorstep.

"No," she muttered. "No, you can't be here." Her heart galloped like a spooked horse, and her knees grew weak and wobbly. She wanted to slam the door shut, but her arms wouldn't obey. She was glued to the spot, unable to tear her gaze away from the unassuming young man who stood before her.

"Quinn, please, I'm not going to hurt you. I need to speak to you," Brett pleaded as he took a step backward, seeing Quinn's obvious distress.

Quinn couldn't seem to find the strength to move. Cold dread had spread from her chest to her extremities. She couldn't get enough air into her lungs, and black spots began to dance before her eyes. She leaned against the doorjamb, terrified she'd faint and leave herself at Brett's mercy. The last time she'd seen him, they had been in the

Talbot vault in New Orleans. He'd looked much as Jude always had—faded jeans, a stretched-out T-shirt, and beat-up trainers. His hair had been shaggy, and he'd had a few adolescent spots. He'd been a kid, but the person who stood before her looked like a man. His hair had been cut short in prison, and his limbs, which had been lanky, were now thick with muscle. He looked strong and fit, and dangerous.

"You need to leave. Right now," Quinn demanded, finally getting her voice back. "I'll call the police if you don't go."

She expected Brett to argue, to try to plead his case, but instead he sank to his knees in front of her. Tears slid down his cheeks, and his dark eyes were filled with pain. "Quinn, I humbly beg for your forgiveness. I know what I ask is impossible, given the magnitude of my crime against you, but I need you to know that I would do anything to turn back the clock and undo the wrong I did you."

The words sounded rehearsed, and Quinn's fear turned into dark, pulsating fury. She was filled with energy and believed she could probably push him hard enough to make him tumble down the steps if he came at her.

"Nothing you can say could justify what you tried to do," she replied, her voice low and charged with anger. "I've heard your apology. Now, go."

Brett rose to his feet and bowed his head in acknowledgement. "If you ever want to talk..."

"Go!" Quinn roared.

Brett turned and walked away, his shoulders squared, much as Jude's had been only a few minutes before. Quinn shut the door behind him and slid to the floor, hugging her legs and resting her forehead on her knees. That was how she'd sat in the vault, huddled against the door, praying that Brett would come back and let her out. It had taken her a long time to accept that he wasn't coming back. That what he'd done wasn't some sick joke, or an attempt to frighten her into keeping his secret. He'd left her to die, alone in the dark, next to the remains of their ancestor Madeline, who'd also placed her trust in the wrong person and wound up not only dead but completely erased from the annals of history. Quinn began to shake violently, her teeth chattering, her forehead knocking against her knees. In her mind, she was back there, terrified and alone, hope slowly evaporating like a puddle after the rain.

She didn't hear the key in the lock, didn't see Gabe wedge himself between the door and the doorjamb to get inside. He dropped to his knees in front of her. "Quinn, darling, what happened?"

"Mum, what's wrong?" Emma cried from beyond the door. Alex, who was still in his buggy, began to cry. Even Rufus began to growl. He burst inside and lifted himself on his paws, his warm nose pressed to Quinn's face.

"Quinn!" Gabe called to her when she failed to answer. He took her gently by the shoulders and pulled her to her feet. "Are you ill? Should I call an ambulance?"

Quinn shook her head and slumped against Gabe, needing to feel his solid presence. He wrapped his arms around her. "Brett," she whispered. "Brett was here."

Gabe held her close, stroking her back gently. "It's all right. He won't hurt you. Come, let's get you some water."

"Is Mum all right?" Emma demanded. She'd pushed her way into the house and was dragging Alex's buggy into the foyer, so as not to leave him alone outside. Alex was howling like a banshee.

Quinn used every bit of strength to pull herself together. "I'm all right, darling. Just had a bit of a shock, that's all. Why don't you put on a video for you and Alex?"

Emma studied her face, searching for any hint of untruth, but seemed to believe her. "All right," she mumbled. "Come, Alex."

She pushed the buggy into the lounge and positioned Alex in front of the television. "What do you want to watch?" she asked, sounding like a five-year-old mum. "Should I put on one of your baby shows?" she asked solicitously.

Gabe walked Quinn into the garden and settled her in the chair she'd vacated only a short while ago, then went into the kitchen. He returned with a glass of water and placed it in her hands. "Drink."

Quinn gulped down the water. It did make her feel better. She set down the glass, closed her eyes, and leaned against the back of the chair, allowing herself to go slack. She took slow, deep breaths until she began to feel calmer.

"I'm going to have a word with Seth," Gabe said.

She didn't reply. She had no idea what to say.

THIRTY-TWO

For a moment, Brett considered taking a taxi back to his hostel but decided to walk instead. He was tired, having landed only a few hours before, but he needed time to think, and after having been incarcerated for over a year, he couldn't take the simple pleasure of taking a walk for granted. He set the GPS on his phone and allowed it to lead him in the right direction. It was a beautiful day, but not hot and humid, like June was in Louisiana. It felt more like April, or even the end of March. The air was cool and fragrant with the aroma of freshly cut grass and gardens in bloom, and the sky was the kind of blue that had nearly made him cry when he'd only been able to see it from the small window of his cell.

He had yet to call his parents and tell them where he was, but that particular conversation would have to wait. Brett inhaled deeply and smiled to himself. What a difference forty-eight hours could make. The morning before last, he'd still been in prison. Yesterday at this time, he'd been at his hearing. And today, he was in London, a free man.

His parents had brought him home after the hearing, and his dad had taken off like a shot to the nearest supermarket to pick up supplies for a barbecue. He was going to treat Brett to a mouthwatering homecoming meal, but although Brett had looked forward to a rack of baby-back ribs smothered in barbecue sauce, freshly baked cornbread, homemade mashed potatoes, and collard greens, he couldn't concentrate on food.

While his mom and dad saw to dinner, he went up to his room and lay on his bed, considering his options. It'd been two hours since his release, and he knew exactly what that meant. As soon as they sat down to dinner, his parents would start in. They'd been admirably restrained on the drive back, but that wouldn't last long. He couldn't blame them; they'd suffered while he was inside, enough to get back together, not something he'd thought would ever happen, given that his dad had spectacularly fucked up their marriage by doing the one thing his mom could never forgive and cheating on her repeatedly. But she was willing to give him another chance, a sure sign from God that forgiveness and redemption were possible. Brett knew he owed them answers, but he didn't have any to give. Before he could commit to a next step, he had to make peace with himself, and he couldn't do that without seeing Quinn.

Of course, announcing to his long-suffering mom and dad that he was flying off to London would set off a maelstrom of protests. His dad, especially, would fly off the handle. He felt awful, Brett knew that. Whereas his mom's focus had been solely on him, Seth had to consider Quinn, and his other daughter, the one Brett had yet to meet. Seth felt guilty for helping him, torn between his loyalty to his daughter and his duty to his son. His poor dad had been put through the wringer, thanks to him. In any case, whatever he did, he had to do it soon, before anyone tipped Quinn off that he was coming. She'd never agree to see him, not that he blamed her, but he needed to speak to her, had to explain and beg for her forgiveness. He couldn't get on with his life without her blessing.

By the time Brett came down to dinner, his mind was made up. He ate with relish, complimented his dad on the ribs, asked for a second helping of mash, and even asked after the business and his dad's most prominent clients. He talked to his mom about her work at the hospital and listened with interest when she replied to his inquiries. He managed to avoid all the questions about enrolling in college for the fall semester and promised his father he'd come back to work in the office for the summer as soon as he was ready. Then, he sprang his surprise.

"Look, Mom, Dad, I really appreciate everything you've done for me, but I need a few days to adjust."

"We won't say a word, will we, Seth?" his mother instantly replied. "You take all the time you need, Brett."

"I just need to be on my own for a while," he explained.

"Are you going somewhere?" Seth asked carefully.

"I'm going to drive down to Key West. I just need a little head space, Dad." Seth nodded, seemingly agreeing with him. "I'm going to leave tonight."

"When will you be back?" his mother asked.

"A week or two. Don't worry, Mom, I'll be fine. I'll just lie on the beach, maybe do a little fishing."

"All right, Brett. We understand," Seth said. "Just keep in touch, okay?"

And don't try to kill anyone while you're there, Brett added mentally. "Sure. Of course."

Having thrown some clothes into a duffel bag, Brett had driven directly to the airport and got on the first flight out to Atlanta, where he'd bought a ticket to London. He'd arrived early this morning, checked into a hostel near Victoria Station that a website for travelers on a budget had recommended, and immediately gone to see Quinn. Their initial meeting hadn't gone well, but Brett wasn't leaving just yet. He'd try again, and again, until Quinn finally listened to him.

In the meantime, there was lots to do. He'd never been to London and had several attractions he intended to visit, starting with the Tower of London. He'd do that later, after he got some lunch and took a nap. The time difference was messing him up. Brett stopped at a quaint-looking pub, enjoyed his first-ever fish and chips and a pint, then returned to his room and slept for several hours. By the time he woke up, he felt like a new man.

I'm free, was Brett's first thought on waking. *I'm really free.*

THIRTY-THREE
JANUARY 1961

London, England

Helen rested her head against the bathroom wall. She was so weak, she couldn't find the strength to get up off the floor. She was sweating despite the January chill, and her stomach, which had revolted again after egg and toast, felt as if it had been turned inside out, and her mouth was sour with the taste of vomit. All she wanted was to lie down and sleep, but Davy was calling her name, begging her to play with him.

Helen finally pulled herself up, washed her face and rinsed out her mouth, and shuffled toward the parlor. Davy was sitting on the floor, a toy plane in his hands. He was holding the plane up, making droning noises as he pretended it was in flight.

"I'm bombing the Jerries, Mum," he informed her. "I'll blow them to smithereens."

"That's nice, dear," Helen mumbled. Remaining in the parlor meant having to listen to Davy's spirited play, so she retreated to the kitchen, where she put the kettle on. She needed a cup of strong, sweet tea. It was the only thing that helped with the nausea and soothed her raw stomach. She wished she had a sprig of mint to put in the tea, but it was hard to come by in the middle of January.

Helen sat down at the table and massaged her temples. She was more than three months gone, but the sickness wasn't abating. In fact, it had got worse. Another five and a half months of this would finish her off. The midwife had suggested a few herbal remedies, but they didn't seem to be helping.

Helen was still sitting at the table, an empty cup before her, when David arrived home from work. "Let's get you to bed," he said when he noted Helen's pallor.

"I didn't make anything for tea," Helen said weakly. "I just couldn't."

"Don't worry, love. Davy and I will go to a chippy. Can I bring you anything back?"

Helen shook her head and instantly regretted it. The motion made her dizzy. She hadn't eaten anything since that morning, but the idea of putting anything but tea in her mouth was enough to bring on the dreaded nausea.

"Helen, you need to eat. You're losing weight. It can't be good for the baby."

"I can't keep anything down," she moaned miserably.

"How about I make you some soup? You just tell me what to do, and I will do it," David said. He looked very concerned and Helen felt a pang of guilt, as if she were somehow responsible for her condition.

"Agnes stopped by earlier. She brought me beef tea. I had a cupful."

"Thank the Lord for Agnes," David said. "I'll go over on Saturday and see if she needs help with anything. It's been hard for her since Jonas passed."

"She'll appreciate that," Helen replied, thinking that as much as she wanted David to repay Agnes for her kindness, she didn't want to be left on her own. She needed help too. The washing needed doing, and the floors hadn't been properly scrubbed in weeks.

"I won't be long at Agnes's," David said, as if reading her mind. "I'll come straight back and see to whatever needs doing. You just make me a list."

Helen nodded. That was all she had strength left to do. She allowed David to help her upstairs, quickly undressed, and got into bed. The sheets were ice-cold, and she shivered as she curled into a ball beneath the duvet. She wished she had a hot-water bottle, but by the time David boiled the water and filled the bottle, she'd be asleep. After a few minutes, her body heat warmed the sheets and she began to relax, allowing herself to straighten her limbs. Within minutes, she was asleep, her depleted body desperate for rest.

"I rang Dr. Ross's surgery," David informed Helen the following morning. She hadn't heard him go out and suddenly wondered what time it was. It was nearly eight, high time she was up and about.

Helen peered at David blearily. "Are you ill?"

"No, but you are. You can't go on like this. Mrs. Ross said there's a new medication that helps with the sickness."

"David, I'm afraid to take tablets."

"Are you not afraid the child will not develop properly if you don't eat?" David challenged her.

"Yes, I am," Helen mumbled.

"Then go see the doctor. If you're still against taking the medication after the consultation, I won't pressure you."

"All right," Helen agreed. "I trust Dr. Ross."

"So do I. Now, have some breakfast, and then Davy and I will walk with you, to make sure you get there safely," David said.

"Won't you be late for work?" Helen asked as she took her customary place at the table while David made her some toast.

"I'll make up the time tomorrow. I need to make sure you're all right first."

Helen smiled at him gratefully. He was so good to her, her husband. *My brother*. The unbidden thought sprang into her mind.

My flesh and blood. She must have grimaced at the thought because David was instantly at her side.

"Are you all right, love? Do you need a basin?"

"I'm fine," Helen assured him. "Thank you."

"Here you are, then. Dry toast and sweet tea."

Helen gave him a grateful smile and took a sip of the hot tea. She experienced a moment of pure pleasure as the hot liquid slid down her throat, warming her insides and soothing her tortured esophagus. "Mm, that's good," she said. "Thank God for tea."

"Eat your toast," David said. "I won't have you going on an empty stomach."

Helen obediently picked up a piece of toast. The bread tasted bland and dry, but at least she didn't feel sick. Having finished, she went to put on her coat and shoes while David rinsed out the cup and plate. Davy was already dressed, ready for their walk. He held the toy truck in his hand. It'd give him something to do while he and David waited for her to speak to Dr. Ross.

David came out into the corridor and reached for his own coat. Before leaving the house, he took Helen's silk scarf off a peg and tied it around her neck, smiling at her when he'd finished. "There now. You look lovely. Doesn't she, Davy?"

"You look pretty, Mum," Davy agreed. "I want you to feel better."

As they walked to the surgery, Helen realized she was relieved that David had taken matters into his own hands. She couldn't go on like this much longer. She was hungry but couldn't eat. Tired, but couldn't get a proper night's rest. And worried about the baby. The waiting room was nearly empty when they got to the surgery, which was a blessing. Helen's back ached too much to sit in a hardback chair for too long.

"Ah, Helen," Dr. Ross said when she entered the examining room. "How have you been, my dear?"

"I'm expecting again," Helen replied as she took a seat on the table. "I'm afraid I haven't been feeling very well."

"Have you been examined by a midwife?"

"Yes. She says the fatigue and nausea will pass, but I'm finding it hard to cope. I can't keep anything down, Dr. Ross, and I feel so tired I can barely manage to get through the day."

Dr. Ross gave her a stern look after performing his examination. "Helen, you're underweight and suffering from exhaustion. Normally, I would send a woman in your condition to the hospital, where they'll feed you intravenously and keep you in bed for at least a week, but I'd like to try something else first."

He walked over to his desk and wrote out a prescription, which he then handed to her. "There's a new drug on the market. It's doing wonders for expectant mothers. It helps with the nausea and acts as a sleep aid, so you can get proper rest. You will begin to feel better within a few days."

"I'm a little nervous about taking medication while pregnant," Helen replied.

Dr. Ross scoffed and waved his hand dismissively. "It's perfectly safe. No side effects reported, only benefits. Give it a go and come back to see me by the end of the week. If the medication isn't helping, then I'm afraid the hospital is our only option."

"I understand," Helen said. She got dressed and left the surgery, the script in her handbag. They could stop by the chemist on the way home and have it made up. She was still hesitant, but it was better than going to the hospital. She'd loved the hospital as a nurse, but she had no desire to be a patient. Besides, she couldn't leave her boys for a week. David would have to take time off work to look after Davy, and the two of them would be worried sick about her if they knew she was so malnourished. She'd try the tablets and see if they helped.

By the end of the week, Helen felt reborn. The nausea had abated, and she was able to sleep solidly through the night, waking refreshed and full of energy.

"I made you breakfast," David said. It was the first Sunday since she'd started the medication, just over a week since she'd seen

Dr. Ross. David had made a fry-up, and the wonderful smell of eggs, bacon, mushrooms, and tomatoes made Helen's mouth water.

"I could eat the whole pan," Helen said. "I'm ravenous."

"Then do. I made it just for you. Davy and I have already eaten. I didn't have the heart to wake you."

He kissed the top of her head as she tucked into the food. It tasted heavenly, and she realized just how hungry she'd been these past weeks.

David refreshed her tea and looked on with a happy smile. "I'm so glad to see you're feeling better. Shall we go for a walk after church? You could do with a bit of air."

"Yes, I'd like that."

"Good. More toast?" David asked, grinning at her.

Helen shook her head. "I don't think I can eat another bite."

David pulled Helen's plate toward himself and finished what was left of the bacon and mushrooms. He wiped the yolk with a piece of toast and sighed with satisfaction.

"I thought you'd eaten," Helen said, feeling guilty for eating nearly all the food. She felt fit to burst, but it was a pleasant fullness, the type she hadn't experienced in months.

"I have, but I can't let good food go to waste."

"I know what you mean," Helen agreed. "I'll be plump as a pheasant if this medication works."

"Don't you go worrying about gaining weight, Helen. You're thin as a rail, and that baby inside you needs nourishment. Besides, I don't mind a bit of plump," David said, smiling at her seductively. "I'd like me a buxom dame with a bum like a drum."

Helen swatted him playfully with a tea towel. "If it's a big bum you want, keep cooking for me and I'll see what I can do."

"Small price to pay," David joked as he pulled her close, clearly glad to have his wife back.

THIRTY-FOUR

JUNE 2015

London, England

Gabe seethed with fury as he approached the building. Selling his flat to Seth had seemed like a good idea, since Quinn's father wanted to have a London base, but now that his flat was being used to house the person who'd nearly killed his wife and unborn son, Gabe wasn't so sure he should have agreed. At the risk of being selfish, he fervently wished she'd never reconnected with any of these people. With the exception of Logan, each and every one of them was proving to be a nightmare.

When Quinn had informed him that Jude had joined the army, he'd been staggered. The idea of Jude in the military was preposterous, but he had to acknowledge, with grudging respect, that he admired Jude for taking such a drastic step. If the army didn't set him straight, nothing would. Gabe genuinely hoped Jude would find the stability and structure he was looking for and live long enough to tell the tale.

Gabe took the lift up to the fourth floor and rang the bell. There was no answer. He tried again. Nothing. Gabe returned to the lobby and approached the doorman, who'd known him for years.

"Afternoon, Perry. I was wondering if Mr. Besson is in residence," Gabe said, hoping Perry would divulge the information without a song and dance about violating the residents' privacy and basically gunning for an incentive to part with the information. Perry wasn't above such tricks.

"No, Mr. Russell. He's not been back since the beginning of May."

"Is the flat in use by anyone else?"

"Not that I know of. Why do you ask?"

"My wife's brother turned up at the house this morning. I assumed he was staying here."

"I'm pretty sure he isn't. He'd have to have signed in when he arrived, and no new tenants have taken up residence since Mr. Besson moved in a few months ago."

"I see. Thank you." Gabe pushed a ten-pound note across the counter and said goodbye. Given the situation, it was probably wise to maintain Perry's goodwill. Gabe exited the building and dialed Seth's number. It'd be just gone nine a.m. in New Orleans, so Seth would most likely be at the office.

Seth answered on the second ring. "Is Quinn all right?" he demanded without any preamble. Gabe normally didn't ring him first thing in the morning. In fact, he didn't ring him at all, leaving all communication to Quinn.

"Depends on your definition of all right," Gabe replied. He was still angry, but his fury was beginning to abate.

"What happened?"

"Brett showed up at our door this morning. Took Quinn completely by surprise. You can only imagine how she reacted."

"Jesus Christ!" Seth exclaimed. "Gabe, I'm so sorry. I should have realized Brett would pull something like this. He told us he was driving down to the Florida Keys for a few days. Needed some alone time, you know? Naturally, we believed him. I should have known he'd try again."

"Try what?"

"He wrote her a letter from prison, you know. She never

replied. In fact, she told me she hadn't read it. I wish she would have. I think it might have helped them both."

"Look, Seth, no offense, but my first priority is not helping Brett."

"None taken. I completely understand. Look, Gabe, for what it's worth, he'll never do anything to hurt her. He just wants to make amends."

"Brett didn't embarrass Quinn or hurt her feelings; he locked her in a cemetery vault and left her to die," Gabe said, having difficulty controlling his temper. "Nothing he can say to her will make her forgive him. Nothing. So, please tell your son to stay away from her, because if I see him, I will give him the message in a less civilized way."

"Understood."

Gabe ended the call. He wasn't angry with Seth, just tired of putting out fires started by Quinn's relations. He had no doubt that Seth would contact Brett, just as he had no doubt that Brett would ignore his warning. He'd come this far; he wouldn't give up after one attempt.

Gabe selected Quinn's number and made the call. She answered almost immediately, sounding wary and upset. "What do you say to visiting my mother for a few days?" he asked without preamble. "We'll be back in time for Jill's wedding."

Quinn considered his proposal for a moment. "If we can come back in time for Jill's hen night, then I'm in. I can use a change of scenery, and your mum misses the children."

"I'll book us into a hotel in Berwick for a few nights."

Quinn took a deep breath before asking, "You called Seth, didn't you? Does he know Brett is in London?"

"Doesn't seem so. Seth's at home in New Orleans. He said Brett took off for a few days, needing time to think. He's here of his own volition."

"Well, that's a relief at least. I'd hate to think Seth put him up to it, after what I've been through."

"He'd never," Gabe replied. "Seth cares about you."

"I know," Quinn said softly. "He's not in an enviable position at the moment."

"No, he isn't. I'll be home soon, love. Start packing."

Gabe ended the call and headed for the tube station. His father had often told him that running away was never the answer, but in this instance, it wasn't really running away. It was a tactical maneuver to outsmart the enemy. Brett would never think to look for Quinn in Berwick, and Gabe did feel guilty for neglecting his mother. Phoebe rarely complained, but he could hear the reproach in her voice when he spoke to her. She'd been lonely since Graeme died, and although she tried to fill her hours with various senior-type activities, she still missed the companionship. She would love to spend some time with the children, and it would make him feel less guilty about going to Spain to visit Quinn's parents. Once back, it'd be almost time for the new term and Quinn would no doubt have a new case to focus on. In an odd way, Brett had done him a favor.

THIRTY-FIVE

The flat was silent, the electronic glow of the laptop screen the only light in the room. Jo sat with one leg folded beneath her, leaning forward for a better look. Daisy had posted several new photos. She'd gone to a party with her sister, Paige, and judging from the photographic evidence, it looked to have been rowdy. Daisy wore a sparkly tube top and low-rise jeans, and, although it was tastefully done, way too much makeup for a girl who wasn't yet fifteen.

Jo wondered if Michael and his wife had access to Daisy's Facebook page. Probably not. Or maybe they were liberal parents who had bought her the make-up and driven her and Paige to the party themselves. Jo pondered that for a moment. What kind of father was Michael? Was he strict, lenient, supportive, or judgmental like his own father had been? Probably all of the above, depending on the day, if she knew Michael at all. He'd never had a strong personality and was easily manipulated, as she had discovered to her own detriment.

The thought made her cringe. Why had she done it? What had prompted her to seduce her own brother? Was it the feeling of power it gave her, or the knowledge that she could use Michael for her first sexual experiment without taking any real risk? Why had she been so angry with him when all he had done was give her what she'd wanted, and why had she felt so betrayed by her parents when all they'd tried to do was parent her? No one's family was perfect; no one's parents got it right all the time, but people forgave each other and moved forward, their bonds unbroken. They didn't stop loving each other, nor did they sever all ties. Perhaps they'd done what any parent would do in similar circumstances, but she had never been able to take their decisions at face value, convinced that they'd judged her more harshly because she wasn't truly theirs, and took Karen and Michael's side over hers because in their eyes, she was never as important.

What type of parent would she have been had she kept Daisy? Would her daughter love her or think her an unbearable nag, or worse yet, a tyrant? Jo would not have been a permissive parent, she was sure of that, but how far would she have gone in rearing her daughter in her own image? Jo scoffed at the thought. Why would she want her child to be like her? What had she accomplished, besides a successful career, that was worth aspiring to? She'd driven away everyone who'd ever loved her, and she was about to do so again.

Some part of her begged her to stop and think, to take a step back, but she was on a collision course with destiny; she always had been. She wasn't one to do things by halves; she was all in. And if it was a choice between one night with Gabe or a lifetime with Quinn, she knew the answer. It had crept up on her over the past few months, while she was trying to sort through the rubbish heap that was her tangled feelings. She wasn't good with women. She'd never really got on with her mother or Karen. She liked men. They were easier to understand, easier to manipulate. Women were too smart not to see through her and put up a protective shield, knowing that sooner or later, they'd need to defend themselves against her.

Jo's gaze drifted back to the laptop screen. Daisy would be a woman one day, was nearly one already. Jo had missed her daughter's entire childhood, and if not for social media, she'd have missed her entire life. For the first time, Jo experienced pure longing rooted in what she believed to be love. Or maybe it was just selfishness on her part. Daisy had nothing to gain by knowing her; it was Jo who'd benefit from the relationship, but she couldn't look away, couldn't quite keep her promise. She wanted to meet this girl she'd made and who was part of her, talk to her, find out what she thought, what type of music she listened to, what made her laugh and cry, and what it would take for her to forgive the mother who'd abandoned her without a second thought.

Ironically, she was on her way to forgiving Sylvia. Having met her again and spoken to her, she no longer saw Sylvia as the bogeyman who lived under the bed. She was a woman: flawed, selfish at times, misunderstood, and reviled for choosing herself over her daughters. She had been seventeen, only a few years older than Daisy was now. How could anyone expect a child to make such a monumental decision when faced with two squalling infants, one of them seriously ill, and no help or emotional support? If Jo was able to finally see the truth of Sylvia's situation, perhaps, in time, Daisy might see the truth of hers, as long as she got to present Daisy with her version of events. She didn't think Michael would ever tell her the whole ugly truth; he was too kind a man to burden Daisy with such a sordid portrayal of her birth mother. Instead, he'd probably told her the sanitized version of the truth, that her mother had been a kid who was foolish, selfish, even cruel. She'd chosen her own self-preservation over the well-being of her child and, despite the support of her parents, had left the fate of her daughter in the hands of her father. Lucky for Daisy that her biological dad hadn't washed his hands of her. Daisy had had a happy life. She was safe, loved, and supported. Her parents clearly doted on her and her siblings.

Jo reached for the bottle of whisky that stood next to the laptop and added a splash to her glass. She had to put the dream of Daisy from her mind. In her own perverse way, she loved the girl and didn't want to do anything to destabilize her life, at least not yet. But knowing that she held all the cards made her decision easier.

She was no longer ignorant of Daisy's fate, nor was she completely cut off from her. All she had to do was send her a message through Facebook, and the knowledge gave her wings. She could contact Daisy at any time, ask her to meet, tell her daughter her side of the story. Daisy might be angry, dismissive, even cruel, but once the thought was planted, she'd get curious, she'd want to know more; girls always did. Sooner or later, she'd reach out, maybe only to berate Jo or tell her that she never wanted to see her, but it would be contact, and once made, there would be room to maneuver.

Not yet, Jo told herself as she closed the laptop, gulped down the whisky, and headed to the bathroom. *Not just yet*. She was tired, and having drunk more than half the bottle, she was ready for bed. Tomorrow was another day, a day in which she'd see Gabe, one way or another. She smiled at the thought. She wouldn't disrupt Daisy's life, but she didn't feel as protective of Quinn. Quinn was a big girl, and she'd have to fight for what was hers.

THIRTY-SIX

JUNE 1961

London, England

Helen stepped out into the garden and sighed with contentment. It had been a long winter and a cold spring, but at last, summer had come, and they had enjoyed a series of warm, sunny days that gladdened the heart. The delicate scent of roses wafted toward her, and Helen walked toward the bushes, bending to smell the fragrant blooms. Primroses were her favorite, partly because of their heady scent, but also because she loved the color. They were a pale yellow, each bloom as big as her palm, and up close the aroma was intoxicating. With David's help, Helen had added to the garden over the past few years, turning it into an oasis of scent and color. She'd planted hollyhocks below the windows and lavender along the back wall of the garden.

She clipped a half dozen roses and took them into the house, arranging them in a pretty jug. She set the flowers on the table and started on breakfast. David came up behind her and wrapped his arms around her round belly, planting a sweet kiss on her temple.

"Maybe today," he whispered.

"Maybe," Helen replied.

She knew it would be today. She'd been having mild contrac-

tions for the past two days, but by this morning they had intensi-
fied, and her water had broken just before she stepped out into the
garden. She was more than ready for this pregnancy to end. She'd
felt much better since taking the prescription Dr. Ross had given
her, sleeping soundly and eating well once the nausea abated, but
she was eager to meet her baby. Although she'd originally wanted
to name the child Annie, she thought she might like to name her
Rose instead, after the gorgeous primroses in her garden. In fact,
she was almost sure it was a girl. Davy had been boisterous during
the pregnancy, but this baby was quieter, calmer. She felt it turn,
but the movements had been gentle, rolling, like a sea creature stir-
ring in its watery world. There were no painful kicks in the ribs or
pressure against her bladder. Mrs. Mason, the midwife, thought
the baby was a good size. She'd felt its head and bottom and
believed it would be as big as Davy had been at birth.

Helen placed a protective hand on her belly. "I think you
should go and fetch Mrs. Mason after breakfast," she said.

David hugged her even tighter, as if he were afraid to let her go.

"Everything will be all right. You just take Davy out when hard
labor starts. I don't want him frightened. He's too young to understand how babies come into the world."

"Don't worry, love. I will look after Davy. Here, let me do that."
David filled the plates with fried eggs, bacon, and toast, and set
them on the table. "You have a hearty breakfast and then go for a
lie-down. You'll need your strength in the hours to come. Davy and
I will go fetch Mrs. Mason."

"Yes, I think I just might do that," Helen agreed as she took a
forkful of egg. She was hungry. Over the past six months, she'd put
on considerable weight, but she wasn't worried. She'd lose the
weight as soon as she was up and about again. She'd go for long
walks with the baby, now that the weather was so pleasant, and
spend time working in the garden while she (Helen thought
giddily) napped. She could already see the sweet face of her baby,
its downy hair a soft brown, and its eyes hazel like David's, or
brown like hers. She couldn't wait to hold it in her arms, sing it a

lullaby, and put it to her breast. She liked being a mum, and secretly thought they might try for another baby in a year or two. She was past thirty, but plenty of women had babies in their thirties, especially if they'd already had other children before. She might be an older mum than most of her neighbors, but it wasn't too late for her yet.

"Just leave the dishes," David told her, but Helen waved him away.

"I feel fine, and the waiting is the worst part. I promise, I'll go lie down as soon as I tidy up the kitchen."

Helen kissed Davy before he left with his father. "I'll see you later. You be good for Daddy, and by the time you return, you might have a little brother or sister waiting for you."

"I'd like a sister, if it's all the same to you," Davy said. "It'd be nice to have a girl, for you, I mean, but a brother would be just as good. So, don't worry about me; I'll be happy with either."

"Okay," Helen replied with a grin.

Helen walked her Davids to the door, finished up in the kitchen, and went back out into the garden. She had no desire to spend several hours lying down in the bedroom. Instead, she walked for a while, then sat down to rest. The pains were coming closer together now and were becoming more difficult to ignore.

"Helen? Ah, there you are," Mrs. Mason said as she stepped out into the garden. "How are you, dear? Oh, it is lovely out here," she said, inhaling deeply.

"I'm well, Mrs. Mason. The contractions are about seven minutes apart, so we have plenty of time."

"That we do, but it's always good to be prepared. I'll see you to the bed."

Mrs. Mason helped Helen upstairs. She placed a large rectangle of oilcloth beneath the sheet to protect the mattress before allowing Helen to lie down. "Let's get you out of that dress, shall we? You'll be more comfortable in your nightgown."

Helen obediently changed. There was no need to ruin a perfectly good dress, and the loose nightgown wouldn't restrict her movements. She climbed into bed and leaned against the pillows Mrs. Mason had propped up against the headboard. The pains were coming quicker now, and she was panting and groaning. Mrs. Mason laid out several clean towels on the bureau and went down to boil water to sterilize her instruments.

Once back upstairs, Mrs. Mason waited for a break between contraction before performing an internal examination. It hurt, and Helen instinctively tried to move away from her prying fingers, but Mrs. Mason pushed deeper, measuring the opening in her cervix with a practiced hand. "You're about seven centimeters dilated, Helen. It won't be long now."

She was right. Within a half hour, Helen was in hard labor. She'd forgotten how awful this part was. The contractions came one after the other, the pain rolling over her like huge waves that knocked her over and squeezed the air from her lungs. She barely had time to catch her breath before the next contraction was upon her. Her back ached dreadfully, and her pelvic bones felt as if they were being forced apart.

"It's time to push," Mrs. Mason finally said. "You're nearly there, dear. Just a little while longer. There's a good girl." She mopped Helen's brow with a cool, damp cloth and brushed her hair out of her face, but Helen barely noticed. The pressure was unbearable as she bore down, but the child wouldn't come. It seemed to be wedged in the birth canal, unable to move forward.

Helen pushed for what seemed like hours until the baby finally slithered from her body and into Mrs. Mason's waiting hands. Helen breathed a great sigh of relief and lay back on the pillows, needing a moment to catch her breath. Her legs were shaking, her back was in agony, and she was drenched in sweat, but she forgot her discomfort the moment the baby let out a lusty wail.

"What is it, Mrs. Mason? Is it a girl?"

"Eh... yes." Mrs. Mason stood with her back to Helen as she cleaned the baby on the bureau.

"Is she all right?" Helen asked. She had no reason to think otherwise, but something in Mrs. Mason's voice made her uneasy.

"Helen, why don't you rest for a while. I'll see to the little one."

"I want to see her."

Mrs. Mason turned around, the baby in her arms. The child's eyes were closed against the light, and she was no longer crying. Her perfect lips were slightly open, and her cheeks as pink as the blooms in Helen's garden. Helen held out her arms and Mrs. Mason placed the infant into them. Helen wanted to look at the baby, but Mrs. Mason's anxious gaze sent a shiver of apprehension down her spine.

"What is it?" she whispered. "Please, tell me."

"Helen," Mrs. Mason began, but a hoarse scream tore from Helen's throat when she finally looked down at the child. She tore at the blanket until the baby lay naked in her lap. Great sobs of grief erupted from her mouth as she bent over the child, rocking back and forth as she wept. The baby opened her eyes and looked at Helen, her gaze puzzled by such a display. Frightened, the baby began to fuss, her cries like the mewling of a kitten.

"Shall I take her?" Mrs. Mason asked, but Helen shook her head. She wrapped the blanket around the baby, more to cover her deformity than to keep her warm. Helen was still in shock, desperately wanting to believe that she wasn't seeing straight after her ordeal, but there was no escaping the truth. The child had no limbs. She was just a torso with a head. It was grotesque, unreal. Helen had never seen anything like it in all her years at the hospital. There had been babies born with disabilities, but nothing could have prepared her for this level of disfigurement. She continued to cry softly, clutching the bundle to her chest. The infant had stopped fussing and closed her eyes, paying little attention to her heartbroken mother as she fell asleep.

Mrs. Mason carefully took the child from Helen and placed her in the cot David had moved into their room before the birth. The little girl slept on, her chest rising and falling with each breath.

"Helen, she's not in any discomfort," Mrs. Mason said.

Helen nodded. "I need to be alone, Mrs. Mason. Please."

"Of course."

Mrs. Mason collected the soiled towels and left the room. Normally, she would have helped Helen into a clean nightgown and changed the bedlinens, but now wasn't the time.

Helen wrapped her arms around herself and rocked silently back and forth, bitter tears pouring down her face. This was all her fault. God had given her one chance to do the right thing, but she hadn't taken it. She'd ignored decency, the laws of nature, and God's own word, and lain with her brother again and again, begetting more children. She'd pretended all was well and thought she could get away with it, and now the Lord had meted out justice, and it was brutal and merciless. What was she to do? How was she to cope with a child who was so disabled? And what could she tell David? She couldn't keep the truth to herself any longer. He had to know what she'd done. He needed to understand why this had happened to them.

Helen couldn't remember how long she'd sat like that, but natural light had faded from the room and Mrs. Mason had come in to give her some water and change the bloodstained sheets. Helen moved like an automaton, allowing Mrs. Mason to stuff her into a clean nightgown. She felt numb with horror, eviscerated by guilt.

"Helen, you must try to feed her," Mrs. Mason said. She placed the child in Helen's arms and the little girl began to nurse, sucking like a normal child. Except for her obvious deformity, she appeared to be healthy.

"What will you name her?" Mrs. Mason asked gently.

"I don't know. You don't need to stay, Mrs. Mason. We'll be all right on our own."

"I'll stay with you until David comes home," Mrs. Mason replied. "I'll make some tea, and you should have something to eat."

"I can't eat," Helen said, shaking her head. "I just can't."

"You can and you should. You'll need your strength in the days to come, Helen."

"To do what?"

"To cope."

"Will she live, Mrs. Mason?" Helen asked. "Can she live like this?"

"I think you'll need to speak to Dr. Ross. He'll advise you."

Helen nodded, sniffling loudly. What could Dr. Ross possibly say? It wasn't as if there was a way to grow limbs. Even if the baby was basically healthy, she'd never be able to fend for herself. She'd need round-the-clock care for the rest of her life. What kind of a life would she have if she lived into adulthood? Helen had encountered plenty of patients with missing limbs at the hospital, had seen their struggle for independence and their anger and frustration at being pitied or perceived as being less than whole. Most of them were missing a single limb, but Annie was quadriplegic. Her emotional struggle would be as severe as her physical disability, if not more so.

At the thought of David seeing the baby, Helen began to cry again. What would he say? What would Davy say? Dear God, how could she explain this to a five-year-old boy? Helen gingerly touched the baby's soft pink cheek. The skin felt like velvet beneath her finger. The baby's head was covered with soft brown curls, her face angelic. She was just as Helen had imagined her, and when wrapped up, she looked like the daughter she'd dreamed of.

This was all her fault, and she would do anything to make things right, but it was too late. She'd gladly have died if this little girl could have been born healthy. Why should she have to bear the punishment for her mother's selfishness? Helen's grip loosened, and she dropped the baby onto her lap, unable to bear the pain any longer. Mrs. Mason took the child and returned her to the cot, before going downstairs to fetch Helen's tea.

"Here we are," Mrs. Mason cooed as she edged into the room with a tray. "I brought you tea and a ham sandwich. Nothing like a cup of tea to revive you."

"No," Helen protested and tried to get up, but Mrs. Mason,

who'd set the tray down on the bureau, gently pushed her back down.

"You're too weak to be gadding about."

Helen sank into the pillows and wished she could go to sleep and never wake up, but Mrs. Mason pushed a cup into her stiff hands. The sweet tea tasted good, and Helen marveled that something could still feel normal after what had just happened. How could anything ever be normal again? Was there any way they could come to terms with this, or was a blood sacrifice required by a vengeful God? She stifled a sob. This wasn't the Old Testament, and no amount of sacrifice would ever make things right again. Her only choice was to soldier on.

Helen nearly spilled her tea when she heard the front door open and Davy's excited voice piping up the stairs. "Can we go see Mum now? Did she have the baby? I want to play with it."

"I don't think you can play with it just yet, but maybe you can hold it," David said in his most reasonable voice.

"Okay. Let's go."

"You wait down here for a moment, while I check on Mum. Go wash your hands," David added.

Helen heard David's heavy tread on the stairs and then he was there, in the room with her and Mrs. Mason, and their child. David looked from Helen to Mrs. Mason, then his gaze traveled to the cot. He looked momentarily confused. He could obviously sense the tension in the room, taste the bitter tang of tragedy that permeated the small space, but he couldn't understand what was wrong. Helen appeared to be well, and the child was sleeping peacefully in its cot. David looked to Mrs. Mason, who lowered her eyes, as if she were at fault somehow.

"David, may I have a word outside?" she said quietly.

David looked at Helen in utter bewilderment but followed the midwife out of the room. Helen heard their muffled voices, then David came back inside, his face white as a sheet. He walked over to the cot and stared down at the baby, as though unable to believe what he'd just heard. Silent tears ran down his cheeks as he bent down to pick her up. He held her against his chest, rocking her gently.

"Hello there, sweet angel," he said. "Don't you worry. Your mother and I will love you till our dying breath, and we will do everything in our power to make your life happy and fulfilling." He kissed the baby on the forehead and turned to Helen.

"So, what shall we name our daughter, love?" His eyes radiated love and support, and Helen nearly choked on the lump that welled up in her throat. "What about Annie? I've always liked that name. I seem to recall you liked it too."

Helen nodded, unable to speak. David returned the baby to its cot and came to sit on the bed. Helen leaned into him and buried her face in his neck.

David enveloped her in a life-saving embrace, holding her as if he were trying to save her from drowning in grief. "It'll be all right, Helen. We'll be all right. We'll look after her. She'll want for nothing."

They sat like that for a long while, and when Helen looked up, she saw that Mrs. Mason had slipped out of the room and Davy had come in and was looking down at his baby sister. Helen's heart shattered into a thousand pieces when his thin voice pierced the silence.

"Where's the rest of her?"

THIRTY-SEVEN

Helen stood off to the side, head bowed, as Dr. Ross examined Annie. He'd tried to hide his shock when Helen unwrapped the blanket and laid the child on the examining table, but she had heard the sharp intake of breath and seen the involuntary widening of his eyes.

Dr. Ross pressed the stethoscope to Annie's little chest and listened intently, then looked into her eyes and mouth, and palpated her belly. He then turned to Helen, his eyes warm with sympathy. "Helen, Annie seems to be healthy, on the whole. Her heart is strong, and her organs appear to be functioning properly. I know you want answers, but I can't tell what caused this. I've never seen anything like it in all my years of practice."

"What do we do, Dr. Ross?" Helen asked. It took a herculean effort not to break down in front of the doctor, but he must have been well aware of her distress.

"You do what you would do with any newborn. You feed her, change her, put her down for naps, and take her for walks. She needs fresh air."

"But what will happen when she gets older? How will she live?"

"Helen, there are quadriplegics who lead semi-normal lives. Of course, they need constant care, but they still find some happiness in their lives. Some even learn to use their mouth as a tool."

"A tool for what?" Helen asked, taken aback by the suggestion.

"To pick things up with, even to paint with. Look, Helen, I know you're in despair, and I can't say I blame you, but there's nothing you can do for Annie other than love her. She will need all your support as she grows. How's David handling this?"

"Better than I am," Helen replied truthfully.

"And young Davy?"

"He's confused, and disappointed. He wanted a sibling he could play with, and instead he got one who'll never be a companion to him. He's too young to understand, but she will become his responsibility someday. She'll be his burden."

"Don't say that. Once Annie is older, you might consider placing her in a care home where a medical staff will look after her needs. She needn't be a burden on anyone."

"Thank you, Doctor," Helen said with a deep sigh. "You've been very kind."

"I'm not being kind; I'm being truthful. Helen, I know this is devastating, but it's not the end. Annie will have a future, as will you. Make an appointment for next month on your way out. I want to see Annie every month for the foreseeable future."

"I understand."

Dr. Ross patted Helen on the shoulder as she prepared to leave. "Don't lose hope, my dear," he said. "Not ever."

THIRTY-EIGHT

JUNE 2015

London, England

Quinn inhaled the tantalizing smell of freshly brewed coffee and toast emanating from the kitchen. Gabe was already up and making breakfast. Quinn considered getting up but decided to give herself an extra five minutes before heading downstairs. She was still shaken by Brett's unexpected visit, but knowing they'd be leaving for Berwick on Saturday made her feel more optimistic. She had two days to get through, and she would make sure not to open the door to any unexpected visitors or leave herself vulnerable to being intercepted in any way.

She'd gladly have stayed in the house for the duration, but Colin had finally rung, and she was due to meet him at the mortuary in an hour. After that, Jo was due to stop by. She'd sounded conciliatory on the phone, so Quinn had invited her for lunch. She'd tell her about Brett's arrival in London, since Jo had been very curious about him. Quinn swung her legs out of bed and prepared to face the day, convinced today would be better than yesterday.

The taxi deposited her directly outside the mortuary door,

which was a good thing since it'd started to pour, and she'd forgotten her umbrella. Quinn sighed as she walked down the corridor toward Colin's office. She wasn't as curious about what he had to say as she'd been only a few days ago. Now that she knew what had happened to Annie, she wasn't looking forward to hearing the rest of it. Dr. Clegg had thought the baby had died of natural causes, but he'd also intimated that it'd been dismembered, a theory Quinn was sure Colin would dispute.

"Quinn, good morning," Colin called out. "Go on in. Be right with you."

Quinn let herself into the lab and was pleased to see Dr. Sarita Dhawan in her usual place. "Sarita, welcome back. I was very sorry to hear about your grandmother," Quinn said.

"Thank you, Dr. Allenby." Sarita always used Quinn's title, as if using her name would be inappropriately familiar. "It's not all bad news though," she said, smiling shyly.

"Oh, really?"

"I'm to be married in December," Sarita said. She blushed prettily, and her eyes shone with happiness. "The wedding is to be in Mumbai, since that's where our families are, but after our honeymoon, Shan is coming to live in London."

"What does Shan do?" Quinn asked.

"He's a pulmonologist. He's using the time until our wedding to study for his exam so that he can practice medicine in the U.K. I don't think he'll have any trouble. He's brilliant," Sarita gushed, her blush deepening. "Really attractive too."

"Congratulations, Sarita. I'm very happy for you."

"I wish Dr. Scott was," Sarita replied. She stealthily peeked toward the door to make sure she wasn't overheard. "He thinks I'll have babies on the brain as soon as I get married and leave him. He wasn't pleased with his temporary assistant."

"So I heard. Will you leave, do you think?"

"Of course not. I worked too hard to get to where I am to just chuck it all in. Sure, I want children, but not right away, and I have no plans of being a stay-at-home mum. Shan doesn't want that either. He understands what medicine means to me."

"I'm glad you're on the same page."

"In time, I'd like to work with the police, as a Home Office pathologist," Sarita said dreamily. "It's so much more rewarding than performing postmortems on people who died of heart attacks or cancer. Your extraordinary cases made me realize that I want to solve crimes. These people are beyond my help," she said, jutting her chin toward the two fresh corpses in the lab. Quinn was grateful they were covered with green hospital sheets and she didn't have to see their faces.

"I'm sure you'll excel at it," Quinn replied and meant it.

Sarita's gaze returned to the computer screen when Colin finally walked in.

"Sorry about that," he said. "Had to finish a call."

"No worries. Sarita kept me company. So, what have you discovered?"

Colin walked over to the slab where the tiny skeleton lay like a broken doll. "Well, the first thing I have to say is that I don't agree with Dr. Clegg's assessment. Any of it. Had this child been dismembered, you'd see stubs of broken bone where the limbs had been severed, but the sockets are perfectly smooth, and empty. This baby was born without limbs, which must have been devastating for the parents."

"Do you have any theories on why that would happen? Could it have been a genetic defect?"

"I don't believe so. The child was born roughly fifty years ago, which places it squarely in the thalidomide tragedy era. You're too young to remember any of this, but toward the end of the 1950s, a new drug had come on the market. It was first introduced in Germany and was used as a sedative; however, it also helped relieve morning sickness and insomnia in expectant mothers, and was prescribed to many pregnant women in the U.K. The most severe side effect of the drug caused a condition called phocomelia, a malformation of arms and legs. Given that this child was born without even a hint of developing limbs, I would hazard to guess that the mother began taking the drug very early in the pregnancy and probably continued taking it for several months."

"Was this condition fatal?" Quinn asked.

"No. And this baby did not die a natural death, as Dr. Clegg suggested."

"Are you sure?" Quinn asked.

"Quite. Take a look at this." He beckoned her to come closer to the tiny skull. "If you look here," Colin pointed to the nose, "there's a hairline fracture in the bridge of the nose."

"Do you think the child had a fall and died as a result?"

"It's possible, but not likely. I think this child was smothered. Holding a pillow over someone's face often leads to a broken nose."

"She was murdered," Quinn whispered. She hadn't meant to reveal that she knew the sex of the baby, but she was too upset to notice she'd slipped up until after the words were out of her mouth.

"She?" Colin asked. "Why do you think it was a girl?"

"I don't. I just felt awkward referring to the baby as *it*," Quinn replied, feeling foolish in the extreme. "Were you able to obtain any DNA?" she asked. DNA sequencing would showcase the single nucleotide polymorphism, which would display large chunks of identical DNA if the child had been born to people who were closely related. It would act as tangible proof that Helen and David were indeed brother and sister.

"I'm afraid not. There was no hair left, and the child didn't have nails and had been too young to start teething. We did find several strands of hair on the shawl. They must have belonged to the owner of the shawl, most likely the child's mother."

"Anything?"

"Nothing of interest. I didn't run the full panel of tests since there's no way to compare the DNA to that of the child. That shawl could have belonged to anyone."

"I see. Thank you."

"Happy to help. How are things with you?" Colin asked as he walked her to the door.

"Everything is okay," Quinn lied.

Colin answered with a heartbreakingly sad smile. "He's gone, you know."

Quinn nodded. "I'm so sorry, Colin."

"Yes, so am I. I thought maybe this was just a bump in the road. A very large bump, but one we could get over, but I realized that this wasn't a bad judgment call on Logan's part; it was his opening salvo. Whether he realized it or not, he wanted out, and this was his way of accomplishing that. He hoped I wouldn't forgive him and the decision to break up would be mine. I didn't share this with him—I have my pride, you know—but I'd forgive him anything." Colin's eyes shimmered with tears. "I've never loved anyone the way I love Logan."

"Perhaps you two will be granted a second chance."

"I think not. We clearly don't want the same thing, at least not right now, so this appears to be the end of the road for us."

"Well, if we're to continue with travel metaphors, please allow me to say that you never know where the road will ultimately lead. I never expected to wind up with Gabe. I took his love and friendship for granted until I almost lost it, and then I realized that I'd loved him all along. I was just too blind to see it. Logan might still come round. He just needs a bit of time to drive down the motorway with the top down and the radio blasting."

Colin laughed. "You mean, eventually he'll get a headache and it'll start to rain?"

"Not quite what I meant, but something like that. At the end of the day, everyone wants comfort and security. Everyone needs a destination. There's only so long you can barrel along without knowing where you mean to end up."

"Logan is still in his twenties. From where he's standing, comfort and security seem more like stagnation—a dead end, you might say."

Quinn patted Colin on the arm in a gesture of sympathy. Having spoken to Logan, she didn't think he was coming back, at least not for a while. He needed time to figure out what he really wanted, and she didn't think Colin would wait that long. She could see the resignation in his eyes and sense his desire to let go. "I'm sorry," she said again.

"Thank you. Talk soon?"

"Of course," Quinn replied and stepped out into the street.

THIRTY-NINE

Jo glanced at her watch as she approached the house. ten forty-five a.m. Quinn had mentioned that she had an appointment with Dr. Scott at ten and had invited Jo to come for lunch at twelve, which gave Jo at least an hour alone with Gabe.

Jo tried to hide her smile as she listened to the doorbell chime inside the house. When Gabe came to the door, his expression was one of bewilderment, but he quickly masked his surprise with a smile of welcome. He wore a T-shirt and a pair of track bottoms, and his feet were bare. Alex was sitting on Gabe's hip, his chubby hand holding a sad-looking rabbit by the ear.

Jo smiled winsomely. "Hi. I'm dreadfully early, aren't I?" she asked, doing her best to look contrite. "I was already in the area and thought I'd just come by. I hope that's all right."

"Of course," Gabe said. "Come in." He led Jo into the lounge and invited her to take a seat. His laptop was on the coffee table and Alex's playpen was in the corner, where it would be clearly visible if Gabe was working on the sofa. He settled Alex in the playpen, a decision that was greeted with a wail of protest, and quickly shut the laptop before Jo could read what was on the screen.

"This is for Alex," she said, holding up a gift bag. She'd bought a toy with as many colorful buttons as she could find, hoping it would keep Alex occupied long enough for her to spend some quality time with Gabe. "And I have something for Emma as well," she added hastily.

"Thank you," Gabe said politely. He took the toy out of the bag, removed the packaging, checked it for anything that might be dangerous, and handed it to Alex, whose eyes grew wide with excitement, his displeasure at being jailed in the pen forgotten.

"Can I get you a drink?" Gabe asked.

"Sure. Will you have something too?"

"Coffee?" Gabe asked. "I could do with a cup."

"Lovely."

Jo followed Gabe into the kitchen, where he made them both a coffee.

"Let's take it into the other room," Gabe said. "I don't like to leave Alex alone for too long. He's been quiet for several minutes now, and that never bodes well."

"Of course. Was it hard—to adjust to parenthood, I mean?" Jo asked, looking up at Gabe coquettishly.

Gabe considered her question. "It was more difficult with Emma, since she was four when she came to live with us. It was as bewildering for her as it was for us, but we managed."

"Admirably," Jo agreed. "Emma seems well adjusted. Does she feel closer to you, since you're her biological dad?"

"She goes through phases. Sometimes she wants only Quinn. Alex is going through a daddy phase now," Gabe said, really smiling for the first time.

"Alex is adorable. He looks just like you," Jo said, lowering her gaze in mock embarrassment, as if she'd just realized that she'd told Gabe he was adorable.

"Eh, thank you. We think so."

Alex lifted his face at the sound of his name but went straight back to his new toy, pushing the buttons and watching them light up.

"And where's Emma?" Jo asked innocently. She'd learned

never to underestimate children. They had an uncanny way of sensing what adults sometimes chose to ignore, and if they were as astute as Emma, they also made mention of it, usually at the worst possible moment.

"She's reading in her room."

"She can read?" Jo asked, genuinely impressed.

"She's learning to read at school, but Quinn has been working with her for months. She can read age-appropriate storybooks by herself. She also likes looking at the pictures, but she won't admit to it if asked."

"I should have bought her a book."

"It's not too late," Gabe replied and walked over to the sofa, where he took a seat in the corner.

Jo sat opposite him, folding one leg beneath her in a way that afforded him a view of her tanned thighs. She'd worn a short summer dress expressly for that purpose and had paired it with a short denim jacket and strappy sandals. She looked young, fashionable, and, she hoped, sexually available. Gabe was visibly uncomfortable and kept his gaze fixed on her face, a carefully guarded response that thrilled Jo. He was aware of her attraction to him, and his discomfort proved that he wasn't indifferent to it. She was getting to him. All she had to do was keep up the pressure.

"And what about you? What were you doing when I arrived more than an hour early?" She laughed throatily.

"I was doing some research," Gabe replied. "For a project I'm working on."

"Do tell."

"There's nothing to tell. It's all very dull."

He doesn't want to tell me what he's working on, Jo thought. *It must be important to him.* "Have you ever considered writing a book?" she asked, hoping she'd hit the nail on the head.

"Yes, I have," Gabe replied.

"What's your area of interest?"

"The Wars of the Roses. My ancestors fought on both sides of the conflict."

"I imagine your ancestors fought in every English war before and since as well. Doesn't your line go back to the time of William the Conqueror or something ridiculous like that?"

"Yes, it does. There have been de Rosels or Russells in Berwick-upon-Tweed since the eleventh century."

"Wow, that's really impressive. My father's people had been in England for centuries as well—that's my adoptive father, not Seth. Not sure about my mother. But that doesn't matter now, does it? They weren't my biological parents. As you know, Seth's ancestors were slave owners, and Sylvia's were probably a bunch of illiterate peasants, so I'm not sure I prefer that family tree."

"Many Brits owned slaves," Gabe replied. "You can't hold Seth accountable for something his ancestors did centuries ago."

"Oh, I don't hold him accountable. I simply find it interesting how people's views of right and wrong have changed over the years."

"People have always known right from wrong. They simply chose not to dwell on the morality of their actions as long as doing the wrong thing benefitted them in all the right ways, and given that their deeds were deemed socially acceptable and in line with the government policies of the time, they had all the excuse they needed to pacify their conscience."

"Do all people have a conscience, then?" Jo asked, giving Gabe a wide-eyed look meant to convey her interest in his opinions.

"No, not all," Gabe replied tersely. "There have always been morally ambiguous people in the world."

"Are you referring to someone in particular?" Jo asked, immediately sensing that Gabe was holding something back.

"Brett Besson came by yesterday."

"Blimey! How did Quinn take that?" Jo exclaimed, surprised to hear that Brett was in town. She'd heard much of her American brother but had only seen a couple of photos, since he'd been in prison for the past year.

"Not well. She was badly shaken."

"What did he want?"

"He wishes to make amends," Gabe explained. He'd finished his coffee and set the mug on the coffee table. Jo was amused to notice that he crossed his arms as he leaned against the back of the sofa, as if he needed to protect himself from her.

"Is such a thing possible?" Jo asked.

"Not in my opinion, but Quinn has been known to surprise me."

"You think St. Quinn will give him another chance?" Jo scoffed, glad of the opportunity to make a dig at Quinn's forgiving nature. Gabe's raised eyebrow signaled that she had gone too far, so she smiled and shrugged. "She makes me feel like a right old bitch sometimes," she confessed.

"Just because Quinn is generous of spirit doesn't mean she's oblivious to people's flaws, Jo. She chooses to see the best in everyone, something I try to remember when I pass judgement on people without a second thought."

"Come now, I'd hardly call you judgmental. You're nobody's fool, and that's a quality I admire in a person."

"And you think Quinn is a fool?" Gabe asked, choosing to ignore the compliment and focus on the insult to his wife.

I'd better change tack, and fast, Jo thought. Gabe was becoming increasingly defensive, which wasn't her objective. She'd only meant to stroke his ego, not bring out the knight in shining bloody armor.

"Quinn is no fool. I only meant that she has an innate kindness, the type few people have these days. Someone who sees the best in people is more likely to turn the other cheek."

"Quinn asked Brett to leave. She has no intention of speaking to him."

"He'll be back, I'm sure of it."

Gabe didn't respond. He was clearly done with the conversation and wanted to move on, but Jo had one more question.

"Did Brett say where he was staying?" she asked. She wanted to meet this bloke. Today.

"No, he didn't."

"You know, I can help you," Jo said as she glanced at her watch. It was nearly noon, and she meant to use the remaining time to get closer to Gabe.

"With what?" Gabe asked, surprised.

"With your book, if you decide to write it. Emma is not the only one who likes to look at pictures. Adults do too. I would gladly supply the photos for your book—free of charge, of course."

"Eh, thank you for the offer, but I've no need of photos at the moment."

"Just think, we could drive out to the sites of the great battles of the Wars of the Roses and get some shots. I'm a whiz at Photoshop. I can superimpose images of knights riding into battle, or fighting, onto the modern photographs, but make the warriors appear almost transparent, like a ghost army. What d'you think?"

"I think that's a very creative idea," Gabe replied, looking at her with renewed interest.

"I thought you might like it. Think it over. My offer has no expiration date."

"That's very generous of you, Jo. Ah, there's Quinn now," Gabe said when he heard the key in the lock. His relief was almost palpable.

"Oh, hello," Quinn said when she saw Jo.

"Sorry. I was early," Jo explained. "Can I help you make lunch?"

"Sure, if you like. I just need to change and file this report away."

Quinn returned downstairs a few minutes later and invited Jo to come into the kitchen with her. Gabe took the opportunity to scoop Alex out of the playpen and take him upstairs for a nappy change. He seemed eager to get away.

"So, tell me about this new case. Can I see the artifact you're using?" Jo said as she leaned against the worktop.

"Are you sure you want to do that again?"

"Why not? I'm feeling reckless." *You have no idea just how reckless*, Jo thought as she studied her sister.

"All right. I'll show it to you." Quinn left once again and reappeared a minute later with a brooch in a plastic bag. It was a cheap trinket, not like the beautiful gold and opal hamsa found at the last site.

Jo reached for the bag and held it up for closer inspection. "May I?" she asked.

"Go on."

Jo lifted the brooch out and held it in her hand, closing her eyes to get a better feel. She felt a burning pain in her chest. It took her breath away and nearly turned her legs to jelly. Her knees buckled and she dropped the brooch onto the floor, desperate to make the pain stop.

"What? What is it?"

Jo's splayed hand rested over her heart as she tried to catch her breath. "Pain. Terrible pain."

"Was it a physical pain?"

Jo considered that for a moment. "Yes and no. The physical pain was the predominant one, but there was also great anguish, the kind that leaves you bereft of all hope."

"That sounds about right," Quinn said. "This poor woman had her heart broken, in the true sense of the term. Her baby girl was born severely disabled."

"Children really do have the power to bring you to your knees, don't they," Jo said. She'd never expected to feel such longing for Daisy, but with every passing day, she knew that stalking her online would never be enough. Sooner or later, she'd have to make contact.

"Yes, they do. There's nothing more painful than seeing your child suffer."

"And yet, people keep having them."

"Because there's nothing like it. Have you considered having children—in the future, I mean?"

"Not really, but I might be persuaded to change my mind. If I met the right man, that is."

"Have you ever met anyone you thought might be right?" Quinn asked as she took some vegetables out of the refrigerator.

"Yes, I have. Just recently."

"Is he interested?"

"He might be. It's early days yet."

"Well, I wish you luck. I want to see you happy, Jo."

"I'd like to be." Jo shook her head, as if trying to dislodge Gabe from her mind. "Tell me about this encounter with Brett. Gabe mentioned he'd come round. That took courage."

Quinn groaned. "Can we not talk about that right now? I'm trying to put it out of my mind."

"Sure. Sorry. I am just curious to meet my brother, the black sheep of the family. But then again, he's not the only one, is he?" Jo said. "We've all got a checkered past. Except you."

Quinn didn't reply.

"Do you know how I can reach Brett?" Jo asked, knowing full well Quinn didn't. She just wanted to rattle her cage.

"No, but I'm sure Seth does."

"I'll ring him. I haven't spoken to him in a while, so two birds with one stone," Jo replied.

"How are things with Sylvia?"

"I've decided to give her a chance. Have you seen her recently?"

"No, I haven't. I've been very busy with the program. Rhys has skeletons turning up thick and fast. The hotline was a stroke of genius."

"Yes, he's clever like that, our Rhys," Jo said, a bit sarcastically. "Is he still shagging that Russian?"

"Yes, he is still seeing Katya. He seems very happy," Quinn snapped.

"You don't need to get defensive on his behalf. We parted amicably," Jo said, reaching for a piece of carrot and popping it into her mouth. "Best of friends."

"I'm not getting defensive. I'm genuinely pleased for him. He deserves something real in his life."

"And the Russian princess is real? Somehow I doubt it."

Quinn didn't reply, but Jo saw the spark of annoyance in her eyes. The two of them couldn't be in the same room for long without creating friction. Jo knew her remarks were caustic, but she couldn't help herself. Something about Quinn got under her skin.

Her self-righteousness, Jo thought angrily. *Well, I've had enough of it for one day.*

"Look, Quinn, I'm sorry, but I think I'll skip lunch. I've just remembered, there's something I need to do. Tell Gabe I'll be happy to help him with his project," Jo added, glad to see the look of surprise on Quinn's face.

You thought he'd only shared his dreams with you, lovey? Jo thought spitefully. *Now you can wonder just how much he's shared with me.*

"All right, if you're sure," Quinn replied.

"I'll ring you later." Jo gave Quinn a peck on the cheek and saw herself out.

She'd done what she'd set out to do. There was no need to stay any longer. She was, however, curious to meet Brett. She fished out her mobile and texted Seth, asking for Brett's contact information. Seth replied a few moments later. Jo saved the number and made the call. Brett didn't pick up, so she left him a message, telling him she'd like to meet, then turned for home. Having barely slept last night, she needed a nap.

FORTY

"Where's Jo?" Gabe asked as he came down, Alex in his arms. He lowered the baby into his high chair, and Quinn handed him a sippy cup full of juice.

She passed Gabe a bowl of homemade baby food so he could feed Alex while she finished preparing lunch. "She left."

"Did something happen?"

Quinn shrugged. "She was in a confrontational mood, so perhaps it's for the best. I hadn't realized you told her about your book."

"I didn't mean to. She just happened to ask the right questions, and it was something to talk about. She offered to take some photos."

"Did she? Well, that's something, I suppose."

"What do you mean?"

"Forget it. I have no idea what I mean," Quinn replied warily. "It's just that she's been so snippy lately." She set a bowl of salad on the table and reached into the fridge for leftover chicken. "Is Emma coming down?"

"She'll be right down. She wanted to finish her book. She seemed really engrossed."

"I'm so happy she enjoys reading," Quinn said, instantly brightening. "My efforts are paying off."

"They most certainly are. I love seeing her with a book."

"Enjoy it while you can," Quinn replied with a wry smile. "She'll be asking for a mobile soon, and then she'll be glued to it twenty-four hours a day."

Gabe nodded. "I see lots of kids with phones when I collect her from school. I can't imagine what their parents are thinking, getting them a mobile at the age of five."

"I don't think we should get Emma a phone just yet, but there are benefits to a child having a mobile," Quinn replied.

"Such as?"

"It's a way to track them, should they get lost or, God forbid, taken. It's also a way for them to call for help, should they need it."

"Yes, I suppose," Gabe replied thoughtfully, recalling the time Emma had left the playground because she thought she saw her mother walking past. Jenna had been recently deceased, and being only four at the time, Emma hadn't been able to quite grasp the finality of the situation. She'd wound up at a busy junction, lost and terrified. Thankfully, she'd been quickly located by the police, but things could have turned out very differently had Emma decided to cross the street or kept going instead of standing still and waiting for rescue.

"Are you getting me a mobile?" Emma asked as she waltzed into the kitchen. "I'd like a sparkly pink case."

"No, darling, we're not getting you a mobile," Quinn replied. "We were just talking."

"Oh," Emma replied, her disappointment palpable. "But you said there are good reasons for me to have one."

"There are, and we will get you one once you're a little bit older," Gabe replied patiently.

"Like when I'm six?"

"Maybe once you're closer to ten," Gabe clarified.

"Eight?" Emma haggled. "That's older than six and closer to ten."

Gabe laughed. "We'll see."

"When you say, 'We'll see,' you usually mean 'no' but don't want to say so straight out," Emma said with a theatrical pout. "You don't have to lie to me, you know."

"No one is lying to you," Quinn said. "We are simply not ready to commit to an answer. That's not the same as saying no."

"Whatever," Emma muttered, still in a huff. "Where's Aunt Jo? I thought she was staying for lunch."

"She left."

"Good," Emma said.

"Why is that good?" Quinn asked, surprised by Emma's statement.

Emma shrugged. "She's like a wicked stepsister."

"In what way?" Quinn asked, pausing in the act of slicing a loaf of bread. Gabe had stopped too, his hand suspended in midair, holding a spoonful of baby food.

"Like, she's nice to the prince, but mean to her kind, loving sister, so you know that's her true nature," Emma explained patiently.

"*Is* she nicer to the prince?" Quinn asked, clearly surprised by Emma's observation. She appeared to be paying close attention to what Emma said.

"Obviously. She's always smiling and doing that thing with her eyes," Emma replied.

"What thing?" Gabe asked.

Emma looked down for a moment, then tilted her head sideways and looked at Gabe from beneath her lashes, smiling like the bloody *Mona Lisa*. "This thing," she said, lifting her head and looking from Quinn to Gabe to see if they understood what she meant.

Quinn laughed, but the sound came out brittle and forced. "What an imagination you have, Em. Life is not a fairy tale."

"No, but in real life not everyone is nice either," Emma said as she reached for a piece of bread.

"No, they certainly aren't," Quinn agreed.

. . .

After lunch, Gabe went upstairs to work, but his mind wasn't on the convoluted politics of the fifteenth century. Instead, his thoughts kept returning to the conversation with Jo. She'd been more forward this time, and considerably more suggestive. She'd practically asked him to go away with her, since most of the famous battle sites were not within close driving distance and such an undertaking would require them to spend the night somewhere, possible even two or three. Gabe felt angry and uncomfortable, but also guilty. He was only human, and the images Jo was so carefully planting in his brain were taking root. She was a beautiful woman, and she knew it. She was also comfortable with her sexuality and had no issue with using it as a tool. Unlike Quinn, who needed an emotional connection in order to pursue a sexual relationship, Jo seemed to be the type of woman for whom sex was the endgame.

Gabe wasn't privy to the details of her personal life, but he'd met plenty of women like her during his career. They cast off centuries of double standard and simply took what they wanted when they wanted it. Jo likely had an active sex life, despite not having a steady partner. She oozed sexuality the way some men oozed aggression. Perhaps Rhys had been right to steer clear of her. Jo Turing was not a woman who'd put anyone else's needs first. She came first and foremost in her own hierarchy of life, which was why Gabe was under no illusions about her motives. Jo couldn't care less about him. He was a prize to be won in a contest she'd initiated with her sister. Whether it was jealousy, competitiveness, or just some uncontrollable need to destroy every relationship so profoundly that there was no going back, Jo had set her sights on him, and she wouldn't back down on her own. She was aware of his reaction to her and was enjoying his discomfort, secure in the knowledge that she'd got into his head. She would maintain her residence there until he either succumbed to her advances or involved Quinn.

Gabe closed the document he'd been working on and stared

out the window, seeing little of the garden beyond. He could hardly tell Quinn her sister was making advances to him, not when Quinn was already worried about her fragile relationship with Jo, nor could he tell Jo to back off. He didn't know Jo well enough to predict her reaction to such a confrontation but thought it could go one of two ways—she would either go on the offensive and goad him until he snapped, or she'd laugh in his face and tell him he'd imagined the whole thing and she was simply being sisterly. Either way it went, it would be about as prudent as opening Pandora's box.

Gabe sighed with frustration. All he wanted was to get the bloody woman out of his life and off his mind. She had initiated a tactical assault on his defenses, and ashamed as he was to admit it, even to himself, losing individual battles didn't guarantee she wouldn't win the war, not if she proved successful at getting him to think of her in a sexual context. Neither the short dress nor the way she'd folded her leg beneath her to give him a glimpse of her inner thighs were lost on him. Had she moved her leg a little to the right, he'd have been able to answer with complete certainty whether she'd been wearing knickers. She'd wanted him to look, invited him to wonder, and dared him to resist. She'd silently challenged him to compare her and Quinn, to wonder what she'd be like in bed, and to grow curious enough to want to find out for himself.

"Damn you, woman," Gabe muttered under his breath. "How I wish you'd just go away for good and stop interfering with our lives."

FORTY-ONE

JULY 1961

London, England

Helen lifted Annie from the pram and hurried inside, kicking the door closed with her foot. She leaned against it and shut her eyes as bitter tears of unbearable pain slid down her cheeks. The neighborhood women didn't mean anything by their questions; they were just curious and wanted to chat about a subject that was close to their hearts—children. Helen tried to act nonchalant, but she simply couldn't keep up the charade. The weather had turned warm and poor Annie was hot beneath the blanket Helen used to cover her whenever she went outside.

"God, Helen, she must be sweltering, the poor mite. You were never this fearful with Davy," her next-door neighbor Marge had said not five minutes ago. "Oh, look, she's awake. Can I hold her?"

"No," Helen had snapped. "Not now. I have to go." She'd nearly run Marge down with the pram, she'd been so desperate to get away.

Her neighbors had given her a few weeks to recover from the birth and settle into a routine, but now that Annie was a month old, the other mums were beginning to call on her. Lynn had come twice, and both times Helen had told her that Annie was asleep, and Sarah had sent a lovely gift, with a note that inquired when they might see each other. She'd said she'd be happy to bring her girls for a visit whenever it was convenient. Helen wished she could crawl into some hole and die. It was preferable to seeing the shock on the faces of the women she knew and hearing the platitudes that would eventually come, once they recovered enough to speak. Nothing they said could make a difference. No words of comfort or sympathy could soothe her battered soul. This wasn't a minor defect that wouldn't prevent Annie from living a normal life; this *would* be her life, every hour, every day, every year.

"Mum, are you all right?" Davy asked as soon as they were inside.

Helen had tried valiantly to hide her despair from him, but he'd heard her crying, had seen her anguish. He wasn't old enough to comprehend the long-term effects of Annie's deformity, but he could see Helen's pain and recognize it for what it was, and it troubled him.

"I'm just fine. Something in my eye, that's all," she explained as she kicked off her shoes and walked into the parlor, where she sat down heavily on the settee and settled Annie next to her.

Davy came over and patter her shoulder, his eyes full of understanding. "It's all right, Mum," he said. "People will get used to her." Wise words for a five-year-old.

"Yes, I know."

"Can I go out and play?"

"You can play in the garden."

Davy made a face but complied and went out back. Helen sighed and leaned against the back of the settee. What was she hoping to accomplish? Sooner or later, everyone would know anyway. She couldn't keep Annie under wraps forever. Davy was right, people would get used to her, but Helen wasn't sure she could ever get used to her. She loved the child with her whole being, but every time she unwrapped the blanket, her heart broke all over again at the sight of Annie's deformed body. Her life would be difficult at best, hellish at worst. No surgery could correct her condition and no prosthetics could replace the missing limbs. There was nothing to attach them to.

Helen sighed and wiped her cheeks. Annie was looking at her, her eyes so clear and beautiful. There was a strange awareness in her gaze, almost as if she understood her mother's worries and wished to reassure her that everything would be all right. Helen unbuttoned her dress and held the child to her breast, stroking the little head as she nursed. "Oh, Annie, what's going to become of you?" she whispered. "How will you survive, my darling?"

FORTY-TWO

David gently pushed a lock of hair behind Helen's ear, then used his handkerchief to wipe her tears. Helen was sitting on their bed, a pillow clutched to her middle. She'd tried to reason with herself, and when that failed, she'd turned to the familiar comfort of housework, but the tears wouldn't stop flowing, and the dread she'd felt when she returned from their walk hadn't abated.

"Helen, you can't hide Annie from the world forever. I know this is not something either one of us expected, but we must find a way forward. Is there someone you'd like to talk to? Maybe the vicar? Davy is frightened, and Annie will need your unwavering support as she gets older."

Helen shook her head. "David, this is all my fault," Helen whispered. "I caused this to happen to our girl."

"How can this possibly be your fault?" David asked, smiling at her indulgently. "There's no one to blame."

Helen shook her head stubbornly. "There is. I am to blame. I did something awful."

"What awful thing have you done?" David asked, still smiling at her in that pitying way.

Helen clutched the pillow tighter, as if it could keep her heart from exploding from her chest. She had to tell David, come what may. She couldn't carry this burden any longer. "David, I came across something when I cleared out my mother's room. I found your birth certificate."

"What? I don't understand," David replied, his smile slipping.

"I found a birth certificate for David Edward Edevane. Mother —Edith Brent. Father—unknown. There was also a photograph of a man who looked like you. He must have been your biological father, Edward Edevane."

"Show me," David said. "Please." His voice trembled and the desperate look in his eyes made Helen wish she hadn't been so hasty to burn the evidence.

She shook her head. "I'm sorry, but I burned them. I thought I could make it all go away," she whispered, her eyes swimming with tears. "I was in shock."

"Are you sure you read the birth certificate correctly?" David demanded, his worried gaze pleading with her to tell him it was all a terrible mistake. "You were upset about clearing out your mother's room. You weren't feeling well. Could you have made a mistake?"

"No. I read it over several times. There's no mistake, David," Helen insisted. She understood David's disbelief and his desire to reason this hideous revelation away by blaming it on her distress or pregnancy hormones, but she knew what she had seen, and now that she had finally told him, she wasn't about to backtrack and pretend it was just a misunderstanding. She needed him to believe her, and to comprehend the unbearable strain she'd been living under these past few years.

David shook his head in dismay, still desperate to deny what she was telling him. "Helen, that's mad. How could such a thing be possible?"

"My mother—our mother," Helen corrected herself, "must have had an affair while my father was off fighting the Germans. She could hardly keep the baby, so she left you at the orphanage, making sure to give them your full name, in case she decided to come back to claim you. And she might have, had my father not returned. Then she could have simply told everyone she was a widow, and no one would have been the wiser. They'd assume you were her husband's child."

David shook his head again, like a stubborn donkey. "No, I don't believe it. It simply cannot be. You must have misunderstood."

"I didn't misunderstand," Helen cried, her agitation growing. "I told you, I read and reread that birth certificate a dozen times. And the man in the photo..." How could she make him understand without showing him the photograph that the man she'd seen looked just like him, only younger?

David's shoulders slumped, as if all the fight had gone out of him, and he reached for her hands, taking them gently in his own. "Helen, you should have told me. You had no right keeping this from me." It was a reproach, but he had a right to be angry.

Helen nodded miserably. "You are right, but I wasn't thinking clearly. I was so upset, and so frightened. I didn't know what to do. I was afraid you'd leave me," Helen whimpered. "I'm sorry I deceived you."

"Could it be a coincidence?" David asked, his gaze pleading with her to consider this unlikely new possibility. He was grasping at straws, just as she had when she'd discovered the truth, and Helen felt a stab of pity for him. She had laid this squarely on his shoulders, and he could never throw the weight off, not now that it was out in the open between them. "Surely there's more than one David Edevane out there in the world," David said, but his voice lacked conviction.

"David, the certificate had your birthday on it. March twenty-first, 1917," Helen explained gently. "That would be more than a coincidence. Seeing you in the flesh killed our mother. She knew who you were the moment you walked in, and then once I introduced you, I confirmed her suspicions. Before that night, I'd only referred to you as David."

David sighed, his expression pained. "I know God sometimes

has a cruel sense of humor, but this—" He shook his head sadly. "I can't even say the words out loud."

I can, Helen thought. *I must. I need to speak the words in order to make them real between us. I need to confess to what I've knowingly done.*

"We are brother and sister, David, and Annie's deformity is my punishment for not doing the right thing."

"And what do you suppose the right thing would have been?" David asked. He was white as a sheet, but his eyes held no anger or resentment, only pain.

"I should have told you straight away. We should have had the marriage annulled."

"And what would have become of Davy? Can you imagine what his future would have been like had it come out that his parents were, in fact, siblings?"

"Yes, I can, which was why I burned the photo and the birth certificate and carried on as if nothing had happened. When Davy was born healthy and strong, I thought that maybe God had forgotten about me, but it seems he hadn't."

David shook his head. "Helen, fate brought us together. You could have married any other man, but you married me. We found each other for a reason, and if you believe that God oversees everything we do, then that had to be part of his divine plan."

"What plan?" Helen cried. "David, you're my brother."

"Half-brother, which is about the same degree of relation as first cousins. First cousins have been allowed to marry throughout history. In ancient Egypt, royal brothers and sisters married to produce the next pharaoh. It was a way to keep the blood pure. Besides, we were strangers to each other when we met. We didn't grow up together. We came together as man and woman, not as brother and sister." David was so desperate to make some sense of what he'd just learned, Helen's heart went out to him. He was understandably in shock. The reality of their situation would take more than a few minutes to fully sink in.

"But that doesn't change the fact, does it?" Helen replied

gently. "Our union is incestuous, and our children are a product of sin."

"It's only a sin when undertaken with full awareness," David argued. He seemed determined to reason their predicament away.

"We are fully aware now," Helen reminded him.

"But we weren't when we married. Our son was conceived in innocence."

"But not our daughter."

"You had good reason for keeping this to yourself," David replied.

"Are you saying I did nothing wrong?" Helen asked, staring at David as if he'd just started speaking in tongues.

"I'm saying that you did the most sensible thing under the circumstances. Had the truth come out while we were stepping out, it would have been better for us to go our separate ways, but you were already pregnant with our son. You had no other choice but to carry on. Helen, darling, I don't think Annie's disability has anything to do with us."

Helen wiped away fresh tears. "Oh, David, I want to believe that, I do, but if I told anyone the truth, they'd see it quite differently, especially Reverend Hale."

"Then don't tell him. Don't tell anyone. No one needs to know. We are a family, and we'll remain a family until the bitter end. You've been carrying this burden for so long. Let me carry it for a while. Put if from your mind and focus on our children. They need you."

"Why is Mum crying again?" Davy whined as he came into the room. "What's wrong?"

"Nothing, son. Everything is all right. Mum's just tired."

"Mum cries all the time."

"Come here." David enveloped his son in a comforting embrace. "Mummy is not going to cry anymore. She is going to be much better from now on. Right, Mummy?"

Helen nodded. "I promise. I'm going to get better."

"Well, all right then," Davy said. "I'm hungry. What's for tea?"

"How about chips and egg?" David asked as he stood. "I'll make it. Let's give Mummy a chance to rest."

"You are going to make chips?" Davy asked, his expression dubious.

"I most certainly will. And they will be splendid."

"Okay," Davy replied, his tone betraying a total lack of confidence in David's cooking ability.

David planted a kiss on Helen's forehead. "I'll call you when tea is ready. Take a moment for yourself."

"Thank you," Helen said softly. "I do love you so."

David smiled into her eyes and escorted Davy from the room.

FORTY-THREE
JUNE 2015

London, England

Jo closed her eyes as she slid lower into the heavenly embrace of the hot water. She'd perfumed her bath with a fragrant oil and lit a few candles. Normally, she found taking a long, hot bath soothing, but today the ritual failed to relax her, try as she might to let go of the tension that had been building up inside her since leaving Quinn's house. She'd put it all on the line when she'd proposed that Gabe come away with her, even if only for a few hours. She hadn't expected him to jump at her offer, but she'd meant to plant a seed in his mind, letting him know in no uncertain terms that she was there for the taking. Quinn, in her staggering naiveté, would probably allow Gabe to go off with Jo if she thought she was being a supportive wife and helping him with his project. *What a fool!* Jo thought, her lip curling with derision. Quinn seemed to trust Gabe implicitly. He was a man, after all, and all men were led by their cocks. It was like an antenna that picked up the subtlest of signals.

Maybe Gabe's antenna is broken, Jo thought angrily. Gabe's reaction had been underwhelming, to say the least. He'd politely fobbed her off, doing that passive-aggressive thing where people said something sounded great, while at the same time making it clear they had no interest in pursuing whatever had just been proposed. Was he really so devoted to Quinn that he didn't dare entertain the possibility of a hot fling? God, it wasn't as if she were asking him to leave his wife. For starters, she wanted to fuck him. Badly. Once she got past the hurdle of breaking down his ridiculous moral inflexibility, she'd decide where she wanted the relationship to go. And it would be her decision; it always was. Gabe would do whatever she wanted once she had him firmly in hand. Jo chuckled at the thought. Yes, she would like to have him in hand, and in her mouth, and in every other orifice in her body. She felt a pleasant warmth between her legs that had nothing to do with the hot water lapping at her tender parts. She extended a hand from the tub and reached for her mobile.

"You up for a shag, Timmy?" she purred when Tim answered the phone. "You get a special bonus if you get here before I get out of the tub."

"I wish every call I get was this exciting," Tim replied with a throaty laugh. "I'll be there in twenty. Keep that water hot for me. I'm coming in. Do I get to choose the bonus?" he asked, his voice silky and suggestive.

"What would you like?"

"I've always fancied having a little photoshoot. Stephanie won't let me anywhere near her with a camera. She's too shy, but I know you're not."

Jo laughed. "You can take all the photos you want, but on one condition. My face is not to appear in the pictures, not in all of them, anyway. Everything else is fair game."

"Deal," Tim replied. "It's not your face I'm after."

"I didn't think so. Hurry, darling, the water's getting cold," she moaned and ended the call.

Jo sighed and leaned back against the cool porcelain tub. The thought of Tim taking photos of her excited her. He was right, she wasn't shy, and she'd give him a session he'd never forget. He could even get in on the action, if he liked taking selfies. Jo slid a hand down her body and shivered with pleasure. No one said she couldn't start without him.

FORTY-FOUR

Brett ordered a beer and took a seat at a corner table where he had a good view of the door. Jo was late, but he didn't mind. It'd been more than a year since he'd been out at a bar, and even longer since he'd had a beer. He had been pleasantly surprised to hear from someone at his hostel that the legal drinking age in the U.K. was eighteen, not twenty-one, like at home, so he could legitimately have a drink and not feel like a nun in a whorehouse when he met Jo at the bar. The place was loud and trendy, with lots of well-dressed millennials sipping on craft beers and expensive-looking cocktails. Music was thumping over the loudspeakers. He didn't recognize any of the songs but enjoyed listening to something new. He leaned back against the faux-leather banquette and took a slow sip. After a year of not drinking anything but milk, coffee, and juice, he was afraid to get drunk too quickly.

A slow smile spread across Brett's face when he saw Jo enter the bar. He'd recognize her anywhere. Her dark hair hung loose around her shoulders and she wore tight jeans and a lacy top that did little to disguise the fact that she wasn't wearing a bra. She nodded to a few people she knew and exchanged a few words with the bartender before scanning the place with her dark gaze. Having spotted Brett, she made her way to the table and slid into a seat across from him.

"Well, hello there, little brother," she said, smiling at him. She wore dark red lipstick that accentuated her dark coloring and made her look a little Goth. She looked even more like his dad in person, but that didn't prevent her from being sexy as hell. "You look different than I expected. Older," she said. "Stronger."

Brett met her inquisitive gaze. There was truth in what she said. He had yet to leave his teen years behind, but prison had stripped away the last remnants of childhood, leaving in its stead a world-wary young man. His sculpted biceps were clearly visible beneath the cotton of his shirt, and his chest and shoulders were broader than they had been in the pictures she must have seen.

"Well, I had to grow up fast," Brett replied.

"Why's that?" Her head was tilted to the side and her eyes were sparkling with amusement.

Brett was sure she knew the answer to her question already, but she clearly wanted him to talk about prison, so he replied. "I got jumped a few times in the first few months. Other inmates don't like guys who try to kill pregnant women and unborn babies. I got hammered. After that, I needed a way to defend myself. Not that working out a few times a week would save my ass. If someone wanted to stick a shiv between my ribs, they would've done it by now."

Jo nodded. "You're right about that." She looked like she was about to say something else when a server came by the table. "Shot of tequila," Jo said.

"I'm good with my beer," Brett said. He had half a bottle left, and he intended to nurse it for a while yet.

"Oh, come on. Aren't Americans always drinking tequila? Show me what you're made of."

Brett shrugged. "All right. I'll have a shot."

"Bring eight," Jo instructed the server and turned back to Brett. "Quinn said you came by."

Brett nodded. "Yeah, I did. I only wanted to talk to her, but she got really scared."

"And that surprises you?" Jo asked, smiling at him as if he'd just told her some great joke.

"No," Brett replied. He didn't want to sound defensive, but Jo was goading him, and he felt the need to explain. "I really am sorry. When Quinn was going to out me, I panicked and made the worst possible decision. If I'd explained, Quinn would have listened to me. She might not have understood or agreed, but she would have listened. They think I ran off to Texas to make sure no one found her, but I left because I was so scared. Once I had a chance to think, I realized there was no going back. If I let her out of that tomb, she'd tell everyone what happened, what I tried to do. I ran because I was terrified and sorry for what I'd done. When my dad caught up with me, I was too afraid to tell him the truth, especially since I thought it was too late to save Quinn and the baby. I hoped he'd kill me, so I wouldn't have to live with the guilt."

"But you're alive and so is she. Lucky for us all," Jo remarked sarcastically. "Did they beat your white supremacist notions out of your head in jail?"

"I'm not a white supremacist," Brett snapped. "Look, you have no idea what it's like to grow up in the South. It's not like here. Some conflicts are alive and well, and there's still a clear divide."

"So, are you still a raging racist now that you know you're part Black?" Jo taunted him.

"I was never a raging racist, but I needed time to make peace with that part of my heritage. I wasn't ready to tell the world."

"And now you are?"

"I guess," Brett replied. He was glad to see the server, who brought a tray of shot glasses and set them on the table between them.

Jo picked up a glass and held it up. "Salute," she said before tossing it back.

Brett did his own shot. The alcohol burned his throat. He'd

tried tequila only once before, at a friend's party, and wasn't really a fan, but Jo seemed to like it.

"Come on, let's do another."

"You go ahead," Brett said. "I need a minute."

"Milksop," Jo said, grinning at him. She downed another shot and licked her lips. "So, what now? Will you go back to New Orleans?"

"Not yet. I want to try to speak to Quinn again. Maybe I'll call her husband. He'd probably like to strangle me with his bare hands, but Gabe's a good guy, or so my dad tells me every chance he gets. If Gabe will speak to me, then maybe I'll have a chance with Quinn. I only want to make amends."

"And you think you can really make amends for trying to kill her?" Jo asked. She picked up another shot glass and downed it.

"No, but I still have to tell her how sorry I am, and that she has nothing to fear from me. Ever."

Brett took a sip of his beer. He wished he'd never agreed to meet Jo. He could understand her attitude toward him, and he didn't blame her for wanting to hurt him on Quinn's behalf, but he'd hoped she'd at least listen to what he had to say. She was acting like both judge and jury on a case that had already been closed. He'd served his time and paid the price.

He didn't tell her how severely he'd been beaten, or how scared he'd been for the past year. No words could describe the terror he'd felt every time he walked into the showers. Was there any feeling in the world worse than being naked and defenseless against guys who were twice your size and took pleasure in meting out justice? And what right did they have to judge him? It wasn't as if they were there for tax evasion, or some other white-collar crime. Most of the other inmates were violent criminals, men who'd maimed and killed, mostly for money. Was he so different because the person he'd tried to kill was his pregnant sister? They didn't give a shit about Quinn, they just craved violence, and he'd been an easy target since he'd had no one to protect him.

Jo suddenly smiled, her eyes sparkling dangerously. "She kind of brought it on herself though, didn't she? She can be a self-right-eous bitch."

Brett tilted his head to the side. It was his turn to study Jo. "She didn't deserve what I did to her," he replied cautiously. "She was just excited about finding out the truth about our ancestors."

"And the psychic gift we all share," Jo added, watching Brett for a reaction.

"You have it too?" he asked.

"Yeah, but I don't exploit mine the way Quinn does. For the most part, I ignore it. Why would I want to get embroiled in someone else's life, especially once they are dead? But, I guess, for Quinn, there's money to be made. Her ability has made her a star. She's a household name, for God's sake."

"She's good at what she does," Brett protested.

"Yeah, but the ability to see into the past gives her an edge other archeologists don't have. She's not constructing a story around her findings. She's using the findings to support the facts."

"Look, what does it matter?" Brett asked. "People enjoy the show, and she's not hurting anyone."

"She's pulling the wool over their eyes. Everyone thinks the narrative is based on hard evidence, when in fact, it's based entirely on the visions of one super-ambitious woman."

"You don't like her much, do you?" Brett asked, confused by Jo's attitude toward Quinn. According to their father, Jo and Quinn were basking in the glow of mutual admiration, but the glint in Jo's eyes when she spoke about Quinn and the contemptuous half smile told another story.

Jo shrugged. "She's a hard act to follow."

"You don't need to follow her," Brett replied. "She was ready to move mountains to help you. She would've gone to Afghanistan herself if Gabe hadn't talked some sense into her."

"That's what martyrs do, isn't it? A bit self-serving, if you ask me." Jo picked up another shot and waited until Brett reached for one as well. He didn't want it but felt like she was going to belittle him if he didn't drink with her.

"St. Quinn," Jo said, raising her drink. Brett didn't join in the toast. He was beginning to understand what was irritating Jo. Quinn made her feel threatened, and sadly lacking in whatever it was that made a person feel truly special. He wasn't sure why she was showing him this side of herself, but maybe it was because she'd assumed they were kindred spirits.

"I liked Quinn when I met her in New Orleans. She was cool," Brett said.

"Cooler than me?" Jo asked, teasing him. She was eyeing the last two shots on the table.

Brett didn't answer. "Do you plan to stick around?" he asked instead.

"Where?"

"In Quinn's life. Do you want to be a sister to her?"

Jo thought about that for a moment. "I don't know. She's a bit sanctimonious for my taste. Gabe, on the other hand, is just the right combination of beauty and brains."

"What, you got the hots for him or something?" Brett asked.

Jo laughed. "Can't I pay my brother-in-law a compliment?"

"I don't know. Can you?" Brett asked. He wasn't sure if she was drunk, but her thinking didn't appear to be impaired.

"Gabe is hot," Jo said, picking up a shot glass. "I'm simply stating a fact. Come on, join me."

"I'm done. Thanks. You go ahead."

Jo tossed back the shot, then picked up the last full glass and drained it as well. "So, what'd you do today besides harass our sister?"

"I went to the Tower of London. It was really cool. What did you do?" he asked, wondering how Jo spent her time when at home.

"I had a friend over. He took some photos of me."

"Like a headshot?" Brett asked.

"Not exactly." She took out her phone and showed him a picture. In it, she was sitting on a bed with her back to the camera. She was nude. Her back was arched, her head thrown back, and her hands in her hair. Brett could make out the curve of her breast, but his gaze strayed to her very fine ass, and he quickly looked away, afraid he'd see more than he bargained for. "Want to see a few more?" Jo asked, chuckling naughtily. "They're not as tame as this one."

"I would, if you weren't my sister," Brett replied. He felt like a twelve-year-old boy whose mother had just caught him whacking off. Jo knew he was turned on by the picture; she'd wanted him to be. What was she playing at?

"So, how long are you staying in London? Want me to show you round?"

"I'm good, thanks," Brett replied. He wanted nothing more than to go back to the hostel and crash. He was tired and done with this conversation.

"What will you do when you go back home?" Jo asked.

"Dad wants me to go to college. I think I'd like that, but not in Louisiana. People will recognize my name from the news. Maybe I'll go to New York or Boston, or even California. That'd be cool. I need a new start," he added wistfully.

"But not before you make amends to Quinn?"

"Not before I make amends to Quinn," Brett agreed.

"Well, good luck with that. Ring me if you need anything. I'll be around for a few weeks."

"Will do. It was interesting meeting you, Jo."

"Likewise."

FORTY-FIVE

Brett remained at the bar for a while longer after Jo had gone, nursing the rest of his beer and going over their meeting in his mind. He'd heard a lot about her from his dad, but the Jo he'd encountered was much sharper around the edges, and much nastier. In prison, his gut instinct had saved him more than once, and he'd learned to trust his assessment of people. Jo was bitterly jealous of Quinn. She was like a catty high school girl who'd do anything in her power to take down a rival. He had no reason to think that Jo would act on her petty rivalry, but he'd hate to see Quinn hurt again.

He hadn't told anyone, not even his parents, but he'd found God in prison. Speaking regularly to the prison chaplain had helped him to finally come to terms with what he'd done and his reasons for doing it and to find the courage to ask for forgiveness. He'd promised himself that if he got out of prison alive, he'd not only apologize to Quinn but do everything in his power to somehow make it up to her. She'd never have to know, but he'd know, and that would relieve some of his guilt. He'd seen a picture of Alex on Seth's phone and he'd been sick with remorse. For the remainder of his days, he'd have to live with the knowledge that he'd almost killed that adorable little kid, his own nephew. He didn't suppose he'd ever get to meet Alex, or Emma, but he wished them nothing but happiness. Maybe someday he'd be blessed enough to have a family of his own, and he hoped he would be worthy of them.

Brett finished the beer and headed back to the hostel. He had enough money to hang around London for several weeks, if he chose to, so he'd take his time. He'd try to speak to Quinn again, this time without alarming her. He would try approaching Gabe if that didn't work. If Gabe didn't kill him on the spot, maybe he'd hear him out and agree to facilitate a supervised meeting. Brett didn't expect Quinn to ever forgive him, but he needed to tell her that he'd made peace with his heritage and that, in his estimation, she'd made him a better person. And that he'd do anything, anything at all, to make amends.

FORTY-SIX

JUNE 2015

Berwick-Upon-Tweed, England

Quinn stood on the bank of the River Tweed and inhaled deeply. She liked the smell of the river, and she was enjoying the fresh wind that ruffled her hair. Alex, snuggled beneath a warm blanket, was fast asleep in his buggy, and Emma was playing with Buster and Rufus, throwing them sticks and watching them compete for her attention.

Phoebe pulled her cardigan tighter around her ample middle. "It's brisk out today."

"It was quite warm in London when we left," Quinn remarked.

"I didn't used to mind the cold, but now my old bones can't take it. I feel chilled even at the height of summer."

"You should have moved closer to us," Quinn said. "There's so much to do in London, and the climate is milder."

Phoebe shrugged. "I've lived here all my life. It's home. And I would feel disloyal leaving Graeme. Let's walk," Phoebe suggested.

They strolled along, watching the river as it wound into the distance like a shimmering highway. The wind moved through the trees, the leaves rustling above their heads. After the bubbling cauldron of humanity that was London, Quinn found it pleasantly peaceful.

"You seem sad, for lack of a better word," Phoebe said. "Is everything all right?"

Quinn shrugged. She wasn't sure she wanted to talk about what was troubling her, but Phoebe was an excellent listener, and an even better advice giver. She was able to see the whole picture rather than focus on some minor point as many people did, and she often helped both Quinn and Gabe put things in perspective.

"I suppose I am a little sad," Quinn admitted. "More disappointed, really. When I first discovered I was adopted, I made up all these stories in my head, in which I found my birth family. I desperately wanted to have siblings, so I made up brothers and sisters who'd be my best friends, and we'd have the most amazing adventures together. When I discovered that I have actual siblings, I resurrected the fantasy, and thought that despite not knowing each other during our younger years, we could make up for lost time and become a family. I especially wished for that with Jo." Quinn sighed. "She's—" Quinn raised her hands in a gesture of defeat. "I don't even know how to describe her—prickly, I suppose. She's also defensive, competitive, and guarded. I realize her life's been very different from mine, but I want nothing more than to be her friend, her sister. I have no desire to take anything from her, only to give."

Phoebe nodded as she listened and patted Quinn's shoulder in a motherly manner as she considered the problem. Her gaze was clouded, as if she were recalling something from another time, but Quinn could see the compassion in Phoebe's eyes when she stopped and looked her full in the face.

"Quinn, when Graeme and I were newly married, my sister Flora dragged us to a marriage workshop. I think she was having issues with her husband but didn't want to admit to it, so she made it sound like a learning opportunity for all of us, a chance to work on our relationships and grow as partners, which in my day was practically unheard of. You just got on with things, you didn't analyze them to death. Having met Graeme, you can just imagine his reaction to this kind of psychobabble, but he went, for my sake. He knew I wanted to be there for Flora, and I had promised him we could stop at the pub on the way home. The instructor started the workshop by having all the wives stand with their backs to their husbands, and then asked them to fall backward. Most women did, but a few couldn't do it. Flora was one of them."

"I'm sorry, Phoebe, but I don't follow," Quinn said. She was used to Phoebe's roundabout way of giving advice, but this was too cryptic even for her.

"What I'm trying to say, not very effectively, obviously, is that when you strip away all the layers of a relationship, you're left with the foundation, and it should be built on trust. Nothing else matters if you can't trust your partner to catch you when you fall. This is not only true in marriage, it's true in any relationship between two people. Imagine your siblings standing behind you. Who'd catch you, and who wouldn't?"

"That's a good question," Quinn said, pondering what Phoebe had just said. "I know Logan would catch me. I wouldn't think twice about falling into his arms. Jude, perhaps. Depends on the day. I'd never turn my back to Brett again."

"And Jo?" Phoebe asked gently.

Quinn shook her head, realizing with eye-opening clarity that she knew the answer to this one. "Jo would let me fall."

"Then there's your answer," Phoebe said, nodding like a wise old owl.

Quinn hadn't realized she'd asked a question about trust, but perhaps the question mark had been right there, hovering above her head. Now that Phoebe had put it in perspective for her, she was amazed how clear it all was. She didn't trust Jo. In fact, she wasn't even sure she liked her. There was something about Jo that made her feel guarded, unsure. Even in her most candid moments, Jo seemed to be holding back, manipulating the situation to suit her own ends. Jo was not a sister Quinn could ever truly love. She had too many sharp edges, too many barbs to make dealing with her comfortable.

The realization should have upset Quinn, but just as it had with Sylvia, she felt freer for it. She and Jo didn't have to love each other. They didn't have to be best mates, or even friends. They'd finally met after three decades, they'd talked and shared, and that could be the end of it if that was what Jo wanted. They could meet up for a drink from time to time, maybe even see each other at a family gathering, but it didn't have to be more than that. Quinn had felt wonderfully liberated since she'd decided that she and Sylvia needn't have a mother/daughter relationship. Perhaps it was time to do the same with Jo. "Cut her loose," Seth would say with all his American directness. "If she cares enough, she'll stick around, and if she doesn't, well, then you're better off without her."

Quinn chuckled. She often found herself repeating the things Seth had said in her head and marveling at them. Seth wasn't a deep, self-analytical man, but he was sharp as a tack—another one of his sayings—and he saw people for what they were, not what he wished them to be. Well, everyone except Brett, but that was understandable. If she fell, Seth would not only catch her, but lift her up and set her on his shoulders, from where she could see the world in all its glory. He loved her; of that she was in no doubt.

You win some, you lose some, kid, Seth's voice said in her head. *At least you got three out of six.*

"Yes, I suppose I did," Quinn muttered.

"Did what?" Phoebe asked.

"In finding my birth family, I've gained three people who love me, and three people who'd rather leave me than take me as I am. It's three out of six."

"Not a bad ratio, if you ask me. The better half is in your corner."

Quinn smiled. "Thank you, Phoebe. You've really put things in perspective for me."

"I'm glad I could help. And, Quinn, watch out," Phoebe said.

Her voice had an ominous note to it, which Quinn found unsettling.

"Watch out for what?"

Phoebe didn't reply. Instead, she called out to Emma, who was running too far ahead with the dogs. "Emma, dear, wait for us."

"I'll go after her," Quinn offered. She hurried along the path, leaving Phoebe to push the buggy at her own pace.

It wasn't until much later, as she lay in bed at the hotel, that she recalled Phoebe's warning. Had it been a well-meant piece of general advice, or did Phoebe know something Quinn didn't? She glanced at Gabe's sleeping face. The only way Phoebe would know something was if Gabe had told her about it and had perhaps relied on her sage wisdom.

Quinn sat up and rubbed her temples. She felt a headache building behind the eyes. If Gabe stood behind her, she'd let herself fall without a moment's hesitation. She trusted him implicitly, and Gabe trusted Phoebe, so if Gabe had come to her for advice, he had to be worried. What was he trying to protect her from?

FORTY-SEVEN

Gentle fingers of lights caressed Gabe's face, waking him from a restless sleep. He always felt restless in Berwick, he realized, and longed to return home. Perhaps he still had some residual guilt about selling the family home, or maybe it was the sight of his mother that troubled him.

Phoebe had changed in the year since Graeme's death. She'd become frailer, more resigned to encroaching old age. She'd had no desire to remain in the mansion on her own but living in a retirement community wasn't doing her any favors. She jokingly complained that she was surrounded by old people who only left the community in body bags, but Gabe heard the bitterness underlining the joke. She'd reached an age where life didn't have much left to offer except illness and loneliness. He wished she'd have moved to London to be closer to him and Quinn, and the children. Grandchildren were the antidote to decline.

Gabe looked over at the portable cot he'd set up in the corner of the hotel room. Alex was sleeping peacefully, his fingers closed around the ear of the bear Jude had brought for him. Quinn was asleep as well, her breathing even and steady. She looked more relaxed than she had been in days, and Gabe was glad to have been able to offer her this little break from reality. Hopefully, Brett would be gone by the time they returned to London. In a few weeks, they'd be off to Spain to visit Quinn's parents. The promise of sun and sea did much to lift Gabe's spirits. It'd been a while since he'd been on a beach holiday, and he looked forward to playing with the kids and giving Quinn a chance to rest. She was emotionally overwrought and needed time away from her work and her birth family.

Reaching for the phone, Gabe saw that it had just gone seven. He had several emails, and one text message from an unknown number that must have popped up overnight. Gabe wasn't unduly worried. Sometimes he got calls and messages from students, and they came up as unknown numbers.

He clicked on the text and an imagine appeared on the screen. A naked woman sat on a bed, facing away from the camera. Her back was arched, her buttocks resting on her heels, and her hands were in her hair. Her face was turned just enough for Gabe to make out Jo's profile. He stared at the photo in disbelief. If Jo had been engaging in guerilla warfare before, now she had graduated to a full-frontal assault. The choice of words made Gabe cringe. Would a frontal image come next? He hoped not. He was only human, and the image on his screen was doing exactly what Jo had hoped it would.

He deleted the photo and blocked the number from which it had come, then returned the phone to the nightstand before going to the bathroom, where he turned on the shower. Evidence of his arousal infuriated him, and he twisted the faucet, making sure the water would be cold enough to cure him of this particular need. He stepped into the water, gasped as the nearly freezing spray hit his face, and rested his hands on the tiles, bowing his head.

At first glance, the photo Jo had sent was an invitation. *Come and get me*, it said, but it was so much more than that. It was also a threat. She was letting him know in no uncertain terms that she had the power to destroy his life, not only by getting into his head, but by coming between him and Quinn. Who was to say she'd stop at sending him a provocative photo of herself? She had boasted that she was a whiz at Photoshop. What if she superimposed an image of him into the photo and sent it to Quinn? She could find a photo of him easily enough on Quinn's Facebook page. What if she went so far as to inform Quinn they were having an affair? Quinn would believe him if he denied it, but for just a moment, she would question the veracity of his answer. She would wonder if such a thing were possible. And that moment of hesitation could cost him his marriage. If she lost faith in him, no amount of professing his devotion would change her mind. For better or worse, she trusted Jo and would see her confession as the act of a guilty conscience.

Gabe turned the faucet and released the breath he'd been holding as the water warmed up. His body had responded to the image, but the rest of him was angry and frustrated. What did Jo want from him? Would one night satisfy her, or did she want more? Was she only after sex or was this some elaborate mind game she was playing? If so, she wasn't likely to stop. And what was he to do? Telling Quinn was out of the question; she'd be devastated. Confronting Jo was probably not a good idea either, since he'd be playing right into her hands. Ignoring her didn't seem to be working, so what was left?

This wasn't something he wanted to discuss with his mother or even Pete. Pete was a good bloke, but he had never been known for the subtlety of his approach, and he'd probably advise Gabe to simply tell Quinn, which sounded great in theory but would not play out so well in real life. And he had no wish to worry his mother. It was his turn to support her, not the other way around.

Alex's cry startled Gabe out of his reverie. He turned off the water, dried off quickly, and tied a towel around his waist. When he came out of the bathroom, Alex was standing inside the cot, holding on to the side and anxiously looking around, waiting for someone to pick him up.

Quinn rubbed her eyes and sat up. "Oh, you pulled yourself up, you little rascal," she said, smiling at the child. "How clever are you?"

She got out of bed and lifted Alex out of the cot, holding him close. He rested his cheek against her shoulder and wrapped his arms around her neck, sighing with relief. Gabe wrapped his arms around them both and kissed Alex's sweet-smelling head. If Jo cost him his family, he'd end her, he thought suddenly. He wouldn't stand idly by and allow her to toy with his life.

FORTY-EIGHT

AUGUST 1961

London, England

Helen's hands trembled violently as she reached into the pram and lifted Annie out. The baby was wearing a yellow cotton dress and the matching headband Helen had made from leftover fabric. The dress had cap sleeves and would have come to the knee had Annie been blessed with knees. David put a steadying hand on Helen's back as they walked into the church, Davy behind them. They were greeted by friendly smiles and nods.

"Oh, she's lovely," Agnes said. "Like a little angel."

Several more women made comments, having never seen Annie up close, but then a hush fell over the congregation as they looked closer. One woman covered a gasp with her hand, while others peered more intently, trying to understand what exactly was wrong with the child in Helen's arms. Helen tried to hold her head high, but tears pricked at her eyes and she thought she might be sick. She wanted nothing more than to turn around and run, and never come back. She wished she could just run away from it all, from her secret knowledge, and from her pain.

"Give her here," David said quietly. He accepted Annie and herded Davy to their regular pew.

Helen slid in behind them and grabbed on to the back of the pew in front of them, grateful for the unyielding wood that kept her from falling. She was shaking, and there was a ringing in her ears that thankfully blocked out the whispers and well-meaning comments of her neighbors. Most people had averted their eyes, unable to stomach the sight of her deformed child. She might have reacted much the same had this happened to someone else. She'd have been horrified, and so sorry for the parents who'd been dealt such a cruel hand. What would she have said to them, if anything? What could one say? It was too awful for words, since no comfort or acceptance could ever truly be found.

Helen lowered her head and breathed deeply, inhaling the scent of wood and beeswax polish. The familiar scents comforted her somewhat, but she was too afraid to look up. She couldn't bear the pitying glances or the cruel jibes that would soon follow. If one could count on anything in life, it was people's cruelty.

David settled Annie in his lap and reached for Helen's hand, squeezing it until she finally responded and turned to face him. "You did it," he whispered. "You did it, Helen. It will get easier from here on in."

It will never get easier, Helen thought angrily. Anywhere they went, anything they did, people would stare and comment. Everyone would assume the parents were somehow at fault, particularly the mother. It was always the mother who got blamed for everything. Helen fixed her eyes on Reverend Hale, but she didn't hear a word of the sermon. All she wanted was to grab Annie and run, to lock the door behind them, lay Annie in her cot and cover her with a blanket, then climb into bed, curl into a ball and cry until she had no tears left.

You've already done that several times, her inner voice reminded her. *It hasn't helped, not long-term anyway. This is your life now. Get used to it. Stop being so weak, so frightened. Annie needs you.*

Helen took a steadying breath and reached for Annie, who was becoming fussy. She held her close and rested her cheek against

Annie's head. The baby settled, and after a few minutes her eyelids began to flutter as she grew heavier in Helen's arms. She finally fell asleep, pink lips slightly parted, and rounded cheeks rosy with good health. Her long, thick lashes fanned over her cheeks, and her dark hair curled over her ears. Helen's heart welled with love, and she held her closer, brushing her lips against Annie's smooth forehead. When she looked up, several pairs of eyes were watching her. Some looks were pitying, while others were jeering and judgmental.

"Monster," a woman said under her breath. Helen couldn't tell where the insult had come from.

The service finally came to an end, and Helen stood, ready to leave.

Agnes patted her gently on the arm and smiled in sympathy. "She's lovely," she said again, a little defiantly this time.

"She's grotesque," someone else hissed. "An abomination."

"Say that to my face, if you dare," David challenged the speaker, his voice firm and loud enough for everyone to hear.

No one said another word, but the damage had been done. Helen walked home slowly, her eyes unseeing. Had it not been for David, she'd have tripped, fallen over, and not had the strength to get back up. He pushed the pram slowly, his other hand on the small of her back, a pillar of silent support. Davy walked next to his father, his cheeks flushed and his eyes downcast. He was old enough to understand, and he looked as upset as his parents.

Helen had never been so relieved to see her front door. She left the children to David and went into the kitchen to see to Sunday lunch. Performing mundane tasks calmed her. David turned on the wireless and the strains of a Beethoven concerto filled the house, drowning out Helen's unhappy thoughts.

"Would you like to go for a walk? It's a fine day," David asked after lunch.

Helen shook her head. She couldn't bring herself to leave the house and come face to face with any of their neighbors. She wanted to hide for the rest of her life, if such a thing could be arranged, but if all she could get was a few hours of solitude, then she'd take them and be grateful. "I'll take Annie out into the garden. I'll read while she sleeps."

"Davy, would you like to come with me?" David asked.

"I'd rather stay at home, Dad," Davy replied. He looked sad and tired, his shoulders sagging with the weight of his parents' troubles.

"All right. I won't be long. Just need a bit of exercise," David said.

"Take your time," Helen said.

David gave Helen a quick kiss and headed out the door. Helen closed the door behind him and leaned against it, glad to shut out the outside world. She coped by hiding, but David walked for hours, desperate to release his pent-up frustration.

They hadn't spoken of Edith in any great detail since Helen's revelation. Neither of them had the emotional wherewithal to delve into her alleged affair with Edward Edevane or the abandonment of their son, but Helen knew David thought about it and it gnawed at him. Not only had his mother given him away without a second thought, but she'd been angry to find him on her doorstep. She'd had a good reason for her reaction, but given that she hadn't seen her boy since he was an infant, it would have gladdened David's heart to know that despite her mortification and shock, she was glad to see him, pleased to discover that he'd turned out to be a fine man and had survived the war that had killed so many. Instead, Edith had looked at David as if he were shit on her shoe, something distasteful to be disposed of as quickly as possible.

Had Edith the courage to tell Helen the truth that night, things might have been very different for all of them. Perhaps she'd even still be alive. Helen didn't think sharing her secret would have prevented the heart attack, but maybe if Edith had remained downstairs, Helen could have summoned help when the pains came. It was a foolish thought, she knew that, but she couldn't help wondering what might have happened had Edith lived long enough to tell the truth. Would she have told her the truth? It would have been the right thing to do, but for some reason, Helen doubted her mother's desire to do the right thing was uppermost in her mind. Perhaps she would have kept silent, allowing Helen and David to marry anyway.

Helen had to stop thinking along these lines, but her mind kept looking for ways out of their predicament, even though the die had been cast and there was nothing left to do but live with the outcome. She needed something to distract her from her morbid thoughts, so she fetched her book and carried Annie out into the garden, where she settled her on a cushioned chaise. Helen covered the baby with her shawl since it was cooler in the shade and she didn't want Annie to catch a chill. Davy came out into the garden too. He had his toy truck with him. He liked to roll it back and forth and load the bed of the truck with pebbles from the garden.

Helen tried to read, but the words swam before her eyes, the sentences slithering like snakes. All that emotion had worn her out, leaving her feeling as limp as a rag doll. She laid down the book and leaned back in the chaise, closing her eyes. Annie would be asleep for at least an hour, so she allowed herself to doze off, lulled by the murmur of the wind in the trees and the calming symphony of birdsong. It felt so good to just let go for a while, to slip into oblivion and dream.

Awareness came slowly as Helen surfaced from deep sleep. She didn't rush to open her eyes, just lay there for a few minutes, listening to the rustling of the leaves, the chirping of the birds, and the *vroom-vroom* sounds Davy made while playing with his truck. She felt so peaceful and heavy-limbed, it was a shame to have to get up, but it was time to feed Annie and get supper going.

"Wake up, sleepyhead," David said softly. Helen hadn't heard him come into the garden but was glad he was back from his walk. She must have slept longer than she'd thought.

"I fell asleep," she said apologetically and glanced at her watch. She felt guilty for leaving the children unattended for such a long time, but everything appeared to be much as it had when she first came out into the garden nearly two hours ago.

"I know. You looked so peaceful. Do you feel any better?" David asked gently.

"A little," Helen lied.

"Good. I'm glad to hear it."

"I'll nurse Annie, then get supper started." Helen said as she sat up and tidied her hair.

"Annie's still sleeping. Don't wake her. I can stay out here with the children for a bit," David offered.

"All right."

Helen got up off the chaise and walked into the house, reluctantly entering the kitchen. She was so tired of cooking. She felt like that was all she ever did, besides the washing. It never ceased to amaze her how much dirty laundry four people produced, and how many meals needed to be prepared. When it had been her and Edith, they'd often eaten a cold luncheon or sometimes just fried some sausages for their supper. It didn't seem right not to offer David a hot meal when he came home from work, and Davy was a growing boy who needed hot, nutritious food.

Helen took some potatoes out of the pantry and began to peel them over the sink. Edith had hated peeling potatoes, but Helen didn't mind. It was better than chopping onions. That always made her cry. She finished peeling, washed the potatoes, and set them to boil. Once the potatoes were almost ready, she'd mash them while the sausages were frying.

Helen turned at the sound of footsteps. David walked into the kitchen, Annie in his arms. She was still wrapped in Helen's yellow shawl and it hung around her like a curtain. Helen opened her mouth to say something when she noticed David's expression. The pain in his eyes was like nothing she'd ever seen before, not even when he'd first beheld Annie. He looked bewildered, as if he'd just seen something he simply couldn't make sense of.

"David, what is it?"

"She's—" The words seemed to stick in his throat. "She's not—"

Helen dropped the tea towel she was holding and reached for the child. David surrendered her without protest and Helen held her close, peering into her little face. Her eyes were still closed, and her cheeks were rosy, but there was no life left in the tiny body. Annie's chest did not rise and fall, nor did her eyelids move. She was perfectly still. Gone.

An anguished scream tore from Helen's lips. How could this have happened? Annie had been sound asleep, alive, only a short time ago, and now she was... Helen couldn't even think the word. The finality of it took her breath away. Her legs began to tremble, and she sank into the nearest chair, Annie still in her arms. She held the baby to her face, kissing the downy head and inhaling the scent of Annie's silky hair for the last time. Death had already begun its work, turning a living child into a lifeless doll, but Helen's mind was still grappling with what she was seeing.

"David, I don't understand. What happened? How could she have just slipped away like that?"

David's eyes glistened with tears, but all he could do was offer her a helpless shrug. "I don't know. She seems to have passed in her sleep. Perhaps her condition—"

"Dr. Ross said she was healthy and strong," Helen protested. "We should call him right away. Hurry, David!"

"Helen, she's gone," David said gently. "I think she has been for some time."

"No!" Helen cried, but she knew the truth of David's words. Annie's face was cold to the touch, utterly lifeless. As a nurse, she'd seen many recently deceased bodies. Had Annie had limbs and digits, they would already be growing stiff.

"Let me have her, Helen," David said softly. "I'll put her in her pram until the undertaker comes to collect her."

"No!" Helen cried. "There will be no undertaker."

"You can prepare her for burial yourself, if it will make you feel better," David replied. He looked ashen but talking of practicalities seemed to ease him somewhat.

"I want her buried here."

"What?"

"I won't leave her alone in that graveyard. I want her here, in the garden, where I can look after her."

"Helen, Annie deserves a proper burial."

"Proper? What's proper? She hasn't even been baptized."

"That won't matter. She must rest in consecrated ground, under God's protection."

Helen laughed bitterly. "God's protection? What sort of God would do this to a child? What sort of God would sentence an innocent little girl to a life of misery and deprivation? What kind of life would she have had if she'd grown into adulthood? Can you even begin to imagine how she would feel once she began to understand that something was irrevocably wrong with her? Can you even pretend to know what it would feel like to see other children running, playing, holding an ice cream, or even just wiping their own bums? How would she feel when she became a young woman and saw girls her age going out with fellows, wearing pretty frocks and high-heeled shoes, putting on lipstick and fixing their hair? How would she feel when those girls got married and had babies of their own and walked proudly down the street pushing a pram? She'd have none of it, David. None. She'd sit in her chair and watch the world go by, knowing she could never fully be a part of it, never enjoy the things that others took completely for granted. So, don't tell me about God's protection and love. He had none for my little girl, and I have no time for Him. I'm through with God!" Helen screamed.

Somewhere at the back of her mind, she knew she was hysterical, but she simply couldn't get hold of herself. Why should she? God had just multiplied their already unbearable tragedy, leaving her no emotional reserves to deal with her pain. She was broken beyond repair, utterly undone.

David pulled her into his arms and held her close, the baby between them. "It's all right, love. It's all right. I'll do as you ask. I'll bury Annie by the rosebushes where you can look after her. I'll do as you ask," he repeated. "Now, let me have her."

Helen stubbornly shook her head. "I will hold her until she's ready to be buried. I'll not leave her alone for a minute. She deserves better than to be left in her pram like a forgotten toy. I'll keep watch over her."

"Of course, love. You do that. And then I'll take over. We won't leave her alone."

Helen nodded into David's shoulder, tears pouring down her face. "We won't leave her alone."

FORTY-NINE
JUNE 2015

London, England

Quinn threw the brooch against the wall, unable to bear the pain it brought. Tears poured down her cheeks and dripped into her mouth, salty and bitter. All she wanted was to hold Alex and Emma in her arms and never let them go. The razor-sharp pain that had torn Helen's heart to shreds was her pain. How did any parent ever survive the loss of a child? How did they go on from day to day knowing they'd never see their baby again or hear its voice? How did they fill the void that had been left not only by the child, but by the feelings the child inspired in its parents?

Her heart broke for Helen, but it went out to David too. He'd loved that baby and was doing his best to cope with the terrible secret Helen had sprung on him only weeks before. Quinn admired his stoic strength and unwavering support, but although she couldn't hear his thoughts or see his actions when he wasn't with Helen, she was sure he'd suffered just as much.

Quinn angrily wiped the tears away and stood. She needed to take something for the pounding headache that was cleaving her skull in two. This case was shattering her, and her body was letting her know in no uncertain terms that it wouldn't tolerate this kind of emotional stress much longer.

She went downstairs, took some tablets, and thirstily drank two glasses of water, then leaned against the worktop, gazing out over the sundrenched garden. Once Annie was buried, she wouldn't be able to see anything more since the brooch would be buried with her. The cause of Annie's death would forever remain a mystery, since Quinn had seen no signs of foul play. Perhaps Dr. Ross had been wrong, and Annie had been born with some internal defect. Or maybe it had been a case of sudden infant death syndrome, which usually struck while the child was asleep.

Quinn considered ringing Colin to verify whether the hairline fracture in Annie's nose might have occurred during birth but stilled her hand as she reached for the mobile. What was the sense? Regardless of what Colin had said, Annie had died of natural causes, as Dr. Clegg had initially concluded. It made no difference to the story; it was tragic enough as it was, and she couldn't wait to be done with it. Annie might have died peacefully, but this was the most difficult case Quinn had ever worked on. This death wasn't a result of adultery, treachery, or even bad luck. This case was about people who were good and kind and had done nothing to deserve the tragedy that stalked them. They'd had no say in what happened to them; their story had been written the moment David had injured his arm and went to the hospital where Helen worked, or maybe even before that, when Edith Brent had met David's father during the Great War.

Helen might have believed that Annie's deformity was her fault, but she would discover in time that it was a side effect of the drug Dr. Ross had prescribed. Annie might have been one of the first cases, but she certainly hadn't been the last. Quinn hoped with all her heart that Helen had been able to forgive herself, but she wasn't so sure. Even if she had accepted Annie's disability as the result of the drug, she'd never be able to forget that David Edevane, the husband she adored, was her biological brother. How could she? That knowledge was bound to eat away at her, at both of them, until it destroyed their marriage.

Quinn took a deep breath and headed to the study. She'd given herself time off from the case while they were in Berwick, but they'd returned home last night, and it was time to wrap it up. She had one more thing left to do before she could hand this case over to Rhys. The Google search for David Edevane returned two entries in the London area, and the ages fit. The elder was ninety-eight years old, the younger fifty-nine. Quinn jotted down the information and made a call to Rhys, but he didn't pick up, so she left yet another message.

She hadn't been able to reach him in three days and was beginning to worry. It wasn't like him not to answer her calls. She hoped he was all right and considered ringing his PA but changed her mind. Rhys wasn't a child, and unless she had reason to think otherwise, she had to assume all was well. What happened before had been a one-off, a gut reaction to unbearable emotional strain. Rhys hadn't intended to take his own life; he'd only been trying to dull the pain when he chased a handful of sleeping tablets with half a bottle of Scotch. Rhys wouldn't do something so foolish again. He'd been happy the past few weeks, almost irritatingly cheerful, smiling to himself as if he had a wonderful secret. Quinn shook her head. Rhys was mercurial as ever, but she wouldn't have him any other way.

Gentle sunshine warmed the garden and enveloped her family in a golden haze. Gabe sat at the table, his laptop in front of him. Emma was curled up on the chaise, reading a story, and Alex was napping in his buggy. They looked so happy and peaceful, it brought tears to Quinn's eyes. *Dear God, please don't ever let anything happen to them. Please, keep them safe*, she prayed. Life could change so quickly, and so unexpectedly.

Gabe turned to look at her and instantly shut his computer. "Quinn? What is it?"

She shook her head. "It's nothing, really. Nothing I hadn't known was coming."

Gabe nodded in understanding. "Do you know now?" he asked, not going into detail in front of Emma.

"No, not conclusively."

"What are you talking about?" Emma asked, watching them with interest.

"Nothing, darling. How about we go out for dinner today?" Quinn suggested. She needed to get out of the house and go somewhere where she would be surrounded by people. She wanted conversation to flow over her, music to thrum in her veins, and gorgeous, pulsing life to quash all thoughts of death.

"Yes, let's," Emma immediately agreed. "I want a salad."

"What?" Quinn and Gabe asked in unison.

"I need to watch my weight," Emma announced. "Maya says it's never too early to start."

"So, no chips then?" Gabe asked, his expression all innocence.

"No."

"And no ice cream for afters?"

Poor Emma looked so conflicted, Quinn nearly laughed out loud. "Em, it's all right to eat what you like, as long as you do it in moderation. Your weight is right where it should be. You don't need to go on a diet," Quinn explained patiently.

"But Maya says—" she began.

"It doesn't matter what Maya says. You have to make your own decisions in life, and if you want a salad, then you can have one," Gabe replied, "but don't do it to please Maya."

Emma nodded thoughtfully. She seemed to be weighing both arguments. "All right, you win," she finally said.

"It's not about winning and losing, it's about what you think is the right thing for you to do."

"I want Maya to like me," Emma said, her eyes begging for understanding. "I want her to be my friend."

"Em, your friends have to like you for yourself, not for what you eat, what you wear, or what kind of house you live in. Why do you like Maya?" Gabe asked.

"I don't know," Emma whispered.

"Do you want to be her friend because she's fun to be with or because she makes you feel good about yourself?" Quinn asked.

"No."

"Then why?" Gabe persisted.

"Maya is popular. Everyone wants to be her friend."

"Is that the only reason?" Quinn asked.

Emma nodded. "I like Jenny, but she's not popular. Maya says she's dumb."

"No one is dumb," Quinn said patiently. "You need to be friends with children who make you happy, not ones who make you doubt yourself. Would you like to invite Jenny over for a play-date one day?"

"Can I?"

"Of course, you can."

"Can I ring her now?"

"You can ring her now, but she can't come over today. Tomorrow afternoon would be all right, if it's okay with her parents," Quinn replied.

Emma jumped off the chaise and ran inside to make the call.

"Did you think about dieting at five?" Gabe asked, shaking his head in dismay.

"Me? No. I wanted to dig things up," Quinn replied with a straight face.

Gabe laughed. "Me too. I kept hoping to find an ancient sword."

"Clearly, you were digging in the wrong place. Should have just cracked open the kitchen floor."

Still laughing, Gabe scooped up Alex, who'd woken up, and carried him into the house. "Come on, sweet pea. Let's get you changed, and then we'll go out for dinner, compliments of Mummy's depressing job."

"Don't remind me," Quinn moaned, but the pall of depression had lifted. Her own family was alive and well.

FIFTY

Quinn woke early on Monday morning. Everyone was still asleep, so she went downstairs and made herself a cup of tea, which she took out into the garden. Today, she would chase up the Edevanes and see if she could get any further information to pass on to Rhys. She still hadn't heard from him, which was worrying. If he didn't return her call today, she'd have to call Rhiannan and see if he'd been in touch or if he showed up for work this morning.

On a more positive note, Quinn hadn't been accosted by either Brett or Jo, which was a definite improvement on the previous week. She fervently hoped Brett had returned to the States but had no way of finding out for sure. She'd ring Seth later in the day. Maybe he'd be able to enlighten her. Knowing that Brett was no longer skulking around would certainly make her feel more at ease. And Jo? She no longer cared what Jo decided to do. Perhaps it was for the best if they didn't see each other for a time.

Quinn took a sip of tea and smiled. Jill's wedding was at the weekend, and then they'd be off to Spain. She couldn't wait. She'd bought Alex an adorable swimming costume and would get him a set of buckets and shovels for the beach once they arrived in Marbella. He'd love to play in the sand. Emma had asked for an inflatable unicorn ring that she could use in the pool. She'd found one online and showed it to Quinn, who'd had no choice but to order it for her. Emma had set aside several books she planned to bring and, to Quinn's great relief, announced that she would be leaving Emme and her extensive wardrobe behind. The doll would have needed a case of her own, Quinn mused.

She'd finish packing within the next few days and collect her and Emma's dresses from the shop on Wednesday. Jill's hen night was on Thursday. In the past, it would have been a rowdy affair, but being five months pregnant, Jill had opted for a nice dinner with her girlfriends rather than a boozy bar crawl that would end in a hangover and serious regret. Quinn was glad Jill was keeping it low-key. She had no desire to spend the night drinking and fending off come-ons from blokes who were too pissed to even see her face clearly. The only come-ons she was interested in these days were from her husband.

Having finished her tea, Quinn returned inside and glanced at the clock. It had just gone eight, so not too early to ring the care home. Someone would be at reception.

"I'm sorry, love, but Mr. Edevane passed just over a year ago. He was a nice gent. Lovely manners," the woman who answered the phone said. "I can't give you any further information, but you can look up his son. He came to visit regularly. Nice bloke. David, his name is, same as the father."

"Thank you. I will," Quinn had said and ended the call. Speaking to David the Elder had been a long shot anyway, given his advanced age. And even if he were still alive, what right did she have to come in and start asking him questions about his family, when remembering what happened that summer could only bring him pain? It'd be easier to speak to the son, if he were willing to grant her an interview.

Getting in touch with David Edevane junior proved easier than she'd expected. He owned a sporting goods outlet in Croydon and agreed to meet with her when she rang asking if she could come round. Rhys would have liked her to take Darren along, but she didn't think Mr. Edevane would appreciated their interview being filmed. If he agreed, then they'd put something on the calendar and do it in a more formal setting. Quinn found the shop without any difficulty and walked to the small office at the back.

"Mr. Edevane? I'm Dr. Allenby. We spoke on the phone."

"Oh, hello, there," David Edevane said. He looked very much like his father and had the same friendly smile. "Can I offer you some coffee? I have a new package of Jaffa cakes," he added, smiling guiltily. "They're a particular weakness of mine. I hide them from my wife. She's trying to get me to eat healthier."

"I love Jaffa cakes," Quinn confessed. "One won't hurt."

"That's what I always say," he agreed. He poured them both coffee from an old-fashioned coffeemaker and set the package of biscuits on the table between them. He tossed several sugar packets on the table and produced a bottle of milk from the tiny fridge in the corner.

"So, what's this about, then? You're from some program, you said on the phone," David said as he took a noisy sip of coffee.

"Yes, I host the program *Echoes from the Past*. Perhaps you've heard of it."

"Sorry, no. Doesn't sound like something I'd enjoy. *Top Gear* is more my thing. What's it about?"

Quinn explained the premise of the show, then carefully introduced the subject of Annie. "Mr. Edevane, Mr. and Mrs. Brock, who I believe purchased the house from your parents, discovered human remains in the garden several weeks ago."

David nodded. "That'd be Annie. My sister," he added.

"We would like to make Annie the subject of an *Echoes from the Past* episode. Do you think you might give us permission to do that?"

David looked thoughtful. "Normally, I'd say no to this kind of thing—not that people routinely ask to make a program about my family—but I think I owe it to my mother and all the other children who were born deformed because of that awful drug. My parents didn't know it at the time, of course; no one did. Annie was one of the first babies to be born with deformities, but there were many more after."

"Mr. Edevane, can you tell me Annie's story? And would you be willing to do it again on film?"

David chuckled. "Can my missus be present for the interview? Oh, she'd love that. Always wanted to be on the telly, my Shona. She'll probably buy a new hat."

"Yes, of course, your wife can be present. Also, I need you to sign a release form stating that you give us permission to tell your story." Quinn slid over the release form she'd brought and handed him a pen. "You can take some time to think about it, if you like."

David signed with a flourish. "Nothing to think about. All the people this might have hurt are long gone. I'm the last of the line."

Quinn returned the form to her bag and took out her mobile. "Do you mind if I record our interview?" she asked.

"Not at all," David Edevane replied with a careless shrug.

"Thank you. Do you remember anything about that time?" Quinn asked, knowing that David would have been five when Annie died.

"I was just a little lad when Annie was born, but I remember. What happened that summer haunted me my whole life, and my dad too, of course," David said sadly. "I'm not proud of it, but I hated her. I'd waited and waited for a friend to play with, but what I got was a sister who looked like a loaf of bread with a head."

Quinn thought that was quite a cruel description of his sister, but as David had pointed out, he'd been very young at the time. She supposed in his mind, he always thought of Annie as he had then.

"My mum, who'd been loving and kind until Annie's birth, turned into a recluse who cried whenever she thought no one was looking. It was supposed to be a happy time, but it was awful and frightening. And confusing. No one would tell me anything, and Mum pretended that everything was normal, which it obviously wasn't."

"What about your dad?"

"Dad was better at keeping his emotions in check, but he was devastated, as you might imagine. He became more withdrawn, silent. I thought it was all because of Annie, but there was a bigger story there, one I didn't fully understand until I was older."

She smiled encouragingly at him. "And what story would that be?"

"You know how they say truth is stranger than fiction? Well, that was the case with my parents. My mum, Helen, met my father at the hospital where she worked. He'd had an accident and came in to get patched up. Mum was a nurse. Their courtship was fairly routine. They took a liking to each other, stepped out a few times, and decided to get married. Well, that all sounds grand, doesn't it? Except that my dad was an orphan, left at an orphanage when he was a newborn, but registered right and proper, with his full name and date of birth. He'd never bothered to look for his birth parents. Didn't see the point, on account of not being wanted," David explained. "Well, he found them regardless."

Quinn felt a shiver of anticipation at David's words. So, he knew, and seemed to be willing to talk about it. Quinn was chuffed to be getting the story on tape; Rhys would love it.

"Seems my grandmother had been a busy lady during the Great War. Had a husband at the front and a lover at home. My dad was the product of that illicit affair, and Grandma, God rest her soul, got rid of him before her husband came home and would find out his wife had been playing away. Grass widows, they used to call them. Did you know that? Meant they didn't let the grass grow under their feet."

"Yes, I have heard that term," Quinn replied.

"Well, when Mum brought her intended home for the first time, Grandma Edith took one look at him, heard the name, saw the resemblance to his father, went upstairs, and died. Had a heart attack that very night. I guess the thought of her children getting married to each other was too much for her to bear. Can't say as I blame her," David said, reaching for his third Jaffa cake.

"But your parents married anyway?"

"They didn't know, you see. It wasn't until months later that my mum cleared out Edith's room and found my father's birth certificate and a photo of his father. Edward Edevane, his name was. Well, she was already carrying me and decided not to tell Dad, but the knowledge ate at her. She was terrified of living in sin, as she thought of it. People were a lot more afraid of divine retribution back then, weren't they?"

"Did your parents tell you all this?" Quinn asked carefully. David didn't seem at all bothered to be a child of incest.

"My dad did, after Mum passed. Do you want more coffee?"

"No, I'm all right," Quinn said, eager to hear the rest of the story. "Please, go on."

"When Annie was born, my poor mum thought it all her fault. She thought God had cursed her for not telling the truth and dissolving the incestuous marriage. Little did she know that the deformity was caused by the drug she'd been taking and that she and my father weren't brother and sister at all."

"How's that, then?" Quinn asked, her ears pricking up. This was an interesting new tidbit.

"My mum became ill after Annie died. Just couldn't cope with the guilt. She begged my father to bury Annie in the garden, didn't want her alone in the cemetery. He was against the idea, but she was so distraught, he did as she asked. As you might imagine, the neighbors grew curious when Annie just disappeared, started asking questions, so Mum refused to leave the house. Had Dad bring in whatever she needed, and she carried on as if Annie were still alive. She sat by Annie's grave every day, talked to her, sang lullabies, and read her stories. Her mind had turned. She became more and more withdrawn and erratic, stopped bathing and forgot to eat, and grew angry whenever Dad tried to talk to her or get her to leave the house.

"After several years, my father had no choice but to put her into care. He couldn't look after her himself, and he had me to think about. You can just imagine what that would do to a child, watching his mother carry on like that. Mum grew agitated when they came for her, didn't want to leave Annie. She bit the nurse and assaulted one of the doctors, so they had to sedate her to get her out of the house. It was truly awful. I cried for days after she was gone."

"I can't imagine how you must have suffered," Quinn said, overcome with pity for that little boy who'd not only lost his sister, but the mother he'd adored.

"Dad suffered too. He went to see her every week, brought her flowers and her favorite sweets. I always went with him, but after a time, I stopped going. Just couldn't bear to see what had become of her. She'd been pretty once. A real classy dame. I have some photos, if you'd like to use them in your program."

"Yes, that would be very helpful."

"Mum died when I was eleven. There was nothing physically wrong with her. She died of a broken heart, my dad said. He'd told her about the drug and what it had done, but that made her even worse. She blamed herself for not being woman enough to deal with sickness and fatigue during her pregnancy. She said if only she hadn't been so weak, Annie would have been born whole, and would probably still be alive. The knowledge really sent her over the edge. Until then, Dad hoped she might still come home."

"You said they weren't actually related," Quinn prompted.

"No. Once Dad realized she was never coming home, he sold the house. Couldn't deal with the memories of the life they'd shared before it all went wrong. He had to find the deed to the house in order to sell it, and that was when he came across Mum's birth certificate. It was inside the envelope with the deed in it. The names looked as if they'd been tampered with, and he got curious. The mother's name seemed to have been written over, and the father's name was in a slightly different shade of ink. I don't know why he did it. I suppose he needed closure, or something to occupy his mind, but he went to find the midwife who'd delivered my mother. Thankfully, she was still alive, but old and frail. Dad fixed some things for her around the house. The poor dear couldn't do it herself and didn't seem to have the money to hire someone. She was most grateful. Told him the whole story."

"Which was?"

"She'd known my grandfather's family, you see. Knew the Brents all her life. My grandfather had a younger sister, Ellen. She died of influenza in 1928. Ellen got involved with a married man when she was sixteen. He strung her along for several years and abandoned her altogether when she became pregnant with his child. Ellen left behind a two-month-old daughter when she died."

Quinn nodded, understanding dawning. "And your grandparents took in the child and altered the birth certificate to show that she was theirs."

"They did. Didn't want Mum to go through life with the stigma of having been born a bastard. And they were only too happy to take her in. Seems they weren't able to have children of their own."

"So, Helen and your father were not related by blood?"

David shook his head. "No, they weren't. Grandma Edith never became pregnant with her husband, which must have been a source of great frustration for her, since she knew she was able to have children. I reckon she'd have taken Dad back had her husband not returned from the front, but he did, so Dad remained at the orphanage while Edith raised someone else's daughter. Dad said she'd never been warm or loving to Mum, and often wondered what kind of mother she'd have been had she kept him. Seeing him that day must have been too much for her. She knew, of course, that Mum and Dad weren't related, but having the son she'd abandoned as a son-in-law was not a situation she could live with, I suppose."

"And your father? How did he fare after all this?"

"Better than Mum. He was a strong person, my dad, and kind. He was both parents to me until I was old enough to strike out on my own."

"Did he ever remarry?"

"No, but he did have a lady friend in his later years. Got tired of being alone, I suppose. I never begrudged him a little bit of happiness. He deserved it. He'd been through hell. You see, he was never really sure if Annie died of natural causes. Mum had been so distraught, so worried about what would become of her, that for a split second he thought she might have, you know..."

"He thought she killed her?"

"He thought she might have smothered her with a pillow, for her own sake. Not much of a life she would have had, our poor Annie. Some of those children with phocomelia did all right for themselves, but they had something to work with. Disabled, but still capable of looking after themselves. Annie would never have been able to fend for herself, and my mum would lay down her life taking care of her. It'd have killed her in the end, just as the guilt drove her mad. I wish my dad would have discovered the truth while there was still a chance of turning things around, but it was too late by then. Mum died believing that everything that happened had been down to her."

Quinn wiped a stray tear away. Her heart broke for Helen and her family. How cruel life could be, and how random. Had Annie been born whole, the Edevanes might have survived as a family. Helen might have eventually discovered the truth of her birth and been able to forgive herself for keeping the secret she'd thought was so explosive. She'd have had a normal life, and so would Annie.

Sighing, Quinn stopped the recording. "Thank you for sharing your family's story, Mr. Edevane. I'll be in touch regarding a formal interview."

"You just let me know when you plan to film. I'll need some new togs. Will there be a fee, do you think?"

"I'm sure something can be arranged," Quinn replied. She couldn't speak on Rhys's behalf, but she was sure David Edevane would be generously compensated for his story. After all, he was the first descendant to come on the program to tell the tale in his own words, having been there at the time the events took place.

Quinn and David shook hands, and she left him to finish the Jaffa cakes. Having heard the whole story, she wasn't sure if she felt less or more upset. She didn't believe for a moment that Helen had smothered that child, nor had she seen it in her visions. Was it possible for a person to block something out so completely that it would be erased from their memory? She didn't think so. Helen hadn't killed that child any more than David had. Annie had to have died of natural causes. Quinn breathed a sigh of relief. For some reason, knowing that made her feel a little better.

Pulling out her mobile, she rang Rhys again. The call went directly to voicemail. This time, Quinn left a snippier message. "Rhys, ring me back, or I'll send in the cavalry. I'm getting worried. And I have some very interesting news for you. Ring me," she added forcefully.

Her mobile vibrated before she reached the tube station. "I appreciate your concern, but I've never been better, and there's no need to send anyone," Rhys said. His voice sounded like warm honey, and she thought she heard the rustle of crisp sheets.

"Are you still in bed?" Quinn demanded. "It's a weekday, for God's sake."

Rhys responded with a throaty laugh. "I'm on my honeymoon."

"You're what?"

"I'm in Paris. Katya and I were married on Saturday. We'll be back in London tomorrow night."

"Eh... congratulations. Well, this is a surprise," Quinn said. She knew she sounded less than congratulatory, but it seemed Rhys had jumped into this relationship with both feet. She only hoped he wouldn't get hurt again.

"Be happy for me, Quinn," Rhys said, his voice rippling with feeling. "I've had many relationships in my life, but nothing has ever felt this right. I feel like—I don't know how to explain it—like I've finally come home, I suppose."

Quinn smiled and shook her head in wonder. "Then may it be a home filled with joy, and with the laughter of children. I'm happy for you, Rhys. Truly."

"Thank you. Now what was this news you had for me?"

"It can wait. Go spend time with your wife."

"My wonderful wife went out to buy croissants and coffee. We're having breakfast in bed."

"It's almost noon," Quinn replied with a chuckle.

"Which would explain why I'm so hungry."

"I'll talk to you when you get back, Rhys. Au revoir."

Quinn disconnected the call and descended into the tube station. She only realized she had a silly grin on her face when several people gave her amused stares. *Good for you, Rhys,* she thought. *You deserve to be happy.*

When Quinn got home, Alex and Nicola were in the garden. Alex was sitting on a blanket on the grass, and Nicola was rolling a ball to him. He rolled it back and laughed with glee.

"Hello, Mrs. Russell. How did your meeting go?"

"Very well, thank you. Where's Emma?"

"She's at her friend's house. Mr. Russell took her round."

"Did he say when he'd be back?" Quinn asked. She couldn't wait to tell Gabe about her interview with David Edevane and Rhys's happy news.

"No, he didn't. He said he had an errand to run."

"Okay. Nicola, would you mind feeding Alex and then taking him for a walk? I just need an hour or so to finish some work."

"Of course." Nicola scooped Alex up and carried him inside.

FIFTY-ONE

AUGUST 1961

London, England

The sun had come out after three days of pouring rain. Helen got up early, made a cup of tea, and sat by the window, watching a sparrow hop from branch to branch. She'd refused to bury Annie in the rain. She deserved a beautiful day filled with sunshine and the smell of roses as she was laid to rest, and today would be that day. She tried not to think of the eternal darkness or the loamy smell of the earth that would swallow her baby. Annie was no longer there. She was in a place of warmth and light, and joy.

Helen finished her tea and walked into the parlor, where David slept on the sofa. She was momentarily angry with him for falling asleep, but the grayness of his face and the harsh set of his lips, even in sleep, reminded her of his suffering. She'd maintained vigil over Annie since Sunday, agreeing to sleep for a few hours only when David took over.

Letting him sleep, Helen picked up Annie and took her into the kitchen, where she set about preparing her body for burial. She washed her thoroughly, brushed her downy hair with a baby brush, and dressed her in the pretty yellow dress she'd worn on Sunday. It was the color of sunshine, and of the primroses that would watch over her during the summer months. Once finished, she wrapped Annie in her yellow shawl and pinned the ends with her *H* brooch, to keep Annie from getting cold. Even after three days, Annie looked like she was sleeping. Her eyes were closed, her lashes fanning her pale cheeks, and wisps of hair curling over her tiny ears. The only mark of death was the pallor and the bluish tint to her lips, but Helen chose not to focus on that. She bent down and kissed Annie on the forehead, before going to wake David.

"It's time," she said simply as she touched him on the shoulder. David opened his eyes, took in her determined face, and sat up. "Would you like a cup of tea first?" Helen asked.

David seemed surprised by the question, but nodded, his eyes still clouded with sleep. He followed Helen into the kitchen. "Jesus Christ," he muttered when he saw Annie laid out on the kitchen table.

Helen didn't reply. What was there to say? She watched in silence as David drank his tea. He didn't sit at the table, but stood by the sink, his gaze firmly fixed on the tree outside the kitchen window. *He's already let her go,* Helen thought as she watched him. *He's ready to move forward.* The thought made her angry, and sad. Annie had been gone for only three days, and she wasn't ready to accept her loss. She didn't think she ever could. She turned away so David wouldn't see her tears. She'd cried enough over the past few days to know that he could no longer handle her grief. He hadn't said so out loud, but she could see in it his eyes—the acceptance, tinged with relief.

"Should I go on, then?" David asked as he put the cup in the sink.

"Yes. We'll wake Davy when we're ready."

David nodded and left the kitchen, going to fetch a shovel. Helen remained inside. She couldn't bear to watch. Twenty minutes later, she roused Davy from sleep and summoned him out to the garden. Still in his pajamas, Davy hung back, refusing to look at the hole in the ground. It was heartbreakingly small, like a grave for a beloved family pet, and about three feet deep. Helen was surprised when David brought out a length of oilcloth.

"What's that for?" she asked as she held Annie closer to her breast.

"It's to wrap her up," David explained. "To keep moisture, and eh… well, roots away from the body," he explained, looking relived to have come up with something that didn't sound as gruesome as what he had to be thinking. "Let me have her, Helen."

Helen shook her head. "No."

David didn't argue. He simply stood back, giving Helen time to say goodbye. Neither of them made speeches or read from the Bible. They simply stood, heads bowed, eyes downcast.

"Mum, I need to pee," Davy said, breaking the silence.

Helen nodded. She silently handed Annie to David, who wrapped her in the oilcloth and laid her in the makeshift grave. He looked to Helen, who gave a small nod. David filled the tiny grave and leaned on his shovel, looking to Helen for instructions.

"Go on, Davy," Helen said. "And don't forget to wash your hands and clean your teeth. I'll make you some breakfast," she added as she turned to go back inside.

"Helen," David began, but Helen held up her hand.

"Don't say it, David."

"Say what?"

"How it's for the best that she left us. I know what you're thinking. She'd have had a miserable life, deprived of all the things that make life worth living. She's better off, in your opinion."

"Well, maybe she is," David replied defensively. "Would you want to live like that, Helen? Would you want to spend your whole life watching other people doing the things you never can? Would you want to see the pity and horror in people's faces when they met you for the first time, or any time? Would you want to be so completely helpless? I know I wouldn't. I'd rather be dead, so you know what? I'm happy for her. I'm happy she doesn't have to suffer or ever know what she'd been cheated out of."

"I cheated her," Helen cried. "I sentenced her to this."

"You did not, and I won't hear you say that," David snapped. "What happened to Annie was a tragedy, but neither you nor I are responsible. I refuse to accept the blame for something I didn't choose to do. This happened to us, to her, to Davy, but we didn't cause it. We're the victims, not the perpetrators."

"Speak for yourself," Helen said, her voice low and angry. "You want to absolve yourself, go ahead, but I don't have that luxury. You never knew the truth, but I did. I made the choice to ignore it, to pretend everything was all right. This is my punishment, my cross to bear, and I will bear it for as long as I live. Please God, may it not be too long. I can't bear the thought of Annie all alone."

"Helen!" David exclaimed. "Please, don't say that. We need you, Davy and me. We will move on from this. Maybe even have another baby," he added gently, hope shining from his eyes. He made a move to touch her, but Helen drew back as if she were repulsed by him.

"There will never be another baby, David. From now on, we will live as brother and sister, not as husband and wife. I will atone for my sin."

"Helen, you're not—"

Helen held up her hand. "Don't say another word, David. I've made up my mind. You do as you must. I will understand if you wish to divorce me or if you find another woman, but I can no longer be a wife to you."

Helen turned and walked into the kitchen. She'd thought her heart would break once she told David of her decision, but all she felt was numbness. Some door had closed in her soul the moment Annie passed, leaving her unable to walk out of her prison. All she could do was serve her time, atone for her sin, and pray that her baby didn't spend an eternity in purgatory.

* * *

Quinn tossed the brooch down on the coffee table and buried her face in her hands. The desolation that swept over her felt like a huge black wave on a dark, stormy sea. She couldn't remain standing in the face of its power, its deadly force. Quinn lay down on the sofa and curled into a ball, silent tears falling for Annie, Helen, David and their son.

FIFTY-TWO

JUNE 2015

London, England

The photo had popped up just as Gabe was getting ready to walk Emma to Jenny's house for her playdate. This time, it had come from Jo's own number, and the picture wasn't as tame as the first one. She was still sitting on the bed, her hands in her hair, her face slightly turned away from the camera, but this time, she'd sent him a frontal shot. Her full breasts, tipped with rosy nipples, were center stage, and her legs were parted just enough to give a glimpse of what was on offer. Gabe stared at the image, unable to tear his gaze away. Jo was beautiful, no doubt about that, but she was also feral, and hungry. The look on her face said it all: *Come and get it.*

"Daddy, what are you staring at?" Emma demanded. "Let's go." She slung her pink backpack over one shoulder and walked purposefully toward the door.

"Coming, darling," Gabe replied, shoving the phone into his pocket. He said goodbye to Alex and Nicola and headed out the door, his mind still on Jo.

He listened to Emma prattle on endlessly as they walked but could barely focus on what she was saying. The image of Jo's naked body was still in his mind, refusing to go away no matter how hard he tried. She was brazen, he'd give her that, and persistent. He hadn't responded to the last photo, and Gabe was sure she knew that he'd blocked the number it'd come from, but there was no stopping her. She was all in, so he had no choice but to react.

Gabe left Emma at Jenny's house with the promise to collect her in three hours, then headed for the tube station. If Jo wanted to play, he'd play, he decided, but he'd make the rules.

Gabe quickened his step as Jo's building loomed ahead. Now that he was here, he was eager to get down to business. If she was all in, so was he. He was done with playing dumb. That strategy clearly hadn't worked, and if anything, his refusal to acknowledge her advances only served to spur Jo on. He rang the bell and waited for her to answer.

"Come up," Jo purred into the speaker.

Gabe took the steps two at a time, his heart pounding with anticipation. His breath caught in his throat when Jo answered the door. She was completely naked, her dark hair cascading over her shoulders in shiny waves. She smiled seductively and stepped aside to let him in.

"What took you so long?" she asked.

"I had an errand to run," Gabe replied huskily. He approached her slowly and looked down into her upturned face. The look in her eyes nearly undid him, but he meant to take his time and prolong the pleasure. He encircled her waist and pulled her closer. "Tell me what you want, Jo," he said as he looked deep into her eyes.

"Have I not made it clear?"

"You have, but I need to hear it. Say it. Tell me what you want me to do to you."

"Ah, so you're a talker," she replied, her voice silky and seductive. "Okay, I will tell you exactly what I want you to do. How graphic would you like me to get?"

Gabe pulled her against his overheated body. "I want you to get really dirty," he growled. "I know you're not shy."

"Why don't I demonstrate as I talk?" she offered and led him into the bedroom, where she lay on the bed and spread her legs.

"Can I record it?" he asked.

"Only if you promise to whack off to it later," Jo replied.

"Oh, I promise," he drawled, training his mobile on her. "Go on," he invited.

Jo didn't disappoint. She had none of Quinn's shyness. She told him exactly what she wanted and used her fingers to illustrate. Gabe could smell her arousal and feel her desperate need for him. He wanted to stop, but he kept filming, wanting to get as much as he could.

"Say my name," he ordered her.

"Gabe," she purred. "Put down that phone and fuck me, Gabe. Better yet, set it over there, so you can have the entire Jo Turing show for your viewing pleasure. Come, I bet it'll turn you on to watch it later."

"You've no idea how much," Gabe replied.

Jo withdrew her hand from between her legs and licked her finger for the camera. She was so ready.

FIFTY-THREE

Quinn hauled herself off the sofa and trudged to the study. She had to type up her notes from the David Edevane interview, and then she would be nearly finished with the case. Once Darren recorded the formal interview, she'd step away until it was time to film the episode, which wouldn't be for a few months. She'd have time to put some distance between herself and Helen's unbearable pain.

Quinn opened a new document and began to type, describing David in the introduction. He seemed well adjusted and pleased with his accomplishments, but Quinn couldn't help wondering what his life might have been like after Annie's death. He'd been too young to understand his mother's feelings, but old enough to remember what she had been like before. Had Helen still devoted herself to him after Annie's death, or had she been so lost in her grief that Davy became just another reminder of the child she'd lost and the sin she believed she'd committed? Quinn hoped Davy had still felt her love, even if she wasn't always fully emotionally present.

The text alert on her mobile buzzed, and Quinn reached for the phone, glad of the interruption. The text was from Gabe:

Quinn, I'm so sorry, but I had no choice.

Quinn clicked on the attached video file, and Jo's sultry voice filled the study, demanding, pleading, seducing, betraying, and cruelly destroying Quinn's love and trust. As frame after frame flashed before Quinn's eyes, she no longer heard the words, or even saw the images. She was trembling, her extremities suddenly ice-cold. Black spots danced before her eyes as her stomach turned itself inside out, giving her just enough time to grab for the rubbish bin beneath the desk before she was violently sick.

Quinn continued to heave long after she finished vomiting, her body still reacting to the shock of what she'd seen. She finally set down the bin and rested her forehead against the cool wood of the desk. Mercifully, the video file had come to an end, and she no longer heard her sister begging Gabe to fuck her. It was the right word, Quinn thought queasily. She didn't want his love, or even his affection. She wanted him to be unyielding, rough, sadistic even. She wanted him to hurt her, to use her, to exploit her, but all the while, she'd be exploiting him. Jo had a void in her soul that no man could fill. She needed anger, aggression, and pain to make her feel alive, to help her get off.

Bitter tears of heartbreak slid down Quinn's cheeks. She'd begun to suspect that Jo wasn't what she'd originally shown herself to be, but this... this was the cruelest, most heartless thing she could have done. To go after Gabe, to try to destroy Quinn's marriage and family was vicious.

Taking a steadying breath, Quinn forced herself to stand up and left the room, pounding down the stairs in her haste. She needed a breath of air, a whole gale of it. She felt like she couldn't breathe. As the full implications of what she'd seen hit her, her heart hammered against her ribs and she was panting. She thought she might faint. She stumbled toward the door and yanked it open, nearly falling into Brett's arms.

"Quinn, are you all right? What's wrong?" Brett exclaimed as Quinn leaned against the wall for support. Brett took her by the shoulders and forced her to look at him. "Are you going to pass out? Should I call an ambulance? What's the number?" He looked panicked and Quinn nearly laughed at the helpless look on his face. Of course, he wouldn't know the number for the emergency services in the U.K.

"I'll be fine," she said and sat down on the step, her head in her hands. "You know, I thought my brother leaving me for dead was the worst thing a sibling could do, but once again, life has proven that I know nothing of human nature. I'm not fit to be a mother, naïve as I am."

"What are you talking about? Who did what?" Brett asked, sitting down next to her.

"You'd like to know, wouldn't you?" Quinn asked, pinning him with her gaze. "Here. Have a gander."

She clicked on the video file and shoved the phone in Brett's hand. She had no idea why she'd done that, or why she wanted to subject herself to hearing Jo's filthy words again, but at the moment, she felt completely unhinged. Maybe she wanted to humiliate Jo, or maybe she wanted Brett to tell Seth, because she certainly wouldn't confide in him herself.

"Jesus fucking Christ!" Brett exclaimed as Jo's seduction took a more physical turn. "Oh my God, Quinn. Now I can never unsee this," he cried, shutting off the phone and setting it between them on the step.

"Neither can I," Quinn replied with a maniacal giggle. "Are we irreparably damaged?" she demanded. "All three of us?"

"No," Brett said, shaking his head vehemently. "You're the best of us, Quinn, and I will do everything I can to make this okay for you. I will spend the rest of my life making up for what I did. I swear. I will never let you down again."

"Nothing can make this okay, Brett. Jo has willfully tried to destroy my marriage, my family, my trust in Gabe. And do you know what the funniest part is? She probably doesn't think she did anything wrong. She simply went after something she wanted; the feelings of others be damned. She must have figured that if Gabe went for it, then it wasn't her fault if it was the end of us. It was on him."

"Quinn, she will regret what she's done. I know she will."

"And how do you know?" Quinn exclaimed. Her pain had turned to white-hot fury. Had Jo walked in right now, Quinn would probably have caused her grievous bodily harm.

"I just know."

"Please, go now. I can't do this with you. Look, if my forgiveness is so important to you, consider yourself forgiven, but please, don't come here again. Go home, Brett. Your parents love you, and you have your whole life ahead of you. Don't ruin it."

"Thank you, Quinn. That means everything to me, even if you probably have no idea what you're saying right now."

Brett leaned forward and kissed Quinn on the cheek, then he was gone. Quinn barely registered his absence. Her heart rate had slowed, and she was breathing more evenly now, but there was a hollow in her heart where her sister used to be. She would never see Jo again. She would never speak to her, or even follow her online. Jo was dead to her.

Quinn looked up blearily when Gabe walked up the path. He crouched next to her and cupped her face in his hands. "Quinn," he whispered. "I'm sorry. I couldn't think of any other way."

Quinn leaned a little closer, not to kiss him, but to reassure herself he didn't smell of another woman. She needed proof, for her own sanity. Jo was too clever for her, too ruthless, and too willing to cross boundaries, and steadfast as Gabe was, he was a man with a healthy sexual appetite. Few men would be able to resist what Jo had offered so graphically, especially if they thought they could get away with it. Quinn refused to fall into Jo's trap and start doubting Gabe, but for just a moment, when she'd heard her say his name and invite him to fuck her as if it were a regular occurrence, she'd doubted, and that made her even angrier because that was exactly what Jo wanted. She wanted to drive a wedge between them, to sow seeds of mistrust.

Quinn couldn't even begin to imagine what Jo had stooped to

over the past few weeks to drive Gabe to such a place of desperation. He'd been willing to compromise himself to show Quinn what Jo was up to and shown no small amount of self-restraint. Any hotblooded male would have tossed aside the phone and fucked her into oblivion, and Quinn would have been none the wiser, unless Jo had sent her the video herself, using indisputable evidence of infidelity to torpedo her marriage.

Now she understood why Phoebe had told her to be careful. Gabe must have confided in her and asked for advice. He must have felt cornered, possibly even tormented with guilt at having to come between the sisters. Never in all her days had Quinn hated anyone the way she hated Jo at that moment. She wished she could turn back the clock to the day before she'd learned she had a twin sister. She would have been better off, safer. Her family would have been secure. They were still secure, but somehow less so today than yesterday.

Gabe reached for her and held her close, and Quinn's eyes filled with tears of relief as she inhaled his familiar scent. He didn't reek of Jo, nor did he smell as if he'd just showered. He hadn't touched Jo. He hadn't betrayed Quinn. He'd proved to her yet again that he was hers alone. Gabe had never needed armor and a sword to be her knight. He was Gabriel de Rosel, and he had those all-important traits modern men no longer thought necessary. He had honor, and loyalty, and faith. He wasn't a man who was easily broken.

"Quinn, I love you," Gabe said, lifting her head so she had no choice but to face him. "I have always loved you, and I always will. I wouldn't betray you with Jo, or any other woman. Ever. Our family is the heart of me, and if I were to lose you and the children, I'd have no reason for being. I know you're hurting right now, but this was the only way I could put an end to it, to show you what she was up to and to humiliate her brutally enough to make sure she got the point."

"Has she?"

"Oh, I think so. She won't be bothering me again."

Quinn nodded as tears slid down her cheeks. She wasn't upset or angry anymore. What she felt was blessed. "I love you, Gabe," she whispered. "Now and forever. And I will never let you go. I would have fought for you, and I would have won, because what I feel for you is so much more than lust."

"You'll never have to fight for me," Gabe said as he pulled her to her feet and led her into the house. He kicked the door shut and captured her mouth with his, his fingers unzipping her jeans and pushing them down over her hips.

Quinn yanked at his belt. Her hands were shaking, and it took several attempts to unbuckle it, but she finally got it open and slid her hand into Gabe's trousers. He was rock-solid, his skin hot beneath her fingers. Gabe pulled off her jeans and knickers and lifted her up, his hands cupping her bare buttocks. Quinn wrapped her legs around his waist and grabbed a fistful of hair as Gabe rammed his way inside, sending a bolt of desire shooting through her. Their joining was hot and fast, their bodies colliding like two celestial objects and erupting in a ball of fire that was raging desire. It was all the validation Quinn needed that Gabe was hers and hers alone, and their commitment was mutual.

They were still trying to catch their breath when they heard Nicola's voice just outside the door, talking to Alex. Quinn quickly pulled on her jeans while Gabe disappeared into the bathroom to tidy himself up.

"How was your walk?" Quinn asked, reaching for Alex, who wrapped his arms around her neck as if he hadn't seen her in days.

"Lovely. Sorry it took longer than an hour, but I couldn't get him off the swings. He cried every time I tried. He's ready for his lunch now."

"Thank you, Nicola," Quinn said. "I'll see you on Saturday?"

"Absolutely."

After Nicola left, Quinn took Alex into the kitchen, washed his hands, and settled him in his high chair. She was already feeding him by the time Gabe joined them in the kitchen. He took a bottle of water out of the fridge and drank it in one go before taking a seat next to Quinn.

"Promise me you won't confront Jo," Gabe said, giving her an anxious look. Now that the anger and passion had been spent, he was obviously afraid Quinn's thoughts would turn toward finding a resolution.

"I have no intention of confronting her. I don't need to."

"No, you don't."

"You win some, you lose some," Quinn said under her breath.

"Is that another one of Seth's wisdoms?" Gabe asked as reached out to take Alex's hand.

"It's another one of life's wisdoms. Are you hungry?"

"Starving," Gabe replied with a smile. She wasn't sure if he meant for food, but she took it that way.

"I'll make lunch. Can you finish feeding Alex?"

Gabe took over and Quinn walked over to the drawer where she kept the menus. "I thought you were making lunch," Gabe remarked.

"I changed my mind. I want pizza, and by the time it gets here, Emma will be home. I can collect her from Jenny's."

"I'll do it. You look like you need a few moments to yourself," Gabe said, smiling at Quinn's disheveled appearance.

Quinn nodded her thanks. She did need a few minutes.

After Gabe left, she deposited Alex in his playpen, turned on the baby monitor, and made for the bathroom. She needed a quick shower, and a change of clothes wouldn't hurt. As the hot spray hit her, it occurred to her that she felt free and light. Life was about expectations, and she no longer expected anything from Jo. Come to think of it, she no longer expected anything at all from her birth family. She'd take what they were willing to give her and give what she felt was appropriate in return. It would be a win-win for everyone. Quinn stood under the water for a few minutes, allowing it to wash away her fears, doubts, and unrealized dreams. It was liberating as hell.

FIFTY-FOUR

Shards of broken glass littered the hardwood floor, the mirrored pieces a mosaic of color. The gilded frame still held on to several jagged pieces, like broken teeth that reflected the sobbing woman on the bed. Jo was still naked, but the siren of an hour ago was now the slave: exposed, vulnerable, and humiliated. Her skin was cold, the tang of her unsatisfied desire nauseating and shameful. The crystal heart from the nightstand, where she kept certain pieces of jewelry and occasional stashes of cocaine, lay unbroken amid the wreckage of the mirror. She'd thrown it at Gabe's head but missed, striking the mirror that mercilessly exhibited her bitter humiliation.

She'd really thought she had him, but she'd underestimated his love for her sister, and for his children, who would be collateral damage if Jo got her way and bound him to her in the only way she knew how. Oh, he'd wanted her, she'd seen it in his eyes, and in the massive erection that had strained against the fabric of his trousers, threatening to break free. He'd used every ounce of self-restraint he could muster, taking his time, giving her enough rope to hang herself with. He'd been vicious and cruel, and so much more desirable for it. He wasn't a weak, gullible man, his will undone by the sight of her slick, throbbing desire. He was strong and determined, and vengeful. He'd sent that video file to Quinn in front of Jo, his gaze spearing her with its intensity as he told her exactly what he was doing and why.

"Is she really that great of a lay?" Jo had hissed, angry beyond words.

Gabe had shaken his head, looking at her with something akin to pity. "You really don't get it, do you? I don't suppose you ever will. You have a chip missing, Jo, the one that's programmed with real human emotion. My love for Quinn is not just about sex. I love her kindness, compassion, intelligence, sense of humor, and even her empathy, something you clearly know nothing about. You're a selfish, bitchy, bitter woman who's so self-absorbed, she doesn't realize life is passing her by. Enjoy your conquests, Jo, and your awards. I hope the memory of your past glories will keep you company when you're old and alone, spurned by anyone who ever cared for you. You've lost a true friend in Quinn, someone who'd have had your back no matter what. She'll never forgive you for this, and neither will I. Don't ever contact us again."

Gabe had walked out without a backward glance, leaving her shaking with helpless fury and frustrated desire, but her rage had quickly turned to despair, and her burning passion for him into a pile of cold, acrid ashes. Never had a man rejected her so completely, and never had she loved the man in question the way she loved Gabe. She didn't think she would ever recover from the blow he'd dealt her, but life went on; it always did. She'd learned that early on.

At long last, Jo got off the bed, walked into the bathroom and turned on the taps. She was already thinking how to spin this, should Seth, Sylvia, or Logan ask what had happened to cause a rift between her and Quinn. She certainly wouldn't tell them the truth, and she doubted Quinn would either. St. Quinn would be discreet, choosing icy self-righteousness over a volcanic eruption of anger. She wouldn't confront Jo, probably would never even acknowledge what had taken place. Quinn would simply erase her from her life, as if she'd never existed, choosing to believe her husband over anything Jo said.

Jo leaned against the slick tiles as hot water cascaded over her shoulders. She could still come back from this, she mused, turning her face up to the spray. She could tell Quinn that Gabe had preempted her finding out about their affair by sending the video and carrying on as if nothing had ever happened between him and Jo. The file didn't conclusively prove that he hadn't slept with her before the footage was filmed. He'd simply been covering his tracks, going on the offensive to disguise his guilt.

Yes, that just might work, Jo thought as she allowed herself a small smile. Gabe would never give her what she wanted, but she could still take him down, destroy his credibility with Quinn, retain a tentative link with her sister, and make him squirm. Quinn might not believe her, but anyone with even an ounce of common sense would question Gabe's story and his motives for sending that file. Jo wouldn't take his rejection lying down. She would humiliate him at every turn, undermine his precious marriage, and wipe that smug smile off her sister's face. *What happened this afternoon was merely Act II. Act III is yet to come, and it will be explosive,* Jo thought, her eyes narrowing with malice. No man made a fool of her and lived to tell the tale.

She turned off the water, dried herself off, and walked into the kitchen, where she reached for the broom. The first thing she would do was put her bedroom back to rights, and the second, plan how to approach Quinn. She wouldn't seek her out today or tomorrow, or even next week. She'd let her stew for a few weeks. By the time she returned from Marbella, she'd be ripe for the picking, the pain of Jo's betrayal dulled by several weeks of sand and sun. And then, when Gabe thought he'd got away with it and exiled her from their lives, she'd reappear, tearful and remorseful, ready to beg Quinn's forgiveness and confess all.

The shards of glass made a clinking noise as Jo swept them up and tossed them in the bin. She picked up the crystal heart and opened the lid, taking out a small bag of cocaine. She'd been keeping it for a special occasion. She'd thought she might even offer to share it with Gabe, but she had need of it now, and she'd do anything it took to restore her equilibrium. She weighed the pouch in her hand, then reached for her mobile. It was no fun getting wasted alone. She'd call Tim, and if he wasn't available, she'd ring Callum. He was due back in London. Maybe he'd already arrived. It really didn't matter who came round, as long as he had a big cock and a small brain. She was done with cerebral men; they were too dangerous.

Surrey, England

Quinn held open the door as Gabe carried Emma into the guest house. Her head was against his chest, and her mouth stretched into a beatific smile. She'd danced for hours and had finally fallen asleep in the car on the way back, unable to keep her eyes open any longer.

Quinn got the key from the sleepy clerk at the desk and followed Gabe upstairs. She knocked on the door and Nicola let them in. She was wearing a silky dressing gown and her hair was held back with a headband. Alex was asleep in his portable cot, and Emma's pajamas were all ready for her on her bed. Gabe laid her down and removed her shoes.

"Should we just let her sleep?" he asked.

"Not in that dress," Quinn replied. "The lace might chafe her skin." She carefully unzipped Emma's frock and pulled it off, leaving her in her undergarments. "There, she'll be much more comfortable now." Quinn covered Emma with a blanket and planted a kiss on her forehead. "Good night, sleepyhead."

"We're just next door if you need anything," Quinn told Nicola.

"We'll be just fine. If the children wake early, I'll take them downstairs for breakfast. You deserve a night off," Nicola said with a smile. "How was the wedding?"

"Beautiful," Quinn replied, smiling at the memory. "I can't remember the last time we danced so much. And Jill and Brian made a lovely couple. They are so happy."

"Where are they off to on their wedding trip?" Nicola asked.

"The Maldives. Jill's always wanted to go. She is calling it their babymoon," Quinn said dreamily. "I like that idea, taking a holiday before a baby."

"What are they having?"

"A girl," Quinn replied.

"Have they settled on a name yet?" Nicola asked, clearly eager to chat for a while. She must have been bored, spending the entire day alone with Alex.

"Jill likes Zoe, but Brian prefers Hannah. They will decide once the baby is born. Jill says she needs to meet her daughter to know which name fits best."

"Is it possible to know that early?"

"Yes, I think it is. Sometimes the name just feels right."

"Come," Gabe said, holding out a hand to her in his impatience. "I'm tired."

By *tired*, he meant he wanted to go to bed, but not necessarily to sleep. Quinn followed him to their room and kicked off her shoes, sighing with relief. "That's the last time I wear four-inch heels," she said with feeling. "Unzip me, please." She turned her back to Gabe and waited, but he didn't help her. "Gabe?"

Turning back, Quinn was surprised to see Gabe sitting on the bed, his mobile in his hand. His gaze was fixed on the text he'd just opened.

"What is it? What happened?" Quinn asked.

Gabe looked up, his eyes full of shock. "It's from Logan. There's been an accident."

"Who was hurt, and how badly?" Quinn demanded, sitting down next to Gabe. She had that sick feeling one got just before being confronted with bad news, fearing life was about to be forever altered. "Is it Jude?" she cried, when Gabe didn't answer immediately.

Gabe shook his head. "It's Jo. She was hit by a car."

"Is she badly hurt? Was she taken to a hospital?"

"She'd dead," Gabe replied. His voice was strangely flat, devoid of all emotion.

Quinn's hand flew to her mouth as Gabe's words penetrated her brain. Dead. Jo was dead. For one brief moment, she felt confused, but then the grief came, and Quinn buried her face in Gabe's shoulder as he held her close. She didn't grieve for a sister who'd betrayed her; she grieved for a young woman whose life had been cut short. She'd no longer expected to have a relationship with Jo, even a casual one, but the finality of death was always brutal and shocking. Jo had been selfish and cruel, but she didn't deserve to die, not like that, alone, in the middle of the street, beneath someone's tires.

"Have they arrested the driver?" Quinn asked.

"Hit and run," Gabe replied. "Didn't even stop, apparently. She lay there in the street for some time before someone called emergency services."

Quinn nodded, unable to comprehend how someone could be so heartless. To hit a woman and drive away, as if nothing had happened, probably too concerned with their insurance premiums to risk involving the police. They hadn't even called an ambulance or bothered to check if their victim was still alive.

Gabe unzipped Quinn's dress and she slid it off, changing into a soft cotton T-shirt. She climbed into bed and curled into a ball, relaxing slightly only when Gabe came to bed and pulled her into his arms. They lay like that for a long while, not speaking, not doing anything but breathing and coming to terms with this new reality. Tomorrow was a new day, in which Quinn would no longer have a sister, and Seth and Sylvia would no longer have a daughter. How unpredictable life was, how random. You had to live now, today, every moment, making your own happiness and forging your own path. She'd questioned Rhys's rush to the altar, but what was there to wait for? Tomorrow wasn't guaranteed. Nothing was.

Quinn lifted her face to Gabe, and he captured her mouth with his, his hand sliding under her T-shirt. Their coupling was urgent and rough, but precisely what Quinn needed at that moment.

After, Gabe stroked her back gently. "Go to sleep, love," he whispered. "Go to sleep."

And she did. That night she dreamed of Jo, not as she had known her in the last few weeks, but as she had been when they'd first met: vulnerable, frightened, and so receptive. In her dream, they were hugging and crying, talking over each other as their emotions swept away all the barriers, and they basked in the joy of finding each other and the wonder of knowing that they had the rest of their lives to nurture their relationship. It had been a beautiful beginning, full of promise and brimming with love.

When Quinn woke, gentle beams of sunlight warmed her face. Gabe was awake, watching her, his eyes full of concern.

"All right?" he asked as he reached for her hand.

"I will be."

"Yes, you will," Gabe replied, giving her hand a sympathetic squeeze. "The children are awake. I heard them go downstairs."

"Then let's join them," Quinn said, and got out of bed.

"Yes, let's," Gabe said. "Shall we tell Emma about Jo?"

"No," Quinn said. "Not yet. She was so happy yesterday. Let's not ruin this moment, or our holiday. We'll tell her after we return from Marbella. It's not as if she was used to seeing Jo often. She'd only met her a handful of times."

"So, we're we still going to Spain?" Gabe asked carefully.

"Absolutely," Quinn replied. She would never take another day for granted, not now, not ever.

FIFTY-SIX

Brett picked up his carry-on and headed for the gate, glad his flight was finally boarding. He'd done what he came to do; it was time to go home. Now that he'd made amends to Quinn, he was full of plans and brimming with hope for the future. It was too late to apply anywhere for the fall semester, but he could take a few classes at the community college in the meantime; they had a more flexible admissions schedule. He'd also work with his father over the summer to repay Seth for his efforts in getting him released from jail. He would never take anything for granted again, not even something as simple as buying a cup of coffee or having a shower in private.

Having shown his ticket, Brett boarded the plane and took his seat. A woman with a baby sat down next to him, and he smiled at the chubby infant, making a silly face at him. The baby laughed, and the woman smiled at him, probably glad that he wasn't the type of person to complain about sitting next to a baby on a transatlantic flight. Brett leaned back in his seat and looked out the window as the plane taxied toward the runway in preparation for takeoff. He'd thought he'd feel guiltier but surprisingly experienced no remorse. He'd read about Jo's death while waiting for his flight to be called. "Award-winning photojournalist killed in a motor accident," the headline had read. It hadn't been an accident, but Brett was the only person in the world who knew that. He'd planned it carefully, making sure he didn't get caught this time.

His roommate at the hostel, Swen, had rented a car for the duration of his stay. He'd intended to drive down to Cornwall, then swing around and head north, toward Scotland, where he was meeting up with some friends. Swen went out at the crack of dawn every morning and spent the whole day sightseeing, hitting every museum, gallery, memorial, and bar along the way. He was dead to the world by nine, and he left his car keys in plain view. Last night, Brett had borrowed the keys, and the car. He'd smeared dirt on the license plate, making it nearly impossible to read, then called Jo and asked if he might come by to say goodbye. Jo had agreed.

"Do me a favor. Can you wait for me outside? I have a hard time making out the house numbers in the dark, but I'll see you standing there."

"You're a total weirdo, you know that?" Jo had said but agreed to come out. She'd sounded weird, almost as if she expected him to say something more.

Yeah, I know what you tried to do to Quinn, you filthy whore, Brett had thought, but hadn't said anything out loud. He had no way of knowing if Gabe was guilty of anything, but he didn't think so. He wouldn't have sent that video if he was.

He'd never met Gabe, but he'd spent time with Jo, and it didn't take a doctorate in psychology to see that she was royally fucked-up. His dad liked her, loved her even, but he hadn't seen the side of Jo she'd shown to Brett, nor had he seen that video. Brett grew hard just thinking about it. His dear sister certainly knew how to play her instrument. Had some woman done that for his benefit, he wouldn't have been able to resist. He probably wouldn't have lasted very long either. God, she was hot. He wasn't ashamed to admit that. It wasn't as if he'd grown up with her. She was a stranger to him, a beautiful woman who clearly had no inhibitions.

Maybe now that he was free, he could find himself a girlfriend, an older divorcee perhaps. Cougars were always horny, desperate to be satisfied by guys who lasted longer in the sack than their middle-aged husbands. And they were more open, eager to try things they hadn't done in their youth. Or maybe they had and wanted to relive the fond memories. He didn't care. He just wanted a woman who'd put on a show for him like Jo had for Gabe. He'd watched a little porn when he'd returned to the hostel. He'd needed to get his rocks off.

The engines roared, and the plane hurtled down the runway, the wheels finally leaving the tarmac and bearing Brett toward the safety of home. But as the aircraft tilted to the side as it changed course, offering Brett one last glimpse of London spread out in the distance like the glittering city of Oz, he couldn't help reliving the crime in his mind, going over the details of last night.

Jo had been standing by the curb when he arrived, her hair pulled back in a ponytail, her hands in the pockets of a denim jacket. She was alone, and the street was deserted. Brett had experienced a moment of hesitation but recalled Quinn's heartbreak, and it spurred him on. Jo was evil. She had beauty, brains, and talent, but she'd chosen to use her gifts to destroy the life of the one person who seemed to really care for her. She had no compassion for anyone, least of all Quinn's children, whose family might have been destroyed thanks to her. Jo didn't care about anyone but herself, and her death wouldn't be much of a loss to anyone, not even to his father, who had yet to learn what a bitch he'd brought into the world.

Brett had gunned the engine and plowed onto the sidewalk, hitting Jo head-on. He heard her scream, saw her body fly into the air as if she weighed no more than a child, then land with a satis-fying *thunk*. After that, all was silent, and he drove away, not both-ering to look back. Even if she wasn't dead, she'd be too mangled to think about seducing any man for months to come, maybe even years.

The rest had been easy. He'd performed several evasive

maneuvers before finding an open carwash, where the unsuspecting employees had washed all traces of Jo away, leaving the car looking shiny and new. He'd returned to the hostel, dropped the keys on the table, and gone to bed, his conscience untroubled by what he'd done. This time, he'd got the right sister.

FIFTY-SEVEN

Jo never saw it coming. The blow was so forceful, it lifted her up and for a few terrifying moments she was airborne, hurtling through the dark night on wings of excruciating pain. And then she landed on the ground with a sickening thud, her limbs splaying at odd angles, as if she were a broken doll. Her head rolled to the side, and a trickle of blood ran down her chin and onto her shoulder. The pain was so visceral, she thought her heart would stop from sheer shock, but then all sensation began to recede, replaced by a creeping chill that spread from the tips of her fingers and toes inward, toward her major organs. Unable to move, she stared up at the star-strewn sky, its distant vastness making her feel tiny and inconsequential.

Jo tried to turn her head, to call for help, but when she finally managed to cry out, her voice was no louder than a whisper on the wind, a desperate plea no one would ever hear. The street was deserted, the night pressing down on her like a soft blanket that was about to smother her. Jo began to tremble as tears of white-hot terror slid down her cheeks, the realization that this time, there'd be no dramatic rescue, no second chance. This was it. Her life was at an end, and what a legacy she was leaving behind. A trail of tears. She'd cut a swath through life with her angry sword, had taken what she wanted, leaving nothing but carnage in her wake. Well, now she was the carrion, left mangled and defenseless to be picked over by the crows that wore the disguise of family. Perhaps she deserved it, she thought, confronting the truth head-on for the first time in her life, for what she'd done couldn't be forgiven, or forgotten by those she'd hurt. She'd tried to destroy something precious and sacred, and this was her punishment, her just reward for her vanity and indifference.

"Why did you do it, Brett?" she whispered hoarsely, her clouded gaze no longer seeing the sky or the stars, only the murky shadow of death hovering above her. There was no time to ponder Brett's motives or hope for retribution. As death cradled Jo's head in its gentle hands, her final thought was of Daisy, her daughter's beautiful face swimming before her closed eyelids. Never having known Daisy was her only real regret, but for just a moment, Jo imagined she heard Daisy's voice, telling her to be brave and to let go. And she did, leaning into death's comforting embrace and leaving behind a woman who'd been irreparably broken long before this night.

FIFTY-EIGHT

SEPTEMBER 2015

London, England

Quinn got off the lift and walked toward Rhys's office. She nodded to Rhiannan, who was typing furiously, and went right in. Rhys was expecting her. He sat behind his ultra-modern desk, his lean cheeks glowing with a golden tan and his auburn hair streaked with coppery highlights.

"Welcome back," he said, smiling hugely. "How was Marbella? I didn't realize you'd be away for a full month."

"It was so amazing, we decided to extend our holiday," Quinn replied. "The kids loved it. Emma learned to swim, and Alex started walking," she added, smiling wistfully. Her baby was growing up. He was still unsteady of his feet and preferred to hold on to furniture as he made his way across the room, but he was definitely on his way.

Rhys smiled. "It was a well-deserved break. And how are you, otherwise?" he asked carefully.

"I'm all right. Really."

Rhys nodded. He'd come to Jo's funeral and stood beside Quinn, as she and Gabe took their place beside the open grave. A surprising number of people had turned up, mostly because Jo was well known in certain circles, but no one had seemed particularly overcome with grief. It wasn't until Gabe pointed it out that Quinn had noticed that other than herself, Sylvia, Karen Crawford, and Michael Crawford's wife and daughters, who'd never even met Jo, there were no other women present. Jo didn't seem to have or need female friends, and she clearly didn't get on with her colleagues either.

Logan had stood next to Sylvia, his eyes downcast as he listened to the words of the minister. He'd looked almost unrecognizable in a dark suit and somber tie. Quinn had been pleased to see Colin next to him. At one point during the service, Logan had reached for his hand, and Colin had taken it and held it until the casket was lowered into the ground.

Seth and Sylvia had stood apart, united in their grief. They didn't really know or like each other, but for better or worse, they were Jo's parents, and the pain of losing her had been evident in their faces. Kathy had stood off to the side, there for Seth, but not truly a part of his loss. Quinn hadn't been overly surprised that Brett had chosen not to accompany them. He must have heard the news as soon as he landed in the States and hadn't been ready to return so soon. He hadn't really known Jo, so it was understandable that he'd felt no desire to attend her funeral.

"Do you believe in fate?" Rhys suddenly asked.

"I don't know. Why do you ask?"

"Perhaps it was Jo's time. She was meant to die in Afghanistan but was saved by passing American troops. Maybe her death was the universe autocorrecting itself," he mused.

"Do you really think so?" Quinn asked, surprised that Rhys would take such an unorthodox view.

He shrugged. "I have no idea. Just theorizing. I hate to think that life is so random. I suppose believing that there's some sort of pattern makes it easier to accept a senseless death."

"I honestly don't know, Rhys. Having seen what I've seen, I tend to think a person's life is a series of choices made in response to certain situations. Death and tragedy are unavoidable, but some people tend to court disaster, while others do everything in their power to stay the course."

"Do you think Jo was the former?"

"I do think Jo liked to stir things up, rattle people's cages."

"But her death was an accident," Rhys pointed out.

"Yes," Quinn replied. "It was."

"Did they ever find the person responsible?"

"No. They were able to determine the make and model of the car from CCTV footage, but the license plates were covered in grime, and the driver's face was obscured by a baseball cap. The police had nothing to go on."

"Shame, that."

Quinn nodded. "Look, Rhys, there's something I need to tell you, and I hope you'll understand. I won't be doing another season of *Echoes*. In fact, I don't want to use my gift ever again. I'm done with wading through other people's misery. It's having too much of an impact on my life and my family."

"You're under contract for one more episode," Rhys reminded her.

"And I will honor my commitment, but I'm under no obligation to use my psychic ability. I will give you the archeological facts and you can build a story around them, as you would do if I were anyone else."

Rhys nodded. "What will you do after we're done filming?"

"I think, in time, I'll pick up a few classes at the institute. I miss teaching, and I need to stay close to home for the next few years." Quinn smiled shyly, her face suffusing with heat.

"When are you due?" Rhys asked, correctly interpreting her blush.

"End of March." She couldn't be sure, but she thought she'd conceived the day Gabe had her against the wall after sending her the video of Jo. It had been an awful day, one she didn't care to dwell on, but something beautiful had come out of it, and they were thrilled. It was only later, once they were already in Marbella, that she'd realized she'd forgotten to take her birth control pills several days in a row, having been emotionally overwrought by Helen's story, and realized she no longer had need of them. She'd thrown them in the bin before she'd realized she was pregnant but was still glad she'd made the decision independently of the news.

Quinn had had her first scan a week ago, and the picture of their baby was proudly displayed on the refrigerator. It was too soon to tell the sex of the baby, but Gabe insisted it was a girl, and Quinn secretly agreed. They could both be wrong, but whether they had a boy or a girl was irrelevant. As long as the baby was healthy, they would be happy with either.

Before her conversation with Rhys, she'd given little thought to Jo. Having left for Spain the day after the funeral, she'd put Jo from her thoughts and focused on time with her family. She still mourned Jo on some level, but the grief didn't go deep, and life without her was much as it had been before her. She'd had several communications from Jude and Brett, and although she was still wary of having any dealings with Brett, she had replied, determined to give him the benefit of the doubt.

"Sounds like you've thought things through," Rhys said, leaning back in his chair.

"I have. It's time to look forward, not backward."

"It sure is. Katya and I are expecting as well," Rhys said, beaming at her. "It's a girl."

"Oh, Rhys, I'm so pleased for you. How's Katya feeling?"

"Happy, hungry, amorous," Rhys replied, blushing furiously enough to make Quinn laugh.

"Well, I hope you're taking care of all her needs."

"I'm at her beck and call, whatever she desires," Rhys replied with a coy smile. "Katya has no issues with gaining weight. She's all about the baby," he said. "And I like her plump. It's sexy as hell."

Quinn smiled. She loved seeing Rhys happy. He deserved it, and he'd be a great dad. She was sure he was already a wonderful husband.

"I have to get going," Quinn said. She handed Rhys the file containing all her findings on Annie Edevane. She'd written it all up before leaving for Spain, needing to put the image of the child from her mind. Had she not been a mother, she might not have taken this case so to heart, but that poor deformed baby had nearly broken her. Perhaps it was what she'd needed to allow herself to move on without her gift. She'd always have it, but that didn't mean she had to use it.

"I'll see you next week, Rhys. Regards to Katya."

"See you," Rhys replied. He looked at her as if he were searching for something in her gaze but then smiled and waved his hand. "Off with you."

EPILOGUE
AUGUST 1961

London, England

Davy set down his toy truck and studied his mother. She looked so beautiful and peaceful, her face dappled with sunshine. The deep groove between her brows disappeared when she was asleep, and there was a half-smile on her lips, as if she were dreaming of something nice. He missed his mother. She hadn't been the same since Annie was born. She was always crying these days, and his father reminded him of a coiled spring. His parents, who had always made him feel safe and loved, were in the grip of emotions he couldn't grasp, but he knew they were deeply unhappy, and afraid.

Getting to his feet, Davy walked over to the chaise where Annie was lying, covered in his mother's yellow shawl. She was so sweet when she was asleep, almost like a normal baby. But she wasn't. She was broken, and everyone now knew, and their lives would never be the same. He'd heard the jeers and the cruel words as they left church. Any day now, his friends would start to taunt him and say things about his sister, possibly even about his mother, and then he'd have to fight, and he didn't want to fight with his mates.

He liked playing with them, and soon they'd all go to school, and maybe be in the same class for years, so this would follow him around until he was a grown man. He didn't want to be laughed at because of Annie or made to feel different because of her deformity. And he knew he would be, because had Annie been someone else's sister, he'd be tempted to say cruel things and jeer with the rest. Annie looked strange, frightening almost, with just that head atop a body that looked like a gingerbread man whose arms and legs had already been eaten.

Davy sighed as he looked at Annie's face. He couldn't understand what had happened to his sister, or what his parents might be going through. They were grownups and their feelings were as incomprehensible to him as the sermons Reverend Hale delivered in church. All those strange words and sentiments bored him silly, but he did understand death. Death was final. It changed everything, usually for the worse. But if Annie died, things would be better. His mother would be happy again, and his father would pay attention to him and take him out on adventures, like he used to. They could have another baby, a good one this time.

Davy picked up one of the smaller pillows and held it over Annie's face. She didn't even twitch, just lay there, like a lump. After a time, her chest stopped rising and falling, and he knew she was dead. Davy put the pillow back and went back to his truck, filling the bed with pebbles from the garden. He was a little frightened of what he'd done, but he'd done it for his parents, and for Annie.

She was better off dead, like a dog that was put down when it was injured. She'd play with the angels now. Maybe even grow limbs, and wings. She'd be like one of those fat little cherubs he saw in religious paintings. Yes, everything would be all right now. He'd saved them all.

A LETTER FROM THE AUTHOR

I hope you have enjoyed this installment of the Echoes from the Past series. If you want to join other readers in hearing all about my new releases and bonus content, you can sign up for my newsletter.

www.stormpublishing.co/irina-shapiro

I love hearing your thoughts, so if you enjoyed this book and could spare a few moments to leave a review that would be hugely appreciated. Even a short review can make all the difference in encouraging a reader to discover my books for the first time. Thank you so much.

And, as always, thank you for your support. I hope you'll stay in touch —I have so many more stories and ideas to entertain you with!

Irina

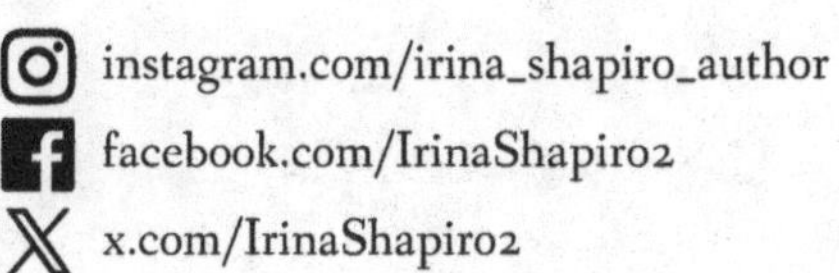

www.ingramcontent.com/pod-product-compliance
Lightning Source LLC
Chambersburg PA
CBHW010429170726
48283CB00011B/3125